Fairy Cursed
By Renee Field

Fairy Cursed

Renee Field

Published by Renee Field, 2015.

FAIRY CURSED

First edition. November 23, 2015.

Copyright © 2015 Renee Field.

ISBN: 978-1928178071

Written by Renee Field.

Dedication

TO MY HUSBAND, BRIAN and to my four children who anchor my soul. To my father, who took us as a family to Cape Breton many summers to experience the love of the people, the flavor of the food and fall in love with the scenery. I miss you Dad every day.

Chapter One

CAEL PULLED HIS BLACK leather jacket tighter around his chest. Goddamn wind. He was sick of it. Ever since he arrived in Nova Scotia the wind had kicked his ass. It had even followed him to the Highlands of Cape Breton where the temperature had dropped. His kind had never tolerated the cold well. In a thousand years living on this ragged Earth he'd never grown accustomed to it. It went against his nature and brought back those bitter dark memories of his early life. But so did a lot of things these days. Take traveling to Canada on an Internet rumor that the Stone of Fal was located in an old cemetery in the Highlands. Highly doubtful.

Six hours of traveling on a bus from Hell wasn't helping his mood. The warmth of Hell would be welcome and much more comfortable. Shut up! Cael knew it was a bad sign when he started to tell his subconscious to stop talking. Finally, able to stretch his long legs, he rolled his shoulders, flexed the muscles in his arms and inhaled the scent of pine trees mixed with the exhaust from the bus.

Maybe I'm finally going crazy. He wished he could plead insanity, because he knew without a doubt he had as much chance finding the sacred Stone of Fal as he did a needle in a haystack.

The squeaky old ladies' voices came from behind him. They were talking about him. People always did. Cael knew he radiated bad vibes, and the black clothing he wore helped add to that impression. He resisted the urge to turn around and growl, baring his teeth just for the fun of it. Instead, he stalked off and pushed his way past the bus crowd without a second thought. Moving his legs felt good. He had been so angry the vehicle he'd reserved at the car agency wasn't available that for one moment he'd thought about buying a first-class ticket back to the Cayman Islands, his island paradise, the place he'd called home for the past decade.

However, when he had reached for his wallet where he had shoved his confirmation number on a small torn piece of paper, he couldn't believe it. His wallet was missing. Managing to get one of the stewards on the plane to look for it, he was informed it wasn't on the airplane. He'd been robbed!

Serves me right for trying to drink myself to oblivion, again. He huddled his form against the hearty cool wind. All he had left was the sixty dollars he'd converted into Canadian cash. That was it. No plastic cards, no license, and no friggin' passport. Of that, he was left with a twenty after paying for a one-way ride to the Cape Breton Highlands on the bus made by Hades himself.

If he had his powers none of this would matter to him. Since he didn't he was left with that edgy, angry feeling that wanted satisfaction—and that wasn't going to happen, either.

He trudged on down the paved road, wanting to put as much space as possible between himself and humanity. Eyeing the darkening sky, he frowned. Dusk was descending fast and he was in for a cold night. *Too bad it won't kill me.* His limbs might bloody well freeze and he'd be uncomfortable all night but he'd make it. He'd live. And that was the crux of things. He wanted out. Wanted death, like a warm blanket, or better yet, a glass of dark Jamaican rum.

He swallowed. He was parched and hungry. It was times like this when he would recall the luxurious life he had at one time. He shook his head. That life would never be his again.

He trudged on. He'd check out the cemetery, hike his way to a place of civilization and then call his banker in the morning to get cash. A night with the elements might do his soul good. He laughed loudly, startling a few ravens eating road kill at the side of the road. *I definitely need a drink. Wrong, I need my head examined.*

4

An hour later he found a watering hole and slinked into the small tavern. Armed with twenty bucks, he was relieved it was happy hour. Two glasses of cheap copper-yellow rum sat in front of him. Another slowly made its way to his stomach. Since he had foregone food, dining on alcohol would have to do. He enjoyed the sting of heat from the rush of the liquor as it coated the back of his throat. For a moment he let down his guard and closed his eyes to his surroundings—loving the blackness that engulfed his mind.

TARA MCNEIL KNEW SHE shouldn't have come to meet her friend, Katie MacLeod. She should have known better. Her friend's breathy tone of voice on the phone was a dead giveaway that something was up. Instead here she was, being forced by one of Katie's twelve brothers to make herself at home in MacLeod's Tavern. All of Katie's brothers tended to think of her as their baby sister.

She took off her warm plaid jacket, carefully draping it over the tall bar stool. A hot chicken pot pie dinner materialized in front of her within seconds followed by a warm apple dessert with a heavy dose of real whipped cream. She eyed the dessert eagerly while her friend's voice filled the small bar.

Besides singing, Katie played the violin while Alec, the oldest brother played the drums; and the set of twins, Keelan and Keegan, jammed away at the guitar and piano. They were actually really good—all of them. Every single one of the MacLeods could play at least one or two musical instruments. And it seemed that tonight, all twelve of Katie's big Highlander brothers were in attendance.

As well as the band members, Angus and Ross were behind the bar, Neil and Scot were acting as bouncers and Alistair was cooking tonight—hence the double dose of whipped cream. Devlin and Brody along with Curran and Fergus were huddled together in a corner booth probably arguing about hockey.

Every single one of the MacLeods was a hunk. They were known throughout the Highlands for their tall lumberjack physiques and dark looks, which they jokingly claimed came from the druid blood that ran in their veins.

Sure, why not. A little fantasy in this small town couldn't hurt anyone. Tara took in the bar scene in a blink. The small, log cabin style tavern always made her feel comfortable. Her eyes glanced at the paintings that lined the walls, noting the mosaic jeweled gems and shells she and Katie had glued to the dark paneling. They were like fingerprints, each piece representing an aspect of their friendship and adventures in Skir Dhu, Cape Breton.

Tara caught Alistair edging her supper toward her, taking the dessert out of reach just to annoy her. "Tease," she mouthed at him; a genuine smile lit up her face.

Every single MacLeod, including Katie's father, Devon and her mother, MacCallah made eye contact with Tara when she walked in the place. It was their way. Had always been and as usual it eased her heart.

"And now for a special treat, everyone...give a warm hand for our very own Tara McNeil, who has agreed to sing what we believe to be a very old Gaelic song for us tonight." Katie winked and dramatically waved at her.

What? Tara gulped. Surely to God she's not expecting me to get up there and sing.

"That's your cue, Tara," said Alistair, from behind the bar.

"I...I...I'm not singing, Alistair," stuttered Tara. She tried hard to ignore Katie's on-stage pleas, turning her attention to her food.

"Ah, come on, it's just us, Tara. No need to get all tongue-tied and all." Alistair yanked the food away from her before she could steal a spoonful.

Tongue-tied? More like a full-blown stutter coming straight at you. That was part of Tara's problem. When she got nervous she became a stuttering idiot. "Hey, I was eating that."

"Now stop over thinking. You know you never stutter when you sing, and you get to eat it after you sing us a song. Just a wee song...It's not going to kill you." Alistair gave her one of his big, beautiful, friendly smiles. The warmth of his chocolate brown eyes made her feel slightly calm.

No, but my voice might kill all of you. Painfully so. Tara simply shook her head.

"Come on, Tara-girl. Sing for us. Okay, audience I think our Tara needs some encouragement. Open up your pockets to our girl here and let's see if we can entice her to the stage." Katie gave her another exaggerated wink.

Tara's eyes widened as a ball cap appeared from somewhere and people throughout the tavern placed their donations in it. "What's she doing?"

Tara knew practically everyone within the tavern. Besides the MacLeods it was filled mostly with unemployed coal miners, who like her father were living off a tight fixed income. Katie's mother waved at her from the kitchen door and her father grinned at her. Great, everyone is working against me here.

"Okay, Keegan says we've got one hundred and twenty-five dollars and change here, Tara-girl. So, come on up...you don't want to disappoint us now, do you?"

You are so going to regret this Katie. I will get even. Tara's heart pounded. The only other time she'd sung in front of an audience had been at a church supper and that was twelve years ago. She hadn't liked it then and highly doubted she would now. However, Katie was right. These were her people. They had donated their hard-earned cash for her. And boy could she use that money. For a moment she wondered if Katie knew how desperate her living situation had become. With that money she could pay half the oil bill and keep the phone for another month.

Swallowing her pride and with a double-dose of trepidation Tara moved toward the stage. It's no big thing...I can do this. I know everyone, so what could go wrong? Nothing. Tara's little pep talk with herself motivated her toward the stage. She forced herself to breathe through the nervous, butterfly feeling eating away at her insides as she made her way through the small crowd of people.

"Ahh, now, ladies and gentlemen, here she comes. Our own Tara McNeil." Katie gave an exaggerated cat whistle at her and then made a hasty exit.

Tara knew she did that on purpose to avoid coming face to face with her. Chicken!

"What are you singing, Tara?" asked Keelan, helping to haul her up onto the stage.

Wiping her sweaty hands on her faded jeans, Tara said, "A ballad, an old one my grandmother taught me."

"Okay, we'll follow your lead when you're ready." He turned to the rest of the crew and waited for her to begin.

Never. I'll never be ready for this.

Thank God the stage lights were aimed directly at her. It made seeing the audience almost impossible. Almost wasn't enough though. Anxious knots of dread clenched inside her stomach, making her throat feel parched. Tara swallowed; afraid she'd start to stutter any minute. She didn't want to see anyone. Chicken that she was, Tara closed her eyes and sang.

Thank God humans discovered how to make alcohol. Cael twirled the third glass of yellow rum around, wishing again it was the dark Jamaican type he had developed a fondness for. Then every single hair on his body stood on end. A warm tingly sensation fired itself from the pit of his stomach straight to his groin. His breath hitched with anticipation, and desire coiled hot and heavy, singeing his body taut with ferocious passion.

Blast it, someone is singing a Tuatha Dé Danann ballad. He swallowed fast, downing the rum in one gulp. The alcohol burned hard as it went down his throat. He shifted forward on the small, hard wooden seat trying to see who it was.

The angle he sat at made it difficult for him to see the woman but the voice...her words, beckoned him forward. Her words were a throaty-dark rumbling promise of the same wicked carnal delights that had made up his existence at one time. Visions of limbs locked in passion, of tongues dueling, of a lover crying out in pleasure caused his cock to become painfully aroused as he absorbed the song. He forced his mind to pay attention and not delve into old memories, best forgotten.

Come to me, lover mine.

Feed my heart, lover mine

Seek my heat, lover mine

And together we'll fly, lover mine.

He edged closer. He had to see her. Had to seek the source of the voice who spoke the Tuatha Dé Danann language with such eloquence that a fierce longing for his own kind, a desire he had thought long dead, broke through the effects of the three glasses of rum he'd consumed on an empty stomach.

His first impression of the woman was that she was small. Almost child-like in her appearance, but she stood regally proud on stage. He noticed her hands were fisted and her eyes were squeezed shut. She was uncomfortable being the center of attention. She turned and with the stage lighting he saw curly, long chestnut hair with streaks of red and yellow, reminding him of the lush colors from the S'alabah, the passion tree that grew in Tir Nan Og, his homeland. The place he'd been exiled from for eternity.

She wore faded blue jeans and a bright red sweater. He could make out the outline of small breasts as she took a much-needed breath at the end of the song. And she was half Tuatha Dé Danann. Half-fucking fey!

Damn! Of that he was sure. But she didn't look one bit like a Tuatha Dé Danann. She wasn't tall like the women of his race, pale or white haired. She was small and earthy in appearance. She was an exotic mix of innocence and mystery that fired his imagination and his cock to rigid attention.

Cursed to live his life as a mere mortal—to experience hunger, thirst, lust, and sorrow for eternity—he could still recognize his kind. But he'd never seen a hybrid, a half-human, half-Tuatha Dé Danann. They simply didn't exist. Oh, sure they existed in folklore but he knew better. His kind didn't like humans. They viewed them as pets or insects, either one depending on Queen Mir's mood.

Belonging to a Tuatha Dé Danann Royal House, Cael had been chosen personally by Queen Mir to be her champion. For half a millennium he served her well, until he'd been cast out a thousand years ago. Why? Because I bloody well stuck my nose where it didn't belong.

That's what he liked to think but the reality was had he not interfered; the evolution of humankind would have taken on an entirely different path. One he thought they didn't deserve.

So, he had done the unthinkable. Well, that's not true either. He was sure others had thought it but their brains had obviously been more awake and in-tune to Queen Mir's rage for the ancient Druid race.

Often in the past Cael wished his brain could have shut down at that crucial moment when Mir made him choose between his race and the cursed humans. It hadn't then and wasn't about to now. Daring to interfere had cost him greatly. But did he regret his actions? No. Did he wish for an alternative punishment? Hell yes! Did he seek revenge? You bet.

That, however, did not explain the tempting apparition in front of him. Her aura was so bright that now without the stage lights glaring on her, he was amazed he hadn't seen her enter the home-styled bar. *Then again my bloody eyes were shut! Pathetic warrior that I am.*

Plus, he'd been too intent on drowning his miserable human-like existence in alcohol. Anything to dull the ache of loneliness that filled his mind. If he had a soul he'd say that was filled with loneliness too, but he didn't have one.

No soul. None whatsoever. No Tuatha Dé Danann, born of a race from the beginning of time, had one. No Druid either. Only the blasted humans—Eve's daughters and sons were blessed with the gift of regeneration. It was a cruel twist to immortality that he often wished for a soul.

"Sit down, Mister."

Cael ignored the gruff, baritone voice that belonged to the imposing man who now stood in front of him—obscuring his view of the tiny woman. He shouldered the man out of the way so he could stand directly in front of the stage. His sight was fixed solely on the woman, whose aura hummed at him, lush with sensual passion and a promise of carnal delights that quickened his blood.

"Who taught you the tongue of the Tuatha Dé Danann?" Cael spoke using the high royal intonation she had used in her song. This was a riddle he wanted sorted out, now, not later.

"What?" she answered in English.

Amber eyes glanced his way. They scorched him. That one quick calculating perusal reminded Cael so much of the sexy, come-hither look his queen had at one time cast his way that it took effort not to growl and spring to the stage to demand an answer.

"You either sit or we'll make you leave."

The man once again attempted to block Cael's view of the intoxicating woman who was trying her best to hastily exit the stage. Like before he didn't bother responding. The threat of harm held little value to Cael. In fact, the dark part of him welcomed a fight. Two burly figures abruptly blocked his path as he moved to the right of the stage.

"She ain't for the likes of you, Mister."

The dark-haired man now stood directly in front of him. Cael punched the man in the face. Yes, every time he did that it hurt like Hell. He shrugged it off, eyeing the second man. In a blink he was surrounded by a dozen dark-haired men. A vibe of intense power swamped him. It had the feel of druid to it but that was impossible.

No more so than finding a wee feyling that speaks my language.

He slipped his leather jacket off, letting them get a good look at his arms. *If they are Druid then they will know what they see. They will know what I am. Better yet, what I am capable of.* Cael's eyes dared them to come at him, while he tried to pinpoint exactly where the woman had gone.

He sensed the silent communication amongst the group as their power whispered to the dark recesses of his brain. He crouched, ready for action. The punch to his back hit him hard. He lurched, almost falling to his knees. *Now, that won't do at all. Thanks for playing fair.*

Two tried tackling him from behind but it didn't matter. He was bred and trained as a warrior for his queen. He was Tuatha Dé Danann to the core, even if he no longer wielded the power inherent to his race. He certainly hadn't forgotten how to fight.

Cael laughed loudly, the eerie booming sound ringing in the small tavern as two men tried to grab his arms. He kicked and punched his way out of it, shaking them off with practiced ease.

"Halt!" bellowed a voice, causing all twelve men to instantaneously cease their attack.

All the men were panting, giving Cael time to get his bearings and look around. The word had been spoken in his language, but it lacked the proper accent.

Will wonders never cease! I end up in this backwater hole and run into wanna-be fairies. And if another bloody person speaks my tongue I'm going to rip it out of them. Cael wiped his nose. It was bleeding and he was winded. Still he flexed his fingers and stood tall. He took the time to eye every single man that surrounded him—letting each, in turn, feel his dark rage. He practically hummed for them to come at him again. More than a couple of the men would sport black eyes in a few hours. He wished he felt something for his actions but he didn't.

"Move aside Alec." An old man pushed his way through the feisty crew.

Cael eyed the man's approach, sensing the deep druid power that vibrated around him. He judged him to be in his late sixties, and power clung to him, effortlessly. Cael cleared his throat. "Who are you?"

"Name's Devon. You're not welcome here."

"The woman, where did she go?" Cael scanned the crowd. *I lost her. I bloody well lost her.* He gritted his teeth in frustration and wiped his sweaty hands on his jeans.

"She's not for the likes of you."

The Druid grasped Cael's forearms hard in a traditional warrior embrace. The intimate action stilled Cael's thoughts. It had been such a long time that for one moment he almost let the Druid's inner eye scan his thoughts. Quickly Cael blocked the probe that was testing his strength.

That wouldn't do at all. He was surprised to feel such a strong current of power flow from the Druid. *Well, well, well, a pure-blooded Druid, of the Lunar warrior clan, hiding in the backwoods of Cape Breton. Will wonders never cease?* The knowledge that he was dealing with a Druid stirred a restless part of him that recalled a time best forgotten. In that time, he and a Druid Priest, who he once called friend, used to test each other's powers. That time was so long ago that for Cael it almost seemed like it had never been.

Not breaking contact with the stranger, he snarled, "I want the woman."

"I be knowing what you are and we will protect her from the likes of you."

The Druid glared at him, while the surge of power singed Cael's forearms.

"We will all protect her," said one of the Highlanders, who had initially moved aside for the older man.

"It's not like I'm going to harm her. I just wanted..." I am not going to explain myself. It's none of their business.

"We be knowing what you want even if you don't. The answer is still no. Now, get out before I let me boys beat you to a pulp," snapped the old man.

Cael knew the old man said that more for show because there was no way in this lifetime the other Highlander Druids could actually do serious damage to him. While he might get broken ribs and all, his skill was too advanced for them.

Not that it mattered, anyway.

Bloody Hell, nothing like having burnt and blistering skin to top my day off. Cael didn't flinch as more heat radiated from the old man straight to every nerve ending on his arms. Moving would be a dead giveaway that he felt anything at all. As strange as it was he knew this was a test.

"Pop, get out of the way so I can finish what he started," snarled a dark-haired Highlander, whose lip was cut open.

He was the Highlander Cael's fist had made first contact with. A feral smile lit up Cael's eyes, daring him on. Cael sensed the darkness resting deep within this one Highlander and took the time to carefully appraise him.

"Cut it out, Alec. He's leaving."

The old man finally let go of Cael's arms, so he could step in front of Alec, blocking the dark vibe that radiated out from the younger Highlander. Cael didn't bother glancing down. He knew there were burn marks on his skin. To Hell with it. She's not worth it.

He turned, picked up his leather jacket that had been trampled during the brief fight, and marched out of the tavern. Most of the patrons had already left when the first punch had been thrown. He pushed his still-burning arms into his jacket, noting the night was as dark as his mood.

The moon was obscured by heavy cloud cover, the temperature was even colder than before and Cael swore he saw his breath as he trudged uphill. Fuck the road. At least he knew where he was going—straight up.

Finally, something simple for a change. It had taken one inquiry to discern the location of the Highland cemetery. Had he known he was that close after getting off the godforsaken bus, he'd have hiked there and back. But then I would have missed out on that wee bit of adventure and that voice. A fleeting smile creased Cael's face.

Just thinking about that throaty-sexy voice made him hard. Yeah, a few scrapes were worth it. Too bad I'll never see her again. Then again, why bother with her? By tomorrow I'll have proven to myself that the blasted rumor is nothing. I'll have hitchhiked back to civilization, have my banker wire me money and then get my ass back home where the sun shines!

However, none of that made him feel any better. In fact, all he kept thinking about was the sultry voice that set his cock on fire. He had forgotten how much he enjoyed the slow, pounding rhythm of the song. And Cael knew that song, well. Too well, in fact, recalling the last night he'd spent coupling with Queen Mir and her consorts.

Yeah, better not to think of the past or that night. If I keep thinking about that, my cock might bloody well freeze straight up. He winced at his own humor. But Hell, after a thousand years living this life it was a miracle he was still sane. Not one hundred per cent, but nobody's perfect.

Chapter Two

"WHY'D YOU DO THAT?" Alec stared hard at the stranger's back. He was angry at himself that he'd been beaten and the rawness of the emotion triggered that dark speck within him that he kept hidden from his brothers and most especially his father. His skin tingled with the hum of dark power and it took a lot of effort not to close his eyes and savor the euphoric high he felt. Instead, he fingered his swollen eye and cut lip and inwardly cursed.

His father ignored him and turned to the others, motioning them all to move behind the bar so they could talk privately.

"Where's Tara?" asked his father.

Angus tucked his black shirt back into his jeans. "She's with Katie. They're safe. They're in the back."

"One of us will be needed to watch her now at all times," said Devon. "And the next time you boys want to play macho-man take a good look at who you're facing first," admonished their father, swatting at Alec as he passed.

"What's he mean by that?" asked Keelan, cursing silently that his knuckles were bruised.

Keegan gave his twin a smirk and flexed his own knuckles. "Yeah, Pop, we could have easily taken him on."

"You bunch of dimwits. Did you not see what was on his arms?" Their father was angry and his forehead was creased with worry.

Fergus, the only one of the group who looked unharmed, asked, "Tattoos, what of it?"

"Bloody fools. Have I not taught you nothin'?" Devon sighed. "Those weren't your average tattoos, those be ancient druid marks. That man...ain't a man at all. Those marks for your information

17

belong to only one creature that I know of and trust me, you don't want to 'ave him tangle with ye."

"Are you saying he's a Druid...cause I didn't sense that at all," said Brody, touching his broken nose.

"Bloody Hell, are you not listenin' to me? He's not a man...that there thing you were fightin' was none other than the Damned Tuatha Dé Danann," snapped Devon, ushering his wife over.

Handing cold cloths to Alec and Fergus, MacCallah gasped. "You mean to tell me my boys were ganging up on the Damned Fairy?"

"Ugh, MacCallah, don't be callin' him a fairy. That conjures up a sweet innocence the likes of which that creature ain't ever known. He's Tuatha Dé Danann to the bone, that one. And he's one to watch," said Devon to his wife.

Alec took the offered cloth for his cut lip and eye. "He wasn't fey. That was just a man. He was bleedin'."

"Bleedin' sure, but no amount of punching, no amount of pounding is going to make that creature dead. Trust me on that one lads, that's the Damned One. He's the one exiled by the queen of the Tuatha Dé Danann and we don't want anything to do with him. Wherever he goes trouble follows on the wind. The real question we need to sort out is why is he here in our Highlands and what does he want with our Tara." Devon stepped over a smashed beer bottle and eyed the mess littering the tavern with dismay.

"Alec, you get first watch," continued their father.

Alec shrugged, non-committal. "She's not going to like that, Pop. Tara's finding it hard enough right now. I'm not sure having one of us tail her twenty-four-seven is a good idea."

"We took an oath and we are standing by it. None of you forget that. Her grandmother asked it of all of us before she died. And no MacLeod of mine is about to let our Tara-girl down...you get that?"

Devon turned and walked away from the group, making eye contact with his youngest son, Curran, motioning for him to grab a broom and help clean up the mess. He knew his words would be heeded by his sons. Right now, he had to use his druid power to make sure his friends remaining in the tavern understood it was just a bar brawl, and not something unworldly. That kind of attention wouldn't do at all.

"You heard your father," said MacCallah, following on Devon's heels.

"Great. That's just fucking great." Alec stalked to the back of the stage trying hard to figure out how to tell Tara he was walking her home. He knew without a doubt she'd tell him to go to Hell. After all, she lived less than half a mile down the road. Heck, he could practically watch her walk all the way home from the tavern's doorstep. Alex thought that idea had a lot of promise.

IT HAD TAKEN A LOT of fast talking to finally escape from Katie, but Tara had managed it. She was mighty angry. First she was mad at her friend for coercing her into performing on stage, even though her heart had been in the right place. Secondly, she was alarmed at what had happened. She had seen a tall, imposing man approaching the stage and then he had been swiftly surrounded by all of Katie's brothers.

Katie assured her the stranger was nothing, just a patron who'd had one too many. Tara wasn't so sure of that. She could have sworn the man spoke her grandmother's secret language, but that was impossible. It was simply a made-up language they used to chat amongst themselves. It had been their special way of talking since Tara was a toddler. When Katie had pressed her to sing a song Tara chose her grandmother's favorite, The Lover's Song, which had always made Tara snicker.

I must have heard him wrong. It's just my overactive imagination, she told herself for the umpteenth time as she dumped her hard-earned singing money into her money sock. Come Monday she'd pay a portion of some of the bills. A fleeting smile creased her face. As quick as it came it went. She eyed the piece of toast her father had left behind on his plate. The harsh reality of her life bore down on her faster than a nor'easter.

Her father had always been a man of action—a leader among men. Working in the coal mines had been his life. Some men weren't suited for life underground, but she knew making an honest living and working hard were traits ingrained in him. Idleness had been his first illness after the coal mine shut down. Then had come the harsh reality of having to get by on social assistance—beggar's handout, he had called it.

When her grandmother came down with an unknown illness, they couldn't afford the gas to go to the hospital located over a hundred miles away or pay for the experimental drugs the doctors said might prolong her life. Then shame had taken hold of her once proud father. There wasn't much left of the carefree, courageous man she'd known as a child.

Ahh, well a hard life makes you love the happy times and dismiss the hard ones. Her grandmother's favorite phrase popped into her head as she slipped into a warmer, down-filled dark navy-blue coat with the word "Security" written in bold, yellow letters across the back.

She hated having to lie to her friend but if she didn't relieve Marty soon, her secret would be out. That wouldn't do at all. If any of the MacLeods found out she was working the graveyard shift at the Highland Cemetery, without a doubt she'd find envelopes full of money every morning in her mailbox. As it was, MacCallah left casseroles for her and her father at least twice a week.

To let them know how dire things were financially would ruin her father. His pride was basically all he had left. Tara would do anything to let him keep that, even if that meant she could only afford a few courses each year at the university. Family comes first. That was her personal motto.

What she truly detested was keeping her job a secret from her father. When pressed about the extra income she told him it came from a tutoring job she'd taken on. *Don't I bloody well wish.* But a job was a job and she could do this. In fact, there really was nothing to it, if you got past feeling like crap the next day. Tonight, safely stashed in her backpack were two Celtic history books she had to read if she was going to pass her next mid-term exam with her favorite professor, Dr. Xavier. *And I will pass, damn it all!*

That was the vow she said silently to herself, as she trudged up the hidden muddy path that was her shortcut to the cemetery. Tara didn't enjoy going to university but she'd promised her grandmother that she'd study Celtic History and get her degree. She liked the subject but her goal was to open her own jewelry store one day. That was her real joy in life. The minute her father hit the sack, she'd sneak out to the shed and spend half the night working on a new design. *Funny how most of the pieces I make have druid-like symbols.* Tara shook her head, realizing for the past year that's basically all she had been studying, so it made sense her creative outlet reflected what was being hard-wired into her brain by Professor Xavier.

A hard gust of wind caused her to clutch her arms for warmth. It was a two-mile hike uphill and while it certainly wasn't Tara's dream job, the money did help put food on the table. For now, that would have to do.

"What the Hell?" Tara tripped and fell to the hard, cold ground with a cursed "Oomph!"

"Get off me."

The deep growling baritone voice was next to her. She scrambled back, only to have her hand come into contact with one muscular thigh. She stilled. Her breath hitched. Her heart jumped straight into overdrive.

"Sweet mercy, are you trying to fucking kill me woman...or get laid?"

"No...n...n...no, I'm trying to get up, you moron." Tara twisted her body again and tried to be extra careful her hand didn't come into contact with any more of the man.

"Lady, you're the one who landed on me, not vice versa, but since your hand has woken all of me up, take your time," drawled the husky timbre of the man's voice.

When he did nothing to help her, the sexual innuendo of his words fired her imagination. Instead of feeling fear she felt strangely excited. Then a foul, ripe pungent odor hit her nose like a firecracker.

"Wha...wha..." Tara took a deep breath in and that didn't help matters but she was determined not to stutter. "What in God's names is that smell?" She attempted to back up but couldn't. Her left foot was jammed into a small hole. The smell was nauseating.

She could have sworn the man growled. It was a rumble that vibrated all the fine hairs on her skin. She felt the impact of that one sound all the way to her core and tried hard not to breathe any of the caustic sharp smell into her nose.

"It's not me. It's from that cursed animal that I came across."

The man's rough voice was ripe with its own righteous anger. "Blasted thing came out of nowhere and then the next thing I knew it bloody well pissed this godforsaken stench at me."

"Skunk?"

"I said stench."

"No, it was a skunk. You came across a skunk." Tara wondered then about his accent. There was a sense of familiarity in it. But the fact he didn't know what a skunk was made him a foreigner in her mind.

"Are you going to get off me or are we going to have to hold our breaths for eternity?" snapped the man.

It was then she realized she felt no fear of the man at all, only annoyance. Okay, now that's weird. Delayed shock, that's it. After all, walking across a man who happens to be lying down in the heather in the middle of the night makes a lot of sense.

"My foot's stuck in a hole and if you'll be so kind as to move a bit to your left...Oomph...Your left, not my left...Hey mister, that's my leg," squeaked Tara.

"And what a nice leg it is." The man drawled out the words in a slow, teasing manner, while his hand trailed up from her ankle-high boot to her calf and then to her knee.

Even through the worn jeans Tara felt the warmth of his hand. Goose bumps formed along the skin above the muscle of her leg and every nerve ending sparked with keen awareness. She felt his touch all the way to her breasts which tingled in anticipation. A warm sensation pitted itself in her stomach, her breasts heaved and her nipples hardened. Her entire body stilled, waiting for something elusive, something sharp and unspoken that would change her life forever. Tara took a shuddering breath in and fought not to moan. What's the matter with me?

She shook her head, hating that she couldn't see him while wishing she'd taken her flashlight out of her backpack. But she knew the shortcut to the cemetery like the back of her hand. Well, sort of. She certainly didn't know there was a hole, which currently had captured her right foot, worn boot and all. And, she'd never seen a skunk around the area.

Again, the ripe odor of the skunk's scent streamed its way into her awareness and thoughts, almost causing her to gag.

"Okay, either you help me get out of this hole or I'm going to throw up from the smell," stated Tara, trying to be forceful.

He chuckled, his fingers still inching along the contours of her leg. She felt every sensual tease of his long digits from her leg straight to her now fluttering stomach. It took willpower not to close her eyes and savor the delightful rush of emotions he was evoking within her body. She tingled eagerly from the tantalizing trail his fingers were following along her calf and knee. And who would have thought a knee could be so sensitive. Tara bit her lip to stifle the moan that dared to slip free.

"I'm in agreement with you, lass. Let's get out of here."

Thankful he had an ounce of common sense in him she took a shuddering breath. He finally moved his hand to her foot that was jammed tightly into the small hole. A few twists and tugs later her foot was free, minus her boot.

This night couldn't get any worse. Tara was left trying to maintain her balance on one foot on the steep incline of the hill. She almost stumbled again, and had to grab the man's arm for support. Then the clouds parted and her mystery man came fully into view. Straight blond hair that shone platinum-white in appearance fell in disarray around his face. Pale silver-grey eyes rimmed with black circles glared at her. His skin had a coppery glow. He was flawless in his beauty. The epitome of a rugged Celtic warrior stood before her. Startlingly tall, at least six foot six, he had muscular legs and a wide breadth of shoulders that would make any football player proud. Tara eyed him hungrily like he was her favorite drink, frothy hot chocolate, afraid the moving clouds would obscure her view.

Then he pulled her to him.

"I know you."

His gravelly hard-edged voice left her wanting to rub a finger over his lips. She felt his warm large hands span her waist to help keep her standing upright as she bent to dislodge her stuck boot.

The feel of his hands on her waist through the puffy confines of the feather-down jacket caused her body to hum all over. Not good, not good at all. *Why couldn't I have stumbled on an old man? Nope, I stumble across one drop-dead gorgeous hunk. Too bad he stinks to high heaven. Then again, that's probably not a bad thing because I don't know this man...a warning I should heed.*

She laughed this time. "I don't think so. We've never been introduced. Trust me, I'd remember." Boot unstuck, she slipped it untied onto her cold foot.

"You speak my language."

Instinctively she stilled, frozen to the spot. He spoke her grandmother's secret language. The lilt of his words flowed like a sensual stream off his tongue, evoking a sharp intake of breath on her behalf. A flash of a tall, angry, imposing man jumped into her mind. A thought that she should have run when she had the chance caused her heart to accelerate. But none of that mattered. She was nicely caught, held by tempting hands whose thumbs were stroking her jacket, distracting her earlier thoughts. "A bit," she answered back in English.

"Well, well, well, my night just got better."

He crushed her body up close and personal to his muscular frame and lowered his lips to her mouth before she could protest. She knew then she should scream. Instead her mind digested the taste of rum and something wild and exotic like the combined taste of cinnamon and cardamom. A part unknown within her urged her to yield to it. She fought with herself not to bend her body to his large, hard frame. Luckily all she could smell was skunk. But even that didn't matter as much anymore.

What was happening to her had never happened before. Sure, she'd been kissed a few times, but not like this. Not by a man who knew what it meant to be a lover. Not by a man whose lips were molding her own to his, demanding she comply, willing her to open to her own passion. His tongue stroked her own, dancing and dueling with hers, forcing her mouth to yield to his skill. A skill that should have shocked her. Instead, she welcomed it, tilting her head, adjusting her stance without thought to accommodate his desires. Tasting, taking...feeling the rush of sexual power that fueled their mingled breaths. His powerful hands roamed up and under her coat to clutch her back. The heat of his flesh scorched her, fueling a rush of warmth below, causing her to want to rub her legs around his thighs. She whimpered, lust and need swamped her senses, making her dizzy.

"Ahh, that's what I thought. There's more of my kind in you than you know."

His tone was quiet and mocking. Abruptly, he backed away. Tara shivered from his absence as the cold wind of the night brought common sense back to her.

She wiped her long hair out of her face as the gusts picked up. Thank god the smell was back with a vengeance. It washed her with its cold dose of reality. What the Hell am I doing kissing a man I don't know? Letting passion rule my bloody head?

Then a loud engine roar filled the unsettling silence. "Is that a car?" She asked the obvious question.

"It's a limo to be precise, but the better question is what is it doing climbing that road in the dead of night?" Instead of moving further away from her the man took another step into her space, like he too missed the warmth of their embrace. She froze, uncertain if she was afraid of the man or the car that was winding its way up to the cemetery.

Tara took an uneven step back on the hill and tugged on her coat. She needed to distance herself from the man and force the nervous feeling running freely through her body to settle. The lights of the limo climbed to the cemetery. "The only thing up there is the cemetery."

"Great, that's just fucking great." He stepped further away from her. "Stay here."

In a blink the stranger was gone as if he'd been absorbed into the black abyss of the night. At the same moment the clouds once again obscured the moon.

What? Go to Hell. Tara had no intention of staying where she was. First she had to get away from the godforsaken smell and secondly she had to relieve Marty before he had a fit.

She sank to her knees, took out the flashlight from her backpack and hiked the pack over her shoulders. Tightening her boot laces, she proceeded to march up the hill, determination urging her on.

Just who does he think he is? Then it dawned on her. Oh my god, I kissed a man and I don't even know his name. Thankfully no one could see her face because she knew it was flaming red.

Chapter Three

CAEL'S BODY WAS ON fire. *Boy, do I need a cold shower in more ways than one.* He stunk. *Bloody little bugger.* He jogged up the rest of the hill, keeping his eyes peeled for any more devilish creatures of the night. The darkness didn't affect his eyesight. In fact, he preferred it. The white limo was parked at the cemetery gate, which was slightly opened. No one was in the vehicle. His skin prickled with unease.

Over the years he'd learned to rely on his warrior-honed instincts, which screamed evil and danger. *Great, just great. Nice bloody Internet rumor.* The last thing he wanted to deal with was a grave robber. He'd seen enough of that in his day. In fact, he'd about seen it all. Living the life of a human for a thousand years tended to dull his sensitivity toward the living, let alone the dead. But that didn't mean he liked that kind of callousness. *Hell no. Let the dead sleep.*

Then the sweet coppery scent of blood assaulted his nose. He crouched low to the ground and moved forward until he saw something. Lying in front of him was a young man who looked to be in his early twenties, dead. Not a nice death either. His death had been painfully slow. He wore a jagged cut across his neck like a necklace. They'd let him bleed out. *Bastards! Looks like I'm going to get my fight after all.*

Cautiously, Cael edged forward. His side was slightly painful from the bar brawl he had initiated at the tavern a couple hours earlier. There wouldn't have been a fight if the Highlander Druids had simply let him talk with the woman who had sung a Tuatha Dé Danann song with such elegance that a fierce longing for his own kind had gripped Cael. The same woman he'd kissed. The same woman who is half-fucking fey. A walking, talking, kissable fey!

Cael's lips still tingled from the woman's lush lips and his cock throbbed...the burn for release a hot poker scorching him. Thankful for the cover of darkness Cael straightened and edged forward.

He couldn't believe his bad luck since deciding to follow the ridiculous Internet rumor. He'd been robbed, in a fight, and the final injustice was having the half-Tuatha woman stumble across him after the wee-beastie pissed on him. Charming. Then again charm never was one of my virtues.

"It's not here, you fool."

The deep voice came from Cael's left. Cael moved in that direction. It was then his eyes were drawn to the bob and sway of a light cresting the hill. He knew without a doubt it was that woman again. He also knew he'd have to take care of the thugs before she got any closer.

"What is that stench?"

"It's not me, Sir," squeaked a second voice.

I don't believe it. That skunk is going to be the death of me. Literally. Cael almost laughed at how ludicrous the situation had become. How the mighty have fallen. Well, so much for the element of surprise. He stepped to where he could be seen.

"So, who is the one who slit my friend's throat? Better yet, who'd like to die first?" Cael was going for the direct approach and looking forward to a good, hard fight. He still felt edgy and unsettled from the effects of the young woman's Tuatha Dé Danann song and from the alluring touch of her passionate, accepting lips. She had teased him, leaving him achy for the pleasure of his own—something he'd never experience again. That thought sobered him, leaving him cold and empty. Cael gave a savage smile, embracing the harsh reality of the life he was forced to live.

A bright white light filled the space. Druid magick. Fucking unbelievable.

He easily dodged the blast volleyed his way. He could have wielded a few of his own, but why bother. Moving closer he dared his opponent on. Then the clouds parted again. He all but rolled his eyes. What? This is my night for bloody reunions. Cael grimaced. The loud chuckle of the man standing directly in front of him caused him to clench his teeth shut in a grimace.

Stater was the last person Cael ever expected to see again. In fact, he'd long thought the sixth-century king dead. The last time he'd seen the conniving human king he had ordered twenty slaves slaughtered simply because he could, which had strangely impressed his queen.

Then Queen Mir had taken Stater to her Pleasure Palace. In truth, Cael hadn't spared the evil mortal king another thought, thinking Mir would tire of him quickly. Obviously, he should have paid more attention to the human, who had somehow figured out how to extend his life over the centuries.

"You know, I don't believe it. If it isn't the Damned Fairy standing in front of me. And as always, you stink." Stater's holier-than-thou voice grated on Cael's nerves.

Should have known better. But the stink remark hit his pride. When he was done dealing with Stater he vowed to hunt the wee-beastie down and kill it with his bare hands.

"So, what did you bargain with, for my queen to grant you immortality?" asked Cael, edging a fraction of a foot closer.

A blast of light stopped him cold. "That's close enough. You know, you should see the look on your face. Talk about priceless."

"Indeed, it is," said the voice to Stater's right.

"Shut up," snapped Stater to the man.

The man bristled but held his peace. Puppet. Once again, it's Stater and his puppets. "You know Stater, you haven't changed one bit. You're still butt ugly." Cael was taunting Stater on purpose. He knew the king was the one who had slit the guard's throat but the bigger question was why. Why was Stater here in the Highlands? What was he after? "One would have thought with the centuries you would have at least grown up or better yet, gotten used to the fact that you'll always be second rate."

"Ahh, there you are wrong," sneered Stater. "You know the last time I heard mention of your name it was around the Fourteenth Century and then there was that small rumor of strange happenings again after World War Two. It would appear that history hasn't been kind to you."

Cael twisted his body slightly sideways to maneuver his feet into a better attack position. "Like I care. So, what's brought you to Cape Breton?"

"Seems I could ask the same of you."

Cael pondered that statement for a moment and his heart lurched. Perhaps Stater is here too, all because of that same blasted rumor that said the Stone of Fal is buried here. Well without a doubt Cael knew he couldn't let Stater find it.

"Looking to steal some more trinkets from some dead people? Pathetic," said Cael. His eyes followed the movements of the servant who had taken two steps back from Stater.

Stater cackled an evil laugh as he motioned to the man next to him to bring forward a tiny, ornate ivory box he held in his open palm. "Do you honestly think I don't know why you're here? You want what I will get. You might as well leave now. As usual you're wasting your damned time."

Cael's skin crawled as he looked at the small ivory treasure chest currently held by Stater. "Still stealing from my queen as usual?" A shiver of dread passed over him. He dared to hope that Stater had no idea what was being kept in the box.

"What? Could this itsy-bitsy box of hers be important? Like I care. After what she did to me...It doesn't matter. Once I get that Stone of Fal I will have all I need. Now, because you're here, I do require one additional thing that blessedly you are good for. My how the Fates have gifted me."

Cael sensed Stater's movement but it didn't help him. The knife pierced his heart in one quick lunge. Bloody Hell! Stater had mastered the druid vanishing spell after all.

"It would appear, Cael, that I have changed. It's amazing what one can learn from your precious queen when she least expects a human to listen...Ahh, the things I could tell you. The secrets I could share. But I won't. Those secrets are mine. I learned that it doesn't pay to play fair. And with your blood...I will soon get my just reward. The next centuries belong to me."

The cackle of his demented laugh hurt more than the knife. Cael fell to his knees, blood pouring out of his gaping wound. The Tuatha dagger had ripped through flesh and muscle, the fierce burn making Cael wonder if this time he'd be blessed with death for good.

"You see, now that I have your blood I can open the veil. Yes, it's time that some friends of mine—you might remember them, the Decies? I see a small flicker of recognition in your dying eyes. Well, it's time they have what they want and I'll get what I rightly deserve. Cael, I trust you'll enjoy the pain while it lasts," said Stater.

"At least the night wasn't a complete waste." Stater tossed the words as he and his manservant both stepped over Cael to saunter back into the limo.

For one moment Cael thought Stater was going to stomp on him. That would have pissed him off completely. As it was he felt completely undignified dying in the dirt. For once he would welcome the pain that accompanied his resurrection.

Did he say the Decies? A vile loathing soared to life in the dying embers of his thoughts. If Stater thought letting the Decies out from their prison was a wise move, the former King of Malyadoom was in for a rude awakening. Decies were not to be trusted. Ever. They would suck the life-force out of every living thing if they had the chance. They were his race's arch nemeses.

If Stater thought he could open the veil with Cael's blood the former king was about to be disappointed.

However, Cael's last thought wasn't about the evil Decies. It was the sweet smell of the woman, the feyling, who had stumbled upon him tonight. Honeysuckle! That was it. She smelled like honeysuckle, once you got past the ripe stench from the creature she called skunk. He closed his eyes, recalling vividly the feel of her plump mouth yielding to his probing tongue and for once in his life he longed for another sample of her decadence.

Then Cael died for the two hundred and twenty-second time—and yes, he was keeping a tally. Revenge was easier that way.

Tara fought not to throw up. She had watched the white limo speed off down the hill as she stumbled out of the thick brush. Turning toward the gate she had come across the grisly discovery of Marty, lying face down in a pool of blood that was seeping into the wet earth. She gagged and fought hard not to dislodge her supper and dessert.

She didn't scream. Sorrow too richly coated the back of her throat. Then she noticed the stranger. He too lay face down in the dirt, blood forming a trickling pool from under his front. His leather coat strewn across him looked like a blanket of death. The senseless carnage and evil of what had happened was hard for her mind to wrap around.

Things like this don't happen here. This isn't a big city where weird stuff like this takes place. This is Cape Breton. Why? Why did this happen? Tears streamed down her face as she rocked herself, numbly, her mind trying to fathom what she had stumbled upon...what had happened.

Then a group of pale blue sparks of light floated close to her, catching her eye.

What the Hell are those? Tara continued to hug herself as the damp, harsh chill of the night seeped into her bones. The blue sparks of light moved, as if they were seeking something. They hovered over the stranger lying face down in the dirt and then a flame of blue engulfed him, soaring through his body with amazing speed and agility.

She heard his scream but that was impossible. He's dead. Isn't he? She watched in eerie fascination as his body arched off the ground. His large body contorted at twisted angles while his large frame buckled in on itself, the blue glow filling all of him. The light even streamed from his open mouth, eyes and nose. He floated and was held rigidly in the air by some unknown force.

Then he cursed. The blue glow instantaneously dissipated, leaving him to fall to the ground. At the last moment he moved his body to catch it from falling back into the blood-soaked earth. Cat-like, one arm held his weight. His knees bent to catch the rest of his body as he miraculously landed on the balls of his feet. Then he bounded up to his full towering height.

"Stater, here I come!" His shout was one of agony and a curse, all at the same time.

Then Tara realized he had spoken in her grandmother's secret language, again. Shock rippled through her conscious, stilling her from taking flight.

Just what did I stumble upon? While he looked like a man, now standing and flexing his body like he was checking to make sure all the parts were working, Tara no longer believed what her eyes told her. She highly doubted he was human.

"For the love of my queen I just don't believe it," he mumbled to himself.

As of yet she hoped he was unaware of her presence. She moved her feet back a step and wiped her tears away. He turned abruptly toward the slight sound. She stilled and held her breath, hoping the dark of the night would absorb her form.

"Bloody Hell...tell me it isn't you."

Instinctively she backed up, her boots scrunching the wet ground underfoot with loud sloshes. He moved toward where she was, somewhat leaning on the side of the gate, not far from Marty's body, but not too close either. She glanced quickly at Marty. Guilt smashed hard into her.

If I had been on time he'd be alive. The reasoning hurt more than she could bear, while common sense told her that could very well be her, lying dead on the ground.

When the stranger got closer, the clouds parted once again as if on his whim. She saw clearly that he was holding his chest. His wound hadn't healed. Blood dripped freely down his chest. He gritted his teeth in pain, while he advanced with defiant purpose toward her.

The knowledge she could, and probably should run bore down on her. But she didn't. She hadn't feared him earlier and highly doubted he had killed Marty. After all, he had been dead too. It was the had been part she wasn't too keen to think about.

"Since you came when I expressly told you not to, you've got something I need."

The words sounded more like a growl. He stood within arm's reach of her. There was a strange, angry look in his black-rimmed, silver eyes that caused her stomach to clench in anticipation and dread.

"Wh...wha...What?"

He grabbed her. His body was hot and solid—providing her with much needed warmth. Thankfully he no longer smelled like skunk. Instead she digested the scent of wet leaves and the forest combined with his strong musky hot masculinity. The mix was intoxicating, causing her stomach to flutter with a wild yearning, and a strange harmonic note filled her mind.

Then he kissed her. And it wasn't a kiss that warranted hesitation. He simply took, forcing her mouth to open, to yield to him. His warm hand framed her face, cupping her to him, anchoring her mouth to his so he could devour her as he pleased. Tara wasn't sure how she managed to keep standing. His other large hand grabbed hers. Then a slice of searing pain soared through her passion-induced brain when a sharp instrument pierced her palm.

"Wha...what did you do?" Tara abruptly moved away, noticing he didn't hesitate to let her go.

"Like I said, feyling, you've got something I need."

He moved a step away from her. Feyling? The tender endearment brushed away the sting from the cut. Truthfully it wasn't much of a slice, but still she used her other hand to close the wound, hoping it would clot quickly. Talk about strange.

She watched through suspicious eyes as he took the small jeweled knife he'd obviously used to cut her palm and let three drops of her blood fall into his open hand. Then he spoke a strange rhythm of words that resonated deep within her. All the hairs on her body stood on end—electrified with a strange need for something she couldn't describe while the harmonic notes within her mind zinged through her consciousness filling her with warm light. A feeling of ecstasy sang like wild surging wind through her veins.

"Cover your ears, now!" He barked the order at her.

When she didn't immediately comply, he took a feral step toward her. "I said now!"

This time she didn't hesitate. Feeling slightly ridiculous she covered her ears with her hands. Miraculously, the small cut had healed so she didn't worry about the blood. The minute her ears were covered the notes soaring through her mind ceased.

The man was speaking again. He knelt down to the ground, took a handful of wet earth into his hands, mixed it with her blood on his palm and then proceeded to smear it into the wound on his chest. Awk. Okay, I am now clearly delusional. Just how is that going to help?

Strangely...it did. Her eyes widened in fascination as the wound healed spontaneously. He gasped in pain and then a wolf-like smile lit up his handsome face.

"Well, well, well, feyling, it seems you and I are destined for each other." He stood to his towering height and then his hips moved; his long jean-clad muscular legs advanced once again toward her. He oozed sex and sensuality and seemed inherently aware of it.

Not good, not good at all. This time Tara didn't hesitate. She bolted. Turned into the dark of the night and ran unimpeded straight down the steep hill.

"You can run but you can't hide."

His warm chuckle reached out to her in the dead of the night. His words seemed to brush the hairs on her nape. They left her warm and tingly. She shook the feeling off as she ran like her very life depended on it. And, for once, Tara feared—it did.

Chapter Four

ALEC CURSED UNTIL HE was blue in the face. This night is becoming ridiculous. Tara was gone. He, like his sister Katie, had assumed she'd gone home to watch the hockey game with her father. Thinking he'd gotten off easy after his father had assigned him to watch over Tara, all because the Damned Fairy had shown up in their tavern and taken a strange liking to Tara's quirky song, Alec had breathed easy.

He flexed his fingers, noting none were broken from the fight. Even though he sported a black eye and cut lip he was pleased he had landed half a dozen punches on the Damned Tuatha Dé Danann. Alec still didn't understand why Devon, his father, the ruler of the Highland Druid Lunar Clan, wanted them to stay clear of the Damned Fairy. And just why was he in our tavern and how did he enter without one of us being aware of it? Those two questions tormented Alec. He and his eleven brothers were trained as Druid warriors yet not one of their senses had been alerted when evil had walked through their own front door.

Two hours later, after he and his brothers had cleaned up the mess in the tavern they all felt a dark thread reach out to tweak their druid senses.

Immediately, Alec knew Tara was once again in trouble. This time he didn't know if it was from the Damned Fairy; and yes, he was going to call him that as soon as he saw the creature face to face, consequences be damned, or if it was something more sinister.

All of them felt the pull of the druid magick that ran in their veins. He more so than his other brothers, especially when it came to the use of dark druid powers. So how had they missed picking him out of the bar?

"Where's Tara?"

Trust Brody to ask the obvious. "Home watching the game with her Pop," Alec had answered only to be punched hard in the shoulder by Alistair, who still wore his chef's apron even though he too had joined in the brawl.

"Their TV broke months ago. She fed you a lie and you walked right into it." Alistair yanked off his apron and reached for his long, worn leather jacket. "Come on you guys, we've got to find her fast, before Pop finds out we couldn't even keep Tara in plain sight for ten friggin' minutes."

No one said a word. They had all grabbed their coats, leaving two employees to take care of things at the tavern.

An hour later they weren't any closer to finding her. And that fine tingling of druid instinct told Alec things had gone from bad to worse.

"What the Hell is that running down the hill?" snapped his brother Ross, who had ended up with a broken nose from the fight.

The next instant, the thing running down the hill barreled right into Alec. Why couldn't it have hit Ross or even Brody for that matter?

He almost tumbled but years of warrior training meant his reflexes had already kicked into automatic. A quick movement and his arms were safely wrapped around the thing.

"Alec, oh my ga...god, pl...please tell me it's you."

Tara's breathless voice rushed at him. "Where have you been?" he asked, not meaning to sound as gruff as he did.

She buried her head into his chest and cried. Aw, shit. Again, why couldn't she have stumbled into one of my other brothers? "It's okay, Tara, you're safe now."

"Yo...you don't understand...Marty..." She stuttered and hiccupped. Then a gush of fresh tears streamed down her face. "He's dead. His throat was slashed...and then that man...he...I don't know what he did..."

Did? If he laid a hand on her, that Damned Fairy is a dead man walking. The dark part within Alec he always kept on a tight leash growled in eager anticipation. Ignoring the calling, Alec tried his best to soothe his sister's friend.

"Get your hands off her!"

Instinctively, Alec's druid knowledge recognized the inherent power behind the Tuatha Dé Danann words, but it still took a lot of willpower for him to disobey. Instead he forced himself to embrace the power of the words and turn toward the voice while shielding Tara behind his body. "So, the Damned Fairy has come to play." Alec relished the opportunity to finish what they had started in the tavern.

He felt Tara's pull on his coat. Where the Hell are the rest of my brothers? As if on cue, he felt the familiar presence of them as they materialized out of the night to form a tight circle around him and the Damned Fairy.

Alec pushed Tara toward the brother at his back. His mind didn't even register the Damned Fairy moving, but when Alec looked back Tara was in his arms.

"She's coming with me."

The fairy gloated at them all. Then in a blink of unimaginable speed Tara and the fairy were gone.

"So much for a good fight. Coward!" yelled Alec into the night. The punch to his gut felled him to his knees. Bloody Hell!

They all heard the Damned Fairy's laugh as he slipped unseen once again into the dark with Tara.

"Pop is going to skin us alive," admonished Brody, helping Alec up.

Alec knew exactly how his Pop would feel because he also felt like beating himself up. That blasted fairy is nothing but trouble.

He vowed to return a few good blows of his own to the Damned one the minute he captured him. And he would. The knowledge of that fueled the sinister part within Alec, leaving him feeling slightly satisfied.

CAEL WISHED HE COULD explain what had come over him. He couldn't. He didn't like that one bit. The sight of the still unnamed woman being held in the arms of one of those Highlander Druids had caused him to see red. Those same Highlander Druids who had tried and failed miserably to take him down. All because he simply wanted to talk with the woman who was half fey.

Cael wondered if she had any idea of her heritage. Highly doubtful. If his queen found out about her the woman would be dead within seconds. Queen Mir's view of humans was that they were either pets or bugs, depending on her mood. The Tuatha Dé Danann didn't intermingle with humans. But someone had. That cold knowledge left him mystified. Why? Why would a Tuatha do such a thing to risk Mir's wrath?

Cael knew Mir's rage first hand. She didn't have a soft spot within her heart. Even after years of loyal service as her personal champion she didn't hesitate to exile him from Tir Nan Og when he didn't do exactly as she wished. Instead she tossed him out to the human realm of Earth and made him immortal.

Ignoring the muttered curses from the woman he clutched tight over his shoulder, he wondered what had come over him. Must be an after effect of the spell. Yeah, that's it. He'd feel more like his old self, which didn't give a damn about anyone, in another few minutes. Then he'd find out the woman's name. Using his druid senses, he'd been able to hone in on what he hoped was the Stone of Fal. Now he was heading toward it.

"Put me down," she said, once again wiggling in a feeble attempt to launch herself from his shoulder.

He smacked her ass. "Stay still. We're almost there."

As his hand touched her backside his nostrils flared and other more finely-tuned senses jumped to life. *My bloody cock has a mind of its own. Maybe allowing the creature he was to come out and play would be a good thing. Might certainly please my cock, which liked swatting the woman's ass a little too much.*

Worse was the knowledge she had liked it too. As sweet and innocent as she was he couldn't forget that she was part Tuatha Dé Danann —a sexual creature to the core. In fact, it was said that when Queen Mir had her first orgasm her joy and unfurled powers had reached out to create the planets known to humans as Mars and Venus. Cael had long ago learned that when it came to his queen, she was full of unusual surprises.

I've got to get my thoughts to focus on something other than slipping my cock between this lass' thighs and sliding my shaft into her tight, welcoming sheath. And it would be welcoming. Her Tuatha dew would taste like fine, aged wine, ready for the taking.

Her bite on his shoulder did the trick. He let her down, none too gracefully. She flopped hard, landing on that luscious ass he'd been holding. Her "Oomph!" of surprise caused him to feel a momentary inkling of guilt.

He shook his head. Guilt was a useless human emotion. It was a weak, pitiable feeling, one laughable to his kind.

"What happened to Marty?"

She came to her feet in one fluid movement. Cael was reminded again of how small she was. Almost child-like in appearance, but she stood proud and graceful before him. He noticed her hands were warrior-braced on her hips and he liked the pose a little too much. The wind kissed her long chestnut hair with streaks of auburn and blonde, reminding him again of his homeland. The feeling hit him square in the gut.

She wore faded blue jeans and the bright red sweater she had worn on stage peeked out from her winter jacket that had the words "Security" written across the back. She was a rush of sexual purity. A perfect picture of lust and innocence packaged just right for him. He wondered if she had any idea how earthly graceful she was. His senses caught her scent, honeysuckle and fresh soap. He gritted his teeth, almost wishing he smelled that wee-beastie stink again.

She watched him warily, backing up even further from him. He could tell by her startled expression she had found out where he had taken her. They were standing next to a private burial mound, located in a small clearing overlooking a steep bluff with a forest of old pine trees towering behind them and the sea crashed directly below them. The view was breathtaking.

"I didn't kill him, if that's what you're thinking. He was dead when I got there. But trust me, we have bigger things to worry about." Cael fell to his knees on the sacred burial mound.

"Why did you bring me here?"

She brushed her long-streaked hair off her face, twisting the strands to tuck under her jacket. Then she moved to where he knelt. This was her chance to run, yet she didn't. Instead curiosity won her over. Those were qualities he liked about her. She was a brave little feyling. Again, he wondered how much she knew about her heritage.

The elements knew what he was about to do and the night's wind was howling its own protest as the moon once again shone its full power on them. "What's your name?" A desire to at least learn the name of the woman who'd done more to rattle him in the last few hours than any other mortal had in centuries stole over Cael.

"Tara McNeil. What's yours?"

He turned his face to look at her. "Cael."

There was a brief flash of recognition and fear she tried to quash. "Cael what?"

She notched up her chin, her amber eyes wide while she bravely gave him a piercing look.

"You know who I am, Tara, so just say it." He said the words in the Tuatha language, loving her surprised and wary expression. Part of him admitted that he too loved the ritual flow of the words he hadn't spoken since he'd been kicked out of Tir Nan Og.

"You are not Cael, the Damned Fairy. That's just a story my grandmother told me to scare me to death. And who taught you my grandmother's secret language?"

She stood up, ram-rod straight to glare at him. She was slightly angry and he noted a hint of awe had crept into her voice.

He preferred the awe. "Sadly, I am Cael. I have to say that the Damned Fairy part is highly amusing but I prefer being named as the Damned Tuatha Dé Danann. It has a more elegant ring to it. Fairies make me think of gentle, fun-loving creatures, and Tara—that's not what we are." Cael returned his attention to the ground and began digging again. "And it's not a made-up language. The language your grandmother taught you is the royal Tuatha Dé Danann."

She placed both hands over her ears attempting to ignore him.

"This is not happening to me. None of this is real. I must have drunk something at the bar. Yes, that's it. When I wake up, which I will, I'll be safe at home tucked into my bed. All of this is just so laughable," she said out loud to herself, as she paced back and forth.

Cael let her have her rant. He knew exactly how she felt. A thousand years ago when his queen had done the unthinkable, he'd felt the same way—not that he was about to share that vulnerability with her. He hoped she would be quicker to adapt than he had been.

Sadly, it had taken him a good week to realize no amount of pleading or begging was ever going to get his queen's attention again. It had been the worst week of his existence. First came the hunger, then the cold, then the feeling of loneliness that had been so intense he had wondered then if ending his life would be better.

His race were not solitary beings. They were creatures that were always in groups, or at least in twos, and always touching each other. Born a sensual being to the core, he hadn't realized how much he would miss those casual touches; and he had.

The sad reality was he found out the hard way that not only had his queen banished him but she had left him with the gift of punishing immortality. He never aged but he could die like a human. To be immortal as a mere human, well let's just say his first encounter with death had been painful. Dying was painful enough, but being resurrected had been excruciating, unimaginable agony. If there was one thing Cael knew first hand it was that Mir's sadistic streak ran red like blood. His punishment for daring to disobey her would never end. She made sure of that. His only hope was the Stone of Fal, and now that slim promise was fading fast.

"Will you stop digging at my grandmother's grave," snapped Tara, moving in anger toward him. To stop him.

She had obviously stopped her rant and was at least willing to accept his presence.

So, it's her grandmother. Would figure.

"What are you doing?"

"She has something I need." Cael continued to dig deeper. The mound was still fresh which thankfully made his task easier. She stomped directly in front of him. Dirt flew into his eyes. He blinked and growled a low warning at her. "Get out of my way, feyling. I've got to get the trinket."

Bravely she pushed at his shoulders. "Trinket? You...you...you are disgusting. Grave robber! Leave her alone."

Her strength momentarily surprised him. He grabbed at her outstretched arms and together they rolled down the hill. Asserting his dominance, he pinned her beneath him before she could attempt anything else. As it was she bucked and clawed at him and her knee was attempting to inflict some serious pain at the bulge between his legs. That wouldn't do at all.

Cael knew he could use his druid magick to hold her in place but at the moment he liked the wild fey-cat she was. Instead he did what he wanted to do. He plunged in to kiss her, again. Never giving quarter he molded her tender lips to his. He forced her soft, pliable lips to yield to his, and felt the moment when she became aware of him as a man. She stilled and stopped fighting, waited...but he didn't relent.

He snaked his tongue in between her lips when she took a breath and felt the combined heat of their passion roar over them. He wondered if she felt it too. On some strange level they were inherently connected. The second her arm snaked to his head, pulling him tighter to her frame, Cael felt the quickening of Tuatha lust soar through the marrow of his bones. Her fingers, hesitant in their approach, brushed slowly through his hair, like she was thoroughly examining every strand on his head. The feel of her small fingers playing with his hair was more intoxicating than the dra'jal—the mead his kind drank to heighten sexual pleasure.

Just when did she start kissing me back? The harsh reality of the situation caused him to groan loudly. He knew he could continue to kiss her senseless and better yet, slake his lust. Her body was more than willing, and he knew without a doubt that it would make his cock feel better, but he couldn't continue. He had a job to do and bedding the woman would have to wait.

He forced himself to let go of her lips. Cael leaned back onto his knees, keeping her tiny frame pinned between his muscular thighs. Drugged yellow-amber eyes gazed at him in sensual awareness. They scorched him. Only one other Tuatha he knew had eyes that color, his queen. Immediately, Cael released her.

He watched her blink. Anger flared to life in an instant. Then embarrassment. He wondered if she was angry with herself, because he knew she'd kissed him back with equal passion.

"I don't mean to show your grandmother any disrespect. If I don't get her trinket then my kind are doomed." He stood and graciously offered a hand to help her up. *Why am I telling her that?*

She ignored it. Like before she moved with fey grace to stand on her own two legs.

"I can't let you do that." Her voice sounded tired and small. "It's disrespectful."

"I'm afraid, my little feyling, there is nothing you can do to stop me." Cael moved once again to the small mound to resume digging.

"She might not be able to stop you but we will," said a voice that was starting to grate on Cael's ears.

"Bloody Hell, don't you Highlander boys have something better to do, like go kick a wounded dog?" Cael didn't bother to stop digging.

"Now, Alec!"

The shout came from Cael's left.

Nights weave world, wield to thy own power. Drugged to life, forced into exile, adhere to our words. We free you to force compliance. We free you to our obedience. Hear our words. We are your Masters. By the power of the moon, stars and universes we demand you take him to your breast. We demand your will.

The words were harsh in their power. In unison all thirteen Highlander Druids chanted the powerful druid sleep spell. Their combined voices worked as one to wield enough druid magick that Cael knew he couldn't fight his way free.

"Aww, shit," mumbled Cael, as he fell face first into the dirt for the second time in that many hours.

Chapter Five

"WHAT DID YOU GUYS DO to him?" asked Tara, startled wide awake to her senses.

She still felt the lingering feel of Cael's mouth on her swollen lips. Still tasted the wild, wicked delight of rum soaked with the hint of cinnamon and cardamom that clung to him. She licked her lips, the taste of him enticingly strong on them. His essence was like a forbidden drink or drug. Tara shivered with carnal awareness, while the brush of sexual teasing reached deep within her essence. A fierce longing to run her hands through his hair, or trace the outline of his warm, inviting lips left her breathless and achy.

He was Cael—the Damned Tuatha Dé Danann; of that she had no doubt. And she had kissed him. Kissed him with a passion that stole her breath, left her body vibrating for more, yearning to feel every inch of him. The silky, flower-petal-soft feel of his shiny platinum-colored hair had teased her fingers in a way she couldn't describe but could remember vividly. She wanted him. Craved him. The knowledge of that bruised her heart.

How could I want him? He was the very person she had been told to stay away from all her life by the two people who mattered the most in her world—her grandmother and her father. They had instilled a deep fear of the Tuatha Dé Danann in her. While Tara had always thought of those stories as fables, she was beginning to wonder how much of what her grandmother told her could be true.

She looked at Cael again. Even in sleep everything about him was rough and his body still looked tense. There wasn't a tender spot on his warrior face and she highly doubted he had any soft places within his heart. He embodied every dark story she'd heard and a shiver of trepidation rippled through her conscious.

How could I disrespect their wishes so much and let any man kiss me? Wait a second, it was me kissing him senseless too. Tears welled up in her eyes.

"It's okay, Tara-girl, you're safe now."

Katie's father, Devon, stood next to her. Misunderstanding the reason for her tears he hauled her into his frame for a father-like hug.

Tara wished she didn't like it so much but she did. They were her support system when she felt so very much alone. Between trying to help her father, who seemed to be shrinking away before her eyes more and more each day, paying their bills and going to university as she promised her grandmother there was hardly any time for her pleasure. Thinking of pleasure made her face redden as she recalled the powerful feeling of Cael's lips on her own.

"Pop we've got to move him. Where to?"

Tara watched Alec give Cael's prone body a small kick to see if he really was asleep.

"To the cave at the back of Kelly's Mountain," said Devon. "Neil, bring the pick-up. You boys put him in the back and remember he's going to be extremely angry when he wakes up so we've got to move quickly." He barked orders as he forcibly ushered Tara down the hill.

"Tara, honey, I'm taking you home, okay? You've been through enough tonight. Your father needs you. Don't you fret about that there man...me and me boys will take care of him and he won't be bothering ya again. Fear not, Tara-girl."

Devon forced her shaking body to move. Silently they made their way down the steep incline. Tara realized then she must be in shock... must have imagined all this. How else could she explain what had happened to her in the last few hours?

"Wha...waa...what are you going to do with him?" she asked.

"We need to keep you safe, Tara. I know it's been hard on you, losing your grandmother and all but we're your family too. You can tell us anything. Right now, though, you need to get home and sleep." Devon forced her quivering body into the passenger side of the small car.

Tara realized later, once he'd dropped her off and personally escorted her to the door that Devon hadn't answered her question. *Just what are they going to do to Cael? And why on earth should I care or even think about him? He's not real. The Tuatha Dé Danann aren't really real.*

Sadly, that night all she could think about was him—how his black rimmed, silver-grey eyes had looked so sad and lonely, how his powerful kisses had melted her insides and how good the feel of his hard, muscled body held flush to hers had felt. She tossed and turned in her bed, trying to force sleep to overtake her mind that was over analyzing things. She fought with herself to forget the passion, to erase the feel of him nestled close to her. The knowledge he was real was a potent fix. The awareness that the Tuatha Dé Danann existed and that one was currently in Cape Breton slammed into her with vivid intensity, awakening a strange longing for adventure.

She clutched her blanket for reassurance, as a sliver of light crested through her window. Dawn was near. She yawned and then finally gave in and closed her eyes for good, still hugging the intense memory of Cael's cinnamon-cardamom kisses.

THE SOFT WHISPER OF voices brushed into Tara's sleepy mind. She rolled over. Her body was on fire and her throat parched. She felt shaky with a desperate need for something that seemed just out of reach. Her breasts felt swollen and her nipples ached and tingled. There was an uncomfortable throb between her legs. *What's happening to me?*

"You awake, Tara-love? It's morning and not like you to sleep in."

Her father's voice came from the other side of the door. Tara tried to croak out an answer. Her skin felt eerily tight on her body. Sweat trickled between her breasts.

"Tara, you all right? I'm comin' in," said her father, opening the door a crack. "Oh my god girl, what's happenin' to you? Alec, go get your ma, Tara's sick," her father yelled down the stairs. Concern was etched tightly in the lines drawn around his mouth.

An instant later Tara heard the front door slam and the sound of running feet outside. The noises vibrated through every tight vein and nerve ending in her now overly sensitive body. She clutched her ears shutting out the droning sounds. Her head thrashed from side to side as an intense wave of heat rippled through her body.

Her father ran into the bathroom and returned. "Here Tara, take a drink, this will help."

He forced her head up off the pillow. Tara gingerly sipped at the cool water, and then spat it out. The water burned in her mouth. She longed to cry from the pain but couldn't. Her eyes were so dry and brittle all she could do was continue to blink, praying that would help. It didn't. It caused them to hurt like Hell.

Next, she felt a damp cloth on her forehead. Searing white-hot pain slammed into her. She shook her head from side to side to force the cloth off. When her father finally realized what she wanted, he removed it. The look of horror on his face told her all she needed to know. Something most definitely wasn't right.

A moment later the front door opened with the sound of MacCallah running up the stairs. She paused a moment outside Tara's bedroom before knocking gently to open the door.

"When did this happen?" MacCallah was brisk and all motherly as she strode into the bedroom, appraising everything with her bright blue eyes.

Tara looked at her pleadingly, her body on fire.

"She awoke like this," said her father, his voice full of choked emotion.

"Alec, when you brought her home last night was she like this?"

"No," he replied. "Ma, I need to tell you something."

Through a haze of pain, Tara watched MacCallah follow Alec out of the bedroom. The door closed silently behind them. Muffled voices and strong curses followed swiftly.

Something is not right. What's come over me?

"It's going to be okay, Tara. I'll call the doctor. He'll come over and check on you. It's just a fever. You're going to be okay, Tara-love." Her father was using his reassuring voice...all quiet and patient, as he sat on the side of her bed, obviously yearning to reach out to touch her, but afraid to do so.

The door opened again with a quiet creak. "Ahh, Jim, I've got to talk to you for a minute, okay?"

MacCallah motioned him to follow her outside the door. Tara blinked. It can't be good news. She felt humiliated and afraid. Her body didn't feel right. Her skin felt stretched and itchy with a need she couldn't describe. What terrified her more was that every time she closed her eyes she saw Cael and she just knew it wasn't an illusion, or a fever-induced vision.

He lay staked with his arms outstretched and his legs shackled with heavy irons that had engraved symbols on them. He writhed in pain and agony and he was cold, frustrated and hungry.

How can I see him? How can I feel what he's feeling? Her thoughts were a jumble. Part of her hated she was thinking of him when she had no right to when she was obviously sick with some strange sudden illness.

Her father came back into her room. A stony expression marred his face. He sat beside her with unspilled tears shining his eyes. "I'm so sorry, Tara. I tried to protect you all my life. We tried...both of us, but she knew this day might come. We thought here in Cape Breton that the chances were slim. She assured me the Fey would not come here. She promised you'd be safe." He gave a snort. "She said they hated this type of weather." He choked back a sob, his eyes pleading with her to understand what he was saying but she couldn't follow his logic.

"You know you've always been special, you've always been different, but no matter what, you will always be my Tara-love, don't ever forget that. Devon's on his way over. He'll take you to him. Come back to me someday." A sob tore from his throat.

What is he talking about? Her eyes pleaded with him for a better explanation. Nothing was making sense—her body or her father at the moment.

"We've got to move fast, Jim. Sorry about all this. We never expected this to happen. The boys say they thought she was safe from him." MacCallah gave her father a reassuring hug. "I promise we'll make him do the honorable thing."

"You'd better," said her father, giving her one last pained look.

Tara watched him leave, his shoulders slumped. He looked like he'd aged twenty years in the last five minutes. She felt the injustice of what was happening to her and how it was affecting her father. The last thing she had ever wanted was to be a burden to him and now, as she lay almost delirious because of some strange illness, she knew it was slowly killing him.

"You tell him he'd better take care of her, or I will come after him." Her father's voice boomed loudly on the small staircase.

Tara had no idea who they were talking about. Take care of me? Who's going to take care of me? What's going on? She wished she could speak but her throat burned so much that was impossible.

"Katie, you can't go in there," said Alec.

Tara heard the loud scuffle. "Get out of my way, Alec. She's my friend."

"No, Katie. You can't go in there. You can see Tara when she's better, but for now, you must leave," said Katie's mother, MacCallah, her tone announcing she wouldn't take no for an answer.

"Okay, Ma, will you tell her I'm thinking of her," said Katie, heeding her mother's stern voice.

Tara heard Katie and another person, she supposed it was Alec, make their way down the rickety staircase.

She closed her eyes, slightly delirious with the throb and pain her body was trying to process. She thought she had seen MacCallah come back into her room, but the black abyss of unconsciousness took hold of her too soon for her to be sure. Even though she swore she heard MacCallah muttering to herself, "That Damned Fairy is going to pay for this!"

Chapter Six

CAEL WAS GOING TO MAKE them pay for humiliating him. That is once he'd figured out a spell to unlock the manacles chained to his wrists and ankles that were made of solid iron and engraved with the ancient druid symbols holding him in place.

They were smart. He'd give the Highlander Druids that. Still though, he was fuming mad. Sure, he'd been humiliated before during his long human-like existence when he had been forced to live as a mere mortal but he had always known he'd even the score. And he would again. That knowledge calmed him. He stopped straining against his chains and rested his head on the hard, cold unforgiving ground.

He knew the Highlander Druids had brought him to a cave. He sensed the use of old druid magick working within the cave's walls, but little else. He hadn't seen any of the Highlanders since he'd awoken hours ago, screaming the many ways he planned to exact revenge on them.

Now that he was somewhat calmer he scanned his surroundings. The painted druid symbols on the walls told him all he needed to know. He was going to have to fight tooth and nail and use every trick he'd learned to escape from this prison. And he had to escape, which was funny when he thought about it.

He'd come to Cape Breton to find the Stone of Fal to end his miserable existence, this time for good. Only with the use of the sacred green emerald, born from the tears of the first Tuatha Dé Danann queen when she gave birth to her daughter, could he finally die.

The Internet rumor had been wrong. The stone wasn't in a Highland cemetery. It was, he bet, being held in the hands of Tara's dead grandmother, who had obviously been a true Tuatha Dé Danann at one time in her life. How she'd come to be a mortal woman was a question he was going to work out later. Now though he was racing against time trying to find the stone before Stater did.

"When I get free, book your funerals boys." Saying the words out loud with the empty cave as his witness didn't give Cael the satisfaction he was looking for. And satisfaction was something he was going to get.

The cold knowledge Stater planned to free the Decies—vile, evil creatures that would suck the energy out of every living being, left him mystified. Why? Why would he want to do that? The better question is what did Mir do to him that he sought to destroy all of Tir Nan Og?

Over two millennia ago the Tuatha Dé Danann had fought the advances of the insidious Decies species that had appeared out of nowhere. One day Tir Nan Og had a beautiful crystal-clear blue sky filled with the ancient Reikas, sky beings, who were distant cousins to the Tuatha. The Reikas looked more like the fabled fairies of lore, with their beautiful crystal-clear wings and all, than the Tuatha Dé Danann. The next morning, his race awoke to find that the beings living in the sky realm had disappeared. Shortly after that the sky had started to decay from blue to a purple-pink hue while other parts of his homeland were in complete darkness.

He closed his eyes as the bitter memories of his childhood assaulted him. Tir Nan Og wasn't at all the fairytale place humans thought it was. The darkness, the cold and the hunger had been his early constant companions when he'd been a child but once he learned how to harness his Tuatha heritage and embraced the warrior within him, that had slowly changed.

After many wars, Queen Mir's sister, Facia, who was known for her warrior abilities, finally managed to capture the Decies King.

Queen Mir had him and his minions imprisoned in her miniature treasure chest.

The realization Stater had stolen the treasure chest that housed the Decies King and his minions caused Cael to strain again against his chains. He knew if Stater got his hands on the sacred emerald he would force Mir to give him what he wanted, rulership over mankind. From what little he knew of the human king, he never played by the rules. Without a doubt if the Stone of Fal fell into Stater's hands then humankind and his race would die.

The power of the stone was that it granted the deepest wish of whoever held it. For Cael that wish would be to finally die, to end his existence in peace. Stater, on the other hand, would simply use it to force Mir's hand and the only way to do that was to set the Decies free.

If the humans knew anything at all about the Decies they'd all be running for their lives. Cael almost laughed with that thought. Like I care what happens to them. But that wasn't entirely true and he knew it. While he'd become more of a skeptic over the centuries, humans constantly surprised him. Their boundless determination and energy to conquer the unknown, while not always good, did allow them to advance as a race. That insight had at one time given him joy. At the same time, another more painful memory surfaced, one he had thought he'd banished long ago from his immortal memories.

Brown eyes gazed at him in wonder. A mop of jet-black hair fell in disarray around the small child as she attempted to swipe the curls out of her perky face. A dash of freckles flew across her tiny nose and red rosy lips cracked a smile at him.

Cael once again fought the chains. He tossed and turned his head, squinting his eyes shut, trying to force the memory away. It was no use. What must it be now, close to five hundred years? Still the seeds of the memory grew, engulfing his chest with deep racking sorrow. At one time that sorrow had fueled his anger. Now it simply left him feeling hollow.

Tiny hands folded themselves around his large fingers. "Bounce me again," chimed the lass, his lass. He had done just that. If he could have he'd have bounced his child on his knee for eternity—anything to keep her alive. But Fate was cruel and wicked. He'd learned that hard and fast.

Cael closed his eyes, wearily resigned now to the stream of memories even as he gritted his teeth. He could still smell the sweet, sticky sickness that had painfully taken away his little girl, Ashling's life. Cael had married Anya, a gentle, carefree woman after she'd been raped by a neighboring clan member. He had always known the child in her womb wasn't truly his but birthing the babe had awoken something fierce within his lonely heart. He had loved Ashling, his vision-child, the minute she took her first breath. When the sickness took hold of her Cael had fought against her death for weeks just like he had for her mother. He had been happy but it was too brief. And the loss made living seem meaningless and unbearable.

Ten years was all they'd had. Not even a blink to his kind. Sadly, he'd found joy, comfort and a sense of belonging with Anya. She had loved him for the man he told her he was. He had tried at first to tell her about the Tuatha Dé Danann, but she wanted none of that. She wanted the picture he had painted—of a gentle Irish shepherd, a caring husband and a doting father. Worse was the knowledge that he'd wanted it too. The life was a lie but it had brought a reprieve from his loneliness.

Someone should have warned him that the feeling of emptiness and pain of losing one's child would be all consuming. "Pa, I'm gonna see ma again." That had been her last sentence. Cael held to hope, knowing his daughter had a soul that would grant her resurrection and peace everlasting. That painful day crashed through him again.

He remembered exactly how he'd held Ashling, his vision-child, in his arms until she drew her last gasping breath. He had cried and howled in rage to the Fates all day. But at dawn the next day he'd dug her grave and buried her next to her mother. Then he'd walked away from Ireland for good. He had never gone back. A part of him would have sold his druid knowledge to Mir then if she had asked, anything to save the child he had come to love. When Cael realized all his druid powers wouldn't heal her, the injustice of what his queen had done to him had roared wickedly to the surface.

The ripeness of the memory always left him feeling weak. It had been the one and only time he'd given into the need to feel wanted, loved and comforted. He'd take cold, isolation and loneliness for eternity if that meant never experiencing that horrible sorrowful emotion that had consumed him for centuries.

That was when he'd tried a thousand ways to end his life—all to no avail. He'd cursed his queen then and still cursed her today but he'd do the right thing. He had to get to the Stone of Fal and give it back to his queen. Then, somehow he'd make her listen to the real threat Stater posed and if need be beg on his knees for her to end his miserable human-like existence for good.

The crunch of many boots on the ground broke through Cael's reverie. About bloody fucking time, Highlander boys.

Three Highlanders came toward him. The eldest, the one he'd punched in the face on his first encounter, and later, in the gut when he had tried to mock him, sported a bruised eye. Cael glared hard at him, provoking him as the Highlander kicked his foot.

"That all you can do, Highlander?" Cael taunted him. "Let me loose and let's just you and me go at it."

"Sit down Alec," said the old man coming forward to kneel beside Cael's head.

Cael braced himself. This man, while old, could wield druid magick with a force to be reckoned with.

"You're getting what you want, you damned Tuatha Dé Danann. You had better take care of her, or so help me...I will make you die over and over again."

"Look, old man, been there and done that a hundred times so if you're wanting to kill me get in line," snapped Cael, eyeing the old man.

The old man continued speaking like he hadn't heard a word Cael said.

"You will do the right thing. There's a priest waiting outside who won't ask any questions but you will do the right thing. Am I clear?" glared the old man.

Clear as mud. What is he talking about? However, Cael didn't voice any objections. He'd heard priest and the words "waiting outside" so that meant they were going to free him. Then you had all better run. He gave a feral smile and nodded his head affirmatively.

Sure, I'll confess some earthly sin if it will set me free.

"Alec, undo his ankles. We'll keep the wrist ones on for safe keeping," said the old man.

"Take them off now, old man or no dice!" shouted Cael, no longer feeling inclined to play the game.

"After the ceremony," replied the old man.

"Pop, I can't believe you're allowing this. After all we went through last night. It's just not right," said the man, who Cael knew wanted to beat the shit out of him.

Cael glared a savage smile at him, wishing the Highlander would come at him.

"Stay in your place Keegan. I told you this isn't up for discussion. If we don't she'll die."

Die? Who will die? "Will someone please tell me what's going on or better yet tell me how any of your human activities concern me." Cael rubbed his ankles that were now free. The iron manacles were still clasped tightly around both wrists, and while he would normally at this point fight his way to freedom, he didn't because something wasn't right.

"Bring her in," said the old man.

Cael blinked. Cradled in the arms of yet another Highlander was Tara. Every hair on his body crackled. "What the Hell did you do to her?" He attempted to lunge forward.

With one word from the old man the druid symbols on the iron manacles glowed to life, halting his progress. He stood rock still, incapable of moving an inch forward as electricity slammed through every nerve ending in his body.

"We didn't do this to her. You did."

"Like Hell," said Cael, yearning to reach out and take the woman in his own arms. He didn't like her being cradled in the arms of the tall Highlander one bit. "Let me go," he commanded, staring at Devon.

Silent communication passed between the two of them and then with one word, Cael was free. He stood still, knowing he'd somehow passed a test of wills.

"Take her to the priest outside. You've explained things, right MacCallah?" asked the old man.

"Names. I'd like some names. You all look the same to me," snarled Cael.

"You want civility...you Damned Tuatha Dé Danann, fine. This here is me wife MacCallah, sons Alec and Keegan. Alistair is holding Tara. The rest of me boys you don't want to meet at the moment. They'd like nothing better than to beat you into mulch. And before you come back with a nasty retort, we're going to settle this and then we'll leave you for the night. As much as this is killing me and all of us, we're letting you take her," stated Devon.

"Take her? Take who?" Cael was clearly surprised by the turn of events.

"Tara, you bastard," snapped Alec.

Bastard! I don't think so. The druid spell worked its way fast into Cael's consciousness and in a flash Alec was on his knees, cradling his head.

"Stop it you two!" snapped the woman, MacCallah, stepping between them.

Cael did just that, vowing to let the Highlander know at a later date how unkindly he took to that word. Then he realized all of the Highlanders were concerned for Tara. A strange, unknown emotion awoke within him.

He shook his head. He didn't need to get sidetracked. He needed to focus, get free and get that blasted Stone of Fal.

Tara. They are going to let me take Tara...but where? Cael growled in exasperation. Something wasn't right.

Then Tara moaned. The sound cascaded through his system, causing him to suck in his gut. Something is most definitely wrong.

He stepped closer to the Highlander called Alistair to look at Tara. Sweat beaded and pearled on her forehead. Her eyes fluttered open for a brief moment but obviously the effort was too much for her because she closed them wearily. Does she even recognize me?

He turned his head and looked at the woman called MacCallah. "What's wrong with her?"

The woman's cold penetrating look scorched him. Great, they think I did this to her. Why must everything be pinned on me? Before she could say anything, Cael voiced his thoughts. "Look, I have no idea what's wrong with her. Maybe she's got the flu or something. I most certainly did not do this to her." Cael ran his hands through his hair.

"Yes, you did." Devon's calm soothing voice unnerved Cael.

Cael simply shook his head.

"Tara's half Fey. You knew that, and still you claim ignorance. Shame on you. Shame indeed. The only cause of her sickness is you. She's had a taste of you and if I'm correct she's going through the—"

"Sh'lam'alah." Cael gulped and his eyes rounded with disbelief.

"Just what the..." Alec gulped, realizing what he'd been about to say in front of his parents. "What exactly is that?"

"The burning. She's going through the burning." Cael turned toward MacCallah and held out his hands, looking at Devon. "Take these off. I won't flee. Honestly, I never meant for this to happen and yes, I confess that I...well, okay...Hell I kissed her and yes, she kissed me back, but if for one moment I thought she'd go through this, I'm telling you I would never have boarded that fucking bus in the first place." Come to think of it I should have bought a ticket back home the minute I landed in this friggin' place. Nothing has gone right from the get go.

Another low moan reached out to caress the fine hairs on his skin. A wave from Devon's hands and the manacles were released. Cael approached Tara slowly. He looked Alistair squarely in the eyes and then held his arms out. Alistair nodded and then handed over the tiny woman into his arms. She weighed almost nothing and she was burning hot. Her womanly scent slammed hard into him. His nostrils flared in sexual awareness. His cock jumped to attention as he fought the sizzling desire that circled and fired all his cells into anticipation of acute bliss.

"You'll do the honorable thing by her," said MacCallah, not relenting in her mothering role.

Cael simply shook his head. "No, I can't." He voiced the words knowing they were wrong. He could and should, but he was afraid. He didn't want to get attached to another being. He couldn't deal with that grief again.

The woman stirred in his arms. Her amber eyes opened and a heated, sensual smile curved her lush lips. "You, I was dreaming about you. Very naughty things..." She sighed, closed her eyes and thankfully stopped talking.

"Well, I do believe this is a first. Can't recall ever hearing tell of a Tuatha Dé Danann blushing." A small tense smile creased Devon's hard-clenched jaw. "And you will take her or you will remain in chains the rest of your miserable existence."

Cael bristled. Deep down he knew he'd do the honorable thing and that's what made him mad. *This isn't why I came here.* He half-heartedly thought about telling the Highlanders about Stater and the Decies but then thought better of it. They couldn't help anyway.

"You understand that by giving her to me I will fuck her thoroughly," snarled Cael. He had used the crude words cruelly to ensure there was no mistaking his purpose.

All of the Highlander Druids inhaled sharply then growled a low warning. But it was the woman, MacCallah who stepped forward to confront him.

"Bed her well, make her whole. We need our Tara-girl back."

With that the woman promptly turned and marched out of the cave, regal in her grace though her backbone was ramrod straight with disapproval.

Cael sighed. "Fine, get me your priest. We'll do it your way and tonight I'll be doing it my way." He couldn't stop the slow, seductive smile that stole over his face at the vision of giving into the lust he'd felt from the first moment he saw her. His feyling.

Tonight, make no mistake about it she was going to be his in all ways. He strove hard to dampen the erotic images that popped into his mind but it was no use. Already rock hard, his cock pulsed eagerly. He grimaced, as she squirmed once again in a slow, seductive movement he felt all the way to his toes.

Chapter Seven

"SAY I DO," MUMBLED the gruff voice deep inside Tara's head.

She could barely manage it. "I do." She sighed and snuggled in close to the feel of a warm, muscled chest that brought her instant relief from the bone-chilling cold. She longed to reach out and lick the man's skin. *What is coming over me?* Tara inhaled the wild masculine scent of him. It immediately calmed her, stopping her body from shivering with the intensity of the fever she was sure she had.

A short time later she felt the soft, yielding cushion of a mattress. Then gently, a wet tongue reached out to lick her parched lips. Her eyes flew open as did her mouth. A new searing heat slammed hard into her.

"It's going to be okay, feyling. I'll be gentle."

The man's rough baritone voice flew into her body, teasing her with a wave of sexual awareness. His hands skimmed over her highly sensitive skin causing her to moan and writher. He replaced the burning ravaging within her, the strange sickness, with a savage pulse of desire that caused her legs to buck for more. Strong, intent...the feel of his hands, his tongue, his lips, his body was her medicine, licking away the pain to replace it with fevered passion she willingly embraced.

She heard him mumbling strange words that tickled her ears, causing the fine hairs on her body to tingle in anticipation. The weight of him settled between her parted legs and a large hand pressed down on her mound. She squirmed with need. *When did I take off my clothes?*

Then his lilting words wordlessly spoken deep within her mind, reached into her subconscious, enticing her with wicked promises, and playful loving. The erotic play of them made her pant with a heavy need, her body meeting his, needing the heat of flesh to flesh to take away the chill of the fever she was sure she had.

"So wet, so ready, my little feyling," he said.

The sweet endearment sounded vaguely familiar to her. Tara inwardly laughed. This was after all her erotic dream so that made sense to her.

His mouth found her breasts. He proceeded to savor and feast on them, applying a lover's skill to them that had her achy all over. With detailed precision he suckled her breasts, taking the time to tease her nipples. She curved her spine up to meet him, demanding more as he suckled hard on first one and then the other nipple until they were tight buds, aching even as he plucked and tweaked them, merging pain with pleasure. She felt his fingers glide over her cleft, parting her swollen nether lips. Then he slid a finger deep into her, pumping her, causing her body to grind with need. She arched again, trying to draw her knees up, demanding he go deeper.

His small chuckle kissed her skin.

"Ahh, feyling, so like my kind, so ready. I'll try to take away the sting of this, so relax."

Her legs were pushed open more, exposing her to his gaze and demands. His hand held her slick opening wide and then she felt the hard, round tip of him enter her with one long thorough stroke. A small prickle of pain, like that of a paper cut, flew through her but then he moved with sure, swift strokes deeper and deeper into her body. A second later she was begging for him to move even faster. She embraced the pounding rhythm of flesh against flesh like her fever, needing the heat of him seared into her slick skin.

She drew her knees up and felt his hands grasp her ass, positioning her to his liking. He demanded. She took. She accepted, needing his masterful skills, pleased the heat penetrating her body was quaking into ripples of pleasure. He thankfully picked up the tempo, drawing her into him as much as he could. It was heaven. She no longer felt on fire or feverish. Instead, she soared with the pleasure of freedom. Wild, unfettered she let her erotic dream of passion take her to a height she thought she would never embrace...let alone climb, if she was conscious. Savage piston thrusts from the man had her groaning loudly. With each penetration he hit a highly sensitive spot in her body. She ground down hard. He stilled, letting her chase the promise of fulfillment.

"Ahh, feyling, come for me, come for me like I know you want to," said the man, his body shaking with desire. He moved his hand to apply light and hard taps to her small nub of pleasure, which was swollen and achy for more. The minute he tweaked it between two of his fingers she fragmented.

Instantaneously she came. Climbed and soared into a magical land where her body floated free of form and substance. Heat surfaced over her skin, her mind connecting with the warmth of his passion.

She heard him growl, "Ahh, Tara my feyling."

She loved the feel of his vibrating voice and then he came. The hot gush of his seed caused her nipples to harden even more as he pumped deep inside of her, almost touching her womb. Immediately a second climax claimed her consciousness. She screamed in ecstasy and her entire body went taut as desire swamped all her senses, again. The combined powerful release awoke a tenderness within her mind she hadn't felt earlier. For a moment she wondered if the emotion was hers or his. Then realizing again this was her dream, she smiled with pleasure, pleased with her fantasy lover, even as he applied butterfly kisses to her feverish skin. Small nips and licks of passion skimmed her body as the man fed all his thankful passion into her.

"Fucking unbelievable," he murmured.

His weight settled like a warm safety blanket over her. Tara's body felt completely satisfied. Contentment like she'd never experienced before stole into her weary bones and tired dream. Talk about having the best erotic dream of your life. Tara gave into the urge to close her eyes as her knees dropped down. A warm, soft cotton blanket magically wrapped around her body as she closed her eyes again to snuggle against a solid wall of heat and muscle.

THE SMELL OF HOT COCOA and warm bread brought her awake.

She opened her eyes and immediately sat up in the bed and looked around. Next to her in the bed was Cael, staring at her intently. Tara blinked a couple of times, her brow furrowing in puzzlement before she dared to speak.

"Wh...what...where am I? Why are you here? And what did you do to me?" She took a deep breath in and forced the nervous stutter to subside. Tara clutched the cotton quilt closer to her skin. Oh my god, I'm naked! "And wh...where are my clothes?"

A loud cough from the other side of a large red curtain that acted as a makeshift barrier drew her attention. "Are you decent in there?"

"Nope. But bring in the cocoa and bread anyway. I'm famished," commanded Cael, moving to bring his prone body closer to hers.

Immediate heat traveled up her naked skin. Tara gulped, trying like mad to figure out what had happened to her, and why Cael was lying next to her naked. She couldn't help but eye his spectacular chest. Coppery muscles flexed with each breath he took. Her eyes were instantly drawn to the dark blue and black symbols that covered both arms. Intensely erotic, she watched him subtly flex his arm muscles for show. She looked at his face and caught his grin. "Stop showing off," she snapped.

"Ahh, my feyling, but you like what you see and I like to show off." He gave her a playful wink.

What is happening here? Tara tried to think but then in walked MacCallah carrying a tray which was the source of the smell. Two mugs of steaming hot chocolate, a plate with some cut up cheese and apples and a loaf of fresh bread. She hadn't realized how hungry she was until then. Her stomach rumbled.

"Ohh, Tara-love you're looking much better," muttered MacCallah, trying to keep her eyes downcast.

Now this is awkward. "Would someone please tell me what's going on?" she asked.

MacCallah simply kept her head down while Cael took a hot mug and sipped the cocoa like this was an everyday occurrence.

"Not bad at all," he muttered to himself.

Tara sighed in exasperation.

"I thought you would have told her," said MacCallah, now eyeing Cael.

Tara didn't like her tone. "Told me what?"

"We had sex last night," said Cael, crudely, reaching out to twist off a piece of the fresh bread.

Sex! I don't think so. Wouldn't I remember that? "Okay, I'll give Katie this one. It must have taken a lot of work to set all this in motion. You almost had me there for a moment," said Tara, bravely reaching out for the other mug of cocoa.

"You are such a bastard," snapped MacCallah to Cael.

"Come on, you two. This isn't funny anymore." Tara no longer liked the joke her best friend and it would appear, her mother, were playing on her.

"You should have explained things to her," said MacCallah, once again ignoring Tara.

"Actions speak louder than words," drawled Cael.

"I'm going to leave you now Tara, but we're not far. Cael will explain it all."

MacCallah gave her a pained and worried look. Tara knew MacCallah had caught herself, almost like she had wanted to lean in and give her a hug before she gathered herself and turned to leave them.

"You know, this is no longer funny. Why am I in a bed...better yet, why am I in a bed that's in a cave and with you?" asked Tara, shakily holding her cup, feeling her throat start to constrict as her nervousness increased. Her heart was fluttering wildly and while a lot had to do with the hunky specimen of Fey power next to her an equally large part had to do with the fear eating away within her that told her she wasn't going to like what the Damned Fairy said to her.

She felt Cael's fingers reach out and gently take the steaming mug from her. He placed it on an old fish barrel that had been turned upside down to act as a makeshift table.

"Okay, Tara, first off none of this was my idea, even though I confess to playing a small part in it. Secondly, I'd like to get out of this cave as much as you. Third, I fucked you senseless last night." A wolfish grin flashed hard and cold across his face. He held her hand but his tone was even. She sensed urgency behind his words he tried hard to mask. She also sensed he was angry, the emotion a tight coil of powerful energy that rippled beneath his human veneer.

Tara knew what he said couldn't be true. She'd simply had an erotic dream last night. She'd remember a man, especially this stranger, this Damned Tuatha Dé Danann taking her virginity. Tears pooled into the corners of her eyes. None of this made any sense.

"I wouldn't do that," she said, in a small sad voice.

"Not normally, but the sex part had to be done and I must say it was done nicely," said Cael.

"I don't remember it," she declared, turning away from him.

"What?"

His tone was incredulous. Tara filed that one away for future ammunition. "Really, I don't. But if you say it was good, it must have been."

"Feyling, the word good does not describe what we did here on this very mattress last night. Try mind shattering...fucking amazing sex. Now you either get me the Hell out of here or spread your legs for me again," said Cael, that portrait of being human long gone as he asserted his dominance.

His grip on her arm tightened slightly. He wasn't kidding. "You are a gross disgusting pig!" Tara pushed at his shoulder so he'd get the hint and move further away from him.

"That's not what you thought last night."

A real genuine smile lit up Cael's face, reaching to his silver eyes and her heart swelled. Thank god he doesn't smile often. Why aren't I afraid of him? Why don't I fear this Damned Tuatha Dé Danann when I know what he's capable of?

"Okay, saying I believe you, which by the way I don't, that doesn't mean I'm going to stay in bed with you any longer."

With false bravado Tara reached for a piece of the still warm bread. There was a devilish glint to his eyes that caused her nipples to harden. She hugged the quilt tighter to her body, needing any type of shield or weapon to keep her sane.

"You honestly don't remember anything of yesterday?"

He reached out to hand her the mug of cocoa like this was a normal conversation. "Not much. I remember what happened to Marty...oh my god, Marty,"

"It's been taken care of and there was nothing you could have done, Tara," said Cael. For once there was real sincerity in his voice. "If I had gotten there quicker I would have ensured your friend was still alive."

She gave a small nod, realizing the truth behind his words. Then the stories her grandmother told her about the Damned One slammed into her and chilled goose bumps clamored along her skin. Forgiveness was something he was not known for. The nightmare tales told to her didn't paint Cael as the chivalrous knight in shining armor type, more like the bogeyman who lived for vengeance.

Tara gulped, not wanting to recall the tales or events of the past day. "What happened to me? I remember waking up feeling hot and feverish."

"I bet you did. Did you feel like you needed something...something that was just out of reach?" Cael downed the rest of his cocoa in one gulp and placed the mug on the barrel.

"Yes, that's it."

He lazily leaned back to cross his muscular arms over his broad shoulders so they could rest with his head on the pillow. Her breath hitched in her throat. He was such a fine specimen of a man that he stole her breath away. But then again, that's what the Tuatha Dé Danann are known for—their stunning sexy looks and their trickery and he's not really a man. Best to keep that in mind.

"That need was for me...just so we're clear. You and I are connected and as much as you don't like it, I like it even less, so until I can reach my queen you're stuck with me. And oh, I forgot to mention one other thing."

She nodded for him to continue, noting his eyes were once again glacially cool.

"Sex. That's the other thing you'll be needing from me and lots of it my feyling, so get used to me fucking you. I know after last night I've certainly resigned myself to the task. But, I won't shirk my duty to you."

He cast a knowing look her way. Without a doubt Tara knew he had used that word on purpose.

So what? Let me assure you, it, whatever the 'it' is, most certainly it won't happen again. Tara tangled her fingers through her hair in an attempt to take some control over something. When even her hair failed to obey she harrumphed in annoyance.

"You know, this is laughable. How did any of this happen?" She tried hard to ignore the heat of his body so close to hers or the delicious exotic scent of him that rubbed her just the right way.

"Actually, it's all your fault."

"Come again?" she said.

"Feyling, now that's something I could do for a long time with you..."

She jabbed at him with her pointy finger, hating the double-entendre he'd implied. "Stop that, you know that's not what I meant. How is this my fault?"

"Simple," he said, catching her hand to bring it up to his lips. She watched through half-closed lids as he placed her pointy finger in his mouth and then proceeded to suck on it. She felt the shock and sensuality of his actions slide like an intimate lover's caress all over her body.

"You're half Tuatha Dé Danann and I used to be a Tuatha. It all comes down to our sexual natures. Each male and female of our species goes through the Sh'lam'alah, the burning stage when we become acutely aware of ourselves as sexual beings. In the land of Tir Nan Og where I come from we learn the art of pleasuring when this happens. To deny oneself the act...well, actually, I've never known a Tuatha to deny themselves the act, but I digress, sex feeds our bodies. It's as simple as that."

She laughed. "So, you're basically saying I'm going to become a slut and sleep with every man I see."

In an instant her face was framed between his large hands, the silver of his eyes a glare of barely-controlled menace. "There are no more men for you. You are mine. Get that," he snapped and then Tara knew he was going to kiss her even though his eyes gleamed with anger.

When he did, she was surprised by the tenderness of it. She felt him fight to leash in his temper and that warmed her. All of this was too new for her mind to digest. She tried recalling all the legends her grandmother had told her about the Tuatha Dé Danann. Nothing was helping. Nothing she'd heard joined with the man who held her face captive between his warm hands while his lips tenderly evoked a passionate response from her body. The fact her mind liked it as much as her body was not a good thing. Then his words echoed in her brain. He thinks I'm a Tuatha Dé Danann. That's impossible.

Abruptly she backed her head away, pleased that he released her face. "I'm not what you think I am."

"Ohh, I know, you think you're human—wrong on that score feyling. I would wager that either your mother or grandmother was a true Tuatha Dé Danann. Somehow she escaped Tir Nan Og and chose life with mortals to die a mortal death. Wasn't she lucky, Mir!" snapped Cael.

Tara wasn't sure who he was talking to any more. She had the distinct feeling he was lashing out at someone else.

"Anyway, why she chose that mystifies me, but her blood...you could say her fey blood runs in your veins. So that's why I'm calling you a feyling. You're actually half Tuatha Dé Danann and half human."

"But my mother wasn't fey. You're crazy."

He groaned and ran his hands through his long platinum hair. She fought the desire to reach out and touch his silky strands. She knew firsthand how satiny soft his hair was and the urge to slide her fingers through his petal-kissed strands took her breath away. His hair was almost feminine in its appeal but with his chiseled looks he pulled off looking manlier that was humanly possible. Again, a subtle reminder he was anything but.

"Some days I admit to being crazy, but not today. Look, I'm not a scientist. We're made differently than humans," he said. "I'd bet my life that your grandmother, or mother came from Tir Nan Og. You can certainly speak my tongue."

"What?"

"You can speak the Tuatha language and not only that, but you speak it with the royal intonation...whoever taught you knew exactly what they were teaching you."

Tara bit her lip. She didn't say anything as she digested that bit of information, so he continued on.

"Since you don't believe a word I say anyway, I'm going to stop explaining. What you are going to do is help me escape from this prison. Is that clear?"

Now this was more like the Cael she'd heard about—demanding, unyielding and selfish to the core.

Reaching across his body, her breasts accidentally touched his chest. She heard his indrawn breath as she reached for the tray with the sliced apples. "Escape on your own," she snapped back, pleased with her retort, as she bit down hard on the apple piece.

She was on her back in a heartbeat. The apple slice dropped somewhere in the makeshift bed. He towered over her and then he bucked against the vee of her legs. She felt the long, hard width of his erection, the thickness and rock-hard arousal he felt for her and couldn't help a small whimper of desire from escaping.

"Don't fucking play with me. I could fuck you here all day and it wouldn't be enough for you. I could make you come so many times your head would be dizzy from it and still I could make you beg for me, for my touch, for my cock to be buried deep inside of you, feyling. At this very moment you're wet, and your scent is driving me crazy, but like I said, we're getting out of here. Now! Before I give into my need to ram my cock deep inside of you. Or is that what you want?" His silver-grey eyes were simmering and glazed as he looked at her but his jaw was clenched tight.

Yes, I want that. I want it all. The knowledge left her feeling weak. She did. She did want his cock rammed deep within her. She ached for the heavy feel of his passion to be wedged tight within her pulsing core. She shook her head, leashing her wild emotions.

"Ge...g...get off me and I'll get us out of here," she said haltingly, hating how breathy she sounded to her own ears.

"That's what I thought."

He chuckled and slowly moved off her and out of the bed. Her eyes widened in shock as she got a good look at all of him for the first time. Fully aroused, he stood before her in all his splendor. His cock, wide and thick stood proud before her and pulsed under her scrutiny. Immediately she squeezed her eyes shut again as her face flamed red with embarrassment.

His throaty chuckle was not one bit amusing. Sure, I'll get us out of here and get you out of my life one way or another, no matter what. Laugh that gorgeous ass off all you want. Ugh, she hated she had thought of his ass, because at that very moment he chose to walk unabashed across the makeshift room, pluck another apple piece from the pile and plop the damn thing into his mouth.

He smiled devilishly at her, like he could read her mind. Without hesitating she threw the first thing her hand came into contact with at him. Too bad it had been her bunched-up bra. Just how embarrassing is that. Apparently enough only to cause Cael's smile to widen and his cock to flex its own answer.

Chapter Eight

CAEL BREATHED IN THE mountain-fresh air. It reminded him of freedom and Tir Nan Og when he had served his queen. Memories of warm sandy beaches, lush yellow fields, forests filled with life and majestic beauty stole through his thoughts. He chuckled to himself and immediately shut out the painful memories. *Must be the woman.*

She stood silently beside him; her gaze wary. She glanced at the crashing sea directly below them with a weary expression. They were back at her grandmother's burial mound, much to her dismay.

"I don't know what you did to me, but don't ever do that again. I think I'm going to be sick," declared Tara.

Cael noted Tara only stuttered when she was nervous, not when she was pissed at him. Her anger usually got the better of her emotions and she never had a problem expressing herself.

"Your stomach will settle in a minute, so don't worry."

"Worry? Yeah, that's funny. I'm more than worried. I'm delusional. I have no idea how you did whatever it was you did to get us out of that cave and here."

She waved her arms, indicating the area where they now stood. Cael liked watching the awe and sense of magickal disbelief that flashed across her face. Again, her innocence slammed into him. *Well, not all of her innocence. Part of that I took great pleasure in taking last night.*

Her gaze drifted from the forest to the wild sea below them. She fidgeted. He knew how she felt. *The awakening of your sexual side left you edgy and emotional.* He hoped like hell she'd learned how to leash that quickly as it was it was starting to seriously annoy him.

"Told you before, you're half-Tuatha. I was able to harness a tiny amount of your essence and will us here."

"Tiny amount of my essence...is that supposed to make any sense to me? And I am not half of anything!"

Tara placed her hands on her hips and Cael knew all traces of her queasy stomach were gone. He wished he could laugh at her antics. However, he had a job to do. While Queen Mir had made him mortal, he could still call upon the druid magick he'd been taught—the knowledge he'd kept from her. Using his knowledge enabled him to harness a small amount of Tara's powers to transport them directly to her grandmother's gravesite and out of that godforsaken cave.

She didn't believe she was a Tuatha Dé Danann. She thought he was slightly deranged. She could be correct in that assumption. *No sane man would go through what I did in the last twelve hours. Should have walked away from her the minute I heard her voice.*

His thoughts got distracted when she crouched down beside him. He inhaled her unique warm honeysuckle scent. Images of last night crashed through him, vivid in their intensity. She hadn't been shy in her loving even though she was new to the intimate act. A smile stole over his features, recalling the two deep claw marks on his shoulders from her nails when she climaxed the second time. He liked that she had marked him. There was a wild side to her that begged to be released. And he planned to do just that. However as much as he ached to pleasure her senseless out in the open, with the wilds of the woods as a backdrop, this was not the time.

A part of Cael also realized his pride prickled. She honestly didn't believe he had fucked her senseless last night. Why didn't she remember it? That had never happened to him before. Women always knew when he had bedded them. He pleasured their bodies well, so well in fact, many had begged on their knees for his affection. And he had been only too happy to oblige. The idea of Tara on her knees caused him to groan. He fought to dampen the desire he felt for the woman crouching next to him.

The other thing that bothered him was that he had lost control and spilled his seed inside of her. He had always taken precautions with women. His actions made his heart and gut clench uneasily. He'd make sure the next time, and without a doubt there were going to be lots of next times, he'd withdraw, or better yet purchase a box of condoms. The last thing he needed was to make the mess they were in even more complicated.

Cael wanted her to recall every vivid detail of their lovemaking just as he did. But she didn't. Maybe it's because she's a hybrid. Maybe the fever of her body caused her brain to shut down. Cael had decided when he awoke he'd watch her and wait to see if she felt the same desperate sexual itch she had earlier. Then, after he made her suffer a little, he planned on using every bit of his body to ensure she remembered it. It had nothing to do with his pride that was hurt because she didn't remember their love-making, he told himself. But the Tuatha he was knew that was a bold-faced lie.

Earlier she had voiced her displeasure about disturbing her grandmother's grave. Now he was getting the silent treatment. He knew she didn't like what he had to do and he couldn't blame her. The idea of opening her grandmother's grave held little appeal to him but he couldn't tell her that. He simply had to do the job, get the Stone of Fal and then wait until the next new moon until he could take his leave of Tara.

By the cresting of the next new moon the sexual side of her nature would have matured enough for her to function somewhat normally. While she'd always have to fight against her inner nature to want sex, he highly doubted she'd take any man in passing. From what he'd learned of her, which wasn't much, he had sensed that integrity and honor meant a lot to her.

Good thing. The idea of her with another man didn't sit well with him. But the truth of the matter was even though they were married by a priest it didn't mean anything. It was two signatures on a silly piece of paper. That was why he hadn't even bothered to tell her or place the simple gold rings MacCallah had handed him, on her finger or his. Why bother? He had simply pocketed them. They meant nothing to him.

Cael made a vow a long time ago to never care for another like he had in the past, especially not when he was so close to finding a way to end his existence. First though he had to convince Queen Mir the Decies were a real threat. Then if need be he'd beg her to end his human-like existence once and for all. She'd like that too. Cael knew Queen Mir would enjoy seeing him grovel. Begging for his own death would be something she'd thoroughly enjoy.

"What are you thinking about?" asked Tara, eyeing him.

Death. Cael continued digging. "Should have brought a shovel," he mumbled.

She laughed, the sound a rich, vibrating unfettered chuckle that flew through his senses in its purity. "Sorry, that was rich," she said, still smiling.

"Rich?"

"You know, funny." She moved a fraction of an inch closer to him. "This is going to take all day."

She was right. He stopped digging and reached for her hand, bringing her body almost flush to his. She didn't protest. Her head came to rest just below his heart. Together they stood, hand in hand almost looking like a normal couple. But looks can be deceiving. He curled his fingers around hers, letting her Tuatha Dé Danann energy once again flow through his system. Cael closed his eyes and breathed deeply and then willed the elements to work for him.

"Oh my god. How is that possible?"

She attempted to take a step back. He gripped her hand harder, hoping she'd understand he needed her undivided attention. When Cael next opened his eyes, the dirt had all been removed from the grave. He jumped down onto the simple cherry wood coffin. "You might want to turn away for a moment." Cael couldn't believe the niceties that were coming over him. Next thing he knew he'd be carrying her over the muddy puddles like some freaking knight in shining armor.

"Good idea."

Pleased she was no longer fighting him; he gave her time to step away. Then he pried open the coffin easily, only to curse.

She ran back and gaped at him. "What? Where is my grandmother?" Her eyes were wide with shock. "What did you do with my grandmother?"

Shock did not begin to explain how Cael felt. Frustration. Edgy and angry to the core were adjectives better fitting his mood. Instead of finding Tara's grandmother's dried up body, the coffin was empty, all except for a small silver bracelet. He reached out to retrieve it and cursed again. "Tara, get down here. This is something you're going to have to get," he commanded. Just my luck. I channel after a Tuatha relic and nothing but a bloody trinket.

"I'm not jumping down there. Just where is my grandmother?" she snapped at him.

Her red-streaked chestnut brown hair streamed around her. Amber eyes flashed heat at him and the wind howled to the surge of her anger. He had to get her under control. Dark clouds had formed directly overhead.

The Sh'lam'alah had helped to unleash her Tuatha Dé Danann powers—powers she was unconsciously wielding as she forced the elements to tune into her mounting anger.

"Calm down. I didn't do anything with your grandmother. But she's left you something. I can't get it because it's got a casting spell around it."

Tara stomped her foot. "Stop that. I don't want to hear another word about the cursed Tuatha Dé Danann, or spells. The only spell I want is for you to be gone. And I am not going down there."

She turned away from the grave. A bolt of lightning cracked through the skies. *Great, I get left dealing with this and trying to get a woman to calm down before she inadvertently fries herself to death.*

He jumped back up, grabbed a small stick and then landed back on top of the coffin. Using the stick like a hook he retrieved the bracelet. Careful to keep it balanced and away from his hands, he climbed, he hoped, for the last time out of the grave. Then he stalked over to where Tara stood.

"I wish I had time to explain all of this to you, Tara, but I don't. I'm just as confused as you are as to why your grandmother's body isn't there, but there is one thing for certain that I do know. Your grandmother left this for you. It has your name on it." He held out the stick as a peace offering.

She eyed him and sighed, one of those long, weary ones that threatened to twist its way into his heart. He almost reached out to take her into his arms. *Get a grip. No ties, remember that.*

"Take the blasted thing," he snapped, forcing her to take the bracelet. Then he turned his back, trying to figure a way to force his druid senses to search the area for another Tuatha trinket instead of the one he'd accidentally uncovered.

So, the Stone of Fal isn't here. Then he recalled that Tara had mentioned something about her grandmother's amulet. *I bet two bottles of my best Jamaican rum that her grandmother's amulet is the Stone of Fal. Now how do I get her to tell me where that is?*

While Cael was off lost in his thoughts, he did keep a watchful eye on Tara. She was a mystery to him. Small in appearance, she had more courage than half the Tuatha Dé Danann he'd known. When faced with the unknown she struggled to understand it and when that didn't work, she forced herself to cope. And the way she walked and carried herself was with pride and grace. She was so earthly beautiful yet at the same time so very much like a Tuatha Dé Danann he had to keep reminding himself that he'd just met her. Recalling once again her passion, Cael amended his thoughts. Okay, met and fucked her.

She took the silver bracelet off the stick and cradled it with a sorrowful sense of reverence in her hands. With one finger she traced the ancient etchings that spelled out her name and then she turned to him. A fleetingly sad smile crossed her face.

There wasn't much he could do, but he didn't like seeing her like this—lost and feeling unsure about herself.

Then again, what did I expect her to go through? Certainly not a joyous self-discovery about her talents and what she really is.

He took a step closer to her, fisting his hands. "Put. It. On," he commanded on purpose, afraid that the tender emotions she evoked within him would be his undoing. She choked back a small sob as her eyes glared daggers at him. His heart tore itself in two. Then Cael reminded himself that his queen had taken his heart and squeezed all the juice out of it the moment she threw him out of Tir Nan Og. He stuffed his hands in his pockets, took a step back and turned, giving her a moment to compose herself.

"Are you always such a cold bastard?"

Cael knew she was smarting from his commanding tone. He gave her another hard-cold look, adding more sparks to her fire. Her cheeks went crimson with anger and her hair swirled madly around her.

Better her hate me than get attached, cause honey, there ain't no "let's discuss the future" happening here.

"I try my best." He tossed the words unfairly over his shoulder.

"You're disgusting. I hate you!"

"Of course, you do. I wasn't expecting anything else."

Cael turned his head to watch how his words provoked her. He was feeling like a cold-hearted bastard at the moment. She quietly slipped the silver bracelet on over her frail-looking wrist. Then a blast of white-hot heat knocked them both backwards.

Cael stood quickly to confront the unknown with his legs spaced wide apart, his body warrior-alert. "Please don't listen to a word I say ever again," he grumbled.

Tara blinked in a daze. Standing directly in front of her was one startled looking man who was so blindingly beautiful she actually rubbed her eyes to take him all in.

Like Cael he had silver-grey eyes and shoulder-length platinum hair. His skin was pale, almost ivory-white in appearance even though he vibrated health and energy. There was a hard, sexy edge to him that caused her breath to hitch. He wore old fashioned clothing—tight fitting white breeches, and a white shirt with a gold embroidered edge that had a vee-cut down the front, providing her with a great view of his muscular chest.

"My, my my...isn't this a sight for sore eyes."

There was a husky and seductive cadence to his voice. Instantly Tara felt her skin tingle with sexual awareness. Cael growled with disapproval. Tara hated how much she liked his possessiveness, especially since she knew he was nothing but trouble. He stood to the side of her now, rigid, his stance very much a warrior—ready to pounce on his prey.

She felt the heat of the blast as the stranger zapped Cael directly in the chest. Confusion and hurt flirted across Cael's face like the zap of death was the last thing he had expected. Relying on instinct, Tara moved to confront the stranger.

"Stop that. You're hurting him." She shouted loudly but the man paid her no heed.

A loud scream tore itself from Cael even though she knew he was trying his best not to make any sound. But who wouldn't scream when they were being zapped to death.

Tara walked closer, her mounting anger soaring to the surface. Not sure of the motive behind her actions, she stepped directly into the path of electricity that streamed from the man's hands straight into Cael's chest. She held her breath, squeezed her eyes shut, and expected the worst. Laughter was the last thing she anticipated. However, the laws of normalcy flew out the window the minute I met Cael.

The stranger's rich laughter irritated Tara. Cael lay stiff on the ground. Immediately she crouched down beside him. He didn't budge or blink when she tried talking to him, and she couldn't feel a heartbeat or pulse. A white-hot rage soared through her. Sadistic bastard! Tara stood up and marched toward the stranger, all but shaking to keep herself under control. The man was still chuckling with glee.

"You killed him. I can't believe you just killed him. What did he do to you?" Tara didn't realize she had advanced within arm's length of the stranger until he leveled those silver-grey eyes directly at her. Eyes a mirror image to Cael's.

He beckoned with a finger for her to move closer. Not in this lifetime. Tara shook her head as a sensual hum penetrated her mind. She closed her eyes to absorb the erotic visions that sprang to life, and inhaled sharply, scenting the stranger's wild mix of exotic spices that caused her to lick her lips. She bit the inside of her cheek for clarity, and fisted her hands together. The stranger was working some type of spell on her. I will not succumb. I will not.

"You, my little crat-acha, are a true delight and surprise. I had no idea that it was possible for one like yourself to have such spark, such beauty. It is an honor to meet you. I am Balor, your humble servant. And you are?" The strange man had the audacity to give her an elegant, old-fashioned bow.

Automatically she replied, "Tara McNeil." The man's speech and manner were in complete opposition to his actions a few minutes ago. *None of this makes any sense.* The bigger question was why did he kill Cael?

Shakily, she asked the obvious. "Wh...wh..." Tara gulped. "Why did you kill him?"

"Kill him? Sadly no."

He motioned to the cluster of blue sparks that had materialized between them. The sparks proceeded to float to where Cael lay. Like before, Tara watched as the sparks engulfed his body and then after a few agonizing minutes Cael was on his feet—looking none too pleased.

"I am going to kill you, Balor." Cael grimaced and advanced in a steady gait toward the man who held his ground.

"Sorry about that. Had to see for myself if it really was true."

Tara could only blink as the stranger strolled casually forward to meet Cael halfway. She noted there was wary amusement in Balor's eyes. Strangely, like with Cael she didn't fear him. However, she did hold her breath, hoping there wouldn't be a repeat performance.

"It is good to see you Balor," said Cael.

There was a hitch to his voice that resonated within Tara—sadness.

"It is good to see you too, brother. It has been too long," said Balor, clasping Cael to him in a hearty hug.

Tara stilled. *Brother! That's his brother. His brother just killed him. Talk about a sick family.* She noted that Cael's normally hard, chiseled facial features had softened. Then, as if he caught her looking at him he quickly regained his composure. There was no doubt seeing his brother again had shaken him.

"And this, brother..." said Balor with a sweeping gesture toward Tara. "This is something I never expected to see. What an earthly delight." He gamely winked at Tara.

Tara heard the low growling warning that originated from Cael, and she was totally ashamed that the womanly part of her actually liked his overbearing attitude.

"Why exactly are you here, Balor?"

"I have no idea."

He then proceeded to walk around Tara like she was a specimen on display. Hands on her hips, she snapped, "Stop that!"

Balor ignored Tara's remark. "You know, if they knew a halfling would look like this there would be more of them."

If he reaches out to touch me I am going to bite him.

Moving closer to Tara, Balor asked, "What is that delicious smell?"

For one moment, Tara thought the man was going to sniff her hair. Ridiculous. But she didn't need to worry. Cael was beside her in an instant pulling her body flush to his, making sure there was no misunderstanding that she was his. As if.

"Ahh, I see..." Balor retreated a step back. "The sweet scent of cinnamon. Lucky you."

"See what?" asked Tara.

Cael's warm hands moved to touch her flesh from under her puffy fall jacket. Tara fought the shiver that resonated through her body as hard as she felt the longing to arch her neck back, bend his head to her mouth and ravish those lips of his.

"When was the last time?"

Cael cut him off with a guarded look. "Last night," he replied, curtly.

Balor gave a small chuckle, and a devilish smile much like his brother's transformed his features, making him appear even more breathtaking. "If you need my services, my lady, please let me know."

A very sultry look accompanied that strange statement. Services? What is he talking about? "Where exactly did you come from?" asked Tara.

"He came from Tir Nan Og and I'd say that you, Balor, know Tara's grandmother. Just so we're clear on things, Tara is mine."

Cael's voice was calm and even but the husky timbre of it streamed through her senses. Tara shook her head to clear her thoughts. Her body was becoming increasingly hot and tingly. She attempted to twist free from Cael's embrace but he was having none of that.

"This is ridiculous. There is no way a man from Tir Nan Og knows my grandmother," said Tara. "Is this some sick twisted joke you two are playing on me? And just so we're clear on things I don't even believe in Tir Nan Og, anyway." Tara couldn't help the small stamp her foot made on the ground. "And Cael, take that 'mine' remark and shove it."

"Is she always like that?"

Balor spoke directly to Cael and ignored Tara's questions. Righteous indignation flared to life within her. Cael's hands slid even further under her jacket, his fingers drifting along her skin. Electricity, hot and powerful swept through Tara in one fast current. The feel of his large warm hands on her skin rattled her thoughts more than she liked.

"What was your grandmother's name?" asked Cael.

"Raelene," blurted Tara.

Balor placed both hands on his hips. "See, don't know any Raelene."

"Could your grandmother have gone by another name?" asked Cael, continuing to inch his hands further under the puffy confines of her jacket. His fingers came daringly close to brushing the undersides of her breasts. A part of Tara stilled, almost wishing his delightful fingers would step over the line and breech the proper code of conduct civilized people portrayed when out in public. The realization he wasn't proper and human resonated quickly the minute his fingers did such a thing. Her back arched, taut with need and her pulse quickened. Shaking free of his hold she managed to escape his clutches, knowing he'd let her go on purpose.

Cael wolfishly gave a small chuckle.

"What? Well, she let her friends call her Rhea," mumbled Tara, running shaky hands through her long hair. She wished she had an elastic to tie it back, hating how the wind kicked it around and into her face.

"Rhea? Are you telling me this is Rhea's offspring? Rhea of Naldolcoh who vanished from Tir Nan Og without a trace over two dream-lives ago?" asked Balor.

Cael licked his lips, ensuring she was watching. A gasp of desire slipped free from Tara. "Stop that!" Tara tried once again to move even further away from Cael's body. "As much as I'm going to hate asking this, what exactly is a dream-life?"

"A dream-life would be the equivalent of one of your Earth centuries. But time moves differently in Tir Nan Og," replied Cael. Like her attempts to distance herself from him didn't matter he stepped back into her space, pulling her quivering body into his much larger one with a finesse that actually impressed Tara.

Tara's eyes glazed over as sexual need swamped her rational mind.

"The bigger question is why Rhea would place a binding summons on you, Balor," said Cael.

Balor knelt down by her grandmother's open casket, and Tara heard him chuckle softly to himself.

"Well you see, a long time ago we had a brief relationship and I gave her a special silver bracelet, using of course my very own special powers. When things ended...and just so we're clear on this note...you can stop that arch of your brow Cael...we parted as friends. Anyway, I digress. I told her if she ever had need of me again I would come to her aid," answered Balor.

"My grandmother died six months ago and she was in her late eighties. She wasn't a fairy or anything like that. This is the most ridiculous conversation I've ever had in my life and Cael, if you don't move those hands of yours I swear I will bite you." Tara snapped the words out quickly, pleased she wasn't stuttering even though her stomach was filled with nervous flutters.

"Is she doing that?" asked Balor.

Tara followed Balor's gaze, noting the roving large black clouds that were once again threatening to bring thunder and rain. There was also a touch of amusement etched deeply in Cael's eyes that troubled Tara.

"I'm afraid so. She won't admit to having powers and worse, she doesn't understand how to use them. It would seem no one taught her how to harness them."

Before Tara could formulate a retort, Cael continued on.

"Tara, as strange as what my brother has revealed to us sounds, I'd say your grandmother really was Rhea of Naldolcoh. Sorry to say I never had the pleasure of meeting her..."

Another soft chuckle floated on the fiery breeze. "Yes, you were banished long before she vanished. There was a rumor going around in the Royal Court that the veil that separates us from the human world had failed, but the queen said that was ridiculous and well, you can imagine, no one dared bring that up again. Not unless they wanted to experience what happened to you, Cael. You know brother, you are quite the legend at home. What's it been now?"

Tara felt Cael bristle...his body becoming rigidly stiff. Still though, he wouldn't release her.

"A thousand Earth years," he said sharply.

"A thousand years. You are kidding. I knew it was long, but honestly I had no idea it was that long. To be truthful, I'm sure if you were to petition Queen Mir she might forgive you...you used to be her favorite," said Balor.

Wanting to steer the conversation back to her, Tara cut in. "You two want me to believe that my grandmother was this Rhea person from Tir Nan Og who just so happened to get trapped here. What are you two, crazy?"

"And you," snapped Tara, forcibly turning her body around to face Cael. "Whatever you're doing to me, cease it right this minute Mister, or else!" Tara knew her face was flushed with desire and her heart was accelerating. She once again felt feverish. "I'm really not feeling well again. I think I should go now."

"You're going to need to tell her and if you're not Tuatha enough to scratch that itch of hers I will do my brotherly duty and help you out." Tara noted Balor's strange remark was followed with an exaggerated sigh.

"Over my dead body," snapped Cael.

They're talking in some sort of weird code that I just don't understand. Tara fought to control her temper. She felt frazzled and there was a wild edge to her she had never experienced before. Her body was once again on fire. And she had the strangest urge to rub her sensitive body up and down Cael's hard frame. I've definitely lost it.

The wind bucked and buffeted all three of them and then it poured, sheets of rain exploding from the heavens to rain down around them, soaking them all to the bone within seconds. Tara blinked through the rain. She'd never experienced anything like this in her entire life. As cold as the rain made her feel it wasn't helping the strange feverish burn that was tickling every nerve ending on her skin, leaving her quivering and feeling shaky.

"Okay, I've had enough of this. Time to go, brother dear. Enjoy your life," chimed Balor.

Cael's eyes turned to give his brother a haunting look. Once again Tara felt the deep sadness that she knew he wouldn't voice. *That's insane. I must be catching whatever they have. And why should I care one whit about him?*

Even as she thought that, his smell—the wild woods and exotic spices that layered him with masculinity, washed into her senses. Tara fisted her hands deep inside her jean pockets, digging the tips of her nails into her palms to stop the ragged groan threatening to tear itself free from her.

Then Tara heard Cael's brother spew forth what she surmised was a string of profanity. She peeked at him. His clothes clung to him, outlining his muscular lean frame and his hair hung dripping wet down his face. *He looks fit to be tied, and angrier than a rabid dog.*

Cael chuckled. She felt his rumble straight to the marrow of her bones. Tara closed her eyes as ecstasy sang through her cells, wishing she could stop the breathless moan that escaped her.

"I am not happy. Why can't I return? This isn't one bit funny, Cael," snapped Balor. "By all that's sacred kiss her...do something to make her stop this pissing downpour."

Before Tara could even begin to question anything he said, Cael pulled her tight to him and his lips claimed hers. They were tentative, gentle and it was the most wonderful, elated feeling she had ever experienced. Her lips opened to welcome his tongue. Tenderly he probed the inside of her mouth while his hands slid through her wet hair, framing her face to his. She loved his explorations. How the tip of his tongue grazed her teeth. How his hands reverently stroked her hair, claiming while calming her quivering body. Who knew how erotic a skillful tongue could be?

His tongue then snaked over the roof of her mouth. The sensation fired itself from the pit of her stomach to her pulsing core, which throbbed with a tight need. She was thankful he hadn't released her. Her legs felt like rubber and she was sure she would have landed once again on her butt.

Tara wasn't sure what was happening to her body but she didn't care. If she could have crawled onto Cael's large frame to alleviate the itch and burn that was cascading through her system she would have. He picked her up and walked toward the canopy of large pine trees. The shelter of the tree branches provided them with some cover from the rain, which thankfully was starting to ebb. Even still, both their clothes clung to them tightly. Besides the pelting rain, all Tara could hear was her and Cael's panting breaths. Passion sizzled between them, almost visible in its intensity.

"You are going to remember. This. Feyling."

He growled the words into her ear and then nipped her earlobe for good measure. His voice stoked the fire within her even more. She arched into his embrace, needing to feel his wet skin. In a few more minutes reason will return and I'll put a stop to this.

Tara wished she felt guilt for the immorality of what she was doing with a complete stranger, one she just so happened to wake up naked in bed with, but she didn't. She loved the decadent feeling he evoked within her too much to fight the attraction.

Suddenly a voice interrupted them.

"Now this is a sight I never expected to see."

Cael moved so fast from her that she stumbled back, bracing her body on a tree.

"Run, Tara, run. Get my brother," he commanded.

Then in a blur of motion, she watched as Cael fought the dark-haired man who had appeared out of nowhere. The man fought back with equal grace but there was a dangerous glint in his steel-blue eyes that frightened Tara enough to heed Cael's warning. She ran from the trees straight into the man's arms. How that was she couldn't figure out. One minute he was fighting Cael and then in the next he was blocking her path.

"You have something I need."

She heard Cael's howl of outrage. A searing hot pain soared through her senses as time slowed. Then, thankfully everything went black.

Chapter Nine

CAEL KNEW HE HAD NO choice. He hated having to ask for the Highlander Druids' help, but he needed it. So much to his own chagrin, he found himself walking back into MacLeod Tavern, minus Tara.

"Sweet fucking mercy, look at the garbage the wind threw back at us," bellowed a tall Highlander by the door. "Thought we had made our point. You're not welcome here, fairy."

Cael ignored him and casually made his way to the bar, hoping they didn't once again start chanting that blasted druid sleep spell. His brother followed after him like a lost puppy. Cael was sick of Balor's blathering and cursing. A part of him wished his brother did have his powers so he could simply go home and leave him alone.

"Worst stench of garbage I've ever seen. What, you came back so we could go at it again? Come and get it, you Damned Fairy." Alec came around the bar to block Cael's path.

"You're not worth my time. Where's Devon?" asked Cael.

"Right behind you," answered Devon. "So, you brought me boys another fairy to play with. Ain't that grand."

Cael wasn't in the mood for anyone's taunting. As it was he could barely keep his brother from engaging in a brawl. He put a restraining hand on Balor's twitching arm to still his actions. "I didn't have to come back but I did. Tara's in trouble." *There, I said it. That wasn't so bad.* A moment later he and his brother were surrounded by angry Highlander Druids. The air was now dark and edgy, all but crackling as the intense energy from all the Druids reached out to tweak all their senses. Hastily, Cael threw up a mind shield around himself and his brother. Why he didn't want them poking into Balor's mind mystified him, but some dark secrets of his past were better left to the recesses of time.

"Five seconds. Explain yourself," commanded Devon.

"Not here."

Devon chanted the ancient druid words quick and efficiently. Instantly, Cael felt the power of the spell wrap around them. They could now talk without fear of being overheard. Five minutes later, after he told them how his brother came to be here, what had happened to them at the gravesite, and what Stater was after, he wanted action.

"I want to kill someone." Balor plunked down on a hard bar stool. "And I can't believe I let you talk me into coming here. Druids! Hateful creatures. Wait until Mir hears tell you can use druid spells; she's certainly going to like that."

"Balor, shut up. You're not going to tell Mir anything. She's left you here for some reason." Cael turned his attention to Devon. "So, you going to help or what?"

Cael fought not to smash his brother as he heard him mutter, "Mir did not leave me here. That was Rhea's doing. And you, Cael...you really have sunk low."

He reminded himself his brother had no idea of Stater's plans or truly comprehended the power Druids could wield. Focusing on what Devon was saying to his sons as they bantered back and forth with ideas on how to rescue Tara, Cael realized he understood these Highlander Druids more than his pampered brother.

He also knew he had to set a plan in motion to get Tara back by tonight. If he didn't the Sh'lam'alah would slowly make her go insane. The longing for sexual fulfillment...for him...was going to be a steady drumbeat racing through her veins until he found her. Then he would deal with Stater and take care of Tara's needs. This is all my fault.

"Before you came to the Highlands we were all fine. Tara was fine," grumbled Alec, repeating exactly what Cael was thinking.

Cael eyed the eldest MacLeod brother, whose lip had healed in a day. The use of dark druid power often had that effect and Cael wondered what toll that daily inner struggle took on the Highlander. He looked into Alec's dark blue eyes, catching a glimpse of the beast that begged for freedom residing deep within the Highlander. There is a darker edge to this Highlander Druid that warrants paying closer attention to. Cael wondered if Alec knew what resided within him. His gut instinct told him this particular Highlander Druid wasn't stupid and that he worked daily to keep himself level and not give into the darker side of his nature.

"Stop it, Alec. Tell us again everything you know about this Stater fellow," said Devon.

Devon moved his bar stool closer to Cael so they could continue their talk. It also positioned Alec out of Cael's range and something within Cael understood that as being Devon's true motive.

Cael grumbled. He'd told them everything he could about the sixth century king. What he had omitted was what he feared Stater would do with Tara and how that would affect Tir Nan Og. They don't need to know absolutely everything. But Cael didn't like the penetrating gaze Devon leveled at him.

He watched as the old man took a long drink from his coffee mug.

"Pop, I just heard. Where's Tara?" asked a woman running from the kitchen door into the bar area.

Great, another female to deal with.

A low menacing grumble of warning from her brothers caused the woman to slow down as they all stood up. Her gaze slowly skirted past them all and then she marched straight up to his brother.

"I know you."

Her bold declaration startled everyone.

Balor groaned loudly. "I'm bloody well dreaming. That's it." He rubbed his eyes wearily and then turned and walked away from the group without another word.

Cael let him go. He wasn't sure what was going on but it was an added distraction they didn't need. He addressed the Highlanders. "Focus. We've got to get Tara back. Her life hangs in the balance. As I was saying earlier, Stater is here looking for the Stone of Fal. Like me, I believe he came here on an Internet rumor that said the sacred Tuatha stone is buried in one of your Highland cemeteries. He took Tara because he was drawn to the bespelled Tuatha Dé Danann bracelet she's wearing around her wrist." The blasted thing I told her to put on. Stupid! Stupid! Stupid!

"Anyway, with Tara going through the..." he coughed, not wanting to divulge any more personal information than necessary, especially with the woman still staring at his brother with a mix of shock of ecstasy. "Like I said, we need to find her. Are there any more old cemeteries around here?"

"Not that I can recall," said Devon, looking slightly weary as he ran a hand through his mop of grey hair.

"Pop, I think we need to track down who started this rumor. That might help us," said Neil.

Cael nodded. He hadn't thought about that but it made perfect sense. Maybe whoever started it had more useful information.

"I'll get started right away on tracing that information." Neil walked to the tavern door and yelled. "Katie, come and help me."

"No."

Her eyes were all but burning with desire as they locked onto his brother's retreating back.

"Katie-girl, go with Neil. Now!"

There was no mistaking her father's harsh command. Cael watched as the young woman struggled with her own independent nature and tradition. In the end she bowed her head slightly at his brother and then sauntered out of the tavern. Cael heard his brother release his breath. What is going on?

Balor came back to claim the bar stool next to Cael. "Care to explain that?"

Balor shook his head. "Not right now. How do you handle this? I'm feeling strange. There is this weird rumbling going on inside my stomach."

The pained look on his brother's face was comical. "It's called hunger. You need to eat."

"Eat! As in human food! What exactly are you saying, Cael?" Balor paled even more, clearly confused by the turn of events.

Cael knew exactly how he felt. One minute you are all powerful, omniscient and then in a blink—nothing. Tuatha Dé Danann didn't eat the way that humans thought. They absorbed the energy of living things in Tir Nan Og and channeled that power back to the organism, causing it to flourish. It was a symbiotic circle of life. Then the harsh realities of his early life in Tir Nan Og washed over him. Cael shook his head to clear those muddy thoughts.

Taking a piece of bread from the tray MacCallah had brought them, he waved it under his brother's nose. "Eat this, it will help."

His brother narrowed his eyes in mistrust. Talk about brotherly love.

After careful consideration Balor snatched the bread from him and bit into it. His brother's eyes closed as he savored the unique texture and taste of the bread. A long time ago Cael remembered how that had felt. Now however, too much time had accumulated. Bread was simply a means to satisfy hunger. Still though, seeing the emotions race through his brother evoked a tender feeling for him.

"This is wonderful. What is it called?" asked Balor.

"Bread." Cael stated flatly. "You will need more food than bread. And Balor brace yourself, but I'm thinking you're human."

He watched as his brother struggled to control his rage.

"Human!" Balor spat. "I don't think so. The queen would not do that to me. I am her..."

"Her what?" quipped Cael, not liking where this was going.

"Her charm of the moon," mumbled Balor, his cheeks full of warm bread, as his face flushed with heat.

All four of the Highland brothers who were near enough snickered. "Her what?" asked the closest one.

Cael thought his name was Curran, but he couldn't be sure. They looked so much alike.

"Yes, Balor, her what?" Cael teased. He enjoyed seeing his brother squirm for a change. He knew exactly what his brother was but he longed for him to say it.

"Was I speaking to you...you human?" said his brother, abruptly standing and causing the stool to fall over. He took a step toward the Highlander who had taunted him. "I am a Tuatha Dé Danann. Show some respect."

Instantly the other three Highlanders flanked their brother.

"Respect, Fairy...I'll show you the true meaning of respect," said Alec.

Cael noted he was always the first to lead, always primed for a good fight. The thought they were more alike than his sibling made Cael step back from the Highlander.

"Leave him be. He's simply the queen's bed sport," said Devon.

All four Highlanders laughed. It was a hearty laugh that calmed the edgy mood hanging over everyone in the tavern.

"Bed sport. Pop, where on earth did you learn that?" said one of the brothers, still heaving with laughter. "That's fucking charming. Bed sport!" All the Highlanders continued to laugh.

For a moment Cael felt sorry for his brother. Then he recalled his brother had zapped him to death just because he could and whatever emotion Cael felt dissipated. Let them laugh their asses off.

Through narrowed lids, Cael watched his brother try to figure out how best to deal with the upstarts. If he still had his powers, Cael knew Balor wouldn't have hesitated to teach them a painful lesson they would not soon forget.

One would have thought that as brothers he and Balor would have been close but they hadn't been. From day one he'd been trained as a warrior for Queen Mir, while his brother was born for the pleasure pillows. After Mir picked Cael to be her champion, they had spent most of their existence apart. That didn't mean Cael wasn't aware of what his younger brother did, it was simply the way things were on Tir Nan Og.

What truly mystified Cael was why Tara's grandmother had bound his brother to Tara. Maybe she thought he'd be able to take Tara to Tir Nan Og and present her to the queen. Cael shivered, a cold knot of dread tightening his gut with that thought. Without a doubt the last person Tara ever needed to meet was Queen Mir. In all likelihood the queen would kill her on the spot. Tara was a hybrid. Her blood was tainted. She was impure. He knew he had to get her back, had to keep her safe from her own heritage.

Taking two steps forward toward the Highland brothers who were still snickering in glee, Balor snarled, "If you don't stop laughing I am going to make you stop."

"You and what army?" Alec crossed his arms over his chest for show, while flashing a feral smile that only added to his dark, charming looks.

Devon stepped into the middle of the group, once again imposing his presence with purpose. "All of you, this is not helping. Must I remind you that we need to find our Tara-girl? Her life is in our hands. We made a promise to Rhea, her grandmother that we MacLeods would keep her safe and so far we have failed miserably. Now all of you are going to put your bloody thinking caps on. As much as it kills me to be working with the Damned Fairy...now, don't get your knickers in a knot," said Devon, eyeing both Cael and his brother. "Stater is going to use Tara to get what he wants. And what would that be exactly, Cael?"

Cael turned, picked up a mug and helped himself to the brew on tap. He gulped it down, thinking how best to proceed.

"What exactly does he be wantin' with our Tara?" demanded Devon, now glowering at Cael.

Cael muttered, "If we're lucky he'll just want her bracelet." He repeated his actions for another drink, wishing he could get drunk and avoid what had to be done.

"And if we're not lucky?" asked Alec, leaning his large frame onto the bar so he could eye Cael.

Gone was the charming smile from Alec's face, replaced with a stony look Cael was becoming all too familiar with. The Highlander was warrior-ready to get back what was his. Cael didn't like that thought. Tara's mine. When Cael didn't answer, Alec moved his body a fraction of an inch toward him. Devon stilled his son's actions by placing a restraining hand on Alec's shoulder.

Cael sighed. "If he discovers she has Tuatha Dé Danann blood he will use it to open Queen Mir's chest and release the Decies."

Devon was the first to curse. Then in a hushed tone he quickly told his sons the vile nature of the Decies. All the Highlander Druids offered their own versions of profanity. He knew exactly how they felt. Cael felt his brother move to his side.

"You didn't mention that." Balor's lips were pursed together. "I can't believe I don't have any powers and now you tell me this. We need to let Queen Mir know."

"What we need to do is get Tara back before it's too late for her," snapped Cael. "Do you have the means of creating a druid circle?"

Alec nodded. "You mean to use the circle for what?"

The Highlander was skeptical of his actions. Cael understood that as well. If he were in his shoes he'd question everything. "If we can pinpoint the Tuatha Dé Danann bracelet Tara is wearing we can find her."

"Aye, I get your meaning. A druid circle will channel after her fey bracelet," said Devon. "We'll have to go back to the cave."

"We will need something of Tara's," said Keegan. "I'll be right back."

A minute later, Keegan returned with a sweater that Tara had left in the bar a while ago. "Here, this should help."

Cael grabbed the sweater. Her scent of fresh soap and honeysuckle perfume flowed through his senses. He fought not to close his eyes in ecstasy to savor her smell. "This will do. Let's move out."

Devon, Alec, Cael and Balor climbed into the large pickup truck. Curran was left in charge of the tavern. It was a tight squeeze, but thankfully no one said anything. An hour later they were back at the cave.

"I'll draw it." Alec immediately sliced his arm, letting the blood drip onto the sacred cave ground to form a small circle.

Cael repeated Alec's actions and let the blood stream from his own arm directly onto the path Alec had created. He felt Devon flank his other side. The ancient druid words streamed easily from all three of them.

He watched as his brother took five steps back from the circle. Still afraid of druid power. Still believing in Queen Mir's lies of ignorance. Brother dear, ignorance is not bliss. Then again if he had never learned the true potential of druid magick he probably wouldn't be in the mess he was at the moment, or for the last thousand years.

"Concentrate, Cael," admonished Devon.

Cael glared at him, pleased to see the old man slightly flinch.

Then the vision appeared. A small log cabin in the woods revealed itself. Tara was thrashing around madly on a tiny, wooden bed. Her legs were tied down and her hands had been roped high above her head. He couldn't help but groan. She looked completely vulnerable. He was pleased to see though she was as mad as a rabid animal and in that moment he couldn't have been prouder of her. Stater towered over her. She actually spit in his face. *Now that's my feyling.*

Stater had the nerve then to use his power to burn the flesh under her arm. Tara cried out in agony. The vision vanished as fast as it had materialized.

Cael was shaking. "I am going to rip that man limb from limb and dissect him slowly." The words were a snarl of revenge.

"And I am going to help you," snapped Alec.

The two warriors glared at each other. Their faces were both masks of cold ice, as fury over what Tara was going through registered in both of them. Cael didn't think he'd ever be able to get the vision of her in agony out of his mind.

"Fine, suit yourself. Now any idea where that cabin is?" Cael's entire body was taut. He longed to kill Stater with his bare hands. And he needed action now, not later.

"He took her to Boularderie Island."

Devon's information was delivered stoically. Cael marched to the cave's entrance. "Great, now point me in the right direction. You coming, Balor?"

"You are crazy. I have no idea how to fight like a...like a human. I'm staying here." His brother then proceeded to move aside the makeshift curtain and lie down on the bed he and Tara had slept on and had sex in last night. Cael watched as Balor crossed his arms behind his head and closed his eyes as if he didn't have a care in the world.

Alec picked up a hunting knife and slid it through the loop at his belt. Cael already had his weapon of choice but he seriously hoped he'd get to use his hands that longed to squeeze the life from Stater.

"I'm coming but it's not going to be easy getting there," said Alec, forcing Cael's attention away from his brother and back to the Highlander.

Cael marched out to the cave's entrance. "Like I care. But boy, don't get in my way." In truth he didn't care who came as long as he got satisfaction. Cael didn't care if he had to swim to get to that island or crawl on his bloody hands and knees—one way or another he'd get there by tonight.

"We're going to need your brother. You need either fey blood to reach that island or weeks of druid spells to hold it in place. And Pop just told me the queen stripped your fey blood of any power. Ain't that grand. You had better hope your brother's blood still has some fucking fey power in it, or we ain't going to be able to get on that cursed island." Alec sauntered past him as he delivered that blow to Cael.

What the blazes? Why do I need Tuatha Dé Danann blood? Weeks of spells aren't going to happen so looks like I'm taking the easy way out. He wanted to ask the Highlander those questions but with time being of the essence answers would have to wait.

"Balor, get your ass out here!" bellowed Cael back over his shoulder. He prayed to the Fates his brother's blood would do the trick. The day was passing too quickly for Cael's liking. And without a doubt he knew the sexual itch and frustration eating away at Tara would be spiraling through her body by now. Again, the image of her tied up and helpless swamped his senses. Then he remembered how she bravely fought her captor to spit at him. He fought the urge to howl in anger while smiling at her stupid bravery.

Balor followed into step next to him. "I told you Cael, I'm not fighting like these humans. I'm a lover, not a fighter."

Cael spared his brother a quick glance, noting he had the nerve to grin. "Shut up. You're coming because that there Highlander says we need Tuatha Dé Danann blood to get on the island. And trust me, my blood won't do the trick. Let's just hope you have some worth in you yet. Besides, it's the least you can do since you seem to have no idea at all why Rhea would have placed a binding missive on you." Cael steeled a glance at his brother as he marched along the shoreline.

"Are you coming or going?" snapped Alec, already in the driver's seat of another old pickup truck that had been parked at the end of the access road.

Cael wanted nothing more than to wrap his hands around Alec's condescending throat. The need for satisfaction rode him hard. When I get Tara back, he and I are going to have a chit-chat. "Get in the back," said Cael to his astonished, mortified brother. Ahh, yes how the mighty fall onto their asses, quickly. "Enjoy the view and ride. I'm sure it's an experience you won't soon forget."

Cael promptly shut the truck door, ignoring his brother's profanity. For once he was thankful when the Highlander revved the vehicle into first and then slammed it into third gear, causing all three of them to bounce down the gravel pot-holed excuse for a road. Without a doubt, his brother would have one sore ass when they stopped. Serves him right for killing me.

Chapter Ten

TARA KNEW SHE WAS ONCE again burning up with a fever. She had no memory of how she'd ended up shackled and tied to a bed with a crazed man now looming over her.

"Where is it?"

His voice was loud and grated on her sensitive hearing. He was almost as tall as Cael. But there the similarities ended. Long, straight black hair was tied back in a fashionable leather tie, while startling, crazed, crystal clear blue eyes watched her every move. Half his face was covered with black-inked tattoo markings and from what she could see of his arms they bore the same etchings as well. Evil looked to be inscribed on him. He terrified her.

"Where is it?"

For the third time she asked the obvious. "Wh..." She gulped in a breath, forcing the stuttering to keep at bay. *This is not the time to act like a fraidy-cat.* "Where is what?"

Either the guy is a complete lunatic and doesn't understand what I'm saying or this is a nightmare I've found myself believing in. The man had a clipped accent which further grated her nerves.

She yanked against the ties holding her in place. First he had placed her in the bonds with her clothes on. Then he'd changed his mind and forced her to take off her clothes. She had known then he had wanted her to fight his order, anything so he could slap her senseless again. Her face already sported bruises and she was sure her nose was broken. With forced bravery and trembling hands, she had followed his command and disrobed. His evil chuckle with her compliance didn't bode well.

Now her legs were spread-eagle on the hard, wooden bed and her arms had been placed high above her head. She tossed her head, fighting against the surge of panic that threatened to swamp her. Without a doubt Tara knew she needed to maintain a level head and not envision him raping her.

"If you could tell me what it is, I might know where it is," she said with more spunk than she felt. Being pissed at her situation did help keep her from giving into a round of stutters.

She forced herself not to cringe as he moved closer. Like a dog he sniffed her. She bit her lip so she wouldn't scream. Then a finger brushed the undersides of her breasts. She stilled her breathing and she was sure her heart stopped. Ohmygod, ohmygod, he's going to rape me.

Fear now reigned free and raced through her nervous system like a wild storm, strong and destructive with the knowledge she truly was helpless.

"You've been with him. Was the Damned Fairy all they say he is?"

The man took a step back like he was disgusted with how she smelled. Tara said a small thank you for that miracle and released the desperate breath she had been holding.

What is he talking about? She didn't believe for one second she'd actually had sex with Cael even if she had woken up naked and in bed with him. No way. Cael's tale was too fanciful by far. She was pretty certain she'd remember a man like Cael taking her virginity. Despite Cael's crude words that he had fucked her, Tara highly doubted the MacLeods would have let him.

The image of her and Cael naked in bed soared into her mind. She tried hard not to think about that because it was so beyond strange it actually scared her more than her current situation. She tilted her chin up at the lunatic, which forced her neck muscles to work overtime. "I have no idea what you're talking about."

A sinister chuckle spewed forth from him. The sound traveled straight down her spine. This man is evil incarnate. It was going to take all of Tara's creative thinking to escape in one piece.

He left her for a moment's reprieve and moved to open the cabin door. Like with her, he seemed to be sniffing the air. Totally weird! Satisfied that all was right he turned his attention back to her. So much for my reprieve.

"I had hoped to have you as my third virgin but alas you've already been taken. But since Cael is known as a Tuatha Dé Danann who likes to share, he won't mind if I sample the wares. Then you are going to tell me where the Stone of Fal is." He moved closer toward her. With an almost lazy attitude he stripped off his shirt.

Her breath hitched. Ugly welt marks and more eerie tattoos covered his body. In fact, most of his skin was covered with the inky-black symbols reminding her more of bruises than professional tattoo designs. When his hands moved to the top of his black leather pants she squeezed her eyes shut and prayed for a miracle. Her heart raced and a strange humming feeling came over her entire body. She felt hot and flustered and that was the last thing she wanted this crazed delusional man to see.

I must be getting that fever again. The man laughed again. The sound caused Tara to open her eyes. There standing in the doorframe was her knight in shining armor. Okay, he's missing the armor, but hopefully he'll have a big gun. So much for my non-violent constitution. Tara grinned like crazy seeing Cael's large warrior-ready body frame the door. His face was so tense it could have been made of granite. Part of her hoped he really was a Tuatha Dé Danann so he could zap her away to safety.

"You think you can defeat me now, Cael, when you haven't been able to before. This should be most interesting." The man turned his attention to her again, as he buttoned his pants and placed his shirt back on with forced casualness. "When I am finished with him, I will finish my business with you."

Pushing her head up as far as it would go, she said, "Not in this lifetime, Mister." Tara was pleased her force didn't quiver. Her courage was re-asserting itself and it had a lot to do with the Tuatha Dé Danann staring with deadly purpose at the evil man. Tara didn't need to read Cael's mind to know he was going to savor getting his hands wrapped around this man's throat and she was going to applaud his efforts.

Then a blast of white light like something straight out of a Hollywood movie zapped Cael. Can't anyone think of anything but blasting the man to death? Tara cried out a warning. Fear for him lanced through her, leaving her breathless with fright. She didn't want her knight in shining armor dead. She needed him alive and kicking.

However instead of the zap hurting him, he absorbed the electrical energy. Somehow Cael managed to turn the zap around. A startled gasp from the crazy man told her all she needed to know.

"You know, Cael, Queen Mir talked a lot about you after your banishment. I bet you didn't know she spied on you." Tara got the distinct impression the man was taunting Cael on purpose to distract him. Cael didn't fall for that act.

"Save it, Stater," snapped Cael.

Stater! Wasn't that the name Cael had yelled when he was resurrected at the cemetery? The terrifying knowledge she had been taken by a murdering mad-man caused her body to shake with renewed shock.

"You know she actually laughed that day when you...ahh, yes, I remember...the day you buried that child. Now let me remember, it's been awhile, but I believe her name was Ashling. Sad thing having to watch her gasp her last breath." The man cackled a taunting laugh, egging Cael on.

"Shut the fuck up and fight. Then again, I had heard you were a talker. Not a man of action."

Tara smiled at Cael's words, watching him deftly move to the left as Stater volleyed another zap at him. He easily dodged it.

"I think Queen Mir is going to like that young woman you've discovered," said Stater, turning his head to give a malicious smile at Tara.

She cringed and then watched as the men prepared to fight. It was like time stood still. Almost in slow motion, Tara watched as the men fought, moving in a warrior dance perfectly choreographed with deadly zaps. Every once in a while a blast hit its mark and the stench of burnt flesh filled the cabin. She shivered helplessly, trapped on the bed.

"You know what Queen Mir is going to do to her," said Stater.

Tara enjoyed seeing Cael move in closer to him.

Finish him off. Just do it. Stop talking and get me free. Instead of saying any of that for fear of distracting Cael, Tara made a mental note of the tattoo marks on Stater's face so she could help the police identify him as the man who killed Marty.

"Like I said, a man who likes to talk. Blah, blah, blah, blah," said Cael. A blink later he had his hands wrapped around Stater's throat. Instead of struggling, Stater laughed. The evil sound bounced across the crumbling log walls of the small cabin.

"You have no idea what I've done to make me the man I am today. If you think I'm about to let the Damned Fairy take it away from me when I am this close, you are sadly mistaken. I will find the Stone of Fal and get my revenge."

Shimmering hot heat filled the cabin and then in an instant Stater was gone. Vanished into thin air.

"What, doesn't anyone know how to fight fair anymore?" shouted Cael.

Finally daring to draw in a much-needed breath, Tara felt Cael's fingers rip apart her bonds.

"Is she okay?"

Tara opened her eyes. Alec stood framed in the doorway. A wave of embarrassment washed over her. Cael immediately positioned his body to block Alec's view. A tired smile flirted across Tara's lips as she looked at Cael's back. She was mortified at having Katie's brother see her naked and completely helpless. Sensing her discomfort Alec took off his jacket and flung it toward Cael. Peeking her head around Cael's imposing frame she mouthed a "thank you" to him. Reverently Cael covered her body with it.

"Get the fuck out!" commanded Cael to Alec.

"She needs to come with us. We need to get her back to the cave. She'll be safe there." Alec didn't move a muscle noted Tara.

Safe there? Safe from what? Surely that crazy man isn't going to come after me again. "The cave sounds great. Anything sounds wonderful besides this place," said Tara, not realizing she was moving her hands up and down Cael's back until he turned and captured her hands, bringing her fingers up to his lush lips. A playful nip on each finger had her gasping within seconds.

The act was intimate and highly improper for the moment. She leaned more into his body, loving the feel of heat that rushed through her system. His warmth engulfed her finely tuned ultra-sensitive nerves. She inhaled his unique scent deep within her body and sighed.

"We need some privacy. Now!" Cael once again directed his attention to Alec.

"Surely that can wait until we're back at the cave."

Tara recognized Alec's defiant tone. However, all her thoughts got distracted when she inhaled for the second time Cael's scent of cinnamon and cardamom combined with the wild woods. She couldn't stifle the moan. Her cheeks blossomed to a burning red when Alec turned his attention back to her.

"I'm not going to ask you again. Leave us alone, Highlander!" snapped Cael.

Tara let Cael help her to a sitting position on the hard bed. She was about to come to Alec's rescue when she felt her core start to pulse for something and her breasts tingle. Her nipples tightened involuntarily. Every nerve ending zoned in on Cael's body now standing next to her. She felt the rough texture of the jacket as it brushed against her pebbled nipples and she had an insatiable urge to rub her body up against Cael's hard frame.

I know I'm finally going into shock. That's it. It's just a delayed reaction and in a moment I'll get to my feet and get the Hell out of here.

Alec mumbled a string of curses and then huffed and marched from the cabin.

Cael's hands framed her face. His silver-grey eyes seared her. Instant heat scorched her insides, churning her stomach with butterflies of desire. Her eyes closed as wild passion for him, for his body, his dominance crashed through her.

"Did he hurt you?" His voice was a choked ragged question. She felt the tautness of his muscles bunch as he waited for her answer.

"A little face slapping but that was it."

"Bastard! That man is going to die," growled Cael, brushing a soothing hand through her hair. The intimate act unleashed the emotions Tara had kept at bay.

"What's happening to me?" she whispered. Tears welled up in her eyes. She closed her eyes, halting the windstorm of turbulent emotions that swirled deep within her.

"Shh, Tara, this is normal...I will make everything all right. Actually, I will make you feel more than okay. I promise."

He gave a throaty chuckle of promise that teased her sensitive ears, while he moved her body closer to the edge of the bed. He now stood directly between her legs. It was a highly sexual pose and the action forced her to raise her head so she could watch him. Her body seemed to have a mind of its own because for the life of her she couldn't stop the ache she felt and the want to have his hands roam freely over her sensitive skin.

"Lie down."

His voice had taken on that commanding tone. She bristled. However, she wasn't sure if she was smarting because she wanted to follow his orders or because following them went against her nature.

Tara did as instructed, letting the jacket fall from her form. She heard his indrawn breath. Shyly, she opened her eyes. He was peeling his shirt off over his head and the view of his six-pack chest and coppery skin, which was in direct contrast to his long silky platinum hair, caused her to groan greedily. He too had black inked tattoos on his arms. Instead of feeling repulsed by them she quivered for the feel of them under her fingers. He smiled a sexy look at her that said he didn't mind her checking out his body. So, check it out she did.

Once again her eyes were drawn to the designs lining both his arms with symbols, somewhat similar to the ones that lunatic wore on his body. But there was nothing evil about the etchings inked into Cael's skin. They were downright sexy.

"What are these?"

"My curse."

A two-word sum up of this Damned Fairy's life, thought Tara. "Curse?"

"Knowledge always comes with a price."

"Is that supposed to make sense?" Tara reached out to trace a large symbol on his right arm. "They look almost druid like."

"They are."

"But you said you're a Tuatha."

"I am. It's a complicated story but trust me I earned those symbols burnt into my flesh and they are druid."

"What do the symbols mean?" Tara realized she was curious now.

Cael shuffled his body more into the vee of her legs. "As much as I'd love to chat all day, I can think of a dozen more pleasurable ways we can pass our time in this shit-hole."

He then proceeded to rub the large bulge in his jeans up against her core. A flame of desire whirled through her entire body, dousing all rational thoughts of the questions she was about to ask.

"Only a dozen ways?" The teasing words freely flew from her without thought and for once Tara didn't listen to her inner nature that told her she shouldn't be letting him do this to her.

"Feyling, we've only got about ten minutes so don't push your luck."

Cael's fingers came to rest on the top part of his zipper. A gasp escaped her when he undid his jeans. Moving to her elbows, she raised her body so she could watch him strip off his jeans. No underwear. The man was gloriously butt naked and proud of the skin he wore.

"We've done this before, haven't we?" Her body was growing increasingly wet with desire.

He nodded knowingly as he grasped what her eyes were daring to look at with glee and willful anticipation. Tara wet her lips eagerly. There before her was his magnificent cock. Proud. Warrior-ready. Built for sex. Those were the earthly words she thought best described him. She eyed him greedily and was thankful that he let her look her fill. She knew she should have felt embarrassed by her brazen actions but she didn't.

"Want to touch?" Cael asked the question knowing full well her answer. Tara wondered then who was the real tease.

She reached a hand out to tentatively feel him. His cock was thick in its width and her small hand could barely circle it. She felt a shudder rack through his body. It thrilled her that he was enjoying her touch. Tara was surprised at how satiny hot he felt in her hand. Like the Tuatha himself his cock was polar opposite to what she had thought it would feel like. Velvet steel. Heat and ice. Cael was a complicated mix she would be hard pressed to sum up in a neat and tidy sentence. A warrior who wielded death with his hands, he caressed her body with butterfly touches that left her sweetly anticipating more.

He pulsed, this proud muscle showing her what it was capable of. She giggled. What surprised her was that unlike human men he had no pubic hair. His cock and weighty testicles were bare to her gaze and they matched the coppery shade of his skin tone.

"Are you laughing at my cock?" asked Cael, a delightful grin softened his harsh facial features.

There was also a devilish glint in his eyes that should have warned her she was playing with fire, but she didn't heed it. When he purposely bucked his shaft again, she knew he was teasing her. "You like doing that, don't you?"

"What I'd like, my little feyling, is for you to take my cock inside that sweet mouth of yours."

Tara got the impression he said it to see if it would shock her. It didn't. Instead it caused her core muscles to clench with anticipation and her mouth to salivate with need. Without saying anything, she sat up and did as instructed, loving his muffled curse of surprise.

"By all that's sacred, you're so hot." He rasped the words out, while gripping her hair in a tight squeeze of passion.

Hot is certainly the right adjective. The skin on his shaft was stretched taut with need as she slowly took it inch by delicious inch, stuffing it into mouth. Her tongue swirled around it. She played with the slit at the top, loving the salty yet flowery taste of his seed. Feeling even braver, she reached out to cup his large testicles, gripping them tightly in her hands, loving the feel of his sac. He bucked his hips forward and grasped her head hard, anchoring her to him.

"That's it...suck it, feyling. Faster...faster."

Tara loved the power she felt. Cael trembled because of her touch, her mouth and her tongue. She felt like a goddess or high priestess—powerful.

Then he pulled his cock abruptly out of her mouth. Without warning, he pushed her back down on the hard bed. She felt the old wood dig into her hips and back. She fidgeted, trying to get comfortable.

In one sweep his eyes took in her maneuvering form. Before she could protest he scooped her up. Instinctively her legs circled his hips as he walked with her over to a wooden chair. He sat down on the chair. She was so wet with desire she was sure he felt her juices on his skin.

"You're going to straddle me."

Cael's wicked words were a deep guttural groan. A command of his need. His want. His desire. His eyes were half closed, as passion stole over his features. When desire overtook him, Cael transformed from a rugged Celtic warrior to a man of passion, softened with the glow of lust that radiated around him. He became beautiful. The feminine word would not be to his liking, thought Tara, but it expressed his magnificent change. So much so that his Tuatha heritage shone through, marking him truly as non-human...a god to be worshipped, a fey to be loved.

The intensity of her emotions, of the desire that tornadoed through her made it feel to Tara that her body was about to combust. She needed him. Wanted him. Ached to have his cock wedged tight within her core. How can this be? What is happening to me that I want this...Damned Fairy?

Sensing her hesitation and her questions of morality, he pulled her tighter to him. The slick feel of flesh to flesh, hot skin to blistering muscles caused her head to lean back with drug-induced passion. He spread his legs wider, forcing her wet core to slide over his rigid cock. She trembled. The thrill of that movement, slick juice sliding over his steel shaft, throbbed her core, teasing her inner muscles for a taste of what he promised to deliver. The muscles in her legs quivered with fierce need. Anticipation and excitement merged into a pulse of intense desire she had absolutely no control over. She fought with her rational mind that said what she was doing was wrong while her body begged for him to continue.

"It's okay, Tara. Trust me, this is normal. You're normal. And I plan on making sure you remember this..." He reached around her to squeeze her ass, cupping her more to him.

She squirmed even more, loving the feel of wetting his cock with her juices as she straddled his lap.

"...and this," he said, moving his head to her heaving breast.

She arched more into his embrace. His teeth nipped and then he laved her nipples until pain and pleasure merged, causing her to fidget with insatiable need. Under his skillful ministrations her nipples puckered into tight buds. His hand cupped her bottom more and then she felt a hand move lower. Two fingers slid through her cleft to open her wet folds. She leaned back, forcing his mouth off her breast with a popping sound.

"You're going to ride me."

With that warning he moved her ass higher and repositioned her body so that she was poised over his wet, glistening cock.

She looked at his large shaft and then into his eyes, noting how the black rings that circled the silver-grey of his irises seemed thicker. It was one stark reminder that Cael, the Damned Fairy, wasn't human and she shivered for the first time as sexual longing and fear of the unknown mixed to form the perfect recipe for the rising desire within her.

Tara eyed Cael's cock once again. Surely I would have remembered having something that large within me. After all I was a virgin.

"It's okay, Tara. Trust me. I fit like a glove."

His eyes heated with warmth and twinkled sexily at her. She loved that even though he too was gripped with passion he was being gentle, reassuring her all would be well. That caused her to relax more into his hold. Slowly he lowered her until her wet opening was directly over his ridged cock head. She felt her muscles relax as the wide tip of him entered smoothly into her core.

Guess I have done this before. Tara moved her body down until all of him was safe and snug inside her. And then she felt it. Like before when she held him in her hand he bucked his hard cock muscle, only this time it nudged a super sensitive spot deep inside of her that had her mewling out loud.

"See, I told you my cock is not a laughing matter, you naughty little feyling."

Before she could respond he was kissing her, branding her with his lips and molding them to his. He forked his tongue in and out, his actions mimicking her as she rode him with short up-and-down strokes.

She was riding him, loving the feel of his tongue and cock inside her. His hands crept back to her ass and she welcomed their kneading attention. He was helping to leverage her, using his arm muscles to force her up and down onto his rigidly hard member. The friction was building within her body. She threw her head back as waves of ecstasy surged within. Her hair spilled around her. His hands tangled into her strands, forcing her neck back so he could nip the pulse that was beating at her throat. Tara welcomed the love bite, as he suckled her neck, biting her...marking her as his.

Then a hand crept to her front and she couldn't help but scream when he daintily opened her folds and pebbled her already hard nub. The pleasure of it was blinding. She couldn't continue to ride him, so he forced her legs to open more as she shifted to allow him easier access to her clit. She leaned back.

"That's it, feyling. I'm going to make you come again and again. Then and only then am I going to give you what your body really craves."

Tara couldn't think straight. Surely she must be having an out of body experience, she thought. She wasn't inherently like this and most certainly a good girl like her shouldn't be liking or wanting this. But she did. She thirsted for it. Wanted him to push her over the edge...needed him to take command and force the pleasure he promised her.

She felt him tap harder on her nub, which had pebbled and swollen with intense need.

"Lie back more, I've got you. " He gave her body a gentle nudge which forced her to be even more exposed and openly on display for him.

His cock twitched inside her, again hitting that special place that caused her to see stars. The combination of his cock moving inside her, even though she no longer was riding him and his finger squeezing and stroking her nub was too much for her. She felt her muscles clench as she came hard on him. Her cream soaked his cock, lubricating them both more.

She felt his other hand move back to her bottom. His finger was dipping into her juices and then he was stroking the crack of her ass, making it wet from her own cream. She squirmed, not sure of his actions. Her body was still highly sensitive from her orgasm, but he wasn't letting up.

"You're going to come again for me feyling."

Once again his commanding tone warred with her desire and reasoning. Desire won out when he turned his attention back to her nipples. He breathed first on one then the other. She shivered as they went hot and then puckered more with the cool air within the cabin. Then he placed one engorged nipple into his mouth and suckled hard. It was an intoxicating feeling that left her breathless and wanting more.

While he administered to her nipples, he kept up his assault on her ass, rubbing her. She squirmed as desire for the unknown rippled through her. She screamed a ragged plea of enough when another orgasm tore through her body as he suckled her nipple hard and tweaked her still sensitive nub. Then he bucked his hips up, sending his engorged member deeper within her. The need to ride him overcame her senses.

'That's it feyling, ride me hard. Let the Fey within you come out to play."

His breath was fast and shallow but still he didn't stop his administrations to her body. His hands felt like they were everywhere. She felt wickedly invaded and loved it. The heady feel of his cock and fingers playing with her other slick passage was totally encompassing. She slid her legs up higher onto his hips.

He groaned loudly, as he cupped her cheeks so he could take over the pace of the ride. It was rough. He bucked his hips hard into her, almost forcing his body off the chair as he plunged his cock in and out of her wet, pulsing core.

Tara didn't think she could climax again but she was wrong. His cock kept twitching at that ultra-sensitive spot and with her new position she was angled just right. She gripped his shoulders hard, letting her nails dig deep as the world shattered around her for the third time.

This time she took him with her. His growl resonated throughout his body and into hers, giving her comfort that she was able to please him. He shuddered as his hot seed spurted into her body, and she soaked it all in. The feel of his energy flowed through her system, quivering all her sensitive nerve endings. Something deep, soul-rich and perfect fused within a part of her, making her feel totally whole for the first time in her life. It was a shocking realization.

"So good, feyling, so fucking good."

He crooned the words into her hair as he lowered her legs back to his waist, rubbing her back as small aftershocks settled.

The knock at the cabin door brought cold reality and reasoning back to her.

"You bloody well done banging her, brother? Or do you need me to cut open my other wrist so I can keep this fucking island where it is. Get your prick out of that woman. I'm leaving now. You might want to pick up that there Highlander on your way off this frigging island. I just punched him in the face. Fuck that hurts!" shouted Balor, ranting like there was no tomorrow.

What did I just do? Tara scrambled to climb off him, but he was having none of that. He tightened his hold on her body and wiped her long hair off her now sweaty face.

Cael pried her fingers open, dumping a gold wedding band in her palm. "I forgot to tell you Tara, we were married last night. So, don't let your conscious think it's wrong. I get to fuck you all I want."

The surge of anger that mounted through Tara left her feeling cold and shaky. "You really are a Damned Fairy, aren't you?"

"Always. And don't forget it."

Chapter Eleven

"KATIE, FOR THE LAST time! Stop bringing food to that goddamn fairy. And no more chocolate cake." Alistair stood guard at the cave's entrance and tried unsuccessfully to stop Katie.

"Don't be so pig-headed." Katie sashayed straight past Alistair without a care in the world.

"If you think I'm letting you in that makeshift bedroom with that creature you are sadly mistaken, Katie-girl."

This time the Highlander Druid moved his burly frame to stop her approach. It was the Katie-girl remark that Cael knew stopped her cold. He watched as Katie shifted her foot and eyed her brother like he was dog food. The scene was highly amusing, but not what Cael needed at the moment.

What he needed and wanted were two entirely different things. What he wanted again was the intoxicating feel of Tara's smoldering skin glistening with the sweaty scent of sex all over his body. He wanted to feel that chestnut-red hair of hers draped across his chest. He craved her honeysuckle scent with a fierce longing that for a moment left him wondering who was going through the Sh'lam'alah. It certainly felt like he was, but he knew first hand that wasn't so. Worse, he'd spilled his seed again. He wasn't an innocent. He was trained in the art of pleasuring a woman. And now this—twice. *What's come over me?*

What he needed was that godforsaken Stone of Fal. Now! Not tomorrow, not another minute from now. He had to get his hands on it. To do so, he also had to get Tara to trust him enough to tell him where her grandmother, Rhea, had hidden it. He knew with every bone in his body that she knew exactly where that sacred stone was.

However, he couldn't approach Tara. She was safely guarded by MacCallah, the matriarch of the MacLeod clan who had looked like she wanted to bash him to death with the rolling pin when he'd sauntered back into the cave. The mood wasn't helped when Alec trudged in cursing a blue streak, and then came his brother, still bleeding and whining. Tara had stomped her way straight over to Devon demanding a thorough explanation.

Cael had tried to explain about the wedding but she had flatly told him to go to Hell.

It wasn't my idea in the first place so what do I care what she thinks. Cael heard Tara hiccup on another soft sob she tried hard to quell. *Bloody Hell. Enough is enough.*

Marching straight across the cave he shouldered his way through the circle of Highlanders, eyed MacCallah and Devon, and then pulled Tara straight into his embrace.

"Feyling, like I told you get used to the idea."

She attempted to squirm free and kick him. "Get away from me!"

Cael growled low and whispered into her ear. "You either settle down, Tara, or I will kiss you senseless in front of everyone, which will only make you beg for more."

He watched as she struggled to both compose herself and come back with a saucy retort. Her tongue-lashing he could deal with. Her tears, he could not. Thankfully he didn't need to worry. Once again her proud Tuatha Dé Danann heritage won out. She straightened her shoulders, notched up her chin and turned her head to eye him like he was a bug that had crawled out from under a rock. Cael fought the gin that threatened to split across his face. Tuatha to the core, this one.

"I need that Stone of Fal, now!" he said, getting straight to the point.

"I don't have it," she said "Even if I did have this stone, I wouldn't give it to you. Ever." She regally disengaged herself from his embrace and moved away from him.

"I thought Earth women were supposed to obey their husbands when they got married," said Balor. He chose that very moment to saunter out of the makeshift bedroom, looking sleepy and sexy in his wrinkled white shirt, which gaped open revealing his muscular chest. Every single MacLeod heard Katie's sexy sigh.

Cael watched as Balor turned in the opposite direction. It was almost like his brother was afraid of the woman. Cael stifled a laugh. His brother loved women, the more the merrier, hence why he had been chosen as one of Queen Mir's consorts. Then Cael watched in surprise as his brother walked out of the cave.

"Where are you going?" he called after him.

"Home," replied Balor.

Cael laughed, which caused all the MacLeods to converge at the cave's entrance.

"Now I know why Queen Mir expelled you. You really can be a bastard at times," said Balor.

That sobered Cael. "How are you getting home, Balor?"

"Damned if I know. What I most certainly know is that I have a better chance of getting home from Ireland than here. Here, Cael, in case you didn't know it is a place they call Cape Breton. We are nowhere close to home. And this weather, how can you stand it?"

Cael watched his brother hunch his shoulders against the darkening sky and cool night air. In less than two hours it would be completely dark. Going home was not going to happen. Sadly, though Cael knew exactly how his brother felt. Even though it went against his nature, Cael couldn't let his brother go. He was too ill-equipped to deal with the real world.

"Get your ass in here Balor. Once we find the Stone of Fal, you get to go home too."

They all watched as Balor stopped walking to turn back toward the cave.

"Take that Stone of Fal and shove it, Cael. I'm only coming back because it's bloody well freezing out there. You know as well as I do just how dangerous that bloody stone is. I don't want my hands on it."

Balor shoved his way past them and ignored the wool blanket Katie held out as a peace offering.

Something is most definitely wrong with him. Cael watched as Tara's friend fought hard to compose herself. She was hurt by his brother's curt actions. Cael was simply perplexed by it all.

Just then Neil raced into the cave. "I found it. I found out who sent that Internet rumor."

"Who?" asked Cael and the Highlanders at the same time.

"The computer source originated from CBU," said Neil, clearly proud of himself.

Hands on his hips, Cael asked the obvious. "CBU? That's what?"

"The local university," answered Neil.

"What department?" asked Alec, his right cheek still swollen from Balor's fist.

Cael hadn't found out yet why his brother had felt compelled to hit Alec. The drive back from the cursed mystical island that needed Tuatha Dé Danann blood to stay in the human realm had been a silent and sober affair. Cael sensed that Alec had been fuming mad over him having to have sex with Tara. Truthfully, he could have waited until they made it back to the cave but he hadn't wanted to. His need for her had been so great he had to take her then and there, plus part of him admitted having the deed shoved in Alec's face pleased him. An equally loud part of him needed to reassure himself she had been okay and that Stater hadn't hurt her. During the course of their lovemaking Cael had used his druid knowledge to heal the slap welts that had marred her face. Tara hadn't realized what he'd done and he wasn't about to enlighten her.

"The computer is registered to one Professor Xavier," informed Neil.

"Why are you talking about Professor Xavier?" asked Tara, finally tuning into the conversation.

Cael wondered if she knew she had moved toward him and not the Highlanders. Her presence was a warm glow that caused all the hairs on his body to stand on end. He didn't bother filling her in. "Okay, I'm going to go and have a chat with this Xavier. Keep the home fires burning." He strolled past the Highlanders and Tara.

Tara abruptly blocked his path. "Leave him alone. He's an old man that doesn't need the likes of you invading his life."

Cael felt Alec flank his side. "Don't worry, Tara, I won't let anything happen to the professor. I'm going with him."

Cael grumbled.

"I'm coming too," said Neil.

Cael stopped walking. "Bloody Hell, don't you boys let a man do anything alone?"

Tara placed her hands on her hips, in a move he had come to recognize as her defiant pose. "And I'm coming too."

"Fine!" he spat. "Want to come along too, brother?" Cael seriously hoped someone would see the sense in them not all walking up to the professor. As it was his dark vibe couldn't be cloaked. He seriously wanted that stone today, sensing the more time Stater had on his hands to find it the worse things would be for them all.

"Shut up," snapped Balor. "You can all burn in Hell."

"Sadly, you know that won't happen for the likes of you," said Alec.

Cael grinned. One point for Alec. Cael noted Alec's normal blue eyes had taken on a slight grey appearance. Yes, this one needs watching. There is a dark force that lives inside him and if my guess is right there will come a day when that power will emerge. One way it will change this Highlander Druid. Cael hoped to all that was sacred the change would be for the best, but the dark part within him screamed that might not be.

ALMOST AN HOUR LATER they were all crowded into Professor Xavier's office with Tara fuming mad he had picked the lock. *What the Hell did she think I was going to do? Knock politely on the door? Not in this lifetime.*

"You know we could all be arrested for trespassing."

It was the third time she had said that to them. Thankfully, the Highlanders had no qualms about him breaking into the professor's office.

"Not that any of you seem to care."

She sighed. He felt that breathy tone of her voice all the way to his toes and that wasn't a good thing. *Bloody distraction. Females, of all sorts, that's exactly what they are. A distraction.*

As they all ambled into the room, looking bug-eyed, Neil asked Tara. "This is like a bloody museum. Did you know he had all these relics?"

Tara nodded affirmatively, her eyes as round as saucers as she took in all the ancient Celtic treasures. Most of the ancient relics were safely locked up behind glass cabinets but a few, like the two ancient Celtic stone holy crosses that Cael knew dated back to around 800 B.C. were proudly on display on Xavier's desk.

Next to the cross was an object that caused Cael to shiver. It was an Ogham script, an ancient twenty-five letter Celtic alphabet, which was really a lot more powerful than humans understood. *At least they don't have any idea how powerful this ancient word system really is.* Cael said a silent thanks for that one, while wondering how the professor managed to get his hands on one.

"I'm going to check out his computer," said Neil, the computer geek in the group.

Cael watched as Neil maneuvered his large body into the professor's wooden chair so he could sit behind his desk with the state-of-the-art computer.

"Tara, you keep lookout," said Alec.

"Who put you in charge of this expedition, boy? Tara, come here. Alec, you keep look out." Cael stared down the Highlander, daring him to interject. For a moment Cael wondered who Tara would obey.

Both watched as she rolled her eyes to the heavens and then proceeded to plop herself down in a dark brown leather chair on the opposite side of the office. Nothing like a strong-willed woman. Okay, nothing like a sexy, strong-willed feyling.

"Great, that's just great. I'll be bloody lookout," mumbled Alec, brushing past Cael so he could stick his head out the door.

"I didn't know Professor Xavier had an Ogham script," said Tara.

She was straining her neck to get a good look at what Cael had spied on the professor's desk. "My grandmother taught me to read this when I was a child."

"She did?" Cael was clearly surprised. The Ogham script was the druid's spell book even though today's historians thought of it as an alphabet of sorts. If they only knew the power behind those letters the world most definitely would not be the same.

The knowledge inherent in the Ogham script was something only the highest of Druid Priests learned. The priest that had befriended him had shared his knowledge of the powerful tablet with him. Back then, though Cael had thought the power of the Druids laughable. Centuries later he came to understand how powerful they really were. Cael was startled out of his thoughts by what Tara said next.

"Yes, she did and she also taught me the hidden meaning of the letters."

"Would this be the same grandmother who taught you the Tuatha tongue?" asked Cael. His voice was laced with sarcasm.

Tara gave a slight nod and Cael watched as she cleared her throat, visibly trying to get a hold of her emotions. It dawned on him then that she must have loved her grandmother very much. For one moment he wondered if he had ever felt that type of love. The mop of curls of his vision-child, his daughter, tore like lightning through his mind. That type of love he vowed never to experience again.

"She called it her secret language. She was always speaking it, talking to the plants or the air around her and when I started to recite it, she noticed. She took me aside and told me it would be just hers and mine, our special secret language. I honestly thought it was totally made up, not real," said Tara.

"It's real all right, Tara. Alive and well in Tir Nan Og," he replied.

"What made your queen damn you, Cael?" asked Tara, changing the conversation abruptly.

Luckily Cael didn't have to answer.

"Someone's coming." Alec gently closed the door behind him as he ducked back into the office.

Cael wanted to question Tara more about her grandmother and more importantly how she came to learn the meaning of the ancient Druid script, but now was not the time.

"I'm almost there...yes, this is the computer where the Internet message originated from," said Neil.

"We've got company. Quick, out the window," said Alec, moving to the small window.

Cael watched Tara shiver. They were on the fourth floor of the university building. They would not be going out the window. But he didn't want to get caught also because that would involve more people and questions. Time was ticking away. However, he did plan to have a heart-to-heart with this Xavier person at a later date. The door opened before he could put a plan in motion and then everything stilled.

There before Cael's eyes was the absolute last person he thought he would ever see. Before him stood the Druid Priest he had called friend for years...the same man who had betrayed him to his queen. Sure, his physical appearance looked remarkably different but it was the cold, calculating sky-blue eyes that pierced him, breaking through the façade. He was the Druid who forced Queen Mir's hand, causing Cael to be exiled from his homeland.

Because of that Druid I have died two hundred and twenty-four times only to be painfully resurrected each time. Because of that Druid Priest I will never truly die. Because of him I will never have true peace.

Cael wrapped his hands tightly around Xavier's miserable throat before the Druid Priest was even fully in the room. He heard Tara, Neil and Alec shouting at him to stop. He felt all three of them attempt to break his hold, but Cael knew something they didn't. He was going to kill the professor while he had the chance. Damn the consequences!

Tara couldn't believe her eyes. Cael had finally snapped. He was attempting to strangle Professor Xavier before their eyes. Pure, unadulterated hatred seized his facial features. She knew that look. It was the same look he had while battling the man he called Stater. Tara knew then she had to try to stop him before he succeeded in his quest to kill the good professor.

"You are going to die a slow, painful death." Cael's lips had pulled back in a scowl of hatred as he growled the words tightly in this throat. The black rims of his eyes had invaded the silver making his pupils appear like they were filled with black ink. The stark reminder of his Tuatha heritage shone like an angry beacon through his hate-filled eyes.

Tara shivered, as the human façade of Cael faded and the full force of his Tuatha blood blazed before them all.

"I knew you would come, Cael. I had—" Xavier choked; his windpipe now almost completely crushed by Cael's powerful hands.

"Let him go. Now!" shouted Tara, once again yanking on Cael's arm in an attempt to get him to release the professor.

Only when the professor started to turn purple did Cael relent. Xavier dropped unceremoniously to the wooden floor. Alec helped the frail-looking professor into a chair.

The terrifying emotions that surged through Tara caused her to fight with her stuttering. "Wh...why did you do that? What's co...come over you?" She took a calming breath and then turned the full force of her anger on Cael, who hadn't taken his eyes off the professor for one second.

"Why don't you ask your good professor here who he really is?" Cael held his body warrior rigid and defiant as he glared at Xavier.

Tara shook her head. *None of this makes any sense. Then again, much of my life in the past few days hasn't made any sense.* She knew exactly who Professor Xavier was. He was the department chair of Ancient Celtic History, world renowned for his expert advice on druid artifacts.

Turning her attention from Cael to the professor, who was now attempting to take a sip of water from a cup on his desk, she moved her hair off her forehead and approached her favorite professor.

"I am so sorry that happened, Professor Xavier. I had no idea..." Here Tara turned for help from Alec and getting none, she continued on. "We had no idea that would happen."

Cael moved two steps closer to her. "Ask him who he really is, Tara!" He growled the words in a low, threatening tone of voice, which unfortunately terrified a part of her she was trying very hard to ignore. That part of her anatomy between her legs, which was starting to weep with passion simply because Cael was close to her.

His unique wild cinnamon-cardamom scent was driving her mad with desire.

This is so the wrong time to even be thinking of sex. She fought hard not to sigh. Plus, she reminded herself she was furious at him for marrying her against her will. Okay, she knew first-hand now he'd been tricked into marriage but that didn't give him the right to agree to the scheme she knew the MacLeods had hatched. Talk about old-fashioned beliefs. Tara tried even harder to ignore the thrilling twitter in her gut when she thought about her and Cael being husband and wife.

"Go ahead, Tara. Ask him who he really is," interrupted Cael once again.

Tara couldn't believe she was doing this. She felt her face flush with embarrassment. She knew they'd be lucky to get off the campus without being detained by campus security or worse, the police. Flashing her eyes angrily at Cael she nodded. "Fine. Like I said, I am sorry about this, but who are you really?" Tara forced herself to look away from the abyss of Cael's heated black eyes, which truly terrified her.

Before Xavier could say anything she felt Cael's hands pull her back toward him. Did he have to do that? Just the feel of his chest through her winter jacket caused her heart to lurch and her skin to tingle with the beginnings of that terrible ache she was getting to know so well. Luckily, this time when she moved out of his embrace he let her go.

"This I'm going to love. Cael, you look like a man who's seen the devil," said Alec, breaking the quiet that had settled in the office.

"He's not a man," squeaked Xavier.

That comment brought Tara up short. "What?"

"He's not a man. He's a Tuatha Dé Danann. To be precise he's the Damned Fairy," stated Professor Xavier, calmly.

135

Tara moved her arm to block Cael's approach. She knew he wanted to have another go at the professor but that wouldn't help. Something is not right here.

"How do you know him?" asked Tara.

An evil chuckle spewed forth from Cael. "Yes, do tell them how you know me, Xavier," replied Cael, mockingly.

Tara watched as the professor ran a shaky hand through his thin grey hair. "I am the Druid Priest that had him damned."

The statement was said so matter-of-factly Tara felt her heart still. Alec and Neil both sputtered.

Before their eyes the frail looking façade of the professor vanished. A whisper of power surged through Tara's veins, forcing her eyes shut. She shook her head to reorient herself. For one moment she felt the shift of another realm, the pull to leave her body and let her consciousness soar through the galaxies. A movement from Cael brought her instantly back to the situation at hand.

There sitting before them was a man who looked no more than the age of Cael, in his late twenties. He had light brown hair, shiny baby blue eyes and he was extremely muscular.

"Holy shit!" said Neil.

"Mother of god!" echoed Alec.

"Bloody fucking right," answered Cael, smugly.

The new Xavier stood. "You have every right to be angry, Cael. But I had hoped you would come here and find me so we could talk."

"Talk, you want to talk. After I kill you, maybe," said Cael, pushing Tara aside.

"Stop that," interrupted Tara, once again blocking his path. "As much as I'd like to know the history between you two and how all this could be, the bigger question I think is why didn't you just send him a note to get his attention?" asked Tara pointedly.

"I couldn't. I had to be sure Stater meant what he said," answered the professor.

"Do you have any idea what my life has been like? Because of you I've been human for a thousand years. Because of you I've...never mind." Cael turned and walked to the other side of the room, grumbling under his breath. Tara was sure he was cursing the Druid for the next millennium for what he had done to him.

Xavier closed his eyes wearily. "Cael, if I could go back and change what I did, I would in a heartbeat, but you know I cannot. Saying I'm sorry isn't going to make any difference now. I am hoping we can put aside our differences for a common good. Once we were friends—"

Cael turned so quickly to advance that he knocked over a large stone druid cross in the process. "Shut the fuck up! Common good," he grinned evilly. "I did that once and look what it got me. Look how much good I've done."

"I had no idea you were petitioning Queen Mir for the humans' betterment. I was told you were...never mind. It won't and doesn't change things. I sent out that Internet rumor in the hopes that you'd find it and come here. I know Stater's here also so you see the peril we are in."

"I can't do anything about that." Cael ran his hands through his hair as he faced the professor.

Tara was sure she was the only person who felt sorry for Cael. A thousand years forced from your true home. A thousand years knowing no matter what you do, you will be resurrected when all your loved ones die. The harsh knowledge of what his life must have been like, knowing there was no hope, yet forced to endure and to live day-to-day while keeping your sanity was not for the faint of heart. Tara wasn't sure she could have done it.

"He will come for her," said Xavier, pointing a finger at Tara.

Tara gulped. Cael was beside her in a flash.

"I won't let him get her. I will take care of him."

"Bloody fucking right we will. No one is touching Tara," said Alec, moving to flank Cael's other side.

Tara didn't need to look at Cael. She knew he was once again glaring at the Highlander. They were like two pit bulls, always testing each other.

"And then what?" Xavier stood up again. "You need to petition Queen Mir and the only way to do that is to draw her blood. You need another Tuatha Dé Danann to open the veil and the timing has to be just so. The next new moon is within a few days and that's your best chance."

Tara felt Cael pull her body closer to his. None of this conversation is making any sense. Drawing blood, new moon, what exactly are they talking about?

"Plain English would be great," snapped Alec, gesturing to Xavier to elaborate.

"Since Cael was exiled from Tir Nan Og he can't use his blood to open the veil between the two worlds, but Tara's blood will do. With it he can then ask for an audience with Queen Mir."

"Wait a sec, are you saying Tara's like him?" asked Alec, turning to give her a look she couldn't read and wasn't sure she even wanted to.

Cael simply nodded.

Tara grimaced. "Not really." Her voice was a soft whisper.

"Can we use his brother's blood?" asked Neil, ever practical.

"No," replied Cael. "All his Tuatha power is gone. We used what power he had left to keep that blasted island in this realm."

"Shit seems to follow you fairies wherever you go," snapped Alec.

"Like I was saying—" interjected Xavier.

Neil cut him off. "But if the queen exiled him, why would she agree to hear what he has to say?" Neil moved to sit on the arm of a chair like this was a normal conversation. Alec kept his stance next to Cael.

Xavier picked up the cross Cael had bumped onto the floor. They all watched as he carefully placed it back on his desk. "Do they know about the Decies?"

"Yes," replied Neil and Alec, simultaneously, while Tara mouthed, "No".

"Let's just say that what Cael has to say about the Decies is something Queen Mir will listen to," said Xavier, sounding like her normal Celtic History professor.

"What exactly do you know?" asked Cael.

"A year ago, I had heard rumors from the other Druids but I thought they must be wrong. All that changed last year when I went to a conference in L.A. Who should show up at the conference but Stater. I honestly couldn't believe my eyes. You know he even told me how he's managed to keep alive all these centuries, but I digress. He told me his plans and I knew I wouldn't be able to keep the Stone of Fal safe much longer. Rhea and I discussed—"

"What a sec, you knew my grandmother?" interjected Tara, clearly confused by the turn of events.

Neil stood up and both he and Alec moved closer to Xavier.

"There are other Druids here?" asked Neil, ever the fact finder in the group.

Xavier nodded. Before they could question him further the professor continued.

"I knew Rhea for a long time, Tara. When she found out what I was, she asked for my help. She told me how she had inadvertently ended up on Earth. She made me put the binding missive on her bracelet to ensure her previous lover would come so that you could have the option of going to Tir Nan Og. I had no idea any of what has happened would occur. If Stater finds the Stone of Fal he will release the Decies and then humankind is doomed."

"Now that has an end of the world sound to it," said Tara, plopping down in the now vacant chair. "But where is my grandmother? When we opened her grave she wasn't there."

"You do know that she's Tuatha Dé Danann, right?" asked the professor.

Tara nodded.

"She's gone back to Tir Nan Og," replied Cael, moving closer to where she sat. "I can't believe I didn't think of that."

Tara shook her head. "I don't follow."

The professor picked up the stone Ogham script. Tara felt Cael stiffen behind her.

"When she died it was an Earth death. She wasn't damned, she was simply lost. A long time ago for unknown reasons the veil separating Tir Nan Og and Earth opened and Rhea accidentally walked through it, only to discover she could never return. When she walked through she ended up here, on Cape Breton. Your grandmother isn't really dead, Tara, she's actually very much alive in Tir Nan Og."

Tara choked back a sob. Could it be true? She desperately wanted to believe it. Every part of her heart swelled to absorb this newfound knowledge.

"She is not going anywhere near Queen Mir," stated Cael, deflating her euphoric bubble like a pinprick to a balloon.

"It's the only way. You need to let Queen Mir know what Stater is planning." Xavier moved his body closer to her and Cael. She felt the heat from the two men as they sized each other up.

Tara stood up, breaking the blistering eye-to-eye contact between the two of them. The very air almost crackled with their energy. She turned her attention solely to Cael. Looking up at him, she said, "I want to go to Tir Nan Og. I want to see my grandmother again."

"No way. Absolutely not." Cael didn't even look at her.

"Why not?" demanded Tara.

Tilting his head down to look at her, he gently outlined her lips with his finger. It was an intimate act that sizzled all her finely tuned senses.

"Because, my wee feyling, she will quite simply kill you without a second glance, all with a smile plastered to her face"

Chapter Twelve

CAEL WANTED TO SKIN the so-called professor alive. His real name used to be Xa'alter, Druid High Priest. Now, he went by Xavier. Cael knew whatever name he went by he was still the Druid who had him damned.

Cael planned for the last word uttered from the Druid's mouth to be a curse, because he was going to kill the priest who had been his friend for centuries. Friend, until he ratted on him, forcing Queen Mir to exile him.

"Still nursing that old wound I see," said Xavier.

Cael's lips thinned and his eyes narrowed to daggers. "If you think I plan on forgiving you any time soon you are in for a big disappointment. Just so we're clear on things, I do plan on killing you."

Xavier laughed. "That's what I've always admired about you...your Tuatha persistence."

"Fuck you," snarled Cael, pleased to see him clamp his mouth shut.

They had silently decided to head back to the cave with Xavier in tow. Crammed into the pickup truck like sardines, Cael was acutely aware of the woman who was squeezed next to him. Tara. Her honeysuckle scent clogged his throat. Her hand had unconsciously rested against his thigh with the abrupt movement of the truck, and he had felt the contact of her fingers through his jeans straight to his groin.

This is not the time to get sidetracked. He forced his mind to think of blood and murder, anything to dampen down the rage of desire that Tara's hand had evoked in his cock. Unfortunately, his mighty muscle was ignoring his pleas.

"How do you plan to keep her safe?" asked Xavier.

"She'll be safe with us," replied Alec.

Neil was in the back of the truck, and for one moment Cael wished he too was. But there was no way he was going to leave Tara alone with Xavier.

"Will she, really...highly doubtful," muttered Xavier.

Cael shifted uncomfortably on the hard leather seat. He put his hand in his pocket to help readjust a part of him that was trying its best to get Tara's attention. "I will keep her safe."

"So, you say, but Stater's stronger than he used to be. You aren't going to be able to keep Tara safe by yourself. You're going to need me."

That's it. Cael growled menacingly. "You underestimate me, Druid. I will keep her safe."

Cael felt Tara shift closer to him. She leaned forward so she could watch him and the Druid. She brushed her hair back off her face, tucking the long, chestnut strands around her tiny ears. Ears he'd love to nibble on.

"Stop talking about me like I'm not here. I can take care of myself."

Before she could say anything more the truck stopped. They had reached their destination. As dusk gave way to darkness, coating the landscape with the pitch of night like a painter's brush, the pickup truck parked at the end of the access road. They all climbed out of the truck to make their way along the rocky shoreline and then up the steep hill that led to the sacred druid cave.

Without thought he took Tara's hand to help her across the slick beach stones. Part of him was pleased when she didn't object. Another part of him was angry at himself and wished he didn't care if she landed on her ass.

Cael eyed the cave, thinking they might as well move some real furniture into the place which was unfortunately becoming a second home.

Devon took stock of their arrival at the cave's entrance. Xavier stepped casually over the rocks and made his way to the old man. Neil and Alec quickly followed.

Tara stumbled over the rocks. His grip tightened on her hand and he instinctively pulled her closer to him.

"You smell really good. Did I ever tell you that?"

Cael groaned. He knew once again she had no idea what she was saying or that her other hand had snaked into his hair. Ahh, the joys of going through the Sh'lam'alah.

"Snap out of it, Tara."

Cael knew he'd said the words harshly, but he'd been trying to watch Devon and Xavier who were deep in conversation. Tara gasped, pulled her hand from his with lightning quickness and was racing over the slippery rocks without a care in the world. In a blink she was at the cave's entrance. Now that's fey grace.

Cael gave his body another minute to adjust to her absence. Down boy. You'll be getting your fix sooner rather than later. His thoughts weren't helping his control. The knowledge that very soon he'd be sliding his cock into Tara's willing heat caused his shaft to buck in agreement. Great, this is just fucking great. Moving along over the uneven rocks, he marched to where the Druid Priest stood with his head bowed deep in conversation with Devon.

Devon leveled angry eyes at him. What? I'm back to being the monster again. Talk about unfair.

"You should have told me what Stater really needed, Cael," declared Devon.

Traitor. Cael wasn't surprised that Xavier had spilled the beans about Tara's Tuatha blood to Devon. He was surprised though that Devon hadn't called him the Damned Fairy. He had been expecting that and realized he was pleased the Highlander Druid had called him by his real name.

"I won't let Stater get her." He stomped past them all, not bothering to explain.

"Xavier here says you aren't strong enough," boomed Devon's voice off the walls of the small cave.

Cael kept walking. He was going straight for Tara. He needed to explain some things to her. However, the cave had been once again invaded by Highlanders.

"Just how many sons do you have, Devon?" Cael's eyes noted the tense expression of the Highlanders, all of whom were either standing or lounging against the cave's walls. Every single one of them looked like they'd enjoy killing him only to watch him be painfully resurrected. The hairs on the nape of his neck prickled uneasily. Things were tense and he knew the cause of it—Tara.

"Twelve. And we will keep Tara safe."

Cael swiveled his head around to eye Devon.

"I am sorry to say Devon, that none of your Highlanders will be able to keep Tara safe. Cael and I will do the job," said Xavier.

Okay, I've had enough of this. "You, Druid, a word," commanded Cael, turning to march on his heels out of the cave. He didn't bother to look to see if Xavier was following. His senses felt his presence. When they had made it halfway down the hill he turned.

"Okay, you and I are going to have a chat."

Xavier laughed. "Is that what you plan on doing to Stater? Chat him to death?"

Cael let the magick reach out to seep into his cells. He welcomed the angry rush of adrenaline that sang through his subconscious. In a flash he used the druid magick he'd been taught to knock the priest on his ass. Hands on his hips, he chuckled softly.

"Just so we're clear on things. I'm going to call you by your real name, traitor. So, piss on your parade, cause you ain't going to be anything but that to me. And look who's laughing now," said Cael.

But that was all he said. Cael felt the world tip and time stand still. He knew the priest had used his powers to bring them both to a private place where they could fight it out unfettered. Death would be welcome but even here Cael knew that wouldn't be possible.

Summoning the energy, he fired a zap aiming for the Druid's heart. If he has one.

Like with Stater, Xavier simply siphoned the power off the zap and redirected it at him. Cael felt his skin burn. Heat lanced his thigh.

"Your aim still sucks," he shouted, already pushing his energy out so he could volley forth a dozen lightning bolts from every direction straight at the priest. Before even one could touch him Xavier vanished, only to reappear behind him.

"Stater will take out your heart," said Xavier, and then Cael felt it.

The Druid Priest's arm reached straight through Cael's back to gently touch his heart. And then he withdrew. The singe of his power felled Cael to his knees.

"Cael, you don't have any Tuatha Dé Danann powers. You aren't versed in all the high druid teachings and you can't keep Tara safe." Xavier moved to Cael's front to face him.

"I could easily kill you. But what would be the purpose of that? I know you can't die. I know what Queen Mir did to you. And believe me when I say if I could change what I did I would. But the universe works in mysterious ways, Cael. Fate has a way of catching up to you. Let me help you. Together we will stop Stater. Together we can keep Tara safe and in the process keep Tir Nan Og safe."

The Druid's speech gave Cael pause. "Why would you want to keep Tir Nan Og safe? The last time I looked Queen Mir still wasn't allowing any of you to visit. Or has that changed in my absence?"

Xavier crouched next to Cael. "You know as well as I do that I have no desire to set foot on Tir Nan Og. My only concern is for Earth's safety. If Stater releases the Decies, humankind will suffer just as greatly as the Tuatha have."

Cael gave a painful scoff. He wasn't buying it. There was something Xavier was omitting. It wasn't like a Druid to care all that much for Tir Nan Og. And as much as the Druids liked the humans, when push came to shove, Cael knew the Druids would never allow the humans to control them.

"When did caution become your middle name?" asked Xavier, echoing Cael's own apprehension. Xavier held out his hand to help Cael up as a peace offering.

Cael cringed. The Tuatha Dé Danann he was to the core rebelled against help. But the man he had become in the last thousand years knew if Xavier could fell him to his knees then so could Stater if what the Druid Priest said was true. As much as it went against his nature he had no choice but to accept Xavier's words as truth. Still though, that was all he was going to take at face value.

Cael brushed away Xavier's hand and forced his sore body to stand. Before he could make a move, the priest placed a hand over his heart. The contact stilled him. He felt the ancient magick invade his body as the Druid who had once been his friend and teacher healed him, channeling the Earth's infinite healing powers to his damned heart. Cael closed his eyes, almost wishing Xavier hadn't done that last bit of kindness. It had been easier hating him. Now he didn't know what to think.

"Stater is going to need a virgin sacrifice before the next new moon to keep his immortal powers. Let's make sure he doesn't succeed," said Xavier.

Then Cael felt the ground rematerialize under his feet. They were back outside the cave. His eyes narrowed when he caught sight of Tara. Her face looked slightly flushed and anxious as her eyes scanned him.

"Is she going through the Sh'lam'alah?" asked Xavier.

Cael gave the Druid Priest a hard-penetrating look. "Does everyone know about the Sh'lam'alah?"

Xavier gave a soft chuckle. "Lucky for you, only Druids. I must say I find the notion highly stimulating."

"That it is," replied Cael, a wide grin spreading across his face. He turned and looked at the priest almost daring him to say anything.

"When was the last time—?"

Cael sauntered past him. "It doesn't concern you."

"You will need to draw her blood and she will need to see Queen Mir," said Xavier. "Cael, we don't have much time."

Cael stopped. "You can help keep Tara safe but that's it. Stay out of her life. She's not seeing Queen Mir and that's final." Cael resumed his pace before Xavier could say another word. He walked straight to Tara, grabbed her body to his before she knew what he intended, and kissed those lips of hers that were driving him nuts before she could utter a single protest. *So, what if she hates me. She doesn't hate my body. And that's just what I want at the moment.*

Tara flushed with embarrassment but couldn't stop the groan that escaped her lying lips. She fought hard to pull back from his warm, crushingly loving embrace. *This isn't me. I shouldn't be doing this. I can't believe I'm even letting him touch me.* But touch her he was. His hands had traveled up and under her unzipped jacket to caress her back in long tender strokes that caused her toes to curl with shaky need.

She took a step back. She needed space and time to get her bearings and her life back in order, something she thirsted for.

"Where did you go?" She hated the breathy tone in her voice.

"That doesn't concern you." He yanked on her arm and forced her to follow him back into the privacy of the makeshift bedroom, which meant walking straight past all of Katie's brothers.

"Get out," said Cael to his brother, Balor, who was lounging with his arms crossed behind his head.

"No way am I going out there. They want to beat the crap out of me. And unlike you Cael, I'm not sure I'll be resurrected."

Balor made no attempt whatsoever to get out of the bed. Tara felt her heart rate increase. Why did he have to take me into the bedroom? She fought hard not to moan again as she eyed Cael's hard-chiseled body. She closed her eyes against the erotic images of what they had already done. If she got any hotter she'd swoon and then she'd hate herself even more.

"Do your business. But I'm staying," said Balor.

"You either get out or I'll kick your ass all the way out." Cael moved to Balor's side and stared down at his brother.

"Fuck you, Cael. I'm not moving."

"That's okay, he can stay." Tara didn't like the tense expression on Cael's face. "Because I'm not staying," she said, turning to part the makeshift curtains. Cael placed a hand on her neck and she froze. His thumb parted her long strands and stroked her soft skin. Tara's eyes closed in ecstasy. It was intimate, a private act that did more to frazzle her than if he had kissed her, claiming her all over again. The heat of his touch went straight to her already wet core, and a spasm of need ricocheted through her system. She savored the feel of his fingertips as they lured her desire to the surface, breaking her barriers with light, wispy caresses, erasing any thoughts that said this was wrong.

Cael flanked his body up tight to her bottom, crushing her with his need. The bulge of his erection rubbed intimately against her. She couldn't stifle the groan of heady lust that swamped every rational part of her body. Like it had a mind of its own, her body swayed closer to his.

"Get out now, Balor. I mean it." The words Cael uttered were a harsh growl filled with power that had the hairs on her body standing on end with crazed desire.

"Fine. Just bloody well fine. You owe me big time, bro," said Balor, slowly making his way past them. "You know I could just sit here and watch. Remember when—"

Tara felt Cael stiffen.

"Get. Out!"

Balor's eyes narrowed coldly but he did as instructed.

Then common sense fled. Cael's hands moved around to cup her breasts and immediately her nipples pebbled to hard points, begging for his lips.

He repositioned her long hair off her shoulders so he could nip love kisses from her sensitive ears down along the back of her neck. "We need to talk.

"Sounds good," she said, not really meaning it. What was starting to sound better to her brain, which had turned off the no-nonsense Tara, was having his heat, his weight hold her down while she gave into the lust pouring through her system.

"You do understand Tara that I can't let Queen Mir discover you," he said. There was wariness and sadness behind his words.

Cael moved her around in his arms so that they now stood facing each other. Tara wasn't sure what was worse...the feel of his rock-hard body tight against hers or those silver-grey eyes of his that could discern every emotion on her face. A face she knew was already pink with embarrassment over what was happening to her body.

"Not really," she mumbled.

He slowly removed her jacket off her shoulders and drew her shirt over her head, leaving her standing in her bra and jeans. Why am I not protesting his actions?

In one swift move he unclasped her black lacy bra and she was left bare-chested. The cool breeze in the cave caused her to shiver. Then Cael's hands were on her engorged breasts and heat rushed through her body. Her womb clenched in eager anticipation.

She quirked an eyebrow at him and looked down at the bra that lay at her feet. "Nice trick." She certainly wasn't cold any longer.

"I aim to please." His voice was husky with its own passion and that pleased her immensely.

"Then please take me to see Queen Mir." Tara took a step closer to him, and moved into his space with purpose. "By the way, you are wearing too many layers."

He chuckled softly and then quickly took off the layers of clothing he wore and within seconds was totally in the buff.

"You like?" he asked, gripping his cock in his own hand.

Tara grinned. She'd gotten used to Cael trying to be crude to shock her. It did the exact opposite. She didn't say anything. Instead, Tara wet her lips, wanting her own hand to be wrapped around his satiny smooth rod.

"I can't believe I'm actually doing this." She reached out to feel his rock-hard erection, loving the soft growl of approval that vibrated through his body. He fisted his hands for control, which heightened her feeling of power. For now, she'd take that. Usually with Cael, Tara felt totally out of control, but at this exact moment she was the one evoking magick with her hands. She savored the trust he was giving her. Taking the time to adjust to what he liked, she stroked him. Then she pumped him, giving into the need to make him burn. His passion leaked from the slit at the top of his shaft and she longed to taste his essence.

At that exact moment, Cael grasped her hair, forcing her head up to look at him. There was hardly any silver left in his pupils, which were now filled with black desire. She thrummed with the knowledge she was the one breaking down this powerful creature simply with her touch.

"There are more than a dozen people right behind that sheet," he said.

Tara's eyes darted to the makeshift drape that had been hung to give them privacy on her wedding night. A night she didn't remember. As if he read her mind he hauled her up off her knees, knitting her body to his. He fingered the top of her jeans. "You do remember the last time we did this?"

Tara nodded. Remember, Hell yes.

"Then I guess we'll have to try to be quiet my wee feyling," he said, a sexy look highlighted his features. "After all, you are my wife now."

She squirmed with that knowledge, too terrified she liked it more than she should. The mushy endearment warmed her more than she thought possible.

"Now look who's wearing too many layers," he taunted, his hand undoing the button on her jeans.

Tara stepped back, closed her eyes and slid off her pants. She felt him take a step toward her and before she could remove her panties, he was crouched between her legs. The intimate action paralyzed her.

"Open your legs for me, Tara."

Tara looked down. Wrong move. Black-rimmed eyes stared at her with intense heat and passion. Cael's coppery body was the perfect combination of strength and supple muscle. His platinum hair was tied back and his chiseled Celtic face was the stuff of legends. He nudged her legs open and then before she could protest she felt him tongue her wet folds through her cotton panties.

She gripped his shoulders for support and bit her tongue to stop from moaning in delight. Then his hands moved to the top of her panties and he expertly slid them down her legs. She stepped out of them.

Now they were both completely in the buff.

"I thought I'd even the playing field." He grinned, giving her one last long look before he reclaimed her core.

Then he worked her in earnest. Tara knew without a doubt Cael thoroughly enjoyed pleasuring women. His tongue snaked into her slick folds, laving her with long, thorough strokes that had her clutching his shoulders and holding the whimpers of desire at bay. Instinctively, she parted her legs more to grant him easier access. His hum of approval warmed her while her cells vibrated with lustful energy. Once she was worked to a feverish pitch, he backed away. The coolness of the cave washed over her swollen clit.

Without talking, he moved her to the makeshift mattress.

"One of these days very soon, you and I are going to do this in a real bed, in a real room and without a blasted audience," whispered Cael, lowering his body to hers.

She gave a small chuckle and realized Cael, the Damned Fairy, was trying to charm her.

"That would be nice," answered Tara, loving the small kisses he was applying to her stomach.

"I think this is my favorite part of you," he replied.

What? What's his favorite part of me? Tara was sure it couldn't be her stomach, because men usually went for breasts or bottom, or both.

"I love the satiny softness of this…" Cael licked and kissed her stomach and then his tongue darted into her bellybutton, causing her to giggle and squirm. "And this right here," he said, licking his way up the side of her belly past her ribs. This time she squealed gaily, the sound loud to her own ears.

"Don't tell me there's a romantic side to the Damned Fairy. Hey, you're doing that on purpose to make me scream," said Tara, attempting to stifle another round of giggles.

Cael mumbled Tuatha words of endearment as he continued to tease her. The silly nonsense of his words flattered the womanly part of her that yearned to feel sexy and beautiful. The realization he said them for her ears only because she understood the language warmed her from the inside out.

Clutching his silky platinum hair, she stroked him, giving into the need to feel him. Then without thought she returned a few Tuatha words of her own. He growled and grinned at her knowingly.

"Say that again, feyling and I won't be responsible for my actions," he said.

Tara did just that, informing him with the lilt of the words and the caress from her hand, exactly what she hoped he would do to her body. Cael grasped her bottom, anchoring her to him, causing Tara to squeal with glee.

"Everything okay in there?" Alec's voice floated through the makeshift curtain. Tara stilled. Oh my god, I forgot about them...all of them. She pushed at Cael in an attempt to get him off her. It was no use.

"Alec, you step even a fraction closer and I swear by everything you believe you will not see the light of day," said Cael, who once again was buttering her body with small nips, licks and kisses.

Tara heard Alec chuckle.

"Bloody Highlanders," snarled Cael. "Now where was I? Ahh, that's right, I was planning to kiss these."

These were her already heaving breasts which didn't utter one protest when his lips fastened on first one pebbled tip and then the other. Tara arched her back off the bed as pleasure spiraled through her body.

"You taste like honeysuckle dipped in honey," said Cael.

Who knew the Damned Fairy was really a poet? "Cael, please stop talking," said Tara, softly inching her own hands down his long sculptured back so that she could cup his ass. She needed action, not talk.

He chuckled softly, drawing the tip of her breast deep into the recesses of his mouth. She felt the pull all the way to her womb.

"Ever the impatient feyling," he said, settling his body over hers in one quick movement that caused her breath to hitch in sweet anticipation.

Her legs opened wider so that his weight could settle more evenly on her. On his elbows, he stared down at her.

"I won't let anything happen to you, Tara." His voice was thick with emotion. There was something he wasn't saying that stole into Tara's subconscious. Something in the past that had hurt him deeply and he didn't want to repeat it.

She smiled reassuringly at him. "Don't lie to me. Now before my body quite literally combusts please do it."

Cael settled lower onto her, the tip of his engorged cock teasing her entrance. Tara moaned deep in her throat, her body wanting and needing to have the feel of him deep inside of her.

"Do it? Yeah that's got a nice ring to it."

In one swift, masculine movement Cael's cock went deep within her wet core. She cried out in pleasure at the exquisite tightness and invasion of his large member as it moved back and forth within her slick folds. Who would have thought her body would crave this but it did, with a vengeance that rocked her beliefs of all she thought real.

She closed her eyes as the weight of him comforted her body. Then the tempo picked up. His hands grasped her bottom, lifting her hips higher. Her head thrashed from side to side as the pleasure, the pinnacle of that bliss burned within her cells.

"That's it my wee feyling, let it happen."

Cael shortened his strokes as the ritual of their actions pitched to a feverish pace.

In and out he pounded as she met and matched him, wanting even more. Before she knew what her body was doing her legs had climbed around his hips, hugging him even closer as her opening expanded to accommodate his girth. She couldn't stifle her groan of ecstasy. She climaxed so hard she ground her teeth into his shoulder as millions of aftershocks soared through her body and mind. With one powerful thrust that she was sure nudged her womb, she felt Cael's hot seed claim her. He groaned loudly into her hair. For one moment she thought he had cursed, but wasn't sure. Through it all he managed to keep most of his heavy weight off her. The tenderness of his actions caused her heart to flip-flop.

"Now that, feyling is doing it like it should be done. I trust you are feeling more like yourself."

Tara knew what he was referring to. Whatever she was going through, her mind, her rational brain, had no control over. It was like the hungers of her body, her sex had to be met. It could rain fire from the heavens but she would not notice. All her body craved was sex. What was worse was the painful knowledge that her body didn't want just anyone. It wanted Cael. It was like he had become her drug of choice, her fix, her salvation. That scary thought sobered her faster than the loss of the feel of his warm weight on hers.

Tara scurried to gather her clothes and shimmied into them. Cael was doing the same, only slightly slower. Once they were both clothed they looked at each other. Tara had no idea how long they had been in the makeshift bedroom, but something had happened between them. It wasn't just the lovemaking. The wary look on Cael's face made her nervous.

"Tell me where the Stone of Fal is, Tara."

That was the last thing she had expected Cael to ask of her. She felt her face heat in anger. *He used me. He thought having sex with me would make me forget his real intentions.* She huffed angrily.

"Why do you want that blasted stone so much?" asked Tara, not really expecting him to answer.

Cael's answer caused her heart to plummet like a rock to her feet.

"Because I want to die for good."

Chapter Thirteen

STATER SNARLED. HE didn't like being denied. And denied he had been—twice since he had set foot on this godforsaken rock. He stared out the large window watching the thrashing sea below, his mood equally as tempestuous. The Stone of Fal should have been in his grasp by now. He knew why it wasn't—because of Cael, the Damned Fairy, as he'd been nicknamed by men who'd dared to toy with the infamous hothead.

That Damned Fairy is sticking his nose in my business and for that I will kill him. It really was a shame that Queen Mir had damned him and not simply made him a mortal so he could die a painful death. Letting Cael simply die wasn't enough for Mir. She liked to play with her kill...trick them into believing she'd left them alone when in fact her eyes had never vacated them. He relished being the one mortal who had escaped her. Better yet, he was her enemy when she didn't even know it. *You are not always smart Mir. Sometimes it is best to simply kill your prey instead of letting it be your downfall.* Stater relished seeing the look on Mir's face when he took over her realm with the creatures she created. *I will be your demise. Me, Stater, the King of Mayaldoom and soon king of mankind.*

There were many times over the centuries when Stater had wondered why Mir hadn't made Cael completely mortal. To think that the Queen of Tir Nan Og had a soft spot for Cael would be unreasonable. Stater highly doubted there was even a blip of anything remotely mushy nestled within Mir's frozen heart. No, she was a queen brutally triumphant with her power, and the keen knowledge of how best to wreak havoc wherever she thought fit.

Stater was a prime example of what her power could do. Queen Mir had come to him in a hauntingly erotic dream, bathing him in light and sweaty sex and all she had asked was he sacrifice his slaves and family. From that moment forth he had become ensnared within her hard-crusted web of lies, deceit, power and sex. The combination had only become more intoxicating over the years as his awe of the queen served to pique her interest.

During those years, Stater had learned secrets she thought beneath him. Dark family deceits, murder and political plotting that would have made any monarch proud. She shared these stories with him because in her eyes he was beneath her. In fact, Mir relished the sordid aspects of how she'd come to power. To emphasize to him that there was no one as cruel, or power-starved than her, the Queen of Tir Nan Og, she confided her dark secrets to him. She never once thought he'd use that trust to his advantage when she tired of him. And that day had come like the previous dream, dark and foreboding that told Stater his time in Tir Nan Og was limited. It was then he plotted his overthrow and thought how best to use the Druids to get what he wanted.

A hard knocking from the treasure chest he had stolen from Queen Mir's realm drew his eyes. He knew who was knocking, begging for release and he had no intention of letting the King of the Decies out. Not just yet. Once Stater's power was at its height and with the Stone of Fal in his hand, well, then he'd let King Belatucadros out. Or if he was lucky he'd find another Tuatha Dé Danann and this time one with real powers. He had tried Cael's blood but like the Damned Fairy himself it was useless.

A cruel grin twisted his face as he recalled how he stole the chest beneath the queen's nose. Stater had timed his theft with great care and craft. He'd waited patiently for years until the full moon was right and then he'd used the blood of an innocent Tuatha to open the veil to Earth. There he had slipped unseen back into the mortal realm and had immediately sought out the Druids he'd learned of from Mir. From there it was easy to gain their trust, especially since he'd also taken a few simple Tuatha relics with him, which he had gladly handed over to the Druids in exchange for knowledge.

Those priests had no idea what type of man he was or had become. By the time he had mastered enough druid lessons, Stater realized his quest for immortality lay in siphoning off the magick from those very priests who had trained him. Their death helped to create his immortality, but like with all druid magick a balance had to be maintained. At each new moon, Stater had to sacrifice a virgin or risk having his life-force sucked out by Earth's balancing forces.

Stater knew letting the King of the Decies out now was like signing his own death certificate. Soon, very soon, Stater would be king of humankind. First though, he had to play his cards right. He had waited too long to become impatient now.

"Your brandy, Sir" said Castor, his trusted servant for the past two decades.

Stater eyed the brandy and the small, jewel-encrusted goblet. Trust Castor to find me a sparkling pebble in amongst this rot. Without acknowledging his servant, he took the goblet and downed the drink in one gulp.

"Lunch awaits you, Sir." Castor bowed his head slightly as he motioned to the adjoining room.

"Lunch is something I don't need. I need a goddamn virgin by tonight and that fucking Stone of Fal." Stater threw the goblet into the roaring fire in the large stone hearth, no longer willing to play the nice master.

He noted a small tremor fly through Castor.

"Sir, if I may be so bold, this is a lunch you will thoroughly enjoy." Castor once again bowed his head and kept his eyes downcast even though he had dared incur Stater's wrath.

The chest knocked again, this time actually moving on the table. Castor took a step back.

"Sir?"

"Ignore it," said Stater. "I will deal with him and you later." Stater narrowed his eyes and grinned as he strode past Castor, noting the fine sheen on his skin.

Stater walked into the adjoining dining room and was reminded once again how Castor had taken the time to find accommodations to his liking. Still though, a little punishment was always good to wield, especially since I am his master and he is my servant. An image of the many whips and paddles already laid out in the master suite stirred Stater's cock.

Stater had been a king and opulence was ingrained in his royal blood. Then everything had changed. His kingdom had been taken away from him when he'd gone with Mir to Tir Nan Og. Soon though, all that will change. Very soon I will force Queen Mir's hand and get back what that bitch stole from me. Revenge is going to be a sweet, brutal reward.

Their accommodation was a place called the Keltic Mystic Lodge that rested on the bluff of a cliff. While not as magnificent as he was used to, Stater thought the place would do nicely for the time being. After all, he had no intention of staying on the godforsaken rock another minute longer than necessary. Castor had booked the entire place and kept enough staff to see to his needs. His other special needs, Stater knew Castor would help him secure.

"Sir, I'm not sure why I'm here. I don't see a piano." The nervous, lilting voice belonged to a young woman, no more than eighteen. She had mousy-brown hair tied back into a tight ponytail and was no taller than five feet.

Stater watched as she hugged her small winter jacket for warmth. Castor moved into the room. With a servant's grace, Castor held out his hands, forcing the woman to give up her coat.

"Sir, I told Lady MacFarlane how much you enjoy listening to the piano. She kindly offered to play for you."

The young woman giggled nervously with Castor's use of the word, "Lady".

Stater nodded, not trusting his voice at the moment. The girl was a virgin. He could smell her innocence and it tightened his groin further with lust. However, more than that her blood sang to him, beckoning him forward with urgent need.

"I took the liberty of serving lunch, Lady MacFarlane. Please have a seat." Castor ushered the tittering woman into a high-backed formal Queen Elizabeth chair. "After lunch I will show you to the drawing room where you will perform for my master."

A small smile highlighted her soft features. Her brown eyes, now as big as saucers, surveyed her surroundings.

Castor pulled out Stater's chair. "Thank you Castor, once again you have outdone yourself. You may leave us. I do believe I would like to get to know Lady MacFarlane a bit better."

The poor woman had no idea how much better he would be acquainted with her by the end of the day.

"My name's Sherry," she said, taking a small sip of water.

"Of course, it is," replied Stater, cutting his veal with deadly precision. Sherry, Brandy, what did it matter? Virgin blood all tasted the same to him. It was the best aphrodisiac his body could ever ask for.

CAEL'S WORDS SHOCKED Tara when they shouldn't have. Deep down she had feared something like that. Why else would Cael be so determined to find the stone and why do I care so much? Questions she had no easy answer for.

When did I get so out of control that I couldn't think for myself? And what about my father? What must he think?

If Tara could she would have placed her face in her hands and wept, but there was a stronger part of her that was steaming mad with the events that had unfolded. The loss of control she had thoroughly enjoyed in her life was not something she was going to accept so easily. Even if she couldn't get a handle on the strange sexual itch she experienced whenever Cael came near, she vowed to re-organize the rest of her life back into its nice, ordinary routine.

She was angry Marty had been killed all because Xavier had started that blasted rumor, bringing both Cael and a madman to her neck of the woods. She was fuming that her body craved Cael, leaving her vulnerable. And she was hurt and angry with her grandmother for not trusting Tara enough to tell her all about this—the Tuatha Dé Danann, her birthright and Tir Nan Og. Plus, Tara felt as if her grandmother had abandoned her, here, alone on Earth, while her essence was now back on Tir Nan Og.

"Here you go, Tara-girl. A nice cup of hot tea, just the way you like it." MacCallah handed a hot mug to Tara without hesitation.

While fingering the gold wedding band in her pant pocket that Cael had plunked in her hand, Tara took the time to look at Katie's mother. The MacCallah she'd known seemed small in comparison to this woman who was clearly the matriarchal ruler of this Highlander Druid clan. It still amazed her to realize that Katie and her brothers were all Druids, descendants from an ancient and powerful line of Druid Warriors. She'd learned that bit of information from Cael, who hadn't hesitated to let her know what he thought of the race.

"Ahh, now Tara, deep in thought are you?" said MacCallah, her brown eyes looked motherly to Tara.

"It will be okay, Tara-girl. We're going to take care of you so don't you worry about that." She reached out and patted Tara's thigh in a kind and reassuring gesture.

"Please stop calling me that," pleaded Tara. She blew over the top of the steaming hot mug.

MacCallah moved closer on the homemade bench. "That's right, you're a woman now, Tara," she said, taking a sip of her own tea, while her eyes stared intently at Tara.

Tara nodded, wondering what motherly advice MacCallah was going to dish her way.

"And as a woman you must know that you aren't helpless."

Tara harrumphed. "Are you kidding? My life isn't my own. I've been thrown into this mess only to discover that the people I thought I knew I never really did. And that man over there, that...that Damned Fairy, isn't making things any better." Tara knew her anger was once again getting the better of her. She blew on her mug trying to distract her thoughts.

"Is that so? What married woman's life is her own, I ask you? Now, saying that, a woman makes her own life, if you get my meaning."

"No," replied Tara, burning her lip on the hot liquid. She was grateful MacCallah had made her favorite brew, Earl Grey.

"You're a woman now Tara, so act like one. Take charge of the situation. State your demands and follow through. I know you don't have much control over whatever it is that takes over your body, but while you don't have that itch follow through on your plans. That there Damned Fairy, as much as I don't care one whit about him, he will protect you. I see it in the way he watches you."

"Yeah, he watches me like a cat watches a mouse before he pounces and eats it," said Tara.

MacCallah laughed. All the men turned in their direction. Tara forced herself to ignore them as she continued to sip her hot tea.

"I would call that something," said MacCallah.

"Like what?"

"Tara, that's your power. The man wants you even when you don't. Use that. Assert yourself. One other thing. Don't judge your grandma so harshly. I'm sure she had her reasons for not telling you who she really was. Rest assured though Tara, she loved you with every ounce of her being. You know it was Rhea who forced Devon to protect you. We all thought she was a bit daft at the time, but Devon promised, never once expecting all of this. Still though, it was almost like she knew you were to be kept safe and protected. Give your grandma that. I believe in my heart of hearts that she was trying to do just that, protect you, Tara. Just like that Damned Fairy is," said MacCallah, finishing her tea in two large gulps.

Tara didn't say anything as she digested MacCallah's advice. She closed her eyes and continued to drink. MacCallah got up off the bench. "So, are you a Druid?" she asked.

"Aye, not a full one though. My mother was taken by a Druid and it would appear that so was I." There was a devilish gleam in her eyes. "I will admit there were times, Tara I fought my destiny, but who couldn't come to love Devon. When the time comes who knows what might befall you."

"L...lo...Love? Yeah, not in this lifetime," sputtered Tara.

"Love isn't a choice, Tara. Love is the most powerful magick I've ever seen and I've seen more druid magick than even Devon thinks I've seen, so trust me on that one. When Cupid's arrow finds its mark, it's pure and true but make no mistake...there's nothing simple about love's magick. But don't keep telling yourself it's not going to happen, because when it does, you're going to have one Hell of a time convincing yourself out of that lie.

With that stern declaration, MacCallah made a hasty exit.

Katie plunked herself down next to Tara, draping her arm over Tara's shoulders just like old times. "So, what's it like?"

The warmth of her friend touched Tara's heart. Katie nudged her. Tara grinned. There was no way she was going to answer Katie's question and her friend knew it. Luckily, Katie was no longer paying her any attention. Balor had walked back into the cave. She watched her friend, who was all but salivating on the spot. Then Katie threw her backpack onto the bench.

"So, what's with you and Balor?" asked Tara.

"Honestly, I don't know. I swear to God he's the same one I've been dreaming about for months now," said Katie, opening her pack to peer inside. "That's great. I can't believe I left my English paper at the house. Now I'll have to hike home and get it. You know how cranky Professor Finn can get."

"Oh my God. I totally forgot." Tara got up quickly from the bench, knocking over her mug in the process.

"That's okay. It's not like you were going to class or anything... hey, wait a sec, you're not seriously considering going, are you?" asked Katie, shoving her stuff back into her backpack to follow Tara out of the cave.

Tara kept walking. She couldn't believe she had forgotten to write her midterm paper. She had two hours before class and planned to use every second of that to accomplish the impossible. She was at least thankful she had made a rough draft of her paper two weeks ago. If I work lightning fast I might be able to pull this off. Yeah, when pigs fly. Then again who knows, maybe pigs do fly in Tir Nan Og. Tara practically ran out of the cave, amazed she could find any humor in her current situation.

"Alec, can you give me a drive home?" asked Tara, spotting Alec walking halfway up the rocky shoreline.

"Is that okay with you?" asked Alec.

Tara didn't even bother turning her head. She knew who the "you" was.

"No, it's not." Cael's voice was gruff with displeasure.

Tara stopped and turned to stare him down. "Look, Cael I don't have time to explain this to you but I'm going home. You can come with me or stay here." With that statement, Tara continued her march along the large stones lining the beach. For a moment she thought Cael would try to stop her and she braced her body for his touch. Instead she heard the unthinkable.

"Fine. I'm coming with you," he said, falling into stride behind her.

Tara's heart did a flip-flop. "Maybe that's not such a great idea, after all," she said, nearing Alec's pick-up truck. The idea of Cael meeting her father caused her to falter.

"Too bad. It's your only option." He brushed past her to open the door to the truck.

Tara almost closed her eyes in frustration. Then she remembered what MacCallah had said about her own prowess. Straightening her spine, she sashayed past him and lightly placed her hand on his arm. "Thank you." She attempted to step daintily into the truck, and instead banged her forehead. She groaned loudly and rubbed the top of her head.

"You okay?" asked Cael.

Hiking her butt onto the cold leather seat, Tara forced herself to scoot closer to Alec in a feeble attempt to avoid touching Cael. "Fine. I'm just bloody well fine!"

So much for that power a woman has over her man. She squinted her eyes when she realized Cael wasn't a man by any means and he had already made it plain as day he wasn't hers. Fine. I will do whatever I need to get through this. The this she was referring to was the way her body automatically screamed with need and lust for Cael every time he came near her.

She swallowed and refocused her thoughts to the paper she had to produce on a two-hour deadline. It would be tough but she was determined not to fail. After all, that English course had cost over six hundred dollars and failing would mean having to retake it next semester, which meant forking out even more money she didn't have. Cael brushed his leg purposely up against her calf. Tara huffed loudly, almost wishing money was the only problem she had to deal with. She stared intently out the window, attempting to ignore his low chuckle that cascaded down her spine and straight to her core, causing her toes to curl with want.

"I so wish I had never stumbled upon you," she said through clenched teeth. "And guess what? My first impression of you was correct. You really are a stinker."

He grinned, narrowed those black-rimmed silver eyes at her and had the actual nerve to tuck a stray curl of her hair around her ear.

"Unfortunately for you my wee feyling, you've grown mightily accustomed to my scent. I know I certainly have of yours. Especially that warm honey¬..."

"Shut up. Just shut up, will you?" Tara's face blossomed fiery red with embarrassment.

"You know, you two are acting more like a married couple by the minute," taunted Alec.

If looks could kill, Tara was sure both she and Cael would have murdered Alec on the spot. He laughed at them. Tara thought he was right. The joke really was on them.

Chapter Fourteen

A HALF HOUR LATER, Cael was going insane. While her father's embrace hadn't been especially welcoming, he was amazed the man had even let him enter the house. His first impression was that the tiny two-story house was homey. Pictures of Tara with her grandmother or friends dotted every wall. Instead of looking out of place, Tara's genuine smile seemed to shine down from the walls. Colorful homemade quilts of all sorts lay sprawled across the worn sofa and chairs, adding to the warmth and comfort of the sparse living room. The kitchen was simple. An old-fashioned wood stove took up most of the space, and a well-worn path on the floor revealed a lot of time and people had huddled around the stove. A pot of hot tea steamed away on top of it and a box with a small amount of kindling lay next to the stove.

Cael sat uncomfortably on the light green rose-flowered sofa, toying with the chipped mug he'd been handed by Jim, Tara's father.

"Think I'll go out back and chop some wood."

Immediately Cael was on his feet. "Let me do that." Anything to get him out of the house, away from the deafening silence and the scent of Tara that was seeping into his skin. He could hear her upstairs and his mind was conjuring erotic images of her in her bedroom. His blasted consciousness and groin had a mind of their own and all he could think about was how he'd like nothing better than to be up close and personal with that wet juicy honeysuckle scent of hers.

"Thanks. Not as young as I used to be. The axe is next to the wood shed."

Cael was out the door before Tara's father said another word. Twenty minutes later he piled the stack of kindling by the back door. Even though the fall weather was crisp, sweat trickled down his back. He took off his leather jacket and draped it over the quickly dwindling wood pile. He turned and looked up. Tara was watching him shyly out of her bedroom window. He waved, watched her cross her arms over her chest and turn to dismiss him. He knew she was peeved he had come along but the truth was he had to keep her safe from Stater.

Cael placed another log on the chopping block. The hairs on his neck prickled uneasily with the rapid flush of druid magick. Something was wrong.

Xavier popped up beside him. It still unnerved Cael that the Druid Priest he had called friend was alive. Should have known better. He always had a way of staying one step ahead of Queen Mir's ire.

"Did you feel that?" asked Xavier.

Cael nodded, leveling the axe with one clean swoop directly into the heart of the log, wishing with all his might it was Xavier's head on the chopping block. The log cracked evenly into two halves.

"He's taken blood from a third virgin. His power is at its height. Tonight, he will come for her."

"Then we had best be prepared," said Cael, sounding more in control than he felt.

Xavier took a step closer. "You can still change the course of this. Draw her blood."

Cael raised his head and eyed him, stopping his approach.

"Queen Mir needs to know Stater is in control of the Decies."

"No one ever controls the Decies as you well know," said Cael.

Cael took a heavy load of chopped wood into his arms and made his way back to the kitchen. Once inside he deposited his load and turned, intending to gather more.

"Who the Hell are you?"

Tara's father stood in the kitchen, staring hard at Xavier. Shit. Cael had hoped the blasted priest would have had enough common sense to stay outside. To make matters worse, Tara came striding into the kitchen after hearing her father's shout.

"I'm Xavier."

"Xavier? As in Professor Xavier?" asked Tara's father, looking completely confused and befuddled. He turned to Tara for support. "Is this man a professor of yours?"

Tara nodded.

"Actually, I'm really a …"

"Okay, that's it. You. Out!" Bluntly Cael pushed Xavier back toward the door.

"What's going on here, Tara?" demanded her father.

Cael watched as Tara gulped uneasily, her eyes silently pleading him for help. Bastard. I will kill you one of these days, Xavier. With one final glance Cael shoved the Druid Priest out the door. He hated leaving Tara to her own defenses but he knew she had enough courage to stand on her own. As tiny as she was she had backbone and honor, two traits he'd not yet encountered in any Tuatha Dé Danann female. That alone gave him pause.

Why don't I draw her blood? Why should I care what happens to her? Let Queen Mir have her.

Shaking off Cael's shove, Xavier stood his ground. "You're thinking of it. You know it's the only way. Just do it. When did you become such a procrastinator?"

The taunt worked enough to give Cael pause. "Shut the fuck up, before I make you!" He moved to within an inch of Xavier. The Druid Priest simply placed his hands on his hips, egging him on.

"Didn't I prove to you that you can't take me on? Cael, if you can't beat me you won't be able to defeat Stater. You won't be able to keep Tara safe. In a blink I could whisk her away from here, from you and I wouldn't leave a trace. He knows she is his only link to the

Stone of Fal. You either get her to tell you where it is, or you draw her blood before midnight. I'm through playing games with you."

Xavier walked away. Cael let the Druid Priest's rant digest and saw the painful truth of his words. The time had come. He had to take action. If not, Tir Nan Og and Earth would be in jeopardy. Could he do it? Could he draw Tara's blood, and let Queen Mir learn of her heritage, her half-Tuatha Dé Danann nature? He shook his head.

What choice do I have? In a flash of insight, he realized he did have one choice. While it might be painful for Tara without a doubt he knew it would force her hand. But could he be that cruel? Yeah, I can.

He grabbed a load of kindling, headed back inside and dumped it into the wood box by the stove. He heard the hushed, muffled voices of Tara and her father in the living room and strode in. Purposefully, he let his powerful presence invade the small space, making them both feel alarmed and uncomfortable.

Raising her head up from the sofa to look at him, Tara asked, "What do you want?"

"You." He turned his penetrating gaze on her, letting her get his meaning. Her cheeks turned crimson and her amber eyes blazed fire in righteous indignation.

"W...wha...what?" she squeaked, her voice wobbling with her effort to stay unaffected by his harsh statement.

Tara's father got up from the sofa. "I think I'll go take a long, long walk."

Before Tara could protest her father's words, Cael grabbed her arm and proceeded to haul her upstairs to her room. Once inside he gently shut the door, allowing her to momentarily flee to the other side. Like the four feet of floor separating us is going to deter me.

He almost laughed at her antics, but knew as painful as it was going to be for him to force her into giving up her secret he didn't want to appear completely uncaring. Well, okay, I can be. This is just a job. If I don't do this two worlds could die. That cold reminder told him he had no choice. Necessity does not have a conscious. Too bad when it came to Tara he wasn't so sure about his feelings. What was simple one moment became knotted and twisted when she was around and that wasn't good.

Cael felt like he was dying for good. Saving Tir Nan Og and Earth meant having to sacrifice Tara's trust in him. But there was no choice. When I'm done she truly will have reason to call me the Damned Fairy and I won't blame her. I truly am dead inside because even though part of me liked the trust she placed in me; it's not going to deter me. I know firsthand, trust is fragile and like human life, short-lived.

He heard her take a deep breath and waited for it.

"You...you...you...you Damned Fairy. Why did you do that? What did I ever do to you? That was the most embarrassing moment of my life. My father knows exactly what you meant by that statement and he probably thinks we're up here having sex. As if." She rolled her eyes to the ceiling to emphasize her point.

Crowding in on her space, Cael said, "We will be." Her pupils dilated in sexual awareness of his intent, and the wild Tuatha Dé Danann part of him that had existed preened in pleasure—her fear and scent sailed straight to his groin.

Cael crudely rubbed the bulging erection in his tight jeans, letting her know his full intention. Her eyes widened more. Her chest fell rapidly in shock at his blunt, crude actions and he noted the wild excitement in her eyes. Sadly, he also read her defiance.

Without speaking, he took off his shirt, tossed it to the floor and took another step toward her. She didn't budge. Smart feyling. Cradling her face in his large hands he kissed her before she could move or protest. Her soft lips parted on their own and he groaned deep in the back of his throat with want and need, loving the part of her that fought him.

She attempted to push him away. He angled her head more, giving her no choice but to surrender to his kiss. When finally he knew she had to take a breath he relinquished his hold on her mouth, letting his hands move freely over her heaving breasts.

"Get off me. I have to finish my paper. I have to go to school."

He liked that she was attempting to once more assert herself. Ignoring her plea, Cael ordered, "Take off your shirt."

"Did you not hear me? Get out! I can't do this."

She was panting in her effort to appear unaffected by his nearness. Cael knew better. She was half-Tuatha. Half a wild feyling and that naked need for sex was a stirring she had to obey.

"Take off your shirt, Tara or I will rip it off you."

"You wouldn't dare!"

He reached out and easily ripped the material in two, leaving her clutching her breasts. Her room was cool, and goose bumps rolled over her skin instantly. Surprised by his actions and angrier than he'd ever seen her, she stuttered aghast with mortification. Cael had a job to do and he wasn't asking for permission. Amber eyes closed to slits and she tilted her chin up in defiance, regally regaining her composure.

"What's come over you?" she asked.

"You aren't to question me again. Take off your pants," he said, gauging her reaction.

"You're a brute, Cael. I will not! Get out!"

She dove for the bed. He grasped her arms and pinned them behind her back in one swift move, forcing her to lie on the bed.

"You either take them off or I will do it my way." There was a part within Cael that recognized he was being more of a beast than he needed to but now was not the time to examine his actions. That would come soon enough.

"What's gotten into you?"

He hadn't answered her earlier question and wasn't about to now. Answering her would be admitting his weakness and just maybe force him to reexamine his options. Time was ticking too fast for him and he knew the luxury of choice was no longer his.

He almost snarled at her, but that wouldn't do. He had to stay in control. "You have thirty seconds before I tie you to the bed and remove them myself."

A slight breeze from her partially opened window chilled the small bedroom even more. The scent of wood smoke and the evergreen forest sailed into the space, reminding him that in the past thousand years Earth had become a home for him.

Finding the Stone of Fal was essential. To do that he had to make her scream with need. Evoke that Tuatha craving for sex so much that desire would run wild through her veins. It would make her hate him even more, but Cael knew it was a sacrifice he had to undertake if he wanted to save both their worlds.

She stilled her movements. "You wouldn't."

She was clearly stunned by his behavior and the swift turn of events. Cael nodded, letting his gaze travel leisurely over her body, lingering on her exposed chest. She shivered slightly; her nipples had peaked to tight brown buds, which caused her to blush more. The bra she wore did nothing to hide her breasts. Instead, they cupped them up to him like an offering. She looked so innocent, yet sexy at the same time. He almost flinched when he realized she didn't believe he really would follow through. "They don't call me the Damned Fairy for nothing, Tara. I'm not asking again."

Holding her down on the bed with one hand he grabbed the rope he had found in the derelict woodshed. Before she knew it her hands were tied to the two bedposts.

Tara thrashed against the ropes, trying in a feeble attempt to get free. Her voice quavered with indignation and lust. "Cael, why are you doing this?"

Cael knew if Tara wanted to she could channel her Tuatha powers to snap the rope, but she wasn't ready to admit to herself her own heritage. *That mistake will cost her but at least it isn't a life or death choice she has to make.*

He lowered his body over hers on the small bed, amazed the wooden frame held both their weights. "Because Tara...as you said before, I take pride in being called the Damned Tuatha Dé Danann." He ripped her bra apart in the middle, exposing her creamy white mounds to his feral gaze. Bracing his lower half over her middle he placed most of his weight on his knees and then without saying a word reached out and tweaked both of her puckered nipples.

Her oomph of surprise was followed with her attempt to buck him off her.

"Keep bucking like that, my feyling and you'll have my cock inside you so fast you won't know what hit you." Crudely Cael rubbed his bulge, again for show.

What I really need to do is get these jeans off before they cut off the circulation to my goddamn cock. However, he didn't want to give Tara any time to think. He needed to push her to the edge and the only way to do that was to make her itch with the need for him so much that her defenses would crumble, allowing him to reach into her mind and extract the necessary information he needed. Cael knew he had to find the Stone of Fal now. Time was running out.

Moving his mouth to her nipples he suckled hard, teasing the tips until they pruned into even tighter buds. He felt her heart accelerate and her breasts swell with passion. Kissing her neck, he applied feather-like nips and slowly caressed her collarbone with his skillful fingers and mouth.

"Why are you really doing this, Cael? This isn't the real you."

She choked on a sob but a wet tear slid undeterred down her cheek. He licked it, tasting her sweet salty essence. It was almost his undoing. Her breathy tone of voice traveled straight to his heart strings, plucking and pulling at them in the trust she had placed in him. Misguided trust. And hearing his name on her lips caused his heart to do a strange flutter. Cael refocused. This is just a job. Nothing more.

"Where is the Stone of Fal, Tara?" He asked the question knowing she wouldn't yield to him yet.

She closed her eyes in annoyance. "So, that's what this is all about. I'm not going to tell you."

She leveled him with a steely, hateful glance, her pupils large and desire-induced. He chuckled a low vibration. "Feyling, when I'm done with you not only will you tell me...you will beg for my cock to slide into your tight sheath and maybe, just maybe, I might appease your need. If I'm so inclined."

"Fuck you, Cael."

"You'd like that, wouldn't you," he said, teasing her for a moment.

She bit her lip in frustration and harrumphed at him in total annoyance. "I won't tell you, ever. Now get off me!"

Cael fingered the top of her jeans and unbuttoned them, exposing her white bikini briefs. Swiftly he moved his body off hers, sliding her pants off her legs. He yanked off her underwear even faster. Naked now to his gaze, he watched her useless attempt to close her legs. She shivered with need, the Tuatha part of her soaring with passion even as a pink hue of embarrassment over her predicament washed over her.

"You bastard. This isn't necessary." She ground the words out through clenched teeth, while lifting her head up defiantly off the pillow. The angry Tuatha part of her roared to life and her hair spiked up with her inherent powers.

That's the wee feyling I know. Cael realized he was proud of her feisty temper. He liked her spunk and courage. Part of him hated himself. Playing the bastard his reputation provided would ensure she hated him for all time, but it was a sacrifice he had to take. If only she'd acknowledge her true powers. Then again there is a part of her that doesn't really believe I am what I am. Spreading her thighs wide he maneuvered his body to rest between her legs. "Tell me where it is, Tara. Now!"

The scent of her arousal caused his shaft to thicken more. "Where is it, Tara?" His finger gently opened her already wet folds.

She held her entire body rigid, not wanting to give into the demands of passion. Another few strokes over her cleft and Cael knew all her reasoning would flee.

A tiny sob tore from her, almost breaking his heart in two.

"I can't believe you would do this to me. I thought I knew you." Her body began to thrash around as it sought its own release from his skillful fingers.

"That's your problem, Tara. You don't know me at all. No one does." Feeling the last wisps of her trust break for good, Cael placed his face intimately between her legs. His tongue gave her a long lick, savoring the honeyed juices that glistened on her folds. Using his shoulders, he nudged her legs further apart and tongued her nub of pleasure until it pebbled as tight as a stone, burning for release.

Her legs snaked up around him, holding his head in place. Her Tuatha passion had taken hold of her reasoning. The minute before she climaxed he used his druid skills and reached out, snatching the precious information he needed. Half her body bucked up off the bed when she came, deliciously hot and wet inside his mouth. He laved her until her body relaxed but he knew she needed more. She needed his cock. That was the only thing that would take the final edge off her passion. It was the one thing he was going to refuse her because time was of the essence and because there was a part of him that realized he wanted more from her. Later he'd examine his feelings.

Without speaking he untied her bonds and walked out the bedroom. He didn't bother shutting the door. For the first time in his life he truly felt like a cold-hearted bastard and a Damned Fairy.

Tara shivered as the rush of ecstasy settled like a cold pit in her stomach. She was mortally ashamed of herself. I can't believe I let him do that to me. Worse, I can't believe he did that to me. Tara wasn't sure who she was angrier with—him or her. She retrieved a new outfit, since most of what she had been wearing was ripped to shreds. She tied her long hair back into a tight ponytail to re-establish some control and order and then marched downstairs. No longer worried about her English term paper she realized instantly what Cael had taken from her. He was going after the Stone of Fal and he would end his life for good. She couldn't let him do that. In the short span of time Tara had come to care for Cael. He might not like that realization but she wasn't about to let him be sacrificed because of his wicked queen.

He was gone from her house. She didn't need to look around. Instinctively she knew he no longer needed her. He had gotten what he needed. No, she corrected herself. He had taken, stolen what he wanted and now she was left feeling like this. The raw need to rub her body up against something almost burned her skin. His wild, untamed scent combined with that cinnamon-cardamom flavor of him lingered in the stillness of the air and she had to gulp in breaths to compose herself.

I can fight this. I will fight this. She grabbed her winter jacket, stepped into her boots and marched to MacLeod's Tavern, vowing to retrieve what he had stolen from her, before it was too late. Thank God I didn't fall in love with him. In her heart, Tara knew that wasn't quite true.

No one knows me.

His words, truthful to the core, brushed at her bruised heart and emotions. She had learned as much as possible from the MacLeods about Cael. Still, knowing he had lived a thousand years of solitude left her feeling sick. How could anyone ever know you, Cael? You learned a long time ago to block off the real you just to keep your sanity.

Can I really blame him? No. But she would not let him get the Stone of Fal without a fight. She couldn't. He had told her his deepest wish. Death. He had confided in her, and as much as she felt betrayed by him, she couldn't let him die.

Chapter Fifteen

BY THE TIME CAEL REACHED the MacLeod Tavern the supper crowd filled the benches and stools. His body still ached with want, his cock was half hard and every time he swallowed he could taste Tara's cream. He fought to banish the image of her lush body climaxing with pleasure as hard as he tried to quash the guilt of leaving her, knowing her body itched for true sexual fulfillment. Life's not fair, she'll get used to it.

He strode in, the door banging loudly behind him.

He cursed in his native tongue. I am a fucking fool. I was bloody well sitting my ass not six feet from the Stone of Fal. Brilliant! He gave Tara that. Hiding the Stone of Fal as part of the tavern's walled backdrop was perfect. No one would ever think of looking for it there nestled amongst the esoteric, colorful mosaic of rocks, paintings, shells and driftwood that were glued to the homey tavern.

In fact, if he hadn't pushed Tara by using the Sh'lam'alah to his advantage then he would still be ignorant. Now, however his goal was within reach. Well, that wasn't quite correct. He still planned on informing Queen Mir about Stater and his plans for the Decies but after that he planned on getting out. Finally, his miserable useless life would be over. No more painful Tuatha Dé Danann resurrections that allowed him to recall in vivid detail the life he had lived in Tir Nan Og. More importantly his death would keep Tara safe. He would make sure of that.

"Bugger, I thought you were supposed to be with Tara," said Alec, as Cael approached the bar.

Cael gave Alec a once over. He had come to somewhat admire this particular Highlander. His constant harping concerning Tara's well-being was commendable, plus Cael recognized the dark aspect within Alec which the Highlander fought. We all have our demons.

"The Stone of Fal is here," stated Cael.

"Shit," mumbled Alec, coming around from behind the bar. "Neil, Scot and Fergus, get your arses over here."

When all four of the Highlander brothers closed in on him Cael sighed. "The Stone of Fal is somewhere on one of your walls."

"You sure about that?" Neil eyed him unbelievingly.

Cael nodded.

"You're full of shit," mumbled Fergus, pushing his way past Alec.

Cael knew the Highlander ached to fight him, but now was not the time.

In a blink, Cael hauled the young Highlander off his feet. There was an audible gasp from the supper crowd. While a part of him could sympathize with Fergus wanting to punch his lights out, he wasn't about to put up with lip from this youngster.

"Put him down, Cael. Now!" Alec's hushed baritone voice was full of steel.

Slowly Cael lowered Fergus back to the bar's wooden floor. Fergus didn't flinch, he simply dusted out the wrinkles in his white, cotton shirt.

"Fuck you," said Fergus, moving off the stool to trudge his way into the kitchen.

Cael leaned casually against the wooden bar. "He doesn't like me much."

"We all don't like you much," replied Alec, watching his younger brother leave. "Are you sure about this, Cael? It seems a strange place to hide such a powerful object."

The slight stir of air in the room warned Cael that Xavier had popped up beside him. He almost echoed the muffled curses from the Highlanders.

"Don't bloody well do that again in this bar!" A dark whisper of anger was reflected in Alec's low voice.

"Careful who you're talking to, boy," said Xavier.

Xavier gave Alec a calculating stare. He knew the Druid Priest sensed the darkness within the Highlander, but minutes were passing that they couldn't spare. Cael however liked how Alec's dark navy-blue eyes reflected a challenge for once aimed at someone other than him. He almost laughed with relief.

Xavier gave one of his sinister smiles to the Highlander who had the grace to take a step back. "Don't get your hackles up, Highlander. No one here is the wiser of how I came to be here."

Play with fire and you'll get burnt. That phrase was probably written by Xavier. "Like I was saying, the Stone of Fal is here. Now we have to find it." Cael ran his hands through his hair in growing annoyance.

"Did you leave Tara alone?" asked Xavier.

The accusation hung heavily in the air. Just then the tavern door opened followed by a gust of cold fall air. Cael's skin prickled uneasily and he knew Xavier and all the Highlander Druids felt the same thing. Evil. It tickled his consciousness, luring him with falsehoods the height of dark druid magick could evoke. It made him reluctantly recall his first painful lesson Xavier had taught him. The consequences of using dark druid magick, of upsetting the inherent balance of the planet, was not something one ever wanted to toy with. Doing so only sucked the essence, the life-force out of you.

Stater sauntered into the tavern with Tara's arm hooked under his. "Lookie, lookie here, what do my eyes see? Why I do believe this is going to be my night."

To anyone else the couple walking in wouldn't seem out of place, but the show wasn't real. Tension filled the small tavern like a small tornado all but bursting to be set free. Cael felt Alec's energy vibrate with that rawness the young Highlander kept hard to leash.

"If you want your Highlander friends to stay alive for another five minutes tell them not to do anything stupid," said Stater, moving within arm's reach of Cael.

Stater's dark blue eyes were dead cold. The former king had made his move. Cael wondered if he knew the power that rested on his arm. He said a silent prayer hoping Stater had yet to discover Tara's Tuatha heritage.

"Let her go," growled Cael. He silently implored each of the Highlanders to do as instructed and not move a muscle, while he took a small step toward Stater.

"I...I...I'm sorry, Cael. I tried to fight him..."

That one stutter, that one choked sob tore straight through Cael. It took every ounce of willpower not to jump Stater and throttle him. The urge to do so beckoned at him.

"Say another word, sweetie and trust me I will ensure you never speak again," said Stater, in his sticky sweet voice. "As for you, Xavier, the position is still open."

Position? What is Stater talking about? Cael had a sinking feeling that once again the Druid Priest was playing him for a fool. With Tara's life at stake that made his stomach clench and dread seeped into his mind. He didn't like being a pawn for anyone.

Calmly Xavier rose from his stool. "The Stone of Fal is here."

The growl that arose from Alec and Cael simmered in its intensity through the tavern.

"You fucking traitor," snarled Alec, who attempted to take a step toward Xavier, who still hadn't moved a muscle.

Cael held out his arm, ensuring Alec couldn't get at Xavier. That was his job. Traitor. Cael was beginning to think that word did not aptly describe Xavier. He went to grab the priest but Xavier easily sidestepped his advance. "You fucking bastard. I can't believe you told him that." Cael's voice was a low whispered thrum of druid magick. He evoked a spell that easily wrapped around Xavier's windpipe. For one moment the Druid Priest's eyes widened and then with the ease of his race he evoked a counter spell that informed Cael he was in for a long, hard fight.

"Like I told you, Cael you should have drawn her blood." Xavier casually moved to stand next to Stater, like that was normal.

Everything was so beyond normal it was scary.

"You can't save her, Cael. Just like you couldn't save Anya and Ashling," said Xavier.

The room quaked with Cael's animalistic growl of outrage. "What do you know about that?"

"If you're implying I had a hand in their deaths, I didn't," replied Xavier, too smoothly for Cael's liking. "But unless you want to let Tara die you will hand over the Stone of Fal to Stater."

The entire time Xavier talked; Cael's eyes were constantly scanning the tavern. He felt the presence of the rest of the Highlanders draw nearer and made brief eye contact with Devon as he cautiously moved from the kitchen to the bar.

"Gentlemen, may I suggest we take this discussion to the back room?" offered Devon.

Cael watched through narrowed eyes as Stater casually stroked Tara's hair. She stood ramrod straight but wisely remained silent. "Ahh, this would be the famous head of the MacLeod Highlander Druid Warrior clan, I believe," said Stater.

Cael didn't like the look on Stater's face.

"Sad to say there aren't any gentlemen here," said Stater.

Before anyone could react Stater fired a volley directly at Devon's chest. Cael didn't have time to move and Xavier simply stood still, his head slightly bowed, as pandemonium and screams filled the tavern.

All the Highlanders rushed to help Devon but Cael knew that was futile. The once proud Highlander warrior was dead, his heart ripped in half by the electric bolt that had been casually tossed his way. Tara sobbed, the sound slicing hard and cold through the chaos to spur him into action, as the rest of the patrons quickly fled the tavern en masse.

Stater moved her body closer to his sensing Cael's intentions. In the chaos that had followed Xavier had moved closer to Cael. The Druid Priest reached out and laid a hand on his arm.

"Get your fucking hand off my arm, you traitor. You know, Xavier, you really need to have that word tattooed on your forehead." Cael growled the words through clenched teeth while he leveled a hard stare at the priest.

"Give him the Stone of Fal, Cael, trust me," he said.

Trust you? About as much as a snake in the garden of Eden. Finally, Cael understood that ridiculous human biblical phrase. He curled his lip, in barely restrained anger and fury over what had happened. "I don't know where the fucking stone is, Xavier. Tara, you tell them where it is."

With tears falling freely down her cheek, Tara choked on another sob. Her entire body was shaking but still she stood straight. Slowly she shook her head.

"Yes, my sweet thing, you will tell me where it is now. As you can see I have a very short fuse." Casually Stater's finger drew a line down Tara's wet cheek.

Cael saw red. "Tara, tell us where it is. It's not worth dying for."

She hiccupped and then tilted her chin up at him. "Is that so, Cael? Then you tell me why you were going to wish for death. You tell me why. Until you promise me you won't wish for your true heart's desire, I won't tell them. I won't tell anyone."

Cael almost crumpled to his knees. He was felled by Tara's words even as Stater fired off a volley directly at him. All this time she had been trying to protect him. The keen knowledge, the brutal fact she actually cared for him rubbed him raw and unleashed something fierce in his heart. She was willing to sacrifice herself to save him. No one...and Cael meant no one, had ever tried to shield him. In his entire existence not one Tuatha, human or druid thought of his betterment, or his feelings. The enormous wealth and gift of her trust, her true feelings stole his very breath from him. The volley Stater fired hit his body with poker hot precision.

The overwhelming well of emotions he was coping with was not something he could explore if he was going to find a way to save them all.

The chaos of the room, the loud heart-wrenching sobs and the mass exit of people from the tavern all seemed to take place in slow motion.

"Look, my sweet thing, I'm going to first fry him, and then every single Highlander in here until you give me what I want. Am I clear?" Stater moved his hand toward Tara's neck, forcing her to watch as Cael stood in silent agony.

With every ounce of dignity, he possessed Cael turned his eyes to Tara.

"Give it to him. Now!"

He saw her fight. He knew exactly how she felt. "Now, Tara. I'm not worth it. Give it to him."

"Do you promise?"

The fact she dared Stater's wrath to ask that infinite question yet again surged through Cael.

"He can't promise you anything, sweet thing. He's going to be dead in five seconds," said Stater, as he chuckled gleefully at the chaos around him.

"Do it, Tara. I won't wish for death. Just give it to him." Cael made sure he growled the words low at her. His jaw was clenched with anger and he knew he looked as mad as he could be.

"Fine. I'll get it," she snapped at him, directing her hurtful words at Cael to ensure he knew she was equally angry with him.

Cael fought not to grin. There before him, standing regally proud and tall even though Stater held her life in his hands was his feyling. She was Tuatha and so much more. She was his warrior-princess, his feyling, who would lay her life on the line for him. Cael knew then he didn't deserve her faith or trust in him, because damned as he was, nothing good could come of them.

"You have ten seconds until I let my powers loose on this place."

She nodded affirmatively. He released her and Cael grabbed a barstool to steady himself.

"Draw her blood," whispered Xavier.

Cael brushed off the priest's help. He didn't want anything to do with him.

"If he gets his hands on the Stone of Fal he will control the Decies. Is that what you want, Cael? One life to save a trillion. You're all out of options."

"Just whose side are you on?" asked Cael. The longing to wrap his hands around Xavier's throat must have shown through because Xavier had the audacity to grin.

"The only side I've ever been on, Cael," said Xavier, tilting his head toward him. "I am Druid. Don't ever forget that. Draw her blood. That's your only chance. That's Earth's and Tir Nan Og's only hope."

Cael gave Xavier a hard, penetrating look. He knew then the Druid Priest's words were correct. He couldn't let Tara hand over the Stone of Fal to Stater. To do so would condemn both worlds. One life to save two worlds. That knowledge haunted his heart.

Do it, said Xavier, using the intimate path the Druid Priest had forged when he had taught Cael how to mind talk. Opening one's mind to another left your own mind vulnerable. The realization Xavier had resorted to such a drastic move forced Cael's hand.

Quickly, he pulled himself together and then in a blur of speed he reached Tara just as her fingers dusted the edge of the stone. Only the tip of it showed but it was enough for him to feel the pull of the

Tuatha Dé Danann relic. The relic was said to be as old as the cosmos. The power it wielded was too immense to fall into enemy hands.

"This is going to be quick," he said, his eyes beseeching her to believe the good in him. For once he wanted that. And that knowledge burned him.

Before Tara could voice a compliant, he drew the sacred jeweled dagger from his boot and sliced both her wrists. She gave a small muffled cry of alarm and then turned her amber eyes to him.

"I trust you," she said. A sad smile creased her face that quite literally tore Cael's heart in two.

Then he cut his own wrists, tying them together as their blood pooled down to the grungy wooden tavern floor. Chanting the ancient Tuatha Dé Danann words he summoned Queen Mir. The pull of Tara's blood would force the queen to intervene. A silent part of Cael wished Mir would come for him but he knew he would never be that lucky.

The full force of the zap fired from Stater sliced deep into Cael's back. Still Cael didn't move. He sheltered Tara's body, while her blood seeped out of her. He kept chanting the words, forcing Queen Mir's hand.

Another volley of fire would have ended things, but Xavier intervened. Surprises never cease with that Druid Priest. Cael swiveled his head to watch as Xavier held off Stater's blows. He saw the priest's strained look and knew he wouldn't last much longer. Cael hoped by all that was sacred Queen Mir would arrive in time.

The flush of life drained from Tara's face. She paled, turning a whitish gray shade. Through the dim hum he heard the Highlanders attempt to reach him. Angry voices of disbelief over what had transpired spewed off their tongues as they all vowed to kill him for hurting Tara. Cael knew this was their one shot. This was their only chance.

When Tara's eyes rolled back in her head and she fell unconscious in his arms, he finally collapsed to his knees. Lovingly, he cradled her body tight to his, their blood forming a sticky red pool around their bodies, staining the floor.

Queen Mir will come. She will. Tara's blood will pull her and force her to intervene. She's just taking her usual bloody time.

QUEEN MIR WAS REACHING her peak. She was almost there thanks to the meticulous attention of two of her male consorts, who had been sexually teasing and toying with her for the past four days. She felt her body building with that lush euphoric feeling and then she felt the call.

A surge of anger rolled through her consciousness, causing the pale silver of her hair to rise on its own. Her lips narrowed in distaste and her eyes burned with cold fury.

"You are dismissed." She forced the breathtakingly beautiful male Tuatha to raise his head, which was resting between her parted thighs. He gave one more sultry lick to her pebbled nub and then without speaking left her.

Queen Mir stood up from the gold settee. Plush red pillows spilled around her. The blood red velvet curtains parted at will. She held out her arms and in a blink a sheer gold-threaded gossamer gown made of the softest material, which was as light as a cloud's touch, was draped around her body by a second male. She accepted without comment his ministrations. She knew the flowing robe made her appear like a Greek goddess. For today, that suited her mood.

"You may wait for me. Hot and hard." She raked a pointy silver polished elegant fingernail down the male's long, erect cock. He swallowed greedily, nodded, and let her look her fill. His hands erotically rubbed his swollen shaft, the only giveaway he too sought pleasure. Yes, he will do nicely.

The door to her Pleasure Palace burst open. Amber eyes narrowed as Dyloulious, one of her personal warriors, strode in. For a moment she admired his physique. Muscular and built like a warrior, he was lean in all the right places. He proudly displayed his chest, the white caped material flowing sensually around him. Dark breeches clad his legs, and a long saber anchored his hips. Mir watched his abdomen muscles flex of their own accord in direct symphony to his leg movements. Then the harsh pull of what had pushed her sexual peak from her shook her resolve.

"Leave, Dyloulious. I don't have time for you," said Queen Mir, haughtily. She had to concentrate on the source of the call.

Dyloulious stiffened, none too pleased to be so easily dismissed by her. For a moment she watched his face contort in fury but quickly he leashed his anger. With a curt nod in her general direction, he turned and marched back out the door, the billow of his cape a reminder she had yet to deal with him. Soon, Mir realized she was going to have to deal with Dyloulious' impudent nature in her own direct way.

Mir desperately wanted to ignore the call that sang to her blood. But she couldn't. It was the one thing as queen she could not do to her race. As old as time, she was bound to aid one of her own. A small, almost unnoticeable frown marred her perfect features for less than a millisecond. She couldn't think who it could be. Rhea was back where she belonged, and the only other Tuatha Dé Danann outside the veil was Cael, but she had stripped his blood of his Tuatha powers so he wouldn't be strong enough to cause her distress.

The mystery of the call slowly enticed her. If there was one thing Queen Mir had come to love during her long life it was a good mystery. Something unique. Something out of the known realm of her controlled existence.

She widened her eyes slightly and then reached out with her senses to let the scent of the blood take her to where she was needed.

Her quiet, breathy sigh and sudden appearance caused every creature to stand still.

"My my, what do we have here?"

Queen Mir let her facial muscles relax into a feral smile. Her eyes took in everything as her mind catalogued and sorted what was of importance. *The nerve. Who dared summon me to this barbaric rock made up of pathetic humans?* She felt the anger mounting within her being and tried hard to conceal it.

"Queen Mir."

Her entire body shivered in utter disbelief. It was Cael, his voice as sultry sweet in its masculinity as ever. The seductive brush of his voice almost touched her alabaster skin. She was momentarily surprised. She had missed him without even knowing it. *But that does not give him the right to call me to this rock.*

A faint female voice spoke. "Mir?"

The soft lilting voice who had spoken her name caused Mir's eyebrows to quirk. She couldn't help but blink in disbelief. "What is it?"

"Tara. She's a halfling, of the blood of Rhea," answered Cael, his voice weak as he rushed the sentence out before his strength faded.

Queen Mir felt her face flush in outrage. *A halfling. A half-breed. The blood of the Tuatha Dé Danann is pure, never to be diluted.*

"She is not to be." Queen Mir's words were cruelly soft but all within the tavern sensed the power she wielded.

"Where exactly am I?" For once Mir felt her skin prickle with unease. Something within this realm and hers wasn't right.

"You are in MacLeod's Tavern, in Cape Breton, Nova Scotia...on Earth." The rough, baritone voice of the tall, broad-shouldered man who spoke, and who at least had the sense to kneel and bow to her appeased her pride.

"And you are?"

"My Queen, I am your humble servant, Alec MacLeod, of the Highlander Druid Warrior clan. Please save her."

"Save her? You mean the halfling. Yes, the call of her blood still runs."

With one wave of her hand, Queen Mir healed the halfling. She didn't want to but the appeal for the quest for answers surprised even herself. *Just how did Rhea conceal this hybrid from me all these years? And why is Cael involved? Not that I care about him.*

The halfling blinked and the movement caught at Queen Mir. It reminded her of herself.

"Cael, he...he...he's dying. Someone do something," pleaded the halfling.

Mir's eyes narrowed dangerously. The halfling had stuttered. She was flawed. An abomination that did not warrant her attention, or life. With one flick of her fingers, Mir knew then she could steal the life of the halfling, but something stopped her.

A tense smile flew across Mir's face. She realized then the spunk and power of the halfling pleased her. She was also slightly awed by the creature's aura. It was brilliant in its purity. A thousand questions streamed through Mir's mind in a nanosecond. Then she gave into the real smile. *So, this is the gift I am to receive. A gift of knowledge. A gift to add spark to my race.*

"You, halfling will come with me."

"No! Save him," demanded the woman again.

"Queen Mir, if I may be so bold," said the Druid Priest Queen Mir had hoped to never lay eyes on again.

"Cease."

With one word the priest fell to his knees and bowed his head at her. *This must be my day of gifts.*

"You, Druid on your knees, bowing your head to acknowledge my power over you...to what do I owe this pleasure? You may speak. Beware, my patience is wearing thin with all this melodrama."

"Cael only summoned you to save you and your world. Stater plans to release the Decies."

Mir knew this Druid Priest. He had been the one who dared to interrupt her when she was presenting her case before the Druid Constellation, informing the all-mighty Druids of the real danger inherent in the human race.

Eve's daughters and Adam's sons were a danger she had sensed from the beginning of her reign, when the idea of the puny humans was a mere rumor. When they actually came to fruition, she had been stunned to discover they were the race blessed with a soul. Their essence would live on for all of eternity. But the blasted humans were ignorant of the gift they had received. And it was that ignorance, that daring to claim they were superior that truly irked Queen Mir.

In the beginning she had attempted to befriend the humans, allowing them to see Tir Nan Og, but then the Druids had interfered. They blocked the inner-eye of sight for humans, making it impossible for the humans to feel the power of her homeland. To this day, Mir felt they had done that on purpose to impose their way within the vast universe.

Typical of men. She shuddered at the thought of the patriarchal, fanatical way of life they used to control the Druid clans that spanned throughout the galaxy.

But this Druid had dared more than most. He had been the one to inform her of Cael's coming treachery. She had at first laughed at him. After all, Cael was her Champion. However, when Cael had approached her later, begging Mir to leave the human race alone, she knew then the priest had spoken the truth. So, Mir did what had to be done. She threw Cael out of Tir Nan Og and cursed him to live as a mortal with his humans on Earth. As an added twist, she ensured he couldn't age and that every time he died he would be painfully resurrected.

Mir was still pleased with her curse. I bet he thought of me daily and not in a kind way. That's right Cael, no one messes with me.

She looked again at the bowed head of the Druid Priest and a tingle of anticipation, sweet in its innocence, teased her spine. His show of subservience to her, Queen of Tir Nan Og, pleased Mir immensely. It was a first for his kind. Stubborn with their knowledge of the power of the universe, the Druids were a true force to be keenly aware of.

Never had she had a Druid on his knees before her. Queen Mir found herself intensely liking his position and the heady power it gave her. She eyed the Druid, noting his muscular broad frame, his unusual sun-kissed browned skin and tawny hair. The longing to touch him seeped into the marrow of her core. Then his words finally penetrated her mind.

A rush of wind spiraled through the tavern. Everyone covered themselves. Posters were ripped off walls, and glasses were thrown into the air only to come crashing madly down around people. Anything that had been loose became a flying projectile.

"Who dares defy me?"

Queen Mir let the full power of her voice cascade and touch everyone within the place.

The vile Decies were a race that wished to control Tir Nan Og. She would not let that happen. She had plotted and connived too hard to get where she was today and she wasn't about to let a mere human take it away from her. She had plans and nothing, especially the Decies, would stand in her way.

"It was Stater. He was here but he vanished a second before you appeared."

Queen Mir watched as the Druid raised his clear blue eyes at her. The color of his eyes warmed a deep part of her she had thought long dead. A heat of sexual awareness rushed through her being. *I want him. I want that Druid Priest.* Queen Mir motioned for him to rise. She was pleased to note he wasn't as tall as her. *That wouldn't do at all. She would never look up to a Druid.*

"Stater is still up to his old tricks. He will quickly learn another lesson in humility." Queen Mir let her words trickle through them all. The wind had settled, her anger dying a quick death but that did not mean all were safe.

"Your Majesty...your queen, I mean, please save him."

Queen Mir let the full force of her stare penetrate the halfling, who dared to speak to her again. "What will you give me in exchange if I save him?"

"What?"

The halfling was clearly surprised by the question and offer. *Too bad Cael didn't take the time to inform her nothing is ever given freely on Tir Nan Og. Then again I may be able to use that to my advantage.*

"Whatever you want," answered the woman.

Without hesitation the halfling stood to her full, small height. Again, Mir felt the thrum of her power. She attempted to take a moment to judge its strength but couldn't. That surprised her.

This creature is highly amusing but she has no idea what I can ask for and take. Before Queen Mir could respond to her demands the Druid spoke.

"I give you myself. Willingly. In exchange, save Cael."

Queen Mir was stunned. She turned her amber eyes to him ensuring he got her full attention. It pleased her to note the small shiver that cascaded through the Druid's body.

"You, Druid, give me yourself. Willingly. To do with you as I please. For as long as I please." She said the words tauntingly slow, allowing him to envision what she longed for.

The Druid moved one step closer to her. "I willingly give you myself for as long as you please. In exchange, restore Cael permanently to his true state and restore Devon MacLeod to his human life."

Queen Mir's mind recited his declaration. *He is smart. I like that also.* He stated his willingness but defined his terms explicitly. The delicious erotic thoughts of what she was going to do with the Druid and have him do to her caused her body to vibrate with a longing she hadn't felt in eons.

"It is done."

Queen Mir let her power reach out and restore the human Devon MacLeod and then she restored Cael to his full Tuatha Dé Danann state. She watched as the halfling retreated a half-step back when Cael stood. She was pleased to hear the awe in the voices of the other Highlanders as they surrounded their father.

I am the Queen of Tir Nan Og and it is best they never forget that.

Queen Mir let Cael take a moment to regain his senses and then she held out her arms for him. He graciously clasped the tips of her fingers and knelt with his head bowed in reverence.

"You honor me, Queen Mir."

The eloquence of his words pleased her. "Cael, it seems you have friends who care deeply about you. Be pleased that I have restored you to your rightful state. I expect you to not displease me again."

The queen watched the silent communication pass between the priest and Cael. *Her warrior did not trust the Druid.* It was a warning she would keep close to her heart.

"I will try my best," responded Cael, letting go of her fingers.

"I have had enough of this. Come halfling." Queen Mir motioned for the young woman to move toward her. She sensed her fear. *Maybe she's smarter than she looks.*

Cael moved closer to the halfling. "Your queen, this is a lot to ask but please indulge me. Let Tara say her farewells and I will bring her to Tir Nan Og."

"Cael, heed my warning. You are not in any position to bargain."

"Someone still needs to find Stater. He has to be stopped," continued Cael. "This is for you, my queen."

Queen Mir let Cael place the Stone of Fal in her hands. She felt the rush of heat from the power of the ancient jewel as it almost burned her hand. She fought hard not to let its power show. The Stone of Fal had been missing from Tir Nan Og and Mir hadn't even realized it.

How could this be? Who dared defy me with this trickery? The cold knowledge that someone was vying for her power seeped into her thoughts like an icicle. Someone within her family, someone she trusted had removed the sacred relic from within her palace.

Fear trickled in earnest for the first time down her backbone. How is this possible? Her mind sorted through the web of deceit she had used to get where she was today. The minute she got home she planned to have a personal talk with her spies to find out what was going on. To be unaware that such a powerful element, which was ingrained within Tir Nan Og had been taken, shook Mir. And for a fraction of a second she wondered if anyone knew the truth of her reign. No, she told herself. That's not possible.

"Fine. Bring her to me as soon as you find Stater. Cael, I would like to have a chat with Stater myself before I let you kill him. Do I make myself clear?"

He bowed his head. "Perfectly."

She motioned him forward. "I see you still have the jeweled dagger I bequeathed you. Hand it to me."

Queen Mir watched as Cael reluctantly handed over his dagger. Dark, crusty blood had dried on the blade. She willed the blemish away and then chanted ancient, powerful words over the dagger she held in the palm of her hand. "Now, my warrior, you have what you need to defeat Stater. Use my tool wisely." She handed the dagger back to Cael, who quickly strapped it back inside his boot.

He gave a curt nod of acceptance but Mir did not miss the pleased look in her warrior's eyes. Ever a fool to please. Then awareness of how he hadn't pleased her when she forced him to infiltrate the Druids reminded Mir she had best watch her back when it came to Cael. His honor served Tir Nan Og and if her deceit was known he would turn on her within a heartbeat.

With a circling motion of her hand Mir opened the veil to Tir Nan Og. "Come Druid, it's time you got used to being on your knees," said Queen Mir, boldly stepping through the veil with Xavier in tow.

Cael still couldn't believe it. Xavier had exchanged his life to save his. Part of him refused to believe it, but even he could not dispute the fact when the priest sauntered through the veil with his queen. The bold wink from Xavier told Cael he knew exactly what the queen intended for him.

"Is everything all right?" asked Devon.

Cael noted the old Highlander looked healthier than ever, and was now standing without any support. His sons were still all protectively flanking him.

"I need to find Stater." He turned and dismissed the Highlanders, taking in Tara's shivering form. Still standing, he knew what she felt. The pull to go to Tir Nan Og. He too felt the seductive, lush call in his blood that bespoke of pleasures beyond the body. Cael draped his arm protectively around her tiny shoulders, bringing her taut body close to his.

"I can't believe it's true. There really is a place called Tir Nan Og. I can't believe it."

Cael let her mumble while forcing her body to walk out of the tavern. He inhaled sharply the sweet scent of the pine trees and crisp fall night air. He could see the beginnings of his breath as the cold seeped into his bones.

As much as the pull of his homeland beckoned him he knew he'd miss Earth. In the last thousand years this rock, these people, had helped shape him more than he'd thought possible. How else could he explain the strange attraction he felt for Tara? A halfling. A hybrid that somehow managed to please Queen Mir. Will wonders never cease.

"Tara, about what I did..."

"I know now why you did it. You were right. You did what you thought was best to save both worlds." Tara cuddled more into his embrace and Cael felt his heart soar with relief.

"Yeah, but had I known Stater would find you." He paused. "Seeing you in his arms when I know how much he enjoys cruelty was almost my undoing."

"Be careful Cael, I just might think you care for me. And we wouldn't want that now, would we?"

The tease of her voice and words caused him to smile. A soft chuckle flew from him, making him feel whole. No, he corrected himself. She, Tara, made him feel whole—alive when for so long he'd been the walking dead. A creature with no home. Mortal on Earth, but not really. Tied to Tir Nan Og with his longing to go home and desperate to die. The emptiness, the rot of darkness that lived inside him had consumed him for so long that Cael felt he'd been given a new lease on life. She shivered and he pulled her even closer, the heat of her body a delicious combustible feeling instantly setting his cock on fire for the feel of her silky honeysuckle skin.

"Cael, please take me home. I need to go home."

Tara's soft voice soared through his mind. He knew how she felt—stunned by the knowledge of what she really was, while equally terrified with the prospect of being forced to leave her comfort zone. Her normal life was truly gone. She knew that and as terrified as she was, she was also equally brave. She would adjust to life in Tir Nan Og. The bigger question was would he?

"I'll take you home, Tara, but then I've got to find Stater. After you say your farewells to your father I will take you back to the cave. You'll be safe there. Now, if you're ready let's visit your father. Since I've been restored, we're going to travel my way." A grin crept over his features.

"What if I don't like your way?" Tara's eyes gleamed with mischief.

"When have you ever not liked my way...and don't you dare say you don't remember because if that's the case I'm likely to lay you down right here, on the doorstep to this godforsaken tavern and stake you against the wall to emphasize my point."

"You're not going to let me forget that, are you?"

This time he gave into the whole chuckle he felt flying through him, renewing him with a zest for life. It pleased him to note her spunk and spark had re-ignited. This was the Tara he knew. This was the Tara he had come to admire and love. The power of that one word tingled all his senses. He didn't want to love her, but he did. And he had no idea what he was going to do with that knowledge because he wasn't free.

Queen Mir had made that clear. Once he brought Tara to Tir Nan Og he'd the Champion again and that meant he wouldn't be able to bind himself to anyone, let alone Tara.

That doesn't mean I can't enjoy her for as long as it takes to bring Stater to his knees. Cael liked that devilish line of thinking. "Feyling, you will never forget me. That's one promise I can guarantee. Now, let's take you home. And just so we're clear on things, I wasn't asking for your permission. It's my way or no way." He pulled her tight to his chest, loving the feel of her curves as they aligned with him.

"Close your eyes," he said.

"Not that again," she muttered. Then she laughed. Her sexy, throaty chuckle was like a warm breeze, fragile in its intensity, as the cold air tried to engulf them.

"You said your queen would kill me and since she didn't, I'm a miracle believer. One day, Cael, I know you're going to ask my permission for something."

Her genuine smile stroked every muscle in his heart. Sadly, the one question he would have liked to ask permission for wasn't his to voice. He was no longer permitted to ask for her heart or her commitment because the moment they returned to Tir Nan Og he'd be forced to serve Mir once again.

"All those stories your grandmother told you and you still don't get it, Tara. I can't be counted on, feyling."

"Those stories are just myths. You...you are real and I do count on you."

Her heart-felt words stirred memories he tried to blacken. No one should trust him because he didn't even trust himself anymore. What had seemed like a simple task had become anything but. In the end, he was still bound to serve Mir and while it wasn't love, it was duty and that was something he wholeheartedly understood. Tara, he didn't understand. How can she have any tender emotions for me especially after what I did to her? If Mir hadn't come we'd both be dead. I'm a killer. A warrior. Trained for it since day one and that's all I'll ever be.

It was only wishful thinking on her part he could be anything but. Cael knew dreaming wasn't something you could live on. After all, for the last thousand years he's been wishing to go back home. Instead, he'd been bound to Earth. Reminding himself of those facts made him breathe easier. This is just a job, nothing more.

The lie to himself ate away at the humanity he had accumulated in the last thousand years.

Chapter Sixteen

XAVIER LET QUEEN MIR'S male consorts disrobe him. Things aren't going exactly as I had expected. He wasn't afraid or embarrassed to be nude, he simply didn't like male hands removing his clothing. It conjured up to many old memories of his life closeted away as a young apprentice. Dark, endless days spent learning the core mysteries of the universe and vast galaxies. He forced himself to endure, as he had in the past, and more importantly not move a muscle. Once naked, he finally had a moment to take in his lush surroundings.

He fought to find the correct words for what his mind savored. *Tir Nan Og truly does defy all words for breathtakingly beautiful. Everything is more, including the scent of the air. And I am the first Druid to set foot in this sacred realm.*

The power of that knowledge spurred him on. As before, when he had conquered the unknown and learned the intricacies of time and spatial dimension, he felt both honored and powerful. *There was power in him being the first Druid allowed into Tir Nan Og. If I ever get back to tell the tale.*

Xavier forced his breathing to a steady rhythm even though his heart was beating as fast as an exploding sun. Everything glowed in warmth and bright colors. The minute his feet had touched the yellow soft-as-velvet grass he felt the hum of power surge through his cells. The very world felt alive with insurmountable, untamed power. *Maybe that's the key to Tir Nan Og. Maybe that's why we Druids could not ever come to this place. But here I am.* He realized then it was only by invitation he'd ended up on Tir Nan Og but for as long as he was there he'd accumulate knowledge of the powerful race.

Xavier looked up. The sky was a strange mixed hue of dark purple streaked with pink. It almost looked like blood dripped from the clouds. It was the one thing that looked oddly out of place. Just then a small whirling bird flew past him. It was a brightly colored hummingbird. Then in the next moment it vanished.

"They are the one creature I allow into my realm from Earth. The power to shield my world from humans holds, but the spell your precious Druid Constellation evoked did not specify other Earth creatures. We call them crat-acha, for the sound their wings make and their beauty," spoke Queen Mir.

Icy anger roared through her words. Xavier knew she was chastising him. Reminding him once again that she, the all-powerful Queen of Tir Nan Og, did not like Druids or the power they could evoke. And she most certainly was not pleased with the invisibility spell the powerful Druid Constellation had evoked on Tir Nan Og to keep the human race safe.

For one heart-wrenching moment, Xavier wondered if she had read his mind. That notion didn't sit well with him. Instinctively he doubled his mind-shields, careful to focus the energy within his body as a small current so Mir would remain oblivious to his intent.

He nodded as he floated next to Queen Mir over the grass toward her Pleasure Palace. He recognized the palace from the stories Cael used to tell. He was glad now he knew what to expect.

Xavier was pleased that his Tuatha friend had his life back. He was also ashamed at himself, for his weakness in believing the Tuatha who had come and declared Cael a traitor. The being had declared that Cael was going to share his knowledge of his druid powers with Queen Mir, so she could destroy the human race for good. When Cael had initially come to the Druids, Xavier had sensed honesty and integrity within his essence. That was why he had petitioned the Druid Constellation to allow him to train the Tuatha in the druid ways. Xavier had naively hoped for common understanding between the two powerful races.

Thinking the being was lying, Xavier had cast into the future, grasping the picture the Tuatha stored within her mind. That picture had terrified him. It showed Queen Mir using druid power to reign over the humans, making them Tuatha slaves. It was a vision he could not ignore.

The only course of action had been to ensure Queen Mir banished Cael before he had a chance to fulfill the prophecy. With the Tuatha's help he had opened a small portal to Tir Nan Og, and begged the queen for an audience. She'd met with him on Earth. Xavier had feed her a lie, informing her Cael was going to petition the Druid Constellation on her behalf to save the humans. He planted the seed and had waited, anxious to hear the outcome. When news traveled to him that Cael had been exiled from Tir Nan Og to Earth as punishment, Xavier had been relieved.

A part of him had feared Queen Mir would kill him on the spot. He should have known better. It was only later once he came to understand he'd been duped, that he heard tell of the curse Mir had leveled at his friend.

Bargaining for his friend's life was unexpected. Xavier figured he owed him that. Plus, it would allow him the chance to find the Tuatha Dé Danann who had tricked him into believing Cael would share his limited druid powers with his Queen. He still smarted with the knowledge he had let the Tuatha use him. Sadly, he was no closer to the why of things. Why would a Tuatha want to exile Cael? None of it made sense.

Beside the brilliant light of Tir Nan Og all of Xavier's senses felt overloaded by the purity of the smell of the place. He smelled flowering fruit trees, perfumed flowers, and the slight breeze carried the hint of a salty sea with a beach nearby. Or maybe I am hallucinating.

"You might be."

Again, Queen Mir's sultry voice brushed like a painter's touch into the canvas of his mind with such ease that a cold sweat broke out on his back. He wasn't used to another being holding power over him. Agreeing willingly to come to Tir Nan Og meant just that.

"You surprise me Xa'alter, or would you prefer I call you Xavier?" Her seductive whispering voice was like red wine going down his throat, slightly tart, sweet and strong in its appeal. Like a good wine he thirsted for her. A part of him feared indulgence would really kill him.

Queen Mir laughed. There was a childish lilt to her soft chuckle that surprised him.

"I prefer Xavier," he said, pointedly.

"Then Xavier, how do you propose to please me?" Queen Mir sashayed across the blue-veined marble floor to settle her body provocatively on a large gold-colored settee. The sheer gown disappeared in a blink, leaving her alabaster body open to his gaze. Perfection stared at him and she knew it. Xavier knew her erotic pose was a friendly reminder of the vast power she wielded in this realm. Her realm.

He walked confidently forward, sat next to her and lightly reached out to trace her red ruby lips. "I thought I might let you in on a few secrets." He let his hand casually amble down to play with her already taut pink-dusted nipple. Her skin was so ivory white in its purity he was surprised to see her body blush prettily.

As powerful as she is, she is still a woman who craves to have her body worshipped. Xavier was careful to shield his mind from Queen Mir because she of all people would not like the comparison. To her, she was much more than that and Xavier would be a fool to ever forget that.

"I like secrets, but only if they are the ones I want to know." She reached out and her pale hand grasped his already semi-hard cock.

He immediately felt her heat penetrate his skin and his cock jumped to full attention. She stroked him while his fingers tweaked her nipple hard, loving the feel of them pebbling to life. He watched her face and was pleased when her amber eyes slightly closed with desire. Her lips parted in a seductive smile.

"I think I shall enjoy your secrets if they are as impressive as your cock."

"I do aim to please, Queen Mir," he replied, moving his hand to her naked mons while she parted her legs, inviting his fingers. This was not a shy virgin. This was Queen Mir, a sexual creature to her core who loved and lived for sex. Knowing that made him grin and his own cock bucked in her hand.

Xavier was excited by her virginal appearance. Mir grasped his hand, guiding it to where she wanted it most. He was only too happy to oblige.

TARA WAS RELIVED CAEL was letting her go home. She needed to see her father. She had to say goodbye. He had a right to know where she was going. It was the least she could do for him. However, the knowledge that she wouldn't be there to watch over him, to help him in his old age gnawed at her. How will he get by?

They materialized on the back doorstep.

"We can't stay long, Tara," said Cael.

"I know. I need to tell him where I'm going. I'm going to make sure Devon and his family take care of him, Cael. I don't want him to worry. For now, though, I need some privacy," said Tara, opening the door to a scene of complete horror.

Her father's head was tipped gruesomely back, his throat had been slashed and a pool of congealed blood seeped from him to trail down the wooden chair, forming a dark reddish-brown circle on the worn wooden floor. The stench of warm blood hit her stomach causing her to gag.

Tara couldn't voice a sound. She closed her eyes, trying to block out the surreal scene. The horror of what she was witnessing was too much for her sanity. Cael's arms grasped her to him. The flow of his power merged into her and then a blinding white light filled the cold kitchen. When next she looked she was back in the cave.

"Cael, my father? Oh my God, my father!" Tara wailed and pounded her fists at him, wanting to punish him for being a part of this...for evoking this evil into her life. He simply accepted her pounding, until there was no fight left in her. She sobbed, grieving with huge hiccups of tears until her eyes had puffed up and her nose felt raw.

"Why? Why? He never hurt anyone. Why?" Tara moaned the words over and over again. Cael's hands lightly caressed her back, in reassuring strokes.

"You! All of this is because of you!" She attempted to step out of his embrace. "Why did you come into my life? I don't want you. Get out! I want nothing to do with you ever again. Everything evil that has happened to me is your fault. Leave me!" She screeched the words at him, needing to vent her emotions that were a tangled mess of sorrow and anger. She felt raw with it and a strange hum of power swam before her. Afraid she was about to faint, when she wasn't the swooning type, Tara dug her nails into her palms to center herself. The pain helped to ground her.

Through the distant fog of her tears and anger she heard Cael calmly telling her what she didn't want to hear. It wasn't him. It was Stater. When in truth all of this was because of Cael, because of the Damned Fairy, because of this man holding her trying to offer comfort. My life as I knew it is over. All my family is gone from this Earth and now I'm left with no choices. All because of him.

"Leave me alone," said Tara, in a small whisper of a voice that he heeded. The warmth of his hands left her feeling cold, and exposed. He took a measured step back from her, and she fought not to sink to the floor in abject misery. "I need to go back. I need to..."

Cael crossed his arms. "No, Tara you're not going back. I brought your father's body here with us. As we speak, MacCallah is cleaning him up and getting his body ready for burial. Take the time you have to be with him and grieve. When I get back we will leave."

Without another word, Cael turned and left her. She shivered with cold, exhaustion and mental fatigue. How could this happen to me? How could this happen to us? And why? Why did Stater kill my father? She backed up until she came into contact with another body.

"Stater killed your father, Tara, to get to you. Cael will take care of him. I heard what happened at the tavern. Sorry I wasn't there."

Numbly, Tara let Balor help her sit on a makeshift bench. She nodded up at him, still too overwhelmed and exhausted to even reply, even though a small part of her wondered where had he been while they were defending their lives against Stater.

"Don't worry. Things always work out for Cael. This time I've ensured things will work out for me, too."

Tara didn't like Balor's sarcastic tone. There was something she was missing. Then MacCallah walked in and cocooned her body in a big motherly embrace that caused her to start crying all over, again.

"You still here, Damned Fairy? I would have thought you'd be gone by now. Funny how Queen Mir didn't whisk you back to your realm when she was here," said MacCallah.

"For your information woman, I'm not the Damned Fairy and Queen Mir no longer needs to whisk me anywhere," said Balor.

Both women watched as the once proud Tuatha Dé Danann walked away from them without another word.

"Something's not right with that one. I smell evil in the air and I don't like it. Those damned fairies, and to my mind, every single one of them is damned, they don't bring nothin' but trouble on the wind. Mark me words we ain't seen the last of that one. And mark me words there's going to be another storm brewing before all this is over," said MacCallah, harrumphing for good measure.

"Here I am rambling, when you simply need to be comforted. Let's go get a cuppa tea. And then we're going to say our goodbyes to your father. None of this makes sense to me, but I must say I was impressed that Cael had at least the good sense to bring you here, and it was mighty nice how he cleaned up your father. That was right civilized and coming from him, I'm surprised."

Tara let MacCallah rattle on, knowing this was her way. She talked to displace the silence. She talked to keep Tara from thinking about what really had transpired. And she talked to ease her pain. All of it helped to a degree, but Tara knew now more than ever there was nothing holding her to this place. Everything she loved had truly died.

Maybe that's exactly what Queen Mir wanted to happen. The thought popped into Tara's mind until it rooted and grew. Then another more fanciful thought struck her.

"Ca...Cael can save him." Tara's voice cracked from her parched throat that was still raw from her overwhelming emotions.

"Ah, now Tara-girl you be knowing that ain't the case." MacCallah handed her a hot cup of Earl Grey tea.

Tara put the mug down on the table. "Yes, he can. Devon was resurrected, so why can't my father be?"

"Well, for one, Cael didn't resurrect Devon. Queen Mir did it. And secondly, that's not our way. Death is a natural progression, Tara."

Easy for you to say, now that Devon's alive. "There was nothing natural about my father's death. Stater killed him. He cut his throat and why? All to get to me. And for what? For that blasted Stone of Fal that I wish my grandmother never gave me. And none of it makes sense. Cael gave the stone to Queen Mir, she got what she wanted and this is Stater's revenge. I'm going after him. I'm going after Cael. He'll listen to me. If he can't bring my father back to life I will make him take me to Queen Mir, where I will ask her."

"Tara, you can't leave the cave. Cael said you're safest here with us," declared MacCallah.

"Safe from what? I don't care, MacCallah. Because of me, my father is dead. I'm leaving."

"Me boys won't let you leave and Tara-girl, I trust Cael on this one. You don't want Stater gettin' a hold of you. There's no telling what evils the likes of him might do to you to exact even more revenge."

Tara knew what MacCallah said was true but she burned to fix things. A fierce need to take back control of her life surged through her mind and body making her feel powerful. While her confidence might not last it did give her a purpose.

"Don't listen to her, Tara. If you want to leave...leave," said Balor.

MacCallah's eyes practically threw daggers at the tall Tuatha Dé Danann. "You're nothin' but trouble with a capital "T." Don't listen to him, Tara."

"How?" she asked, her mind fixed on what she had to do.

"Your half-Tuatha. Use your mind, your powers and simply envision where you want to go and then the next thing you'll know you'll be there," he replied with such conviction she actually believed him.

Tara felt MacCallah move closer to her. "Don't listen to him, Tara. Alec, Keegan thank goodness you're back." MacCallah ushered over two of her sons with a pained look.

Tara knew if she was going to do this now was the time. A few more seconds and reasoning would return, or the Highlanders would in all likelihood place a spell on her to keep her in the cave.

She closed her eyes and envisioned where she wanted to be. She felt her body start to tingle as her mind drifted toward her goal. When next she opened her eyes, she screamed.

This is not where I wanted to be at all.

"You did surprisingly well, Balor."

Stater's snake-like voice crackled evilly in glee and Tara couldn't help but shiver.

"I delivered what you asked and now I want what you promised," demanded Balor.

Tara turned disbelieving eyes toward Cael's brother. "What have you done? Make a bargain with the devil."

Balor moved away from Tara. He crossed his arms over his chest in a pose so very much like Cael that Tara shivered, feeling the need for her damned fairy with a vengeance.

"If the devil will grant me my full powers back then so be it," said Balor.

Stater moved to pick up a small ivory treasure chest. The hairs on Tara prickled uneasily. An icy cold breeze stirred the air around them. It was a foreboding sense of evil and doom that sucked all the hope from within Tara. When Stater brought forth a sharp, brightly jeweled dagger, Tara's body tensed. Before she could blink, he sliced her bare arm. Blood immediately flowed down her arm. He walked back to the small chest and tilted the knife so the blood droplets flowed directly into the treasure chest's seams. Before she could wonder about his intentions, the lid popped open. The roar of the creature that flew forth rattled the windows.

"King Belatucadros, I brought you a special treat," said Stater.

The creature didn't hesitate. His large, grey male body with black spiderweb wings stretched out to their full width. He was spectacular to behold in his evil appearance. Slanted red eyes glowed hungrily. Muscular arms gave way to claw-like hands and his two legs were more insect-like than human. He had no hair that Tara could see but he certainly had lots of teeth. He moved his jaw from side to side, flexing his hawk-like beak which was filled with hundreds of razor-sharp teeth.

"Release my minions now, Stater."

The voice was rusty, the sound shrill in its intensity. It reminded Tara of someone raking their nails down a chalkboard.

"Put that damned vile creature back where it belongs," demanded Balor.

Red eyes narrowed in on Balor and then the creature advanced.

"This is your treat. A discarded Tuatha," said Stater.

"I am not your treat, you loathsome bug," replied Balor, meeting the creature halfway.

"Actually, you are," said Stater.

Balor doesn't stand a chance. Tara watched as the creature sunk its front claws into Balor's neck. His life-force was being sucked out by the monster. Then a blinding white arc of light shattered the room. A reassuring breeze of power immediately cocooned her, and Tara knew Cael had once again saved them. He was going to be mad as Hell at her for having dared to leave. Worse, she was mad at herself. Leaving had once again only complicated matters. If life got any stranger, Tara thought quite literally, she'd go out of her frigging mind.

Chapter Seventeen

"DON'T YOU EVER DO AS you are told?" Cael was so mad he could barely speak. So instead he yelled. It pleased him to see Tara's small frame back up, keenly aware he was holding his temper in check by a tight leash.

He'd been able to use his druid senses to hone in on Stater, only to be doubly surprised to find Tara and his brother there. And the King of the Decies was loose. Things were quickly moving from one disaster to another and he didn't like it. *Why won't anyone listen to me? And what exactly was my brother up to?*

Another second and his brother's life-force would have belonged to the Decies for eternity. Cael told himself he did the only thing he could have. He zapped in and out using the power of the light as his surprise, to whisk Tara and his brother away to the cave.

Now, he didn't know what to do. His brother was drained. The pull of death tore through Balor and Cael wasn't sure he could do stop it.

"Take him to your Queen," said Neil, ever the clever Highlander.

Cael told him to shut up. Thankfully, the Highlander quickly departed the makeshift bedroom. Gingerly, he laid his brother on the mattress. Instead of being pale, his brother's body was flushed pink.

"Kill me."

The harsh voice of his brother broke into his thoughts.

"If you can speak I won't kill you, yet," taunted Cael, hoping to tease his brother into healing. He placed his hands over his brother's heart and willed the healing power to work its magick. Instead he felt the dark black power seep into him.

If the Decies king took too much of his life-force then the poison he used to release his essence will force Balor to convert. Still, Cael attempted to use every trick in the druid and tuatha dé danann books to make things right with his brother.

"Kill me. Now!" screamed Balor, his body rising up from the makeshift bed in pain the likes of which Cael couldn't begin to understand.

The curtains parted and four eyes stared at him. Tara's were still red and puffy from her earlier emotional onslaught while Devon's were clear and to the point.

Devon stepped into the room. "Are you able to save him?"

Cael didn't say anything.

"Then you will need to kill him." Devon laid a sharp ceremonial dagger, which had the ancient druid symbols of protection, honor and mercy on its ivory honed handle. It lay on the upside-down fish barrel that acted as a night stand. It was the standard warrior dagger used by most Druids. "If he converts then we are all in jeopardy. Either you kill him or one of us will."

"Get out!" shouted Cael, evenly, his voice deadly earnest.

Cael felt Tara move cautiously closer. Even through the chaos of the moment he smelled her honeysuckle scent and it calmed him. He didn't like that either.

"Cael, I don't understand. You should be able to heal him. Why can't you?" Tara bent even closer so she could get a good look at his brother who was currently in the same iron-cast chains he had been in when the Highlanders had captured him.

He knew firsthand how much the iron hurt on his brother's wrists and ankles, but he also highly doubted his brother felt that. Plus, Cael wasn't taking any chances. The iron bonds would hold his brother in place ensuring everyone else was safe.

The poison from the King of the Decies was transforming his brother cell by cell into one of them. Really, their warfare was cunningly effective. When they needed more minions, they made them and forced the conversion onto the unsuspecting being. Then that creature truly was one of them. The idea of his brother becoming a Decies disgusted Cael on all levels.

Tara's hand touched his shoulder, breaking into his thoughts. "This is all my fault. I should have listened to MacCallah."

"Yes, you should have," he snapped.

Her hand left his shoulder. In the same instant his brother let loose a blood-curling scream. "Kill me, Cael, for the love of my queen. Kill me!"

"Come here, Tara-girl. This isn't for the likes of you." Devon ushered her out of the makeshift bedroom.

"Can't he put a spell on him, or something," she mumbled, as Devon opened the curtains for her, ushering her out.

"Go see MacCallah. The boys have almost got the grave ready for your father. I'll be there in a minute," replied Devon.

Cael heard Devon approach. "Seriously, Cael, if you can't heal him, we be needin' to kill 'em. As it is we're wasting precious time here when we needs to find Stater and that creature he's released. You know that within a few hours it be a full moon, and if the King of the Decies is still lose all mankind and your cursed kind are doomed."

Cael stood up from the bed. "Cut the lecture, Devon. Save it. I know exactly what I have to do, so shove off."

Devon glared angrily at Cael. "Do you now? So, you be telling me, what it is exactly you're going to do and how me and me boys can help. Is that the way of things?"

Part of Cael liked the fact Devon actually had the nerve to glare at him. Not many mortals would or dared to. Grudgingly, he acknowledged he had come to like the Highlander, and some, but not all of his sons.

"It be simple, Cael. Either you heal 'em or you can't and if you can't, you need to kill 'em. Think of it like puttin' an animal out of its misery," said Devon.

"Fuck off," said Cael. "And get the Hell out of here now, before I fry you." Cael's eyes were deadly earnest as he watched the Highlander finally get the hint and leave.

Cael sat back down next to his brother. He knew Devon spoke the truth but referring to his brother as an animal having to be put out of its misery was painful and wrong. "Fucking humans." Cael racked his mind for a solution.

He grimaced. The only spell powerful enough to stop the advance of the Decies' poison was the death-like one and he'd never performed it before on a human. But he knew first hand that the Druid Priests had. After all, they were the ones who had taught it to him. To be more precise, Xavier had made him learn it.

Before he could ponder anything further, he heard his brother's garbled breath and hiss of pain.

Time is wasting away. Get on with it. Closing his eyes, Cael cleared his mind and fought for the balance of power that hummed through his being. Then he placed both hands firmly over his brother's heart and willed it to slow. He chanted the ancient druid words, forcing the magick of the universe to work for him. Then he felt it.

"Cael, what have you done to me?"

Those were his brother's last words as death covered him in a blanket, blocking all his pain. In that moment, he felt the power of his brother's words, his breath and his will. All of it hovered above his finally-silent body.

Now all Cael had to do was tie his mind, soul and life-force to his brother's body until he figured a way to rid him of the Decies poison. His hands moved in a fast dance above his brother as he used the language of the Druids and Tuatha to force it to do his bidding. Finally, when he was as sure as he could be, he slumped forward, his head resting on his brother's tight, still chest.

Two feather-light hands rested on his shoulders.

"Cael, I am so sorry you had to do this," said Tara.

It took Cael a minute to realize she thought he had killed his brother. Keeping the truth to himself was safer for the moment.

Her arms slid around to his front, her hands warm and inviting on his tired body. She nuzzled her face into his exposed neck. Then he knew it. The Sh'lam'alah was taking hold of her reasoning and more importantly her body, and the timing sucked. Then again, maybe not. His body was already registering desire.

Without any words, he grabbed Tara's wrists, stopping the advancement of her hands. He stood, turned and pulled her body flush to his. His mouth crushed hers, needing to feel her hunger for him. He knew once he took care of her needs she would hate him with renewed passion but he didn't care. He needed her with all his being. And he was going to have her, just not here.

He tore his mouth from hers, pleased to see her eyes still closed and her lips puffy with desire.

"Come." He grabbed her hand and led her out of the cave.

"Just where do you think you two are going?" asked Alec, attempting to block their path.

Cael shouldered his way through the angry-looking Highlanders. "None of your fucking business, boy."

"Then can I assume your brother has been taken care of?" asked Devon.

"Look for yourself," answered Cael.

Hand in hand, he and Tara walked from the cave and down the hill. He would have liked to zap them somewhere but that would be like firing off a flare gun to both Stater and the King of the Decies. *The last thing I need to do is give away the one safe place on this cursed land of rocks, even though my cock is harder than granite and it hurts to walk.* Cael's eyes were glued to Alec's pickup truck.

"Get in," he ordered, pushing Tara's small bottom into the truck.

Alec ran down the hill after them. Cael simply smiled at the Highlander.

"Don't even think of it, Fairy," shouted Alec.

Cael didn't say anything. He'd learned a few handy human tricks over the course of a thousand years and hot-wiring a truck counted as one. He sauntered fully confident into the vehicle and within a minute the engine revved to life.

He waited until Alec was almost within reach and only then did he squeal the tires and take off, leaving the Highlander to eat dust. Slowly, Cael raised his hand and then gave the finger to the Highlander, enjoying every single smug minute of it.

Tara moved her body closer to his. He liked that a lot. Then he noticed she hadn't even bothered with her jacket and that her nipples were straining against her white shirt, already pebbled and peaked. He swallowed, relishing the thought of his mouth suckling on her small buds.

"Cael, where are we going?" she asked, her hand now caressing the inside of his thigh.

"Damned if I know." He hoped to find a secluded spot within two minutes because that's about as long as he figured he could last before pulling the truck over to the side of the road and giving into the urge to ram her senseless. He needed to get some feeling back in his balls, which ached within the tight confines of his blasted jeans.

Ten frustrating minutes later, he pulled over on a deserted dirt road. "Where are we?" he asked Tara.

When she didn't respond, he turned and looked at her. Her face was flushed with desire, her eyes were glazed and her aura shimmered in its intensity. Her long chestnut red-streaked hair fell in disarray to spill in waves half over her shoulder and down her back. She was fully aroused and he hadn't even laid a finger on her.

To heck with finesse. He cut the engine, scooted over and grabbed her tiny frame, thankful that the pickup truck had a comfortable leather seat.

"Take them off," he ordered, referring to her tight jeans.

"You," she replied, edging off her sneakers as she moved away from him to lie provocatively with her head against the window and her legs over his.

Cael didn't need to be told twice. He undid her snap and moved the zipper down. Tara wriggled her butt to help him ease the jeans and her underwear off. Slowly she removed her socks. She was bare from the waist down, looking as lovely as sin. Her nipples were tight and already pebbled, standing out against her tight white shirt. Thanks to the rush of sexual desire fueling her cells, Tara had lost all her inhibitions. Once they were done Cael knew that would be another story.

Cael's cock was on fire. He knew they didn't have time for a long, slow lovemaking which he'd thoroughly enjoy. A man's gotta do what a man's gotta do. Inwardly, he laughed at that human expression. Unzipping his fly, he freed his already pulsing shaft in one slick movement.

Motioning for Tara to sit on his lap, he said, "Come here."

Thankfully, she knew exactly what to do and how to do it. Bless that feyling blood. She tantalizingly crawled over him, parted her legs and hoisted her lush ass up only to slowly plunge her already wet core straight down onto his rock-hard cock.

His hands grasped her hips to help guide her to the rhythm he liked as she kneeled over him. Fast and furious she rode him, intent on seeking her own release. "That's it, ride me, feyling."

Cael's hand moved from her hips to her breasts. He pinched her puckered nipples hard through her shirt. Tara moaned and threw her head back, aching for his touch. He relished her sexual energy. Her aura, vivid in its intensity, flashed colors of yellow and orange around them. Her desire-induced gasps and moans of passion heated the crisp air around them, blanketing them in hot, erotic sex, and fogging up the windows of the truck. The feel of her nails digging deep into his shoulders as she picked up the tempo to ride him, needing and seeking her own release, made him smile. Up and down, side to side she moved with a will of her own and he welcomed it.

Cael shifted his legs slightly further apart, which was hard to do in the tight confines of the truck. Then when he knew she needed it, he stroked her nub, loving the slick feel of her juices.

"Faster, Tara." Her back arched when he tweaked her nub between two fingers. "That's it, Tara, come for me, my loving feyling. Come." His hand moved from her front to knead her bottom. He slammed deep into her. First one stroke and then a second, almost touching her womb. She screamed her release as she came hot and fast, her sex coating her inner thighs to drip down onto Cael's tight balls.

Cael inhaled sharply and then climaxed so hard he swore his eyes rolled back into their sockets. A second later, almost before he caught his breath and his bearings, Tara's small fists were pounding into him and it wasn't a love me tap.

"You beast! I can't believe you did that to me again! After what just happened to my Dad. I can't believe you." She screeched at him and removed herself very unlady-like to get off him.

"You're welcome," replied Cael, sarcastically. He tucked himself back into his jeans and ambled back to the driver's side. Part of Cael almost wanted to chuckle. She was so volatile it would have been amusing if it wasn't so sad.

Tara was a feyling. Her body was going through the Sh'lam'alah of his kind. She fought against her true nature. She hated letting her body control her and yet, by tonight she'd be in Tir Nan Og for good.

He reattached the wires under the steering wheel and started the truck. "Get used to being fucked, Tara. That's what you'll be doing lots of once Queen Mir gets her hands on you for good."

"Fuck you," snapped Tara.

Cael smiled. Gone was the innocent, virgin-mouthed woman he'd met a few days ago and for that he was pleased. One thing he knew first hand, Tara had to develop a thick skin if she was going to survive living for eternity in his homeland.

"Feyling, you just did." Cael gave her a good wink, letting her know exactly what he was talking about.

Her huff told him loud and clear she understood his crude message.

Chapter Eighteen

STATER LIKED BEING in control. He liked to dominate, and relished being worshipped. Above all though, he thoroughly enjoyed having power over others. It gave him a euphoric high. But he wasn't stupid.

"You are at my mercy." He pointedly stared at the King of the Decies.

The King of the Decies turned his head. His glaring red eyes narrowed and flashed to a fiery red-orange glow. Stater felt his skin crawl, awareness settling into his consciousness. Controlling the Decies was not going to be as easy as he had anticipated. King Belatucadros had the audacity to laugh at him. Or at least Stater assumed the cracking cackle was a laugh. Hard to tell with a creature who has a beak for a mouth.

King Belatucadros walked across the red and blue mosaic Turkish carpet, his long spiny arms tucked behind his back. *By the Gods, I hate these things. For one they stink to the heavens and secondly, they are so ugly they hurt my eyes. When they invade Tir Nan Og I'll get what I deserve. That bitch, Queen Mir won't even see it coming.*

"Only until the moon crests completely," said Belatucadros, in his gnarly, gravelly voice that hurt Stater's eardrums.

What world do you live in? There was no way he'd let King Belatucadros totally off-leash, so to speak. That was suicide. "We shall see." Stater noted by the slight twitch in the leathery skin drawn taut across Belatucadros' face he had heard him loud and clear.

Stater sat in the high wingback chair that afforded him room to watch the King of the Decies move back and forth across the carpet. He sipped at the drink his servant brought him, pointedly ignoring the creature leaving claw marks on the wooden floor when he stepped off the carpet. Ahh, yes, sweet virgin blood. Inclining his head in a nod of thanks, Stater relaxed as the flow of blood and the power that came with it filled his senses.

Thanks to Tara's blood, Stater had finally been able to open Mir's treasure chest. Queen Mir's intricate treasure chest was in actuality a prison created to house her conquests, namely King Belatucadros and his minions.

Stater wasn't insane. He knew the perils of releasing the King of the Decies, so before he did that he had struck a bargain with Belatucadros. Using his druid powers, he had been able to speak directly mind-to-mind to Belatucadros. In exchange for freedom, Belatucadros and his minions answered to him for one full day. That was the amount of time Belatucadros had agreed to, even though Stater had attempted to wrestle more time from the crafty king. That however would be enough time to get Queen Mir's attention. Stater relished the prospect of seeing Mir's clear composed complexion tremble with fear. The knowledge she'll be under my power is better than any sex.

Now, all I need is that woman, Tara. With her blood I can open the veil to Tir Nan Og, set Belatucadros free to wreak his havoc and sit back and watch the show. A part of him wished he had saved some of Balor's blood. That certainly would have gotten Mir's attention.

"Where is she?"

Belatucadros' voice broke into Stater's thoughts. The creature's putrid breath smelled like rotting eggs, almost causing Stater to gag. Instead, he calmly forced himself to take another sip of the warm blood his servant had heated for him. For one moment Stater envisioned the life he would soon enjoy for eternity. Opulence at its most extreme.

"Sit. I am trying to cast for her scent."

Before Stater could say anything more, Belatucadros answered.

"I have her scent. She's mine."

A minute later Belatucadros crashed through the wall-length window that overlooked the sea. So much for the front door. As the wind from the sea blew into the living room, Stater calmly sat sipping his warm blood.

"Sir, shouldn't you go after it?" said his servant, removing the now empty goblet.

Stater was pleased to see his hand tremble slightly. After he'd sampled the virgin he'd taken his demonic pleasure out on his servant.

Looking his servant in the eye, Stater said, "No need. Let him do the work. Once he finds her, I will then take control of the situation and get my reward. So will Queen Mir. Finally!" Stater watched as Belatucadros unfurled his long spidery wings to soar through the air. There was something sinisterly beautiful in the grotesque creature when his wings spread out to catch the air currents. Stater laughed at this own thoughts. The only thing beautiful Belatucadros encompassed was death for Queen Mir.

You will never laugh at me again, Mir. I am King and will get what I want in the end...you begging on your knees for my mercy, which sadly I won't feel inclined to give.

Stater felt the dark rush of evil as the ancient powerful king called forth his minions. Of its own volition the chest opened. Bat-like, his followers freed themselves to follow Belatucadros' bidding. For a moment Stater was stunned with how many there were clustered in the chest but then he realized the power behind Mir's spell. While she kept the Decies in a small prison he knew it was anything but. Created with mazes it contained hundreds of rooms, and there were a lot of Decies because Belatucadros used his venom to convert any living creature he wanted.

Lazily, Stater watched as hundreds of Decies filled the afternoon sky. He smiled, pleased with how things were progressing for him and his cause.

Mir, you should never have toyed with me. Your fear that humans would be your downfall is about to come true. Too bad you didn't realize it would be me. Stater felt his cock harden. Taking Mir's reign from her and destroying Tir Nan Og made lust surge through his body. He all but trembled with the need for satisfaction. He stroked his servant's shivering arm planning what he'd do next.

Chapter Nineteen

TEN MINUTES LATER, the small private ceremony was over. Tara's father was buried at the bottom of Kelly's Mountain. A small white cross bore evidence to the man sleeping his eternal slumber underneath the earth. Lying next to her father was Balor's grave.

The hairs on the back of Tara's neck bristled as a cold, sharp gust of wind swept through the Highlands, bringing rolling omniscient clouds. It wasn't the cold she sensed, rather evil—the sulfuric odor pungent and disarming in its intensity.

Cael grabbed her arm. "Run!"

Once again ordering and taking without so much as a "please". Tara's mind wanted to ignore his order but her legs instantly obeyed. She felt the call of darkness like a stain spreading through the now-darkening afternoon sky and knew that evil was coming directly for her. A shrill scream was the only warning the ensemble got as creatures spiraled from the sky, dive bombing at them.

Tara screamed. Panic seized her heart. Not those ghastly things again.

She heard both Cael and Devon muttering words that sounded vaguely familiar to her. While she couldn't understand what they were saying, or grasp the meaning she felt the flush of power scale her skin, leaving her tingly. The language they spoke was Druid. A part within Tara's mind felt like a door was opening up, letting her freefall into ancient knowledge, other realms and something more powerful than she could ever envision.

"I thought they could only come out at night!"

Neil's shout disarmed her thoughts, firmly closing the door to whatever insight the language was about to yield to her. She let Neil propel her forward, after finally dislodging Cael's hand.

Cael moved to position his body closer to hers. "Wrong bedtime story. Get her in the cave now!"

"I can take care of myself, Cael." Even as she spoke she ran straight toward the cave's entrance, still pissed she was following his orders. However, a quick glance at the sky informed her she'd be stupid to refuse him now.

"Take her. Keep her safe," ordered Cael to Alec who was flanking her other side.

"No way, Fairy. I'm in this for the kill." Alec was already reaching for a weapon Tara knew he kept tucked in his belt buckle.

"Highlander, heed me now. Your only job is to keep Tara safe. Do as I tell you and you might live to see tomorrow. They are after Tara. This discussion is over." Cael pushed her more toward Alec.

"What?" croaked Tara. "Why are they after me?" *Why can't they be after Cael for once? And why did my gut instinct have to be right this time?*

"Because Tara, Stater needs that precious Fey blood of yours to open the veil to Tir Nan Og. Once he does that he'll let the Decies feast on my people and then come back to Earth for dessert," said Cael.

She noted he weaved his hands in an intricate pattern to create shielding spells for them, enabling them to reach the cave unharmed.

"For once Tara, do as I say. Run to the back of the cave and stay put."

Cael turned his silver-grey eyes to Alec. "I trust you, Highlander. And that's saying a lot. But, if there is one hair on her head missing...you're dead."

Alec nodded, grabbed her arm and together they ran straight to the back of the cave. *The cave Tara was getting mighty sick of. But this time she followed Cael's command. Well, there's got to be a first time for everything.*

Panting from exertion, Tara attempted to close her ears to the shrill sounds of battle taking place in broad daylight. Terror-induced goose bumps jumped to life on her skin. The sounds of the Decies filled her mind, reminding her of hundreds of people screaming in agony on a battlefield. She shook her head. None of this is real. She still found it hard to believe an alien-looking being complete with his minions was invading uneventful, ever-peaceful Cape Breton. Nope, none of this is real.

Deep down, Tara knew that was wrong. All of it was real. Cael was a real Tuatha Dé Danann, her professor was an ancient Druid Priest, her grandmother was alive, her father had been brutally murdered, and a sixth century king was after her. And the worst part for her was being half Tuatha. Tara's list went on and on. Everything that was happening now seemed to be because of her.

When it all should be because of him! Tara was angry she still had feelings for the Cael when he didn't have one redeeming quality. Even as she thought that she knew it was a falsehood. While she wouldn't ascribe the word "good" to Cael, he certainly had his own unique style of honor, which MacCallah had been more than keen to point out to her.

At least he's out there attempting to kill those things to keep me safe. Guess that counts as one good thing. Then it dawned on her. The King of the Decies wants my blood, just like Cael needed my blood to call forth Queen Mir to get what he wanted. There's really no difference. Both of them take what they want without asking.

The dark part of Cael was ready for this battle. A long time ago he and the King of the Decies had a good go at it. He hadn't been able though to make a dent in the armies of minions the Decies King had created or called forth. It had been Facia, his own leader, his own princess, the Queen's warrior-sister, who had been the ray of sunshine in that ghastly, brutal battle. She had been able to will the elements to work with her. But even she did not come out of that battle unscathed. King Belatucadros had marked her right upper shoulder, weakening her powers. Only at the last moment had Queen Mir stepped in to quickly imprison him in her treasure chest. Naively, Cael thought he'd never see the blasted Decies King again. How he wished that were so.

"To your right, Brody."

Cael watched as Keegan pushed his twin out of the way of an oncoming Decies.

"If they get their claws into you, kill yourself!" yelled Devon.

His strong warning startled his sons, but Cael knew these Highlanders would do what had to be done. Over the course of a few days, he had come to admire their strength and steadfast honor. The fact they would do whatever had to be done to keep Tara safe made him breathe slightly easier. Everyone knew the consequences. If Stater got his hands on Tara then all would be lost for both of their worlds. Today is not a good day to die. Usually he thought the reverse.

"The battle has to end here today."

"You don't need to be tellin' me that, Cael. We stand fast sons of mine...do what must be done to stop these evil creatures today. It ends here."

Cael smiled. Devon's sermon was a morale booster and he welcomed it as much as his sons, who were crouched, armed and ready.

Where is Stater? That question was what worried Cael. The bastard doesn't play by the book. He's using this divergence to draw us away from the cave and Tara. Cael prayed to all that was blessed and sacred Alec would keep her safe. If not, the Highlander was toast. Cael didn't like leaving Tara alone with Alec, but he was counting on that darkness that lived within the Highlander to be enough fuel to keep him focused to his task.

The crisp, swift flap of hundreds of wings caught his attention. The afternoon sky darkened, thick with the sludge of dread, the feeling a vapor that reached out to suck all hope and promise from anyone who stood against the Decies.

"Think happy thoughts!" Cael shouted loudly over the mad clatter of wing beats and shrieks coming from the Decies as they narrowed the space between them.

"Happy thoughts? You're barmy. This is hopeless. We're sadly outnumbered," said Keegan.

"Do as he says," echoed Devon. "They're trying to suck all hope from you...for once I'm asking you to think of a lass."

"Lass?" Keelan quashed a chuckle.

"Aye, that's right me lads. Think of the taste of a lasses' lush lips as she kisses you back, the feel of her warm body tucked up against you...now if those aren't happy thoughts sure to ground you, think whatever you bloody well need. Just think it. Cause that's their first weapon...stealing hope away when that's all we be hangin' on to."

Hundreds of Decies stormed through the clouds, their shrill screeches playing havoc with the Highlanders' hearing.

Cael knew their voice was their second weapon of choice.

Moving to the front of the group he turned and faced the Highlanders. "Stuff anything you can into your ears. They'll use their voice to render you defenseless. Pretend you are. Once they are close, attack. Cut their front claws off quickly and then decapitate them! Am I understood? No heroes today just do your job, your duty and let's kick their asses back to where they came from."

Cael made it a point to look at every single Highlander, his glance staying a second longer on Devon, who graced him with a warrior's nod of approval. So much for a grand army at my disposal. He turned toward the incoming Decies and braced his body for the frontal attack.

The Decies didn't hesitate. They never wavered in their descent. Cael was pleased to note that as scared shitless as the Highlanders were they never faltered. That alone made him respect them a lot more.

"On my mark. One. Two. Three. Now!" Cael moved out onto the open steep hill to prepare for hand-to-hand combat.

The first Decies brave enough to have a go at him died twenty seconds later. Before Cael could turn, he was flanked by two more and then he lost count and track of time as he hacked Decies after Decies, using the only tool at his disposal—the jeweled dagger from his queen. It wasn't much. Not nearly the weapon of choice he'd like to be holding in his hands but these were desperate times.

What I wouldn't give for my favorite sword, though. Amazed he could think at all he realized his survival instinct had kicked into full gear. *Then again, what I wouldn't give for a well-trained army all fully loaded with semi-automatic guns. Bless the modern age.*

With the mad clash of killing and trying to stay alive, or at least one step ahead of the vile creatures Cael took a second to glance at the Highlanders. He groaned. They were all in the same predicament—sadly outnumbered and forced to use simple hunting knives. Cael highly doubted they'd see the end of this day alive. When death was within reach he thought it was highly ironic he thirsted to live. But Death, like Fate and Queen Mir had their own agenda. Cael hoped today he and the Highlanders could avoid Death's appointment.

Dying can fit in my schedule another day.

Chapter Twenty

TARA COULDN'T STAND another minute of it. Alec kept moving from the back, where she was safely hiding, to the mouth of the cave. He cursed until he was almost blue in the face. She knew exactly how he felt. Frustrated and helpless.

"I can't stand it anymore. Tara, stay here. I'm going out to help!"

Part of her yearned to remind Alec of Cael's warning to protect her but another aspect of her didn't like having a babysitter. She knew Alec longed to help his family and she certainly wasn't about to stop him. Too bad I can't help.

She watched numbly as Alec moved a few wooden crates to get at four guns and two boxes of bullets. Tara didn't think that would be nearly enough. What she heard coming from outside the cave sounded straight out of a horror movie. Four guns against how many? From the sounds of it hundreds of those creatures were outside.

"Whatever you do, stay in here!"

Her chin quivered with fear but she nodded. What could she actually do anyway? Tara didn't know how to use a gun, and couldn't use a knife. She highly doubted throwing sticks and stones would do her any good.

A scratching sound from the top of the cave drew her attention. Tara froze. Something was trying to get in. She tried to force herself to take even, calming breaths to stop her accelerated heart-rate.

One of those things is trying to dig its way into the cave, to get to me. She wanted to yell out to Alec to inform him, but he'd already left. Crouching behind some large boxes wasn't going to help her. She needed a weapon or an escape hatch. Tara shivered, hugging her bare arms for warmth. A crackle of energy splayed along her skin. Her hair rose slightly up off her head. I am part Tuatha. Like that's going to do me a lot of good at the moment. More than anything Tara wished her grandmother had imparted her with the knowledge of her Tuatha heritage and how best to harness the power that lurked within her. She pondered what to do, and then it dawned on her. Both Cael and the creatures wanted her blood. It was her blood that had originally opened the veil to Tir Nan Og. If she could open the veil herself, she could get help. Scanning the cave, Tara tried to find something she could use to pierce her skin while calculating how much blood would be needed. She prayed Queen Mir would heed her call. She certainly wasn't about to slit her wrists like Cael had done, but she also wasn't about to watch her friends, who she thought of as family, get slaughtered.

The scratching sound grew more intense and determined. Time was ticking away. Tara moved from behind the crates and found one of MacCallah's butter knifes. Not all that sharp, but it would do. She rolled up her pant leg and set to work.

Five frustrating minutes later, task accomplished. She sat down and started chanting using the royal high tones her grandmother had taught her to call forth Queen Mir. She highly suspected her call was more a begging plea but so what. Tara prayed she was still in her majesty's good graces.

"Then we pulled the ions from the planet Jupiter—"

"Halt." Queen Mir regally stood up as she interrupted Xavier's beguiling tale. Why, I do believe that halfling is calling me again. What nerve. I am not at her beck and call.

"Xavier, go see what that halfling wants. I am most pleased so far with what you have imparted to me. Don't make me wait," said Queen Mir.

With a wave of her pale manicured hand Xavier blinked. Slightly disorientated with the rush of her power, he found himself standing next to Tara, still as naked as a jaybird.

"Wh...wha...what?" squeaked Tara.

Xavier laughed as she squeezed her eyes shut. Still innocent and shy. Xavier thought that by now Cael would have vanquished those two traits. He was partly amused by her reaction, but he wasn't about to chance annoying the queen by keeping her waiting.

He moved behind a large crate to cover up. "Why did you call, Tara?"

"The Decies have been released. Can't you hear them?" She was annoyed he noted.

Xavier listened, letting his senses see everything that needed to be. "Cael wasn't supposed to let this happen. The queen will not be pleased. You must destroy them." He turned to give Tara his full attention.

She almost laughed in his face. "You are kidding, right? I can't even save myself. Look out!" she screeched, as a Decies arm equipped with its deadly claw plunged through the cave's roof, almost touching him.

"Get the Ogham script. Use the alphabet to change metal into gold. Only gold can kill them. You must kill the king. Once he dies so too will his minions." Before Xavier could say anything more, Queen Mir yanked him back to Tir Nan Og.

"That took longer than I expected."

Dark velvet wrapped around Xavier's senses, flooding him with erotic thoughts that immediately fired his druid blood to a fevered pitch. Mir's voice was soft with sultry need, her pose highly suggestive. She wanted him. She'd get him. First though, she'd make him beg for her and if that was all she wanted from him—the first and only Druid to step foot on Tir Nan Og—he'd take that with a smile on his face.

Xavier didn't bother informing her of what was taking place—he knew she wouldn't lift a hand to help humankind. He hoped Tara would do as instructed and prayed she had mastered some of the powers that came with that fey blood of hers. She would need every advantage to stay alive and one step ahead of Stater, who Xavier had sensed was nearby.

"Now where was I...ahh, yes, I was telling you about how we Druids cast time across the vast universe." Xavier positioned his body where he knew Queen Mir would like it the most. He took possession of her moist heat the minute she parted her creamy, alabaster silk legs and was ever so thankful to be the first Druid to sample such wares.

Chapter Twenty-One

TARA WANTED TO CRY, shriek and hit someone. All three emotions burst through her system, hot in their intensity. *Get the Ogham script. Sure, why not? I'll just walk out the cave, down the hill and hike to the university and then break into Xavier's office. And on the way I'll grab a cup of coffee and maybe eat a donut. Ohh, guess what, I won't. The minute I set foot outside, one of those creatures will eat me alive.* "Thanks ever so much for the help, Professor!"

Before Tara could ponder anything further, two Decies crawled through the gaping hole in the cave's ceiling. She froze. Hoping to mask her presence, Tara stilled, not daring to breathe or move a muscle. Not that she could. Fear lived vivid in its intensity inside of her, causing her throat to instantly constrict. She prayed for a miracle or for Cael to come barging in to save her. *So, what if I have a shining knight complex. At least I can live with that.*

"Well, well, well, this is a nice snack," said the scratchy voice that grated on Tara's hearing. She knew that black coated voice that slithered through her veins coating her with dread. Standing before her wasn't just any Decies. *No, bless me. I get the crème de la crème.* The King of the Decies glared at her with such a hungry, feral look Tara felt it vibrate through the marrow of her bones.

She swallowed hard, gulping back her own saliva.

"Don't touch her. She's mine."

Stater's form materialized next to the King of the Decies.

Watching Stater appear was the bullet that propelled Tara forward. She knew the only person who would save her butt was herself. Recalling Cael's brother's words about letting her Tuatha Dé Danann blood channel through her, Tara closed her eyes and envisioned Xavier's office. She prayed that when next she opened them she'd be somewhere else...anywhere else was better than where she was.

Too bad when she opened her eyes she wasn't alone. Guess that was expecting too much. She fought hard not to give into the urge to cry or hyperventilate.

"Why, this is nice. Trust Xavier to position himself in society as the good professor. And lookie here, isn't this a find."

Tara didn't need to look at what Stater was referring to. He moved toward the Ogham script on Xavier's desk with a child's glee-filled look on his face.

If Stater got his hands on the powerful druid artifact the world she knew would surely be lost. Tara drew in a shuddering breath and let the power she now acknowledged surge to the forefront. Before Stater reached Xavier's desk a fierce gust of wind knocked him back.

Tara felt time freeze. In slow motion she watched Stater attempt to grab the ancient tablet while the King of the Decies crouched to attack her. She blinked, wondering how all this could be.

Did I do that? Her heart accelerated with hope. Mustering her courage and with shaky legs she ran forward, grabbed the Ogham script while she could and then raced out the door. Fear coated the back of her throat but she ran as fast as she could down the long corridor of the university and through the maze of large buildings, until she spied the forest. If this was her one hope, Tara would give it her best shot.

She didn't look back, or stop. Once she cleared the campus, she felt the air around her vibrate, shimmering to life. Instinctively, she knew that whatever spell she had accidentally woven had evaporated. Tara dove for cover in the thick, evergreen forest, and kept on running. She had to get the artifact to Cael. He'd be able to use it to kill the Decies. And save her and Earth.

She almost choked on her own thoughts. *That Damned Fairy is the reason all Hell has broken loose here.* Ignoring the cramp in her side she pushed on, swiping branches out of her way. A large prickly pine limb smacked her in the face, cutting her cheek. She trudged on, ignoring the biting sting from the cut and kept to the dense cover of the foliage. Even though it was only late afternoon the sky's darkened cover settled like a storm over the entire area. She felt the pull of that darkness brush something buried within her.

Tara felt cold and shivered all at once, as a dark, unknown power swamped her senses. For one minute the world became black and white, stark in contrast and again she felt the pull to leave her body behind, let her mind travel across a vast expanse of time and galaxies. A smack from another branch instantly broke the feeling. At the last moment she managed to avoid falling face down in the thicket. Clutching the stone slab in a tight hold to her chest, she shook her head and trudged onward.

As scared as Tara was to be tramping through the darkening woods, she was more terrified with what would happen if she didn't reach Cael. She prayed he was alive and kicking because she was no longer sure how she'd cope if something were to happen to him.

When did he become my anchor? She gripped the large stone slab tight to her chest, feeling heat when before the slab had been ice cold. She bent and scurried across tree roots and under branches, wishing things could go back to being quiet and normal. Fear drove a deep wedge within her thoughts when she thought of losing Cael. *Damn, I actually love that fairy.* She welcomed another smack from a branch, vowing to kill Cael herself if anything happened to him.

CAEL WIPED SWEAT FROM his brow. His arms burned at he lunged repeatedly at the Decies. Nothing was making a difference.

For every five he killed, ten more materialized. He realized then druid magick had a hand in things and he knew Stater was it.

Bastard never did play fair. He quickly scanned the Highlanders. Keegan was down, holding his arm while his twin Keelan attempted to protect him. Like that's going to help them. How did all this come to be?

Why couldn't I simply find the Stone of Fal and bloody well die? No. That doesn't happen on my watch. I get a family reunion that kills me, a woman I could fuck for eternity and after a thousand years I finally get welcomed back home. Should be glad about that. I'm not. When I finally do get to go home I end up fighting for the very life I wanted to end. Talk about poetic justice. Cael lopped off another head that had belonged to a Decies, the stench of sulphuric acid hitting him like a firecracker. Bloody smell reminded him for one second of that wee-beastie that had pissed on his leg his first night in Cape Breton. The same night he'd met Tara. Miracles can happen, he reminded himself.

Rushing to Keelan's side to lend support, Cael shouted, "Move your ass, Keelan, or your brother is bird food!"

"He's pretty bad," said Keelan, still smart enough to not let his guard down as a dozen Decies swarmed at them.

"I'll hold them back. Take him to the cave. Get Tara to help heal him. She has enough Tuatha Dé Danann blood in her to at least stem the flow of blood. Don't these things ever die?" Cael spaced his feet wide so he could jab with his right hand while kicking with his left leg. "Move it. Now!"

Thankfully, Keelan didn't need to be told twice. Cael watched as Keelan hauled his groaning brother to his feet. They managed to tumble into the cave's entrance. Earlier, when Cael had seen the Decies fill the sky he'd cast a druid protective spell around the entrance. That was the only thing that gave him comfort—knowing Tara was safe.

"Sweet fucking mercy, these things are harder to kill than cockroaches."

Cael's head swiveled to the side. "You left Tara!" He wished he could plunge his dagger straight through the Highlander who had dared to defy his orders.

"She's safe in the cave, stop worrying," said Alec, lunging for a Decies.

"Can't you follow orders?"

Alec cut off the claws of two Decies who had attempted to eat him. "Fuck your orders, Cael. In case you haven't noticed were being slaughtered. This is my family. Not yours!"

What could Cael say to that? Not much. The Highlander was correct. "Is your father okay?" asked Cael, pleased to note they circled each other while making clean, effective kills. *Not that it seems to make any difference.*

"More than okay. Wish he'd taught me those spells instead of making me memorize the symbols for all the universes, like that's helping me now," mocked Alec.

Cael welcomed the bitter humor. Anything to get his mind off just how tired his arm muscles felt. He narrowly dodged two Decies as they swooped low, aiming for his head. *Not today. I've got a woman I plan to bed before this night is over.*

He crouched to his knees as he plunged his dagger upward, his aim perfect. One down, only another hundred or more to go. "Druid magick is at work. For every one we kill at least two more materialize. I've got to find Stater and kill him. That's the only way we can stop this. Right now, we're lucky they're content to stay and fight us. The moment they get a whiff of more humans they'll be off for easier prey." While he talked, Cael repeatedly made kills.

"Shit, you ain't serious. Man, that sucks. Okay, go find Stater. I'll cover you," said Alec, panting as he veered to the left to avoid a deadly claw.

Cael was pleased to see the Highlander deftly slice off the Decies' arms, rendering the creature useless.

Then the hairs on the back of Cael's neck rose. "That won't be necessary. I see him now. I can't believe it. You said she was safe."

"I swear Cael, she was in the cave when I left," said Alec, panting from the exertion.

"That's great. Why can't she listen to me? Is that too hard? Obviously, yes."

Blinding fury burned bright within him. Coming up the hill was Stater, as cocksure as any peacock. And why shouldn't he be? He had Tara safely in his grasp.

"What's he holding?" asked Alec, gulping for air, as the two of them continued to cut down the army of Decies that were steadily advancing upon them.

"I'm not sure." Cael hoped to all that was sacred it wasn't what he thought. If that's the Ogham script I'm going to kill her. He was still trying to figure out how she had managed to escape unnoticed from the cave to who knows where. Then it dawned on him. Tara had finally learned how to tap into her Tuatha heritage and transport herself from one place to another. While part of him was pleased with her acceptance of her heritage the timing sucked.

When Stater was halfway up the hill he stopped, looked Cael in the eyes and laughed. The sound was carried on the wind. The laugh only made Cael more furious.

"I've won, Cael. Get used to it. Why don't you bargain...or better yet, beg me on your fairy knees to release her. I know you're dying to," Stater cackled, thoroughly enjoying the show.

"You bastard. Let her go!" Cael wished he could run down the hill and have a go at Stater, however the Decies were still coming in full force at them. "Call off the Decies and lets you and me go man to man!" shouted Cael.

Stater pulled Tara closer to him. Cael felt a shiver of repulsion from her storm through him. Her Tuatha powers were mingling with his own and in a time of battle that was not a good thing. Reaching deep within himself, Cael found his center and shielded himself from the terror she was feeling. He didn't need to be distracted. He had to focus. It was the only way they would all come out of this alive. He gnashed his teeth together. Beside him he heard Alec curse a blue streak.

"Man, to man. That's got a good ring to it. You're forgetting something, fairy. I'm a king and you...well, you're not a man and hardly a fairy and soon very soon you will be nothing...just like Tir Nan Og. Today is my day. Today I get my revenge."

Without hesitating Stater took the dagger he was carrying in his hand and drove it straight through Tara's heart. Her scream tore through Cael's consciousness and soared through the darkening sky in deadly earnest.

Cael felt the Highlanders attempt, like him, to reach her. But it was too late. They were all too late. Her blood had been spilt. The fact she had learned to embrace her Tuatha heritage opened the veil between the two worlds—Earth and Tir Nan Og—lightning fast.

Stater stepped through the veil and had the nerve to wave at Cael. Right there, Cael vowed he'd kill Stater slowly, exacting vengeance limb by limb. One moment they were all fighting the Decies and then the next the creatures were gone, having flown through the opening to get to his homeland. Cael wanted to step through but he couldn't. Raw grief poured fast, a torrent through his system. He raced down the hill and gently scooped Tara up into his arms. Her warm blood coated his body. She gasped for breath, fighting to live.

"Save her," said Devon, coming to his side.

"I can't." Cael could barely croak the words out.

"You, fairy, do it," snarled Alec.

Cael felt that dark thread from Alec settle over everyone. He raised his head, noting how Alec's eyes flashed quickly from baby-blue to black. Devon placed a calming hand on Alec's shoulder and instantly the Highlander regained control of his raging emotions. Cael wished it could be that simple for him. He felt cut in half. Void. Empty. Dead. For the first time in his life he felt truly useless, knowing he was incapable of saving the one person who meant more to him than anyone ever had in his long existence. Cael would gladly have ripped out his own heart if that would save Tara.

"You fucking fairy, save her," groaned Alec.

"I can't. Only Queen Mir can save her." Cael choked back a sob as Tara's amber eyes flickered open.

"Ogham script...turn to gold...save us both." Tara's words were a jumble. She fought with all her might to make him understand. Oh, he understood all right. She had gone after that bloody artifact thinking to save them and ended up an easy picking for Stater.

He wanted to shout at her. He wanted to roar at her. Why couldn't you have listened to me? Instead he crooned loving words he had vowed never again to utter in this lifetime. "It's okay love. I've got you. The pain will soon go away."

"Cael, I love you."

The words came out more as a sigh, but he heard them and felt them to the core of his being. They sailed light and airy through his mind and more importantly to his grieving heart.

"I love you too, my wee feyling." His face was stone cold. He fought not to let his emotions get away from him. Cael hugged her closer, burying his face in her small shoulder, wanting to remember her honeysuckle smell and the feel of her warm body until the last possible moment.

He wasn't sure how long he held her. When he had finally gained control of the wild surging emotions wreaking havoc within him, he looked up. The Highlanders had formed a druid circle around them.

"You can't get to Tir Nan Og that way." Gently Cael placed Tara's body on the hard ground.

"We're not going to Tir Nan Og, you are," said Devon. "We're calling in our own reinforcements. If those Decies come back to Earth after they finish with your homeland we're be needin' all the support we can marshal. As much as it grieves me to say this, time is tickin' away. Get to Tir Nan Og and kill those Decies. Make Queen Mir fix things," said Devon.

Cael didn't say anything. He reached down and scooped up Tara into his arms. Her body was already limp, the heat of her essence vacating her quickly. With the help of the circle Cael was able to use his inherent Tuatha powers to jump back to Tir Nan Og, only to reenter Hell.

"Cael, how dare you!"

So much for being in her good graces for more than twenty-four hours. Cael wondered what type of punishment Mir was going to exact on him. Before his feet touched his home soil his body shimmered to rematerialize in her Pleasure Palace, Queen Mir's home away from home.

Queen Mir stood with her arms crossed, a pose so very earth-like, he could have laughed. But laughing would have erased him from history for eternity. No, Queen Mir was mighty angry.

She advanced toward him, not once letting her form touch the marbled floor. "Simple instructions. Tell me, how is it that you failed me once again?"

"I told her to get the Ogham script," said Xavier.

Cael trembled. His anger and realization that it was Xavier who had caused Tara's death sucked all the life out of him. "You. You're the one who told Tara to get that bloody artifact. She might as well have given herself to Stater." Cael gnashed his teeth, wishing he could get his hands wrapped tightly around the Druid Priest's neck. He couldn't. He was still holding Tara.

"I told her to get that script to help you."

Xavier's even, unruffled voice caused Cael to wince. Damn Druid Priest won't ever admit he's wrong. "Ohh, it helped her all right, Druid. She got a knife straight through the heart, thanks to you. You are dead!" snarled Cael, his eyes promising murder of their own.

Queen Mir backed away from Cael to take a seat on her gold settee. She folded her hands together. "Are you telling me, Xavier, that Stater is now in possession of the fabled Ogham script?"

Xavier gave a slow calculated nod.

"And you told this halfling to secure this sacred, blessed, all-powerful tablet to help, how?"

Anyone else might have missed the insolence behind Queen Mir's question, but not Cael. This is amusing her. All of this is a game.

His heart constricted painfully. He was so sick of mind games he would eagerly have bashed in someone's head to end all of this for good.

Cael felt Xavier hesitate.

"I told her to use the script to turn metal into gold," said Xavier.

Queen Mir patted the spot next to her on the settee, indicating Xavier should sit. "Tell me, Druid, why are you telling me this now?" The commanding tone was back in Mir's voice.

Xavier did as instructed and sat next to Mir. "You know we took an oath not to interfere, but Stater has found a way to siphon a high Druid Priest's power and absorb it for himself so that he can extend his life. We never interfered when the Decies were after you because it did not affect humankind. That has changed."

"I see. You would rather all the Tuatha Dé Danann be destroyed then your beloved, ignorant, fragile daughters of Eve and sons of Adam," snapped Queen Mir.

"Speaking of Eve's daughters, I—"

"Do not speak, Cael. I will deal with you and the halfling in a moment." Queen Mir rose with her usual regal grace to tower over all of them.

"You do know she is dead." Cael fought to get those words out.

Queen Mir waved him away like he was an insect. He knew enough to shut up, because there was a part of him that enjoyed watching Xavier squirm for a change.

The long, white goddess robe swished around Mir's feet as she paced, a clear indication she was deep in thought, trying to calculate every aspect to her best advantage. "Metal into gold. You are implying gold will kill the Decies."

"Sort of," mumbled Xavier.

"Druid, you gave yourself to me willingly. You agreed to my terms. It is binding. I could destroy your life in a blink and take all that precious druid knowledge from you."

Xavier stood up and dared to approach Queen Mir.

"You could, but then you would never discover who the traitor is on Tir Nan Og," said Xavier, not even flinching as Mir's normally composed face turned hard and cold.

It was a look Cael knew first-hand. She had that same look when she'd damned him to Earth. He fervently prayed she'd damn the Druid Priest to Mars and let him burn for eternity, over and over again.

Then Queen Mir laughed. The sound was startlingly clear in its seductiveness. "Amusing, Druid. You are implying there is a traitor amongst my subjects. I must say your divergence tactics are interesting—"

"I know there is a traitor amongst your loving subjects, Queen Mir," interrupted Xavier. "It was a Tuatha Dé Danann who came to me, who informed me that Cael was going to ask you to personally destroy us...that Tuatha made it clear that I had to petition you to get rid of Cael. Why? Why would a Tuatha Dé Danann care what happens to Cael, or to the Druids? That's the question I've asked myself for the past thousand years and I still don't know the answer."

Cael shifted his feet, positioning Tara's now slightly stiff body closer to his frame. What he was hearing mystified him. One of his own had wanted him exiled. One of his own was a traitor.

"You are lying," stated Cael. "No Tuatha Dé Danann would dare to think to defy Queen Mir."

"Sadly, there you are wrong, Cael."

Queen Mir's voice was a pouty sigh. She sat back down on the settee. "Enough. I will deal with your accusations later. Tell me exactly how to kill the Decies. They need to be stopped."

"Kill their king and they all die," said Xavier.

"We've tried to kill the king but he doesn't seem to die," said Cael.

"What Cael says is true. You are leaving something out, Druid. I grow weary of this conversation." With a sweep of Mir's hand, they were all transported to where the current battle was taking place.

The land of Tir Nan Og, once beautiful in its serenity, looked like a blood bath. The wide flowery grounds were dotted with dead Tuatha Dé Danann. Thousands of Decies had appeared.

"Those creatures are sucking the life out of Tir Nan Og. When they are done they will move back to Earth. Is this what you want, Druid? They will destroy your precious humankind without a thought."

"If you poison the king with gold, he will die."

"How much gold?" asked Cael.

Xavier looked mortified at the carnage he was witnessing. "You don't need much. Once it's in his system, it will shut him down."

"I will kill him for you, Queen Mir," declared Cael.

Queen Mir turned her amber eyes on him, assessing his worth. In a blink they were all back at her Pleasure Palace, cut off from the battle, cocooned from the shrill shrieks and sounds of the massacre. Wrapped once again in her seductive allure.

As much as myth would portray the Tuatha Dé Danann as invincible fighters, the harsh truth was they weren't. The Decies could easily cut down a Tuatha and suck the life-force out of them, or worse, convert them. When Cael had been chosen to be Mir's personal Champion, he had trained a handful of others to act as warriors for his queen. He wondered if she still had those warriors.

"I will help," said Xavier.

Cael growled low. There was no way he wanted Xavier by his side and especially not in this battle. Eyeing the settee, Cael moved toward it to reverently lay Tara's body on it. Her blood no longer flowed, but the gaping wound in her chest was a painful reminder that she had not gone gently into the good night. Death had taken the appointment meant for him and claimed Tara. That cold knowledge infuriated Cael.

"Leave her with me, Cael. My army is at your disposal. Make me proud of you again," commanded Queen Mir. "Bring King Belatucadros to me. I will finish him myself."

Cael rose and tore his eyes from Tara. It was the hardest thing for him to do. He fought to overcome the grief that ripped through his system. "That may be hard to do."

"Are you implying that you aren't up to the task?"

"No. I simply said it might be hard to do, but not impossible." Cael bowed his head. "I will bring the king to you, but he is not going with me. And I am going to kill Stater," said Cael, his eyes narrowed in on Xavier.

"Still bargaining." Queen Mir's tone was haughty with disapproval. "You were never this demanding when you lived amongst us."

"Yes, well time weighs heavily on a person once they've been exiled," said Cael. At one time he would never have talked back to Mir but he was getting sick of blind obedience.

Mir sauntered over to where he stood next to Tara's lifeless body on the settee. He felt her cold hand on his shoulder and a shudder rippled through him. He fought to mask the effect she had on him.

"Cael, this is the way it was written. I will honor her well. Make me proud of the champion I hand-picked to serve me. Xavier will stay with me. Dyloulious will be your second-in-command. Now let's outfit you properly."

A flourish and flush of Tuatha power swamped Cael. It took a moment for Cael to realize he wasn't wearing his traditional warrior outfit. He nodded, understanding her gift. Gold-lined armor would keep the Decies away from him, allowing him the opportunity to go straight for their king.

He turned to give Tara one last final kiss, but was stopped short.

"That is unnecessary. I have one final gift for you, Cael."

Cael didn't need to ask. The black beast appeared at his side, stamping its majestic feet impatiently, the sound harsh as it resonated on the hard marble floor.

He gave a curt nod. "You honor me." Cael reached for the golden bridle of Queen Mir's dream steed, A'vatra.

"A'vatra will answer only to you now. Be gone," she said.

When next Cael looked he was standing in the middle of the melee with Queen Mir's stallion nudging him to get on its back. Only too happy to oblige, he grinned wickedly.

About bloody time I get my revenge. Queen Mir hadn't insisted on dealing with Stater herself and he was thankful for that. Cael planned on ripping that man apart piece by piece, painfully slowly. For what he did to his Tara, the feyling who had inadvertently saved him, the woman who had made him love her for her feisty spirit, he wasn't about to be gentle. They don't call me the Damned Fairy for nothing. He kicked the steed hard and charged straight into a battle that would have made the god of the underworld proud.

Chapter Twenty-Two

QUEEN MIR WAS DEEP in thought. She didn't like that Xavier thought one of her own was a traitor. Oh, she wasn't naive. She knew she had her fair share of enemies, but she had been careful, or so she thought. As powerful as she was, she thought she had eliminated those that would attempt to steal the throne from her. *Who? Who would dare defy me? And why get rid of Cael?*

"What do you plan to do with Tara's body?" asked the Druid Priest.

Mir was losing her patience and lust for the Druid. He asked too many questions and stuck that nose of his in places it had no business being.

"Rhea will come for her," she replied, dismissively.

As if on cue, Rhea materialized.

Rhea of Naldolcoh materialized on her knees with her head bowed submissively. "My queen, how can I be of service to you?"

Queen Mir didn't say anything for so long that Rhea was forced to raise her head slightly. Mir stepped away from the settee, knowing Rhea would see the bloodied body of her granddaughter—Tara, and the Druid, who both seemed to have a hand in lots of things.

An anguished howl of grief tore through Rhea. She gathered her long, yellow robe to rush to Tara's side.

"You said you would protect her. Bastard!" Rhea's eyes darted daggers at Xavier.

Ahh, this is how it is to be. I should have seen it earlier. I should have trusted the Fates.

"Does he know?" asked Queen Mir to Rhea.

"No," replied Rhea, sobbing over Tara's body.

"Know what?" asked Xavier.

Queen Mir enjoyed the puzzled expression on the stoic Druid's face for once. *Even your druid senses missed this one mighty valuable piece of information.*

"Tara is your child." Queen Mir's voice was loud and clear with conviction.

Xavier moved toward Rhea and Tara. "You lie." His jaw was clenched tight with anger.

Rhea didn't speak but shook her head negatively.

"How?" asked Xavier, his face flushed. He was angrier than Queen Mir had ever seen. It was a look she liked on the normally cool and composed Druid Priest.

Rhea of Naldolcoh rose to her full height. Queen Mir had to admit she was a beauty in her own right. Rhea had ivory colored skin, and long silver hair, which was streaked red and fell to her slender waist. Pale silver eyes that understood sorrow glared at Xavier.

"When I went through the veil I thought I could come back home at any time. I didn't understand that time moves differently on Earth. You...you were the first Druid I had ever encountered. We first made love in an open field and then had a brief two-week affair. I thought that would be it. I thought then I could return to Tir Nan Og, but I couldn't." A shiver settled through Rhea. Her voice barely registered as a soft whisper.

"No, that's impossible. I don't remember you." Xavier's voice was rock cold.

With a wave of her hand, Rhea changed her appearance.

Nice trick. Queen Mir smiled, pleased with the charade Rhea had used to get what she wanted. *They were sisters after all and the blood that ran through their veins was powerful. Their lineage used whatever they could to get what they wanted.* Mir knew that first hand. She was a living testimony to what one could do and would do to get what they desired.

"You!" said an astonished Xavier.

Mir sensed the Druid Priest's mind fighting to put the pieces together. Cautiously, he circled the now dark-haired beauty, the woman who had dared to trick him.

"I never meant to deceive you, Xavier. But if you knew I was really Tuatha Dé Danann you would have taken me to your elders. When I found out you were a Druid Priest, after recognizing the tattoos on your arms, I knew I had to change my appearance. Even though I was stuck on Earth, I still was Tuatha...I still had the power to wield. I used this," said Rhea, her hand indicating her new form, "and my powers to keep my secret. I only came to you when I realized that over time my powers on Earth were weakening. I asked for your help to keep Tara safe. That was your only job. And you failed," accused Rhea, angrily.

Xavier almost stumbled. "You are telling me that all those years ago when I came across you wandering the Highlands and those few weeks we spent together...you're telling me Tara came from that union."

Rhea nodded. "She is of you...your blood. Seems like we broke another one of those precious druid laws, didn't we." There was bitterness in Rhea's voice.

"You knew. You knew this all along," accused Xavier to Queen Mir.

"No. I sensed Tara was different but even I did not know until I summoned Rhea. Once I saw her eyes, I knew." Queen Mir turned her attention to Rhea. "You did well to serve me, Rhea of Naldolcoh. The Fates have blessed us with this gift."

"Gift..." both Rhea and Xavier said in unison.

"A first. Druid blood and Tuatha Dé Danann blood. The power of two beings into one. The knowledge inherent in this halfling will do well to serve us," said Queen Mir. And, more importantly better to serve me.

The Druid Priest gulped and almost stuttered aghast. Mir smiled bravely at him.

"But she's dead," he said.

"To your eyes maybe. Do you not see it Rhea?" Mir asked the question more as a test than anything else.

"The spark hovers above her. Yes, I see what you mean." Hope and relief flooded Rhea's voice, evoking a soft white power that reached out to merge with her daughter.

"Great, that's just great. Will someone explain it to me." Xavier had begun to pace in an angry circle.

Queen Mir walked up to Xavier and cupped his chin. She forced him to watch as blue sparks settled over Tara's stiff body. "Watch, Druid. This is the mystery of Tir Nan Og. This is the power inherent in my race."

Then the sparks soared through her gaping wound. In a flash her body was engulfed in an energy force that channeled through her system. She screamed in agony, the sound cutting in its intensity. Then the blue hue that had engulfed her turned bright yellow.

"That is your blood," said Queen Mir. "Watch what happens."

And watch they all did. Tara's body bucked and twisted, levitating up from the settee. The blue and yellow hues of energy worked their way systematically through her body. They all watched as she subtly changed. Her hair grew longer, fuller as it turned to a deep shade of mahogany streaked with bright red. Her chest healed and her skin tone turned copper, almost gold-flecked in its brilliance. She was the perfect combination of a Tuatha and a Druid, the essence of health and vitality. The essence of power and knowledge. She was the tipping scale—the one Mir would covet with all her powers to glean the knowledge which Tara had inherited.

The power of two powerful races combined. She was a sight to behold. Her aura surrounded her with its clear, pure brilliance. She was the first. She was the key that would enable Mir to secure her hold on Tir Nan Og for eternity. The Fates will not best me. I will not be deterred. She will give me what I need.

"You understand she knows all those precious secrets you hold close to your chest. You understand she is a power to be reckoned with and she's mine," declared Queen Mir, not releasing Xavier's chin, which was clamped tightly between her long, manicured fingers.

"Did you do this for her?" Xavier grinded out his question, which was aimed at Rhea.

"No, Xavier. I did this for all of us." Rhea reached out and gently laid her hands-on Tara's body which had once again settled.

Tara hesitantly rose to a sitting position.

"What happened?" she asked, rubbing her forehead. "My head, what happened? My head feels like it's on fire."

Queen Mir slowly released Xavier and moved to Tara's side where Rhea was gently smoothing Tara's hair in a calm, reassuring gesture that struck a chord deep within Mir. Tara was Rhea's offspring, her child, her legacy. A child was the one thing the Fates continued to deny Mir. And without an offspring, soon her throne would be taken away from her. But by using Tara, Mir knew she'd find a way to get what she'd fought so long and hard for, even if she had to fight the Fates themselves.

"Give it time, my child. The knowledge is vast and your mind is trying to find a way to accommodate your new powers," said Queen Mir.

"New powers?" Tara looked clearly perplexed. "Grandmother?" she asked, finally focusing on who was beside her.

Before Rhea could speak, Queen Mir spoke bluntly. "Rhea is not your grandmother, Tara, she is your real mother and Xavier here is your real father."

Xavier watched as Tara's eyes grew wide with disbelief. I know that feeling well. Tara shook her head and then raised a shaky hand to her forehead as if she were in pain. Pain would be more than welcome at the moment.

"That's not possible," she said. Her voice was velvety soft, almost like she was afraid to discover the truth. "Stater murdered my father."

Rhea stood up from her crouch beside the sofa where Tara had been lying. "Stater murdered Jim!"

Queen Mir placed her hands gently on Rhea's shoulder, to keep her in one place.

"Jim was a good man, Tara," said Rhea.

Xavier watched as Rhea fought to compose her face back into the stoic Tuatha she was. Hearing her words, as she talked about Jim, caused his stomach to twist. Why he didn't like the notion of her with another man bothered him. But it wasn't like he was able or about to lay claim to her. She was Tuatha. He was a Druid Priest. And betwixt the two shall ever meet. He wondered if he got that expression right for a change.

Rhea knelt back down beside her daughter—their daughter! The notion was startling, awe-inspiring and telling. If the Druid Constellation found out about her then there was no stopping what they would do to destroy her. They had made it clear at the beginning of time when the two powerful races merged to live on the planet now called Earth the consequences of any Druid Priest begetting a child from the Tuatha race. Death for the said child and one very long, painful death for him. Of that he had no doubt.

Xavier forced his mind to turn away from his thoughts. It wasn't safe. Mir could easily breach his mind-shields in this realm if he let his guard down.

"I would wish you to only have happy memories of your time with Jim. Our time together was too short. For most of our life together we pretended. Well, I should say I pretended. I pretended to be your grandmother, and he pretended to be your father. But I will give Jim this much, he loved you Tara like his own with his heart and soul," said Rhea, gently stroking Tara's arm.

Xavier wished he felt something, some trace of emotion, as tears trickled down Tara's cheeks thinking of the loss of the man she had known all her life as her father.

"I don't understand how all this could be," said Tara.

Get used to that. Xavier wondered how things had become so complicated so quickly in the short span of time he'd been in Mir's realm.

"Rhea, you have permission to take Tara to Naldolcoh. You two need time alone," said Queen Mir, dismissing both of them.

Xavier moved forward, compelled by some unknown force. "Rhea, when you can, a word with you." He bowed his head to show respect and his true intentions.

He watched her nod once and then they disappeared in the blink of an eye.

"A word, Druid...that sounds amusing. Didn't that little surprise make your day? I wonder what the precious Druid Constellation would think of you now, Xavier. The mighty Xavier...oops, I mean the mighty Xa'alter, overseer of the High Lunar Druid Warriors." Mir stared at him.

Xavier fought not to show any emotion. Not many knew his true title, and those that did were always cautious to never mention it.

"Did you think I did not know about you? I confess at first when I spied you on Earth with Cael in that dirt hole called a tavern I wasn't sure. So, I did some poking around. The mighty Druid Priest, one of the founders of the Druid Constellation...I bet Cael doesn't know."

Xavier had enough. He closed the space between them in a heartbeat.

"Your angry eyes can do nothing. You willingly agreed to my terms to come to my realm and in Tir Nan Og...I. Control.

Everything!" snarled Mir, her long white hair rising as a rush of warm wind whipped through her Pleasure Palace. "Finally, after eons I am going to get what I need, Druid. So be afraid. Because I plan to use Tara to gather as much druid knowledge as possible and then...I plan to destroy every last one of you."

Xavier knew she was right. In her realm he could almost do nothing. It was the almost that caused him to grin.

Reaching out, he used his infinite knowledge of the universe and willed time to distort. Satisfied he'd at least made a statement; he closed his eyes and willed time to return to normal.

Mir's gasp rushed through him. "How dare you?"

His body was flushed tight to hers. His arms encircled her from behind and one hand was boldly caressing her left nipple.

"Do not underestimate me, Mir. That would be your undoing," he said, calmly letting the words tickle her skin. "I may willingly have come to your realm but do not think I am without powers here. I am Druid." The haughty words were said with power, letting Mir understand the full meaning of his statement.

She gave him a crafty smile. "That's why I will kill you all. Your power will be mine."

Mir flashed his clothing off without warning and turned her body into his. Her nails dug deep gouges into his back. She clutched her pale body to his and his cock had a mind of its own.

"The one thing I will miss after I kill you...is your impressive sword."

A girly giggle escaped her and Xavier knew she truly meant to do his race harm.

"Then again, with all the powers I take from your race, I'll be able to get what I want any time I want. The rules of engagement have been changed. Why I never thought of that before mystifies me. That however is about to change."

She gripped his cock in a hard pull and Xavier wished with all his powers he didn't like it so much.

Chapter Twenty-Three

A WAVE OF QUEEN MIR'S hand and Tara found herself inside another palace. While smaller than the opulent room she had been in, it was warm and comforting. White veined marble walls and dark blue marble floors with bright red Turkish style carpets that looked like they belonged in a harem's tent lined the floor. An open hearth sat in the middle of the palace. Four strikingly beautiful female Tuatha Dé Danann were also present. Each had risen when they had materialized. Four beaming smiles that radiated warmth and friendship gazed at her. The feelings overwhelmed her.

"A true honor to finally meet you, Tara," said the tallest of the women, as she moved toward the spot where Tara was rooted. The woman wore a bright red, sleeveless high-waist gown that emphasized every aspect of her fey appearance. She had long white hair streaked in black that fell to her waist and light silver eyes that flickered with intelligence.

"Tara, these are my other daughters. Myla," said Rhea, indicating the tall woman who had approached her. "Sasha, Autumn and Zuerka." Rhea ushered the other three women toward her. "They are your sisters."

"Sisters?" choked Tara, completely overcome. She could feel the warmth and love from these women yet she didn't even know them. Still shell-shocked, she let each of the women embrace her.

Sasha was slightly smaller than Myla's six feet. She had ivory hair but it was curly and fell to her shoulders. The black irises of her silver eyes were so large she looked truly exotic. Autumn, much like her name implied, had hair that was ivory but also streaked with the color's auburn, chestnut-brown and honey-yellow. It too fell to her waist. She had dark silver eyes that looked warmly at her. Zuerka's hair was so pale it looked the color of ivory and she wore it pixie cropped close to her head, which only served to emphasize her light silver eyes. All her sisters had extremely pale coloring.

"We are so happy to finally meet you. And we can't wait for you to tell us what Earth is really like. Mother refuses to say anything about her time there," said Myla.

"Yes, we are dying to hear all about it," echoed Sasha.

"Is it true? You have seasons that follow the moon and white, cold stuff that hardens on your grounds?" asked Autumn.

Only Zuerka remained silent. Tara guessed she was the youngest of her sisters.

Rhea warmly embraced all her daughters. "Girls, I told you not to ask too many questions. Tara is new here. She has lots of her own questions that I plan to answer. Give her time and I'm sure she will tell all."

"Why won't you tell us, Mother?" admonished Myla.

"Before Tara came here I couldn't bring myself to talk about it. It was simply too painful for me. Knowing that I would never see you again, Tara, I just couldn't talk about my time on Earth. But now hope fills me. Daughters of mine, I will delight you with tales of Earth and more, but first Tara and I need some privacy."

Each of the women solemnly nodded and then in a blink they disappeared.

"Does everyone do that?" asked Tara, wrinkling her nose in amusement.

"Usually," answered Rhea. "Come child, let's enjoy a nice cup of your favorite, Earl Grey tea, and talk. I imagine there are a thousand questions in that curious mind of yours."

A bright orange sofa materialized, along with two cups of steaming hot tea. She found the normalcy of the furniture strangely comforting. Tara lovingly inhaled the familiar scent of the tea, letting it conjure safe memories in her mind.

"Are you really my Mother?" she asked, sitting down on the sofa.

"Yes, my child. I am. You don't know how long I have waited to say those words to you. You can't imagine the suffering I have had to endure to keep silent all those Earth years and then when I returned to Tir Nan Og, I so desperately wanted to go back that I thought of nothing else for months."

Tara settled down into the sofa, took a sip of the hot brew and relaxed. "Please tell me everything," she said.

Tara wasn't sure how long she sat listening to Rhea's words...words that spoke the truth, but it felt like a long time. It felt like she was discovering her true self for the first time. And all of it strangely made sense. She had always wondered why she felt so close to her grandmother and now she knew. But it was also slightly unbelievable. How could any of this have happened? Things like this only existed in books or movies, not in the real world. But then again, she was living proof that wasn't so.

Suddenly a stab of pain flashed inside her head.

"That is the knowledge Queen Mir talked about trying to assert itself. You do understand how special you are." Rhea patted her hand like she always did when wanting to get Tara's complete attention.

Tara closed her eyes as the pain settled into a tight knot she felt in her neck. "I still can't believe Xavier is my father. You do know he's the Druid Priest that had Cael banished?"

Rhea smiled and nodded.

"Is there something else I should know?" She was trying to put together all the pieces. She felt like something wasn't fitting.

"The power inherent in us comes from our blood. I need you to understand that bloodline means everything on Tir Nan Og. I am known as Rhea of Naldolcoh when in truth I am Queen Mir's sister. When my sister took the throne, she decreed only she would bear the title of royalty. It is why each of us, her sisters were assigned to a specific place, she likes to refer to as a corner, within Tir Nan Og. We have our own subjects. I administer to my people and their loyalty is to me first, even though Queen Mir likes to think it is to her. I oversee Naldolcoh. Your other six aunts oversee the other corners," said Rhea, pausing to take a sip of tea.

Tara gulped. "You're saying I have seven aunts? I'm finding all of this hard to swallow. I go from believing I have no family left to this. Four sisters, a mother who I thought of as my grandmother, a father, who turns out to be a Druid Priest, and seven aunts, Queen Mir, and six other. Please give me a moment...no wait, give me a year or two to digest all of this." Tara's sarcastic remark reignited her spark.

She placed her empty mug on a clear black table that had materialized next to the sofa, slightly annoyed things could simply be conjured at will. Another rush of power surged through her being, causing goose bumps to form all over her skin.

"No, Tara, what I'm saying is that you are a direct descendant with the same blood line as Queen Mir, only you also have druid blood in you. That alone makes you both powerful and dangerous in Queen Mir's mind. Trust me, our time together will be shorter than we both would like. I have tried to safeguard you all my life. Sadly, I have failed. I had hoped you'd be safe on Earth. Now that Queen Mir has discovered exactly what you are she will use your knowledge to get what she wants."

Not liking the conversation any more, Tara asked, "And that is?"

"More power," answered Rhea, flatly. "Enough. Come, let us find out what mischief my other daughters are up to. I want them to show you the real beauty of our world. I have a few things I must take care of," said Rhea, and then before Tara could voice her objection, her mother disappeared.

Wow! I really don't like that. Good thing she never could do that when I was growing up. Instantly her four sisters reappeared.

"I thought she'd never leave," said Sasha.

"Come, Tara, we want to show you around, and while we walk you get to talk. Tell us everything there is to know about Earth," demanded Myla, sounding very much like her aunt, Queen Mir.

"Did you get rid of your latest sex toy?" Rhea of Naldolcoh rematerialized inside Queen Mir's private feasting garden, knowing exactly where her sister was.

"Are you jealous?" Queen Mir's eyes narrowed as her hand reached out to pick a purple cesta flower which groaned its displeasure. Like most things on Tir Nan Og, the large flowering plant was alive. Its aura shone bright with life around it. When Queen Mir picked it, she absorbed its aura...its powers, but instead of feeding the plant back enough essence to live, Mir siphoned off all the flower's energy.

Once again, Rhea wished she had the backing of all her siblings. She was treading on dangerous waters. However, she was not about to let Mir get away with what she knew she had planned for Tara. It was time for things on Tir Nan Og to be fixed.

Rhea forced herself to appear calm. "No. He means naught to me."

Queen Mir's eyes pinned her. Her amber eyes were so much like Tara's that Rhea had to fight not to show any emotion. She knew her sister was seeking her weakness and that would be her own swift downfall.

"Ahh, Rhea, do not play me for a fool."

"I did not go through the veil thinking this would happen," said Rhea, with more force than she had intended.

"Did you not? Then tell me, why did you set in motion the plan to get rid of Cael?" asked Queen Mir, with a bored tone.

"How did you...?"

"I am queen, you would do well to remember that at all times. And I am not so easily fooled by your trickery."

Rhea moved closer to her sister. "It's not like you think, Mir. I didn't know I would be the one to get pregnant."

"But one of you knew. Who? Let me guess," she said, picking another cesta plant, this time toying with it as she inhaled its scent. "I am thinking Facia has her scared hands in this little bit of mischief. Mischief that will not go unpunished. I'm also assuming she was the one who told you to steal the Stone of Fal from me. Play with fire and you will get burnt, Rhea."

Rhea bowed her head. She knew exactly what type of punishment her dear, loving sister could wield. "Honestly, Mir I do not know. I didn't steal the Stone of Fal from you...I found it lying on the grass when I stepped through the veil and ended up stuck on Earth. I still don't know why I couldn't force my blood to reopen the veil to Tir Nan Og. I am in the dark like you. And, like you I seem to be a pawn in this game."

"Oh, there you are wrong. I am not the pawn. I am the queen. And I have just declared check-mate. You hear that noise, Rhea? That is the sound of Facia's defeat. I will let the Decies destroy that precious rock with all of her loyal subjects. It's about time I took control of her wayward spirit. And make no mistake Rhea, I will find the Tuatha who dared take Tir Nan Og's sacred stone...don't you worry your little head about that.

Rhea gasped. "You wouldn't destroy Facia's subjects."

"Already done. She won't be able to stop them until it is too late for her and her precious subjects. You would do well to heed me. I am not someone to be trifled with. When I come for Tara, and I will come, do not step in my way. I will train Tara in all the Tuatha Dé Danann ways and from her I will learn every single druid trick. Then I will have the power I rightly deserve in this realm and on Earth. My choice of words was clear. Tara is mine. If you interfere I will destroy all your precious daughters in a heartbeat."

Queen Mir's voice rose an octave, a testimony to how angry she was.

Rhea walked past her sister, trying to feign indifference. "I would never step in your way. You are Queen of Tir Nan Og, but beware. The power you seek could very well be your downfall. I had my reasons for seeing Cael leave but it is not like you think. I did not think you would ever banish one of your own, especially your personal champion for eternity. I never thought you could be so cold and cruel. And especially not to Cael."

"There you are wrong. I did what was best for Tir Nan Og. He dared to defy me. He dared to come between me and that cursed race. And now it would seem that you too dare to defy," said Queen Mir, walking around Rhea, cornering her into the tight confines of the lush feast garden.

Rhea held her place. "Remember sister, who it is that helped to place you as queen. I may be Rhea of Naldolcoh but I am not without my own powers. My subjects are yours but their first loyalty is to me."

Queen Mir let loose a shrill, calculating laugh. "Why, my dear little sister...are you by chance developing some backbone, finally after all these centuries?"

Rhea didn't respond to Mir's taunt. "Be careful, Mir. I will not let you use the knowledge that Tara possesses at will. If Tara willingly wants to learn the Tuatha Dé Danann ways then so be it, but the druid knowledge will take time even for her to understand. Let the choice be hers."

"I am sorry Rhea, but you don't understand me at all. The choice wasn't hers the minute she was conceived and you knew that. That is why you spent your last dying Earth breath trying to keep her from me. She may be your daughter of blood, but by that same token bloodline, she is mine. She will serve me, make no mistake about it. I will grant you some time with her and I will pretend that this conversation did not take place but that is all. I may have needed your help at one time to become queen, but trust me, I have secured that right through my deeds many times over. I serve my subjects and they will always serve their queen. Now be gone. This conversation is over."

Queen Mir gave a gentle nod of her head and Rhea found herself back in Naldolcoh. Rhea sighed wearily. So much for sisterly love and understanding.

THE BESPELLED JEWELED dagger gifted to him earlier by Queen Mir was true in its mark. Still as cocksure as ever, Stater wasn't hard to find. He was using his druid magick to fly toward Queen Mir's Pleasure Palace—a place the old king knew by heart.

Cael intercepted him at the crystal pond. He threw the dagger with all the force he could muster straight into Stater's back. Two can play at the coward's game.

Stater halted as the dagger pierced through his black leather jacket and back, penetrating deeply through to his chest. For one moment he laughed thinking he'd been hit with a mere mortal weapon. Then pain and recognition scrunched his features.

"Belatucadros will only listen to me. You can't kill me." Stater pleaded for his life as he fell to his knees.

Cael wanted him to fall flat on his face and then rip him apart. "The King of the Decies answers to no one and you are an idiot for believing otherwise. On the other hand, you will answer to me and I promise it will be painful."

Cael forced the stallion to a halt and jumped down to where Stater knelt. He gripped the jeweled dagger and ripped it out of Stater's back only to plunge it straight into his neck, slicing his jugular open with one swift movement.

"You are wrong, Cael. King Belatucadros does answer to me. Even now I could summon him back inside Mir's treasure chest," gurgled Stater, using his own hand to staunch the flow of blood from his throat.

The name, Belatucadros, registered slightly in Cael's mind. Dismissing it, Cael laughed as he bared his teeth. "Actually, Stater you were right. Today is your day. Your day to die!" Then without any fanfare Cael plunged his Tuatha dagger deep into Stater's forehead, directly between his steely blue eyes. A gurgled sound of surprise rose up as Stater's eyes grew wide with disbelief. Blood rushed out of the critical wound, and Cael realized he'd had enough. Kicking the former King of Malyadoom to his chest, so that he finally lay face down in the dirt, Cael grabbed the Ogham script and walked away, knowing Stater would bleed painfully slowly to his own demise.

A dark part of him ached for vengeance for what had happened to Tara. He'd gained only a smidgen of satisfaction from killing Stater. Cael needed more. He needed to sweat with blood, or die himself. He realized then that a part of him had loved her. And like most things in his life, that knowledge only brought him more pain.

Task one completed he went in search of the King of the Decies, hoping he'd put up more resistance. Cael decided to follow his nose. All the Decies smelled like Sulphur but the king also reeked of rotten eggs. Talk about leaving a trail.

Jumping back on to the fastest steed bred in Queen Mir's stables, Cael said, "Find the King of the Decies for me, A'vatra."

Within seconds A'vatra led Cael to where King Belatucadros stood, slicing down innocent Tuatha as he made a bee-line for Queen Mir's personal chambers. A part of Cael wondered if the king knew where he was going, but he dismissed that quickly. No Decies would be touching his queen today, not while he was in charge.

"Looking for someone?" asked Cael, forcing A'vatra to halt. The majestic steed pranced and snorted as a dozen Decies circled around him. "What, you don't want to fight me on your own, King Belatucadros?" taunted Cael.

King Belatucadros leapt high, landing directly into the prancing path of A'vatra. He eyed the horse as he beckoned Cael forward. Cael took that as his cue.

"Be gone, A'vatra. Safe flight." Cael commanded the horse into the air so he could escape the Decies' clutches. Judging by the huff and snort of the beast he wasn't pleased, but Cael knew the steed would follow his command.

"So, I finally get to fight Queen Mir's Champion. It is an honor," squeaked King Belatucadros, standing to his full eight-foot height to give Cael a mocking bow.

"You know you could really use a bath. You stink," said Cael, withdrawing his long sword.

The King of the Decies took a step toward Cael. "I see Queen Mir still picks her Champion for his beauty and not their skill."

Cael held his ground, not acknowledging King Belatucadros' words. A war of words was not what he had come looking for. A war of the sword better suited his mood. Chanting the ancient druid spell in his head, he willed the sword to turn to gold a second before he raised it. He brought it down hard as he ran, jumped and somersaulted over the king to cleanly slice off his right clawed hand. Like with Stater, the king simply laughed. However, Belatucadros quickly swallowed his crackly chuckle, realizing Cael hadn't been a fool.

"What did you do?" His voice was grating and harsh as he struggled to breathe.

"Queen Mir would like a word with you, so you get to live a little longer," said Cael. "But you won't be needing this." With no hesitation on his part, Cael looped off the king's second clawed hand. Stupid he wasn't. Cael knew he was forced to bring King Belatucadros to Queen Mir, but there was no way he was about to cart the king anywhere when he still had his deadly claws intact. A shrill whistle brought A'vatra to his side quicker than he could blink.

"I take it you didn't go far." Cael patted the steed, who shook his long black mane in response.

"I can give you the antidote to save your brother," gurgled King Belatucadros.

That stilled Cael. "How did you know?"

A knowing light lit up the king's strange violet flecked eyes. "When one of you turns I feel it like a vibration. Your brother did not turn. But he will. There is only one cure. Release me and I will cure him."

Cael chuckled. "Yeah, I was born yesterday. Wait, I was born long before you were. Forget it."

King Belatucadros bowed his head slightly. "Boy, I was born before you were a thought. Don't forget that. Your brother dies or becomes one of us. It's that simple. No amount of Tuatha or druid magick will work." His taunting words had begun to slur as the gold from Cael's sword slowly worked to release the poison throughout his system.

Those words gave Cael pause. There seemed to be a lot of things King Belatucadros knew about him.

"She won't save him," said the king.

A'vatra snorted, bringing Cael's attention back to the task at hand. "Shut the fuck up. You're so ugly it's hurting my eyes to even look at you. You're coming with me."

"Fine, suit yourself," said the king, far too smugly for Cael's liking.

Cael tied the king's arms behind his body, casting a spell on the snug rope to ensure he didn't try anything. Then he jumped onto A'vatra's back and yanked on the rope forcing the King of the Decies to walk, or be hauled on his belly to Queen Mir.

"This would be better if you would let me use my wings," said King Belatucadros.

"Yes, but then I wouldn't get the pleasure of this." Cael yanked on the rope, jerking the king to his knees as he attempted not to tumble onto his face.

"Nice," replied King Belatucadros, moving from his spiny knees to his legs.

"Anything to please." Cael gave another hard yank, not caring if he had to drag the king all the way on his ass to Queen Mir. Actually, a part of him hoped to do just that.

Cael didn't believe that King Belatucadros was going to stop fighting. Mercy wasn't something he was known for.

Watchful and slightly wary, Queen Mir emerged from her Pleasure Palace. She had changed into a coal-black gown that sparkled with a design reminding Cael of the silver dusting of stars. She wore her gold leafed crown on her head, letting the King of the Decies know exactly who he was dealing with—the Queen of the Tuatha Dé Danann.

"She won't save him," said the king walking past Cael, who still sat on A'vatra.

Cael didn't say anything. He didn't want to hear it. Instead he gave one final hard yank on the rope, this time forcing the creature onto his ass. A hiss that Cael took as a growl of displeasure resonated throughout the palace.

"As promised my queen, the King of the Decies, oh wait, soon to be the deceased King of the Decies," said Cael, dismounting to pull on the rope, again. This time the king was having none of that. He scrambled to his spiny legs faster than Cael could blink.

Queen Mir moved forward to stand within arm's reach of the King of the Decies. "For once you have pleased me, Cael. Leave us."

"I will not leave you alone with this vile creature, my queen."

"What, Cael, you have fear that I cannot tame one like him? You worry unnecessarily, but it pleases me," she answered. "But leave. Now!"

Cael bowed formally. He handed the rope to Queen Mir and nodded. "Where is Tara's body?" he asked, desperately needing to know.

"Ask Rhea after you finish destroying those vile creatures that dared to invade my realm," said Queen Mir, her eyes never leaving King Belatucadros.

"Yes, Cael leave us. Some secrets are best shared amongst family, aren't they Mir," taunted the king.

Cael wanted to ask what the king meant but Queen Mir had obviously had enough of him. She spelled him away before he could object.

Chapter Twenty-Four

"EVENTUALLY THEY WILL find out, Mir," said King Belatucadros, sarcastically. The words came out thick, as the gold poison cascaded through his system. He knew he was fighting a losing battle but he would not go down without a good and if need be dirty fight. Green blood from his sliced-off hands dripped steadily onto Mir's pristine marble floor. He gleaned intense satisfaction from that.

Queen Mir yanked on the rope with more force than Cael had been able to muster, causing him to almost stumble. She moved a fraction of a foot closer. "No, they won't."

"Then kill me. Get it over with. Isn't that what you've wanted all these long centuries? Do it!" he snarled.

"That would be too easy on you, Belatucadros. Do you think this is easy for me?"

"Let me remind you, Queen...I am not the one who started this war. You did. This is your curse, not mine."

Queen Mir took another step closer. They were almost equal in height, but not quite. "They say, 'Hell hath no fury like a woman scorned.'"

"Fuck you, if you're looking for an apology, Mir."

"Such scorn, Belatucadros...and here I thought I might release you from a part of your spell." She taunted and teased him, watching his face for a reaction.

King Belatucadros moved forward, ignoring the pain in his arms from the rope cutting into his mangled wrists. "Kill me, Mir. Just kill me!"

In a flash pain felled him to his knees and instantly he realized what she had done.

"Bitch!" he spat; the words clear in their ferociousness.

"I had to see if you were still as breathtakingly beautiful as ever and I must say you are." Queen Mir's voice drawled as she eyed the tall Reikas, known at one time as the powerful God of War, in more languages than she cared to think about.

"Is this your idea of hope, Mir? To taunt and tease me with the curse you leveled at me and my kind?" King Belatucadros slowly stood to his majestic height, his deep thundering voice reminding her that he was once again a force to reckon with.

I am a Reikas King, an ancient God, no matter what that bitch did to me. The rumble of his voice almost brought tears to his eyes. But that emotion died with the curse Mir had leveled at him and his race, eons ago. Emotion was not a good thing to have. The only thought Belatucadros lived for was revenge on his wife.

Mastering speech with a beak had been her idea of a sadistic joke. He tried not to dwell on what she had done to him. He knew her changing him back to his original self was for her glory only. A ploy to remind him she still had power over him—all because he was married to the bitch.

At one time Belatucadros had admired Mir's strength but he had quickly come to realize the rot that sat deep within her essence. Her quest for power was paramount. And that had been her sole thirst from the moment he'd agreed to the binding ceremony the Fates had decreed upon them. The secret binding ceremony, he reminded himself, ashamed he'd given into Mir's idea to keep their marriage hidden.

Belatucadros had tried to love Mir, and maybe a small part of him had for a time, but that had quickly waned. She had only come to his bed seeking what he knew she wanted—a child. And that he had never given her. He wasn't the God of War and the God of Strategy for eons before the curse to be so easily tricked by a Tuatha Dé Danann. I am a Reikas King. I will rule again. I will free my race.

I will get my revenge. Belatucadros shook his frame to unfurl his majestic wings that longed to fly through the air.

The gold poison still sat within his system but by Queen Mir's unusual actions it no longer had the devastating effect on him. In fact, she had even healed his hands. Hands. He tried hard not to pay attention to them but it had been so long that he had almost forgotten the light intricate feel of fingers and thumbs, so accustomed had he become to the heavy, cumbersome claws she, the royal bitch, had cursed him with.

Belatucadros' skin was still the color of cinnamon and his straight long jet-black hair fell in disarray over his face, obscuring the proud, classical facial features she knew by heart. Queen Mir didn't need to see everything. His features were burned for eternity in her mind. She knew his pale violet eyes would still be as startlingly mesmerizing as ever, his nose was slightly too large for his face and his square, cleft chin still attested to his proud heritage. He still wore the bronze Celtic bands his mistress had made for him. The same mistress who was safely enslaved in a second treasure chest Mir kept close at all times.

"Call off your minions, Belatucadros. Let us talk like two civilized beings," said Queen Mir, turning her back to the Reikas King.

"No, Mir, I won't. I've had enough of your lies and deceit. Your parlor games don't even register. My descendants are strong. Stronger than they have been and I will not call them off."

Belatucadros' voice was husky, reminding her of warm passion and hot sunlight, a warrior's voice to the core. It conjured up memories she did not want to dwell on.

"Do you want me so soon to turn you back into the creature I made you?" taunted Mir, regally sitting on the edge of the settee. "Or would you like to see your son that I have so carefully groomed?

While we speak, Dyloulious is slicing down your minions, oops, I mean your descendants, his family," said Mir, letting her voice carry.

"Dyloulious is dead. Your taunts are worthless. Save them. What do you really want, Mir?"

Belatucadros stretched and flexed his muscles, but it was his majestic wings that dared to almost undo her. Queen Mir hated the fact that he was so beautiful. If she had a heart she knew it would be beating extra fast. But her heart had been ripped out a long time ago by the very Reikas King who still stood proud in his warrior-like form in front of her. It is good to remember his deceit and lies.

Queen Mir held out her hand and a bubble appeared, providing them with a view of the battle taking place. A battle that was strategically taking place in Culinibra, the rock—that barren lifeless corner of Tir Nan Og, which she had granted to Facia.

"Do you see your son, Belatucadros, or has it been so long that you no longer remember your bastard?"

Belatucadros took two long strides forward. His rippling muscular warrior legs, almost as thick as the rasta tree in width, bunched and stretched as he walked butt naked closer to the bubble.

"More games, Mir. What a sad case you've become." He turned his violet eyes on her.

"Games are all you left me, Belatucadros. You know I speak the truth. But that is not why I have released you from your spell. I want what you were supposed to give me," she said, rising to stand, so that her black gown billowed around her shapely form.

"And that is?"

"Don't play coy with me, King. You well know what I was meant to have but instead you gave that to your mistress."

King Belatucadros smiled, understanding accenting the deep purple hues in his surreal, violet eyes. "So, it is as I thought. You know, placing me in your little treasure chest did not keep me ignorant of your behavior. I had thought I'd hear of an heir born but it is as the Fates decreed. Your race...that precious royal blood line of yours is dying, is that not so, Mir?"

Queen Mir's anger rushed to the surface. She glided toward King Belatucadros so that she towered over him, her long white hair streaming wildly behind her.

"Give me what I want, Belatucadros!"

The King of the Decies laughed evilly. "No, Mir. I will not. I didn't then and I won't today or any day in the future."

"Then he dies." Mir pointed her finger at the tall, towering form of Dyloulious, who was leading the charge with Cael to stop Belatucadros' minions.

"He died a long time ago to me. The curse had that strange effect on my heart. Kill Dyloulious, I don't care. But Mir." King Belatucadros moved closer to her towering form. "I will not ever give you what you crave and need. You are the last of your line and I know it. And I have made it my mission to see you fail."

"I will get what I want, Belatucadros. I always do."

The King of the Decies smirked. "If you say so."

She stood a breath away from him. So close but so far apart. "You will die then."

He threw back his head and laughed. The sound was surprisingly refreshing. "No, I won't. You can't kill me and we both know it."

He reached out and gently traced her full lips with a finger. "There had been a time when I would have gladly lain with you, but that is long past, Mir. I may be your husband that the cursed Fates decreed but I will not now, or ever, let my cock slide within your dried-up folds. As I see it you have two choices. Kill me and you know you destroy an entire race of people, my people, and...well, we know what will happen then." He smiled. "Or you could let me go."

"Actually, there is a third option. I will the curse to continue," she snapped, stepping back and with a wave of her hand, the King of the Decies was once again transformed into the evil nightmarish creature Mir had conjured up in her mind. "And just because I feel like it, your son, that precious bastard of yours, dies today."

Before King Belatucadros could even so much as flinch, he found himself once again caged within Mir's treasure chest. The darkness claimed his screams of retribution and revenge as sweetly as Mir's taunting laugh filled the Pleasure Palace.

Chapter Twenty-Five

CAEL FOUND HIMSELF smack dab in the middle of the battle. However, he wasn't alone. He smiled. Facia's army of protectorates were well trained and now with Stater dead the spell he had evoked was also destroyed. A clean kill was a kill and no longer were the Decies resurrected.

"It is good to see you again, Cael," said Facia, materializing next to him. Unlike Queen Mir, Facia of Culinibra preferred to fight alongside her subjects. She was highly unique that way. While her face had that classical beauty similar to Queen Mir, there the resemblance ended. Facia had coal black hair with a long white streak that added to her majestic appearance. She was the only Tuatha he knew whose hair color was naturally black. She was taller than Cael by a good foot and always wore a black leather warrior outfit that outlined her slender frame and full figure. But she wasn't to be trifled with.

"That bitch of a sister of mine let them come to my corner on purpose. And for what? Hope she enjoys chatting to that bastard Belatucadros. When I get done here, she and I are going to have a chit-chat that won't soon be forgotten. To your left!" Facia yelled at the man next to Cael.

"Who is that one? He's not one of my subjects." She mowed down two Decies without breaking her rhythm, a long sword precisely held in each of her slender hands.

Cael noted where she was looking while he used his sword to kill four Decies, two that had come at him on foot and two more that attempted to claw him from the air. "That is Dyloulious."

Facia stopped and stood. "Watch my back, Cael. I need to get closer to him."

Her words surprised Cael. What did she want with Dyloulious? And why did she want it now?

"I sense your questions, but there is no time to explain things. I must get to Dyloulious now, or he will die and I cannot allow Mir that victory. Not today! Not after what she has unleashed on my subjects!" Facia's tone was full of hurt and anger—a toxic combination for any Tuatha, but add in one who had been in disfavor with Mir since he could remember and Cael knew that meant things didn't bode well.

"I want an explanation," said Cael. He backed up to provide cover for Facia as she advanced, slowly cutting her way through the throng of Decies that seemed to be converging solely on Dyloulious.

Cael admitted Dyloulious was a good warrior, but even he could see the Tuatha was outnumbered. It appeared as if the Decies were trying to kill him, but that didn't make sense. Why would they zone in on him? He's no one. A simple warrior who had been chosen and nurtured into one of Queen Mir's royal guards.

Facia yelled again, forcing Dyloulious' attention to his right. For a brief moment Dyloulious looked at the two of them advancing. Cael caught an unguarded moment when the warrior realized he'd been marked for death but then like any good warrior he returned his focus to the battle. And Cael knew it was a fight to his death.

"Asyla me'thaut duide 'lo'lasya'rulm."

Every hair on Cael's body tingled in swift awareness of the complicated Tuatha Dé Danann spell Facia was evoking. Even he couldn't figure it out.

Facia sped toward Dyloulious and then in a blur of speed she had him safely embraced in her arms. A heartbeat later, they were both gone.

The shrill screams of the Decies filled the air. It was their screams of defeat. He heard Queen Mir's voice reach out on the breeze and

Cael realized then the King of the Decies must finally be dead, or he had been recaptured. I'm hoping for death.

With the battle finally over, Cael took the time to look around. There were more Tuatha dead than he had ever seen. The ground was littered with them and all plant life around the fallen was also dead. It was a stark reminder to Cael of the link he and his fellow Tuatha had with Tir Nan Og.

Facia rematerialized by his side, atop her own steed who was so blindingly white it hurt Cael's eyes to look at it.

"That bitch did this to my subjects."

A'vatra pranced closer as each beast sized up the other. "Where did you take Dyloulious?" Cael dismounted so he could help with the wounded.

"To a place my sister least expects," said Facia, also jumping from her horse to help her subjects. "This carnage is her way of letting me know I am in disfavor. That is the type of queen Tir Nan Og has now, Cael. A queen that doesn't blink even when she exiles her lover and her Champion to Hell on Earth. But she won't be queen forever. That I am making sure of."

Immediately Cael wanted to rush to his queen's side to assert she didn't have a hand in this destruction, but he was no longer so sure.

"Facia, you're implying Queen Mir orchestrated this. She didn't." Cael ran a weary hand through his hair as he took in the bloodied scene. Over a thousand Tuatha lay mortally wounded or dead.

"Don't be so sure of that, Cael. I am not feeling merciful today. I think I should let her get her just reward. If all my subjects infected by the cursed Decies turn then she will know true justice. Sadly, I am not so cold-hearted. Listen and learn, Cael."

Facia moved away from him and Cael watched. She braced her feet apart, held her arms outstretched wide above her head and chanted again using the royal Tuatha Dé Danann to evoke a spell that shocked him.

Facia was willing a part of herself to each and every Tuatha mortally wounded so that they would not turn into a Decies. She was bequeathing them a part of her essence, her life-force.

She truly loves her subjects. Cael watched as hundreds rose to their feet, bowed to their leader to acknowledge her selfless act and then vanished back to their lives. Still though, at least a hundred Tuatha remained dead. Even Facia's power was not as strong as Queen Mir's and she could not resurrect the dead.

He rushed to Facia's side when she collapsed to her knees. She shrugged off his support.

"Would your blessed queen do that, Cael? That is the question you should ask yourself. Would your queen save your brother if she could? Or would she damn him like she had you?"

"How did you know about him?" asked Cael.

Facia ignored his question and continued on. "Your loyalty to Queen Mir has always been misguided. Remember what she did to you. Remember all the times you died and were painfully resurrected. All because you dared to object. Freedom, Cael. My subjects have freedom, can you say the same? I must leave now and take care of my dead in the ways of my ancestors. Be gone, Cael and remember my words are the truth you seek."

Cael wanted to assist and ask more questions but he found himself willed away to Rhea's corner before he could stand. Once he was on his feet again the shock that greeted him stole his very breath away.

"Cael!" screamed Tara. She flung herself into his arms like a lost lover. Her honeysuckle scent slammed hard into him, causing Cael to reel with need and lust. Out of the corner of his eyes he saw Rhea's four daughters.

Hugging Tara closer, needing to feel the warmth of her life, he asked, "How is this possible?"

Tara wore a dark blue off-the-shoulder gown that outlined her small, lush figure. He could have wept, loving that she was miraculously alive. He'd find out the how later. Right now, he simply needed to feel her, breathe her scent in and hold her tight.

"There is much to explain and we don't have a lot of time. First though, Cael, I will ask for your forgiveness."

Rhea's calming voice struck a warning chord deep within him. He watched as she regally advanced toward him. Still cradling Tara in his arms, he was astonished when Rhea knelt and then proceeded to lower her forehead to the marble floor, so that her body was completely prone, head bowed submissively to him.

"Get up, Rhea, that is unnecessary," he said, gruffly, as Tara disentangled herself from his embrace.

Rhea rose to stand beside him. Cael took a step back, not liking the fact he had to look up to meet her eyes.

"Daughters of mine, please give us some privacy," said Rhea, ushering both Cael and Tara over to a colorful sofa, while her other daughters immediately vanished.

Cael indicated he preferred to stand.

"I will cut to the chase, as they say." Rhea's tone was dead serious. "I am the one who had you exiled. I was the Tuatha who went in disguise to the Druids. We felt Queen Mir was too powerful and corrupt in her ways. We needed to weaken her and we thought by separating you from her she would see the error of her ways. But Cael, I did not know Queen Mir would exile you for eternity. That was not the plan. For that I beg your forgiveness."

Cael eyed Rhea and Tara, sharply, his eyes narrowed. "There is something else you are not telling me. And who is this 'we'?"

Tara shuffled toward Rhea, offering her comfort and support. Cael watched her place a comforting hand on her grandmother.

"Rhea is really my mother and Xavier is my true father," said Tara, her amber eyes scorching his heart. Eyes he thought he'd never see again. Her warm, sultry voice washed through his system and then he fought the gasp that threatened to tear from him as her words finally registered.

Rhea squeezed Tara's hand reassuringly. "Facia and I are the 'we', Cael."

"Fuck!" he snarled. This has been all an elaborate game. Bloody bitches. He willed himself away so fast, a gush of wind whipped through Rhea's palace.

Chapter Twenty-Six

TARA GULPED. "WHAT just happened?"

"You've had a sample of Cael's famous anger. Give him time, he will come back. He'd better," said Rhea.

Tara noted her mother was pacing. It was a classic reminder of what she had done on Earth when worried.

Tara stood up, slightly shaky and feeling once again out of her element. The air of Tir Nan Og overwhelmed her senses. Fresh flowering plants, lush yellow grass and a variety of small animals lived close to Rhea's dwelling, which was more like a small palace than anything else. Tara squeezed her eyes shut, trying in vain to block the flow of vast energy that surrounded every living thing in her homeland. She also realized her emotions were running amuck. She desperately wanted Cael back and ached to be held in his loving embrace. Those few minutes when he'd held her, that was how it felt—loving, true and right. He was her balance in this strange world she now had to call home.

"The Sh'lam'alah still runs strong within you. You must learn to fight it, Tara," said Rhea, running a calm soothing hand up and down Tara's arm.

Wearily, plunking herself back down onto the sofa, Tara muttered, "Is that what this is called? No one told me. It's some type of disease I've got, right?"

A plate of her favorite chocolate chip cookies materialized beside her. Without thought she took two and devoured them.

"I see I need to explain a few Tuatha Dé Danann things to you as a mother, my child. The Sh'lam'alah is the period in our lives when we become sexually mature. It is a natural process for us and we relish it. Unlike humans, you will find that we are very sexual creatures.

Usually when you undergo this maturity a Tuatha will service you for a month until your body naturally acclimatizes to the lust for sex."

"Wait a sec. Are you telling me Cael was simply servicing me?" squeaked Tara.

"At first he was, yes, but I'm sure he's developed feelings for you." Rhea placed a cookie in her mouth, her eyes darting elsewhere.

Tara eyed her mother. Could my world get any more confused? As much as Tara longed to believe what her mother said was true, she was no longer sure. Servicing me. That's what he was doing. He was simply doing his job.

"What happens if he stops servicing me?" asked Tara.

It took a moment before her mother answered. "Actually, in your case I'm not one hundred per cent sure."

Tara narrowed her eyes at her mother. "Give me the worst-case scenario, please," she added as an afterthought.

"If he stops servicing you, as you so delicately put it, well...you could die!"

Tara laughed. "Didn't I just do that?" she stated once she got herself under control. She watched as her mother, who she couldn't pry her eyes from, rose from the sofa to stroll toward the flaming open hearth, which sat in the center of the room. Multi-colored polished beach stones encompassed the fire, providing the slight rustic touch the warm interior needed. Her new home was so much more refined than what she had grown up in that for one bizarre moment she wished for her small, cozy house with its faded sofa, worn floors and all.

Rhea turned to face her and crossed her arms over her chest. "Tara, you must understand the Sh'lam'alah is not to be taken lightly. If you were to undergo this on Tir Nan Og then you would go through the Va'lasta ceremony with the Tuatha of your choice. I don't want to go into technical detail but the Va'lasta ceremony ties you both physically and mentally with the Tuatha of your choice—"

"Kind of like a marriage," said Tara, interrupting.

Rhea shook her head. "Not at all like human marriage vows which only require two signatures on a piece of paper. The Va'lasta ceremony is when you choose your mate to teach you the pleasures of the flesh. The pleasures of the flesh for a Tuatha help to increase the powers inherent in our makeup. It is a very sacred experience and something cherished. I am sorry that you were unable to pick a Tuatha of your choice."

Tara wasn't so sure she was. The physical bond she felt, the ache to be near Cael felt like it was right and more than physically enough. But obviously it isn't enough for him. He was simply servicing me because I didn't give him any choice.

"You could, I suppose pick the Tuatha of your choice now," said Rhea.

Tara went bug-eyed. "What?"

"Technically, you haven't undergone the Va'lasta ceremony."

"But I crave Cael." Tara's face blushed red with that admission. The realization that for the past few minutes she had been talking about sex with her mother mortified her.

"If one of your aunts and I were to help you we might be able to lessen that craving. Plus, what a great way to get Cael's attention." Rhea moved from the hearth to look out the large round window that overlooked a small flower garden.

The quick movement of wings drew Tara's eyes. In disbelief she watched as a hummingbird darted from flower to flower.

"Those are the only creatures Mir allows into our realm from Earth. Since I've returned I've developed a fondness for them," said Rhea, with a soft sigh.

Tara took the time to really look at her mother. How would she feel if she'd been trapped, unable to return home and left in a strange world with no one? She realized then how brave her mother had been. Rhea reached out to hug her.

"I feel like I have to keep touching you to make sure you're real," she said.

Tara smiled. "I know exactly how you feel."

"Think about what I offer. Maybe the Va'lasta ceremony is what you need. It will, though, have to be soon." Rhea pulled Tara even closer.

"Mothers and daughters are not supposed to talk about sex," said Tara. Her face was hot with embarrassment.

Rhea laughed. "What a load of crock. You told me all about your first kiss."

"That was different."

"How so?" asked Rhea.

"I thought you were my grandmother, that's how so," said Tara, her voice a mere whisper.

Releasing her hold on her, Rhea turned Tara so that they stood almost eye to eye. Tara was not nearly as tall as Rhea, so she had to look up at her mother. "You are Tuatha to the core, Tara. I am your mother. I am still the same person you confided in on Earth. I still love you with all my breath and would willingly lay my life down for you," said Rhea.

"Wow, that had a really melodramatic ring to it."

"I'm sure you will quickly discover that things on Tir Nan Og are often very dramatic."

"What's involved with the Va'lasta?" Tara desperately wanted to change the subject.

"I will call my subjects together. All the eligible male Tuatha will come forward to showcase their prowess. Trust me, it's a sight to behold. If you agree, I will start the preparations."

Tara chewed on her bottom lip. Worry, fear of making Cael even angrier and something else gnawed at her, but she chose to ignore her doubts. "Do it."

Rhea pulled her back into another motherly hug. "You are doing the right thing. I will make it so. The ceremony will take place tonight at Queen Mir's Pavilion."

"I thought it was going to take place here." Unease crept into Tara's thoughts.

"Sadly no...Queen Mir always likes to oversee these rituals. But only the male Tuatha from my corner get to compete for your affection. And before you ask, the answer is no. Cael isn't from Naldolcoh."

"But that means he can't compete." Tara moved out of her mother's embrace.

"No, he can if he's willing to petition Queen Mir."

There was a dangerous twinkle in Rhea's eye Tara didn't miss. She was beginning to get the feeling that she was being set up. "Are you sure he will do that?"

"Let us hope," said Rhea. "Now come, we must tell your sisters. They will be so pleased and very excited, and I believe they will want to have a say in what you wear."

"What's wrong with what I'm wearing now? I like this dress," said Tara.

"Trust me, you will like what they choose for you. Now, come. We don't have much time to spread the word.

CAEL WAS PISSED. ROYALLY drunk like he hadn't been for years. He had hoped that by getting blitzed he'd forget everything that had happened to him within the past few days...make that thousand years. Sadly, that wasn't the case. For the love of all that was sacred he couldn't seem to forget the silky feel of Tara's skin, her honeysuckle scent, her wild chestnut-red hair or her courage and independent nature. And he wanted to forget. He wanted it with a vengeance that stirred restlessly within him.

Xavier sauntered into the decadent small building that catered to the whims of Tuatha looking for a bit more adventure than was usually acceptable. Even on Tir Nan Og there were places like on Earth where one could overindulge without feeling guilty or fearing recognition. Well, that was usually the case, thought Cael.

"Any more of what you're drinking?" asked Xavier. "Two," he ordered to a tall, scantily clad female Tuatha who had sauntered up to him, eyeing him with interest. Cael ignored the fact that Xavier sat beside him.

When Xavier's drinks were delivered, Cael watched through slightly cloudy eyes as his old friend, his old nemesis downed them in two gulps. The hot steaming ozzat drinks weren't like anything the Druid Priest had ever tasted on Earth. Cael knew that without a doubt. He prayed the powerful substance would get absorbed quickly into Xavier's bloodstream and cause him to pass out. Xavier coughed a blue streak as the hot bitter liquor burned down his throat. It was a feeling Cael knew well.

"Two more," bellowed Xavier.

Okay, so he's intent on getting pissed but why? Not that I care...Father...He's Tara's real father. The knowledge of that slammed into him. A red angry haze clouded his eyes. He didn't like it at all.

"Are we having fun yet?" Xavier's sarcasm was ice cold. He slid a drink toward Cael as he played with the rim of an empty tumbler.

Cael growled a low warning. Hell, if he wants to help me get loaded so be it. Cael simply took the drink and chucked it back. His eyes stung from the full force of the powerful ozzat. His anger over what had happened to him was still too fresh and he smarted with how he had been played.

"Well, I'm having fun. I thoroughly enjoy being played like some fucking pawn. Now, don't get me wrong...this place..." Xavier wildly threw out his arm to indicate he meant Tir Nan Og. "Is more than I could ever have imagined and to be the first Druid allowed here, well it's an honor. You do know that Queen Mir is playing us both for fools."

Xavier didn't bother to hush his voice. Cael knew that was a dangerous statement to make, even here. Hell, if Xavier wants to prepare his own funeral so be it. Cael downed his third drink in quick succession.

"Shut the fuck up!" Cael growled, wondering if he could stand and make his way over to another seat.

"So, Cael what's it like bedding my daughter?" Xavier's voice dripped with venom.

Cael was across the small stone table so fast Xavier didn't have time to react. Xavier simply laughed. Cael tightened his neck hold that would have easily put the fear of death in anyone else.

Pissed. He's royally drunk. Wish I were. He let go of his hold and slunk back into his seat. Why bother? No one within the small place had batted an eyelash. Cael knew if he wanted to kill Xavier this was the best place for the crime. However, he no longer cared.

Xavier tilted his seat back to observe Cael. "I'm not drunk yet if that's what you're thinking, Cael. We Druids, pride ourselves on our famous drinking ability, plus this is tame in comparison to the stuff I grew up on. Trust me."

"I don't trust anyone anymore," declared Cael, toying with his three empty glasses.

"Ahh, the mighty one talks," said Xavier, tauntingly.

Cael looked him straight in the eye. Maybe killing him is a good idea after all. Before Cael could say anything else, Dyloulious entered and without a welcoming word joined them, dragging a chair over and ordering a round of drinks for them all.

"Bitch!" he spat.

That raised Cael's eyes.

"Are we referring to the one and only grand dame bitch?" asked Xavier, making room for Dyloulious.

"Who the fuck are you?" asked Dyloulious, his large frame forcing Xavier to scoot closer to Cael.

"You don't want to know," answered Cael. "So, what's Mir done to you? Last time I looked you were neatly whisked away by her loving sister, Facia."

"Oh, yeah, I was born yesterday too, Cael. Go fuck yourself. Did you not notice all those Decies coming straight for me...not for you...me. Wonder why? Well, I know. I know everything now." Dyloulious loudly gulped two drinks in quick succession.

"My bet is Queen Mir is behind that," answered Xavier.

Dyloulious placed his elbows on the black scratched stone table and leaned forward to eye the Druid next to him.

Xavier leaned back in his chair so he could flex his arm muscles, showcasing the ancient tattoos that stood out sharply when he wanted them to. "I'm Xavier, the Druid Priest that saved his ass..." Xavier nodded in Cael's direction. "too many times to recount."

Dyloulious cackled a laugh. "You're the queen's latest sex toy. What exactly do you know?"

"More than you are ready for," stated Xavier, his voice calm and clear.

Cael shuffled to his feet, wanting to be drunk and alone, and weary with all the political speculation.

"So, you heard the latest, Cael?" asked Dyloulious, leaning back in his chair as it balanced on two wobbly legs.

Cael didn't even bite. He simply started walking away.

"Yeah, seems your halfling has decided to undergo the Va'lasta ceremony," said Dyloulious. "I'm going to petition that bitch to let me compete. And with what I know now she wouldn't dare refuse me."

Cael turned back toward the table. "You're lying. She's already undergoing the Sh'lam'alah."

"Seems her aunts are helping her with that particular itch and she's asked for the Va'lasta ceremony tonight."

Xavier pulled out Cael's chair, motioning for him to have a seat.

As if. Cael bared his teeth, all but looking for a good fight now.

"Ahh, the games your queen likes to play with you all. So, Cael do tell, what's this ceremony all about? After all, it does concern my daughter," stated Xavier.

"Your daughter! Well, that's just precious. So, you're Xavier, the infamous Druid who got Cael exiled. Man, with the friends you pick Cael, you don't need enemies. Sadly, wait, you do have enemies. Well, old man, I plan to compete for Tara's affection and fuck her well...so well, she won't even remember you, Cael."

Dyloulious brushed make-believe lint off his arm. He was on his ass in a blink, the chair kicked out from under him by Cael's feet.

"Good one," cheered Xavier, already standing, getting ready to fight as Dyloulious bounded to his feet and advanced toward Cael.

Leveling a punch straight to Dyloulious' face Cael snarled, "Stay out of this, Druid."

"So, you'd rather fight me, Cael then fight for your halfling, go figure. Okay, I'm game. This just fits the mood I've been in all day." Dyloulious wiped the blood from his nose as he followed with a swing of his own straight into Cael's gut.

Shit, that hurt. Cael wished he hadn't had that last drink, as his stomach churned.

"The question you both need to ask is why? Why is Queen Mir allowing Tara to undergo the Va'lasta ceremony now? What is she really after?" asked Xavier, sitting back down to watch the show.

"Man, does he always talk in riddles like that?" asked Dyloulious.

Cael circled Dyloulious, not about to let the Tuatha he had helped train get the better of him. "Yup." Cael brought his foot up to slam hard into Dyloulious' gut. One for one. He was slightly pleased to see Dyloulious recover quickly. Damn, I am a good teacher.

"Really, what is this pissing contest going to accomplish? Sure, Cael you can beat him to a pulp, but is that going to change the outcome? Nope. Tara's my daughter...need I remind you two. And she is going to pick a Tuatha tonight. Be a man for once Cael and fight for her," said Xavier.

Cael slammed his fist hard straight into Dyloulious' face again. "Like I said, Druid, stay the fuck out of this."

Dyloulious moved a fraction of an inch just in time to neatly avoid the blow. "Druid, shut up. Unless Cael grovels at Queen Mir's feet he won't even be allowed to compete."

Cael crouched low, intent on putting an end to the façade. He jumped, using the back end of a chair for leverage and sailed across Dyloulious to grab him in a choke hold. The trained warrior struggled and then ceased, the pressure from Cael's arms causing him to go to sleep. As Dyloulious' large body started to slump to the floor, Cael eased him down gently, ensuring his former student didn't land on his face.

"So, you can be humane," said Xavier, as he ordered two more drinks. "Here, this will help." Xavier offered an ozzat to Cael as the server rushed over, calmly walking over Dyloulious' prone body.

Cael took the drink, downed it and then turned and marched toward the door.

"If you love her, Cael, do the right thing. Fight for her. This is your chance. You couldn't save Anya or Ashling but you can save Tara from Queen Mir. Be a man for once!" shouted Xavier.

At the door, Cael turned and looked at the Druid Priest he had proudly named friend, at one time in his life. "There you are wrong, Xa'alter," said Cael, using his real name on purpose. "I'm not a man, nor was I ever. I am a Tuatha Dé Danann to the core. Don't forget that!" He gave an old-fashioned mocking bow to the priest and then willed himself away.

"Fine, suit yourself. It's your loss. Queen Mir will finally get what she really wants."

Those were the haunting words that echoed in Cael's mind many hours later, as he fought like the devil to dismiss the Druid's parting words and to clear the effects of the powerful drinks he had consumed in record time.

Chapter Twenty-Seven

TARA COULDN'T BELIEVE she had been talked into this. While a part of her was curious, an equally large aspect of her was totally terrified. Would Cael show up? That was the question she kept asking herself. However, the harsh reality of what she was undergoing was a constant reminder he had felt indebted to her and was only doing the honorable thing—servicing her. Sex for him meant nothing. It was simply a means to keep her sane, she kept telling herself.

"He will come," said Myla with a conviction Tara did not feel.

Tara turned slowly. If she moved fast the extremely low-cut gown revealed more of her chest than she was accustomed to. "Have you heard if he has petitioned Queen Mir?"

Myla shook her head.

Autumn motioned that it was her turn to beautify Tara, indicating she should sit down so she could apply the face paint that was custom.

"Cael never has played by the rules...come, have a seat. Stop your worrying. He will surprise you. He certainly has always surprised all of us." Autumn picked up a blue feather and used the sharp tip of it to apply a gold outline to Tara's eyes.

Fifteen minutes later Tara was finally beautified to her sisters' specifications. She stood and stared at herself in the long mirror one of them had conjured. She didn't recognize the woman staring back at her.

Where is the country girl? Where is the woman who hails from Cape Breton? Surely this is not the same person. Tara gulped at her transformation.

The sheer blood red dress draped to the floor, and one would have thought it concealed her figure. Instead it did the complete opposite. It was almost slit in half. A gold clasp held it in place just below her breasts. When she moved, her legs and the accompanying matching red panties peeked out to tantalize the viewer. Panties she had absolutely insisted upon. She had been told by her sisters they had gone au naturelle. Well, not her, she had vowed, almost wishing she could wear granny panties. Anything to conceal more of her bottom.

On her head was a crown of deep purple and black flowers picked from Rhea's own scented garden. The same flowers were clasped throughout her hair, providing her with a very fey-like appearance. The flowers gave off a rich aroma that calmed and slightly aroused her. Or maybe that sexual itch is back. For a moment she wondered if the flowers had aphrodisiac qualities. Shaking her head, she felt the weight of her hair slide across her shoulders. The gold outline combined with the dark black eye shadow gave her eyes an exotic appearance. Intricate gold and black bands were painted on the top portions of her arms and thighs. She wore diamond anklets but was barefoot and extremely thankful for that. Her hands and feet were heavily hennaed with gold designs. The sheer, almost weightless material of her robe swished around her body, teasing her already sensitive skin.

"It is time, Tara," announced Rhea, materializing next to her in an equally elaborate dress, face paint and crown. "My daughter, you make me proud. You are a true Tuatha, don't let anyone ever tell you different. And daughters," said Rhea, moving to embrace each of her four offspring. "You have outdone yourselves. Now, Tara before you go, I have one last thing to give you. Come here, child."

Tara moved closer. Rhea gently clasped her right arm and fingered the silver bracelet Tara still wore. In truth, Tara had forgotten she still had it on. "Do you want me to take it off?"

"No, child, I want you to do me a favor. Actually, you could say I am making amends. Be still for a moment." Rhea placed her hand over the bracelet as she chanted Tuatha Dé Danann words that were echoed by her sisters.

"Don't concern yourself with the meaning of the words, Tara, but I do ask if you go back to Earth, give the bracelet to Devon."

"If?" asked Tara, slightly dazed.

"If it's within my power I will make it so. Don't forget to give it to Devon. The power of the words will be revealed to him. Now enough. We must not make my sister wait," said Rhea, once again embracing Tara in a tight motherly hug.

A gentle rush of wind-swept Tara away. When she next opened her eyes, she couldn't believe the sight that greeted her. Rhea had informed her before that the ceremony would take place at the Queen's Pavilion. Three times as large as Queen Mir's Pleasure Palace, the large open-styled gold-toned Greek columns towered up to the eerie pink-purple sky, providing it with that exotic element. Arena styled seats made up the backdrop and it looked to Tara like a thousand Tuatha were sitting on plush colorful pillows. It was now the middle of the night. Bright stars shone overhead, illuminating the place. There was a large open area with black granite flooring where the competition would take place.

"I'm not sure I can go through with this," mumbled Tara, scanning the crowd for any sight of Cael.

"He is not here, child, but don't give up. Faith." Rhea ushered her forward so that they could both approach Queen Mir together, as a united front.

Sitting next to the queen was Xavier, the Druid Priest, her real father. She still hadn't mustered the courage to confront him. Thankfully he seemed even less inclined to acknowledge her. Tara watched as he pursed his lips tightly together to stare out at the assembly, all but ignoring her.

"Tara, come. I am pleased to see you embrace a part of your heritage." Queen Mir beckoned Tara to sit on the high red-backed chair to her right-hand side.

Tara gave a slight bow to acknowledge Queen Mir, her aunt. Rhea sat to the queen's left side, adjacent to Xavier.

"This will be a show like none other. Our male Tuatha are known for their sexual prowess and I am delighted you will get the pleasure of choosing your own mate this time," said Queen Mir, tilting her head slightly to look at Tara.

Tara felt there was something left unsaid by Queen Mir's words but wisely bit her tongue.

"Rhea, my dear sister, I have a special treat for you tonight. We are going to perform the ceremony following the ancient ways."

"What? You cannot, Mir. We long ago gave up that barbaric ritual," admonished Rhea, rigid in her seat.

"Times can change, Rhea. You should understand that."

"Even you, Mir, are not without your mercy. That practice was discarded for a reason," Rhea snapped, her eyes lighting up to challenge her sister.

"Don't talk to me of mercy, sister. You are overstepping your bounds. Now," said Queen Mir standing, her long white gown flowing around her, "let us begin the challenge."

Tara shuffled forward in her chair. "I thought this was a ceremony. Not a challenge." Tara voiced her concern to her mother.

Xavier chose to answer. "It is the queen's indulgence, daughter."

He sneered the words, immediately making Tara feel uncomfortable. *Guess he's not pleased about being my father. Well, that makes two of us.* "Thank you for that lovely clarification, father," snapped Tara, her temper rising to the occasion.

A dozen well-muscled Tuatha entered the open arena. Each was startlingly pale but their auras were breathtakingly beautiful. Their hair varied from their natural ivory color to dyed jet black. Some had it long and tied back, while others used a gold clasp or leather thong. One stood out. Unlike the rest he hadn't bothered to tie his long jet-black hair back. Tara knew just by looking at him that his hair color was natural. It fell straight to his waist and two small tight braids knotted with a red bead framed his face. Even this far removed from the assembly his strange violet-purple eyes gleamed at her, almost like they were assessing her. He cocked a smile toward her, which didn't quite reach his eyes. There was a ruggedness to him that separated him from the others. Tara wished her body didn't like him so much.

Rhea leaned over toward Queen Mir. "Why is Dyloulious competing?"

"Come, Rhea, even you know the rules. He petitioned me and I granted him his request," said Queen Mir.

Tara noted the queen stared hard at the tall, towering Tuatha, almost like she was watching him for her own reasons. Rhea nodded and sat back in her seat, her spine ramrod straight.

Each male wore a white toga and brandished two deadly looking weapons in each hand. Tara gulped. *This is not what I had envisioned at all.* She caught the spicy male scents of the Tuatha and fought not to squirm as sexual longing streamed through her body. *Get a grip, Tara. You don't want just anyone. You want Cael and he bloody well had better show up.*

"Looking for anyone in particular?" Queen Mir's amber eyes were calculating.

"No." Tara calmly sat back in her chair. Her hands were already fisted so tightly that her nails bit into her palms.

A shrill whistle announced the start.

The males moved so fast that at first it was extremely hard for Tara to discern what was taking place. However, within a few minutes her eyesight had adjusted and it wasn't a pretty sight. A few times Tara heard her mother muffle a gasp. She chanced a brief glance at Xavier and he didn't look pleased.

Within a few minutes over half the Tuatha were either lying immobile on the granite floor or they were being escorted off. Four stood glaring at each other, their weapons dripping with fresh blood.

"Those Tuatha that are down they aren't really dead, are they?" asked Tara.

"Sadly, they are." Xavier turned his eyes toward her, giving Tara a pointed look.

"But they are Tuatha. They can't die."

"Don't be so naive child, of course we can die if the right tool is used. A Tuatha mortally wounded by a weapon created with Tuatha power can die," clarified Queen Mir. "Now is not the time for you to be squeamish. For the four champions who remain, you must determine who they each get to fight."

Tara visibly shuddered. "What?"

"Mir, why are you doing this?" asked Rhea.

Queen Mir rose to her full height, indicating with a wave of her hand that Tara should follow suit. "Ask yourself that very question, sister. Now come Tara, I will gladly help you as your aunt, not your queen. Come."

Tara didn't have a choice. She followed Queen Mir down the steps into the open arena. The musky spicy exotic scents of the male Tuatha were even stronger and harder to ignore. Tara clutched her robe tightly to her, almost bunching the material in her sweaty hands.

Using the Tuatha Dé Danann language, Queen Mir addressed each of the four males remaining, offering encouragement and praise. Tara was pleased she could at least make out much of what was being said. Three beamed at her, while the one they called Dyloulious ignored her friendly smile. He didn't pay any notice to Tara. Instead he eyed Queen Mir with pure hatred.

"Dyloulious will compete first with Kalsta, and the winner of that will compete against the other two," indicated Queen Mir.

"That doesn't sound fair," mumbled Tara.

"Did you say something, Tara?" asked Queen Mir.

Tara notched up her chin. *This is supposed to be about me picking. I am getting a sick feeling this is all about her.* "I said, that doesn't sound fair."

Queen Mir looked at her and didn't say anything for such a long time Tara wondered if she had overstepped her bounds. Then the queen casually moved to drape an arm across Tara's shoulders, giving her a small squeeze.

"I said I would give you my guidance as your aunt. Trust me. This is fair. Come, let us resume our seats."

Tara forced herself not to shake off Queen Mir's arm on her. She nodded and let Mir lead her back to their royal seats. Once seated, Mir indicated the challenge should resume. This time Tara had to blink a couple of times so she could actually see what was taking place. She had thought their movements were fast before but now they were a blur of color as Dyloulious circled his opponent with ease and grace. Again, Tara tried hard to ignore his presence. There was something unsettling about him.

When his opponent neatly sliced his arm, he simply chuckled. It wasn't a pleasant sound. Then without any fanfare Dyloulious plunged his dagger straight into the Tuatha's chest. Before the Tuatha fell to the floor, the other two advanced, each intent on the kill.

Kill! I can't believe this is happening. And all because of me. All because I said I wanted to choose. Looks like I only get the winner...and that will be the one still standing with wounds and blood and all. Ooh, that is so charming. Remind me never again to agree to anything here, ranted Tara to herself.

The other two sadly didn't have a chance. Dyloulious seemed crazed from the kill. His surreal violet eyes looked murderous. He cleanly felled the other two Tuatha within minutes. He stepped over the bodies and advanced toward where they sat.

Queen Mir indicated Tara should stand.

"Not what you were expecting, Mir," said Dyloulious, his eyes all but boring deadly holes at Mir.

"Patience is a virtue, Dyloulious. Remember that. Tara is yours. Enjoy." Mir ushered Tara to come and stand next to the tall, angry Tuatha.

"You must claim him with a kiss," declared Queen Mir to Tara.

That was the last thing Tara wanted, but like with everything else on Tir Nan Og she didn't have a choice. She shuffled forward so that she stood at arm's length from the warrior, noting his clenched jaw.

She took a small step to advance but two powerful arms pulled her away in a blur of speed that left her dizzy and reeling.

"Cael! You will answer to me for that act. And you will be punished," echoed Queen Mir's voice.

Cael. He came. He finally came. Damned Fairy! I am going to kill him. Tara smiled with relief and then instantly chastised herself. She hated how her heart and body once again soared with that heady feeling whenever he was near. It was all an illusion. He didn't have any feelings for her. She was just a job to him. Tara gulped at her tears. She needed to attempt to steal her emotions and her body from Cael's dangerous Tuatha effects.

Chapter Twenty-Eight

"PUT ME DOWN," DEMANDED Tara, attempting to squirm out of Cael's tight hold.

He dropped her on her bottom in a meadow of white fluffy flowers that looked like a cross between dandelions and buttercups. The flowers gave off a rich vanilla aroma.

"Enjoy picking your sex partner?" Cael glared at her.

Tara slowly stood up, patted down her gown and made sure it was still tightly clasped in place before she turned away from him to walk in the opposite direction.

"Just where do you think you're going?" he asked, moving so he could walk beside her.

Tara didn't respond. She continued to plod on, trying hard to ignore the steady drum beat of her heart because of his mere presence. He grabbed her shoulders and twirled her around so that they were face-to-face.

"What is it exactly you want with me?" She choked on a sob as emotions rushed to the surface. This man, no this Tuatha, she reminded herself, was what she wanted, needed and longed for. But pride kept her from saying those words. Pride and fear that he only "serviced" her because he had to.

"I don't know." Cael released his hold of her as his silver eyes assessed her. "I do know that I really like that dress." A cocky grin spread across his face, disarming in its intensity.

Tara cast her eyes to her toes that peeked out of the long gown. "Thank you."

He brought her a fraction of an inch closer to his large frame. "Did you really pick Dyloulious?"

It was the soft-spoken manner of the question that caught Tara's attention. *Could it be that the Damned Fairy does have real feelings for me?* She shook her head. "I didn't pick him. He was just the last one standing. I didn't want to pick anyone."

His hand reached out to stroke her hair. "Then why did you agree to the ceremony?"

Tara closed her eyes as the tender administrations of his hand sailed into her body, leaving her breathless. She fought to compose herself. "You are such a moron!"

Cael laughed. "And here I was hoping you were going to say you are such a Damned Fairy."

She shoved him away from her. He continued to chuckle. It only served to make her angry all over again. *Jerk! He's a big fat, no-good, jerk!*

"Dyloulious was only getting at you to get to me."

"Why does everything seem to be about you, Cael. Why?"

"Actually, as it turns out everything is more about Queen Mir." Cael walked over to a fallen log and sat on it.

Tara didn't want to follow suit but she did anyway. She had no idea where she was and it looked like the flowery, vanilla-scented meadow went on for miles.

"Cael, I just want to go home. I don't like it here. Sure, it's beautiful but this isn't me." Tara used her hands to bunch more of her gown around her legs to sit on the log next to him. "I'm more the jeans gal." She gave a small nervous giggle.

"That you are," he sighed. "I know. I'd like to be able to say I can take you home, to Earth, but I can't. I am Queen Mir's Champion and she won't let me go."

"Why? Can't she just appoint another Champion?"

Cael turned toward her on the log, his hand reaching out to stroke her thigh through the sheer gown. Goose bumps formed along Tara's skin.

"I need to make love to you, Tara."

"Need! Not want? That's why I agreed to the ceremony, Cael. You've done your duty to me. I know you didn't have a choice—"

"Do you think I don't want to make love to you, Tara? Is that what all that was about? You think I simply gave in because I had to? Come, Tara, think closely. You've heard the stories about the Damned Fairy...does that fit my profile? I, Cael, the damned Tuatha Dé Danann gave in because a human made me. As if."

He cupped her chin with his large hand and gently stroked her cheek with his thumb. "I care, Tara, more than I want to. You need to understand that I don't want these emotions. They can be dangerous for a Tuatha. We pride ourselves on being in control of our emotions, but that is not the case."

Tara stopped his hand. "You don't want to care about me, Cael. Why? Is it because of what happened in the past with your wife and child?"

Cael froze. "How do you know about that?"

Tara knew she had a sheepish look on her face. "I overheard Mir talking to Rhea about that."

"You don't understand, Tara." Abruptly Cael stood, clearly agitated. "Queen Mir knew what was going on and even when I begged her with all my might she didn't bat an eye to help my wife and child. You have no idea what Hell I went through watching my daughter all but disintegrate before my eyes. If I could have died in her place I would have. As it was a part of me died that day."

Tara stood up. "Mir said the child wasn't really yours."

A hurtful chuckle flew from Cael. "I'm sure that's how she thought of it. I will admit the child wasn't mine by birth but in my heart she was. I helped birth her. I helped feed and nurture her and she loved me, not because of what I was but because I was a father to her."

Tara moved and wrapped her arms around his waist. "I know, Cael. I won't admit that I know the Hell you've been put through, but let me take away a part of that pain. Let me love you." There, she had said it.

He turned in her arms and looked down at her. "How can you? Do you have any idea what I've done throughout the ages? If you knew, you'd never say those words to me."

"You forget, Cael...Rhea knew. I grew up on stories about you. And yes, I will admit they were nightmarish but if I was in your place, if the things that happened to you were to befall me, I'm not sure I wouldn't have done what you did."

"Tara, I killed thousands of humans at will without a thought. That's honesty. Do you know why I left Ireland for good? I left because the day I buried my daughter, Ashling..." he choked.

Tara didn't say anything. Silently she willed him on.

He moved out of their embrace and shuffled further away from her to turn, providing her with a view of his rigid back. He wore a black cotton shirt that hugged his muscular frame. "I slit the throats of more than a hundred people that day. Strangers, fathers, mothers and children. Then when I was done I left Ireland, turned my anger to any war that would take me and didn't flinch when I mowed down hundreds more. During the first war I lost count of the people I killed. I never bothered with guns; I used my hands. My hands, Tara. These hands." He swiftly faced her, holding his hands out to her.

Tara noted the silent tears well in his eyes. She knew it was only his pride that kept him from falling to pieces. Maybe it was what he needed to stay sane.

He stood up and took a step back from the log. At arm's length from her, he stood rigid before her. She stood up and made a move toward him. He stilled her with his hands.

"These hands are a weapon. But ooh, it gets better. After the first war I managed to get to Africa. I was nicknamed the white ghost, invincible with a thirst for blood. Then let's not forget the second war and boy were my talents in demand. Of course, no one wondered why I never aged. Humans only care about one thing when they are looking to win a war. And that's death. Death to their enemy."

The pain reflected in Cael's eyes broke a dam Tara hadn't realized she had created. She moved closer to him, bridging the gap between them in small measured steps. "Cael, I have heard all the stories about you, but let me tell you what I know. I know you are a Tuatha with honor. I know you were damned by your queen because you do care about humanity. I know you suffered unjustly because of your loyalty to Queen Mir. I'm not going to forgive you for the actions of your past but that doesn't change my feelings. I love you."

"No, you don't. You're simply going through the Sh'lam'alah," he stated flatly.

"Oh really, then why was I praying with all my might that you'd come and save me from that barbaric ritual Queen Mir made me witness?"

"Wishful thinking."

"Actually, that's not true and you know it. You did save me from it. I no more wanted to kiss Dyloulious than a warty toad."

A grin spread across Cael's harsh features. "Warty toad? Dyloulious wouldn't like that comparison one bit."

"Cael, shut up and kiss me," demanded Tara, deciding it was time to be forthright. Her body was on fire with that need to have him deep within her. It was a steady throb she felt all over, reminding her how much she craved the unique rhythm they made when their bodies joined in symphony together.

"Oh, I'm going to kiss you all right, but not here. Hold my hand Tara. It's about time I took you in a real bed for once." A genuine grin spread across Cael's face, disarming in its intensity and breathtakingly serene in its honesty.

Cael couldn't believe this was happening to him. But Hell, he wasn't about to look a gift horse in the mouth. Tara was his gift and he wasn't about to share or play fair when it came to her. Her admission of her true feelings for him had cost her. He knew it went again her nature to admit her heart-felt affection but he couldn't be happier if he tried. Well, that wasn't entirely true. Freedom and happiness would be his once he was no longer bound to Queen Mir.

"Cael, is this your bedroom?" asked Tara, her amber eyes wide, as she took in the lush colorful bedroom.

"No, but I have use of it when I need it," he admitted. "Not bad," he muttered to himself, as he took in the dark navy-blue bedspread and roaring fire in the small fireplace. Trust Facia to add all the details, and she owes me a big explanation. Four small S'alabah trees with their unique hues of red and orange added that exotic element that was so much a part of Facia's corner of Culinibra. The trees smelled like a mixture of apples and pears but their scent was more subtle for Tuatha. The scent of the S'alabah, known as the passion tree, was an aphrodisiac to his kind. Nice touch, Facia.

"So where were we? Ahh, now I remember. I was about to taste every inch of your delectable skin," said Cael, using his body to edge Tara toward the large bed.

Her feminine giggle warmed his heart and his groin. "If you want to leave I will let you."

Tara looked up at him. Her eyes flashed coyly at him. "Still wanting to get rid of me, Cael?"

"No. Never." No longer able to keep his hands off her body, Cael grasped her and pulled her small frame tight to his. He inhaled her unique honeysuckle scent, loving that it spiraled through his system. The scent of the flowers in her hair thrummed into his being. Then Cael moved his head so he could claim those lush lips of hers. She didn't protest. Instead she twinned her hands around his back to cascade her fingers through his hair. Her touch was almost hesitant.

He deepened the kiss, demanding her acceptance, tilting her head for better access. His tongue licked her small feisty teeth and he felt her shiver. She grasped his hair tightly, allowing the Tuatha part of her essence to come out and play. When he knew they both needed air he slowly released her lips, but not before departing them with a quick nip.

Breathlessly she asked, "Will Queen Mir come here to punish you?"

Still framing her head with his large hands, he looked deep into her eyes. "She won't come here unless she wants a confrontation with her sister, Facia."

Tara took a small step back. "Facia. Isn't she another aunt of mine?

Cael's body wasn't interested in talking. He willed both their clothing away and loved how she gasped, slightly embarrassed by her state of undress.

"We're going to continue this conversation at another time," stated Cael, once again taking the initiative. He moved her body back until her legs buckled and she fell onto the bed. He loomed over her, parted her legs and then slowly lowered his already painfully aroused cock until it nudged at her slick opening. She braced herself on her elbows and grinned a saucy look at him.

"Cael, you either put your cock inside me now, or I'm going to explode," she said, squirming her bottom around as she tried to nudge him in on her own.

He knew exactly how she felt. Passion edged him on and while there was a part of him that wanted to prolong their intimacy, he vowed to himself he would later, once he'd quenched the fire within him.

He plunged his cock deep within her core, loving how her legs instinctively wrapped around his hips, urging him on. Then he began to pound into her, slowly at first until her groans and moans spurred him on. He picked up his strokes, moving with Tuatha speed now that he knew her body could take all of him.

"Liking this, my wee feyling?" said Cael, taking a moment to almost withdraw so he could tease her.

She moved her legs from around his hips and brought them up over his shoulders. Now it was his turn to groan. "I like this better," said Tara. Her tone was breathy with need and want.

He cupped her ass and fought hard to keep his climax at bay. Thankfully he felt her body go taut as she peaked, screaming out his name, causing him to come instantly. A moment later he gently lowered her legs, rolled to his side and scooted them up the bed so they could climb under the fluffy bedspread.

Tara sighed into his shoulder as he hugged her body close, loving the slick feel of her sweat after their rigorous bout of sex.

A few minutes later a knock on the door interrupted his pleasant thoughts.

"What's that?" asked Tara, her eyes glazed with a sleepy, well-satisfied sexy look.

"That is someone with a death wish." Cael climbed back out of the already toasty warm bed. Out of habit he flashed his warrior clothing on, which instantly brought him fully awake.

"I am only being polite for my niece's sake. You have three seconds to open the door, Cael!" shouted the voice on the other side of the door, which made him see red.

He opened the door slowly, giving Tara time to compose herself.

Facia forced the rest of the door open without fanfare. The warrior-princess strode in, dressed quite literally to kill. Garbed in her traditional black tight chain-mail outfit, along with a leather cloak, she had two daggers strapped to her thighs, death-stars clustered on her forearms and two long swords, one in each hand.

"Another war so soon? Or, are you planning on getting Mir to exile me again, so soon?" snapped Cael.

"I did not tell you that because I had my reasons. I told you everything that you needed to know but not so you could get what you wanted, Cael. I am always on your side."

"Yeah, right. Like you were on my side for the past thousand years, Facia?" Cael snarled the words out as he moved back to the bed. He was pleased to see Tara had mastered enough of her powers to clothe herself. He flashed a devilish smile at her, enjoying her questioning look. It's about time she understood what's going on here. And how we've all been pawns for Queen Mir and her sisters.

"I will not explain my actions to you, Cael." Facia walked over to the bed, held out her hand and waited for Tara to rise from the bed. "It is with genuine pleasure I finally meet you Tara. You are a true gift as my sister, Mir, thinks."

Tara nodded but wisely remained silent.

Patience was never Facia's virtue. "So, Cael, Dyloulious tells me that he has full rights to Tara. Explain."

Cael crossed his arms over his chest. "Technically yes and no."

Facia gave him a look he hated. "Fine, yes, he won that barbaric ritual Queen Mir made them undergo, but Tara claimed me first."

"Did you?" asked Facia, turning her startlingly bright silver eyes to Tara.

Cael watched as Tara clenched and unclenched her small fists. She was unnerved and he knew a thousand questions were swarming through her mind at lightning speed.

"Yes, Cael is who I want." Tara spoke directly to him.

Like with most Tuatha, she seemed to sense the inherent power Facia wielded, her aura a vibrating shade of purple and orange, as the warrior-princess struggled with her own dark powers.

"It is not a question of want, Tara. Did you pick Cael?"

Cael watched her try to formulate the correct answer.

"Well, technically I didn't really pick him, but I do want him."

A blush quickly settled on her face, causing him to grin.

"I got this disease on Earth and Cael was the only Tuatha there to help me."

"Disease." Facia laughed.

The sound startled Cael. He was born under the rule of Facia and trained first by her as a warrior only to later be forced to serve Queen Mir. In all that time he had never heard Facia laugh. *I didn't know she had it in her.* While not cruel like Queen Mir, Facia demanded perfection. Training with her meant putting your life quite literally in her hands. Practice was deadly and only the best were welcomed as her personal escorts. He had longed to be one, but Queen Mir demanded her annual tithe—Facia's best warrior. Hence, Cael had been forced to leave Facia and swear a blood oath to Queen Mir.

When Facia's laughter died down, she gazed at Tara. Cael was pleased to see that Tara didn't flinch under her scrutiny. Even the best warriors had faltered under her penetrating assessment.

"Please tell me you have come to understand that it is not at all like a disease."

"Well, okay, wrong word to use, but what does it matter? I only agreed to that ceremony because my mother, Rhea, said I would get to pick. However, Queen Mir decided to revert the ceremony back to what it used to be...I guess in ancient times. But I would have picked Cael anyway."

Facia's silver eyes grew dark grey and heavy. "Would you have? Cael, did you compete?"

Cael shook his head, no longer liking the way this conversation was going.

"Did you ask Queen Mir if you could compete?" Facia fingered one of her long swords, absent-mindedly.

"Fuck, Facia, you know I didn't. I was here with you."

Tara's gaze turned to him. "Not like that," continued Cael. "I was here trying to get some answers."

Facia proceeded to pace back and forth. "So, you're telling me you didn't know that Tara had agreed to undergo the ceremony?"

Cael gulped. Shit! "No."

"No what, Cael?" asked Tara this time.

"I knew you had agreed to the ceremony, Tara, but no, I did not petition Queen Mir to let me compete."

The only thing Cael heard was Tara's in-drawn gasp. It felt as hard as steel as it penetrated his heart.

The silence in the room stretched by, until Cael couldn't stand it any longer. "I'm sorry. There, are you happy?" he said to both silent women.

Cael watched as Tara fought hard to keep her emotions under control. The hot gust of wind that was starting to sweep through the bedroom was testimony to how hard she fought that battle. He watched as Facia reached out and gently squeezed her hand.

"Control that tempter of yours, niece."

"You knew I had agreed yet you couldn't or wouldn't ask Queen Mir to compete. Why, Cael? Ohh wait, let me guess. Because you don't really care about me. All you care about is yourself. Maybe you are really the Damned Fairy after all." Tara all but shouted the words at him.

Chapter Twenty-Nine

"IT WOULDN'T HAVE MATTERED, Tara. My sister, Queen Mir, would not have let Cael compete under any circumstances," said Facia.

That statement had both of them silent.

"However, saying that, I now have to figure out a way to make all this right. Queen Mir wants Dyloulious killed and I won't allow that. She is not going to win this war."

"War?" squeaked Tara.

"Yes, my child. War! Queen Mir would like everyone to believe that all is peaceful and serene on Tir Nan Og when nothing could be further from the truth. I will try to make this brief but you need to understand the balance of power." Facia let go of Tara's hand so she could continue pacing.

Cael watched as she unsheathed a long, silver sword. His eyes narrowed suspiciously. *What are those markings on her sword? They almost look druid but not quite.*

Facia held the sword up to her face, letting the blunt part of it almost touch her nose. Reverently she placed the tip on the floor and used her powers to keep it suspended.

"Niece, it's time you learned another Tuatha legend," said Facia, walking around the sword. "See that symbol there?" She pointed to a circular symbol that had a closed eye etched in it.

"A long time ago Tir Nan Og was ruled by my mother, Queen Ulah. This is her symbol." Facia indicated the circular etching. "My mother had six daughters who were named princesses. Equal in rank, equal in power. When mother died it was assumed I would be crowned queen."

Tara gasped. Cael decided to sit down on the bed, knowing first-hand how complicated this was.

"I am the eldest daughter so by tradition it should have gone to me." Facia's long dainty finger pointed to a triangular etching that had a flower embossed in it. "Yes, that is the symbol mother had etched for my coronation. However, at that time I was very sick, almost dead. It was believed I would not live long so my other sisters decided that in the best interests of Tir Nan Og, Mir, next in line should get the throne. To do so, they had to will a part of their essence to her, thus tying them to her for as long as she lives. Nice little twist of her plot." Facia's face was hard with anger.

Cael watched as she strode around the balanced sword. Then she picked it up, turned it and re-sheathed it into a gold-embossed cover which materialized. They watched as she fingered the ornate floral designs on the sheath. She stopped pacing to stand directly in front of them.

"However, I did not die, much to Mir's annoyance. When Mir became queen, she willed that each sister must live in a corner of Tir Nan Og. Only in that corner is their power supreme. When Mir willed me away to here, the so-called dead-zone I named Culinibra, my powers grew and I got stronger. Today I know what she really did. Mir wanted to be queen so badly she slowly poisoned me over the years. Don't look so shocked, Tara. That is the least of her crimes."

"Why would she want you dead? You're her sister," said Tara.

Cael was pleased Tara wasn't forcing him to leave her side of the bed. "She wanted to be queen above all else," answered Cael.

"Trust me, there is no sisterly love in Mir's heart. But I have finally learned the real truth that she has fought so hard all these centuries to conceal. To remain queen, she needs to have a child." Facia crossed her arms over her chest, while a feral smile crept to her face.

"Okay, here I don't follow," admitted Tara.

"Before Mir was crowned queen she was secretly married to King Belatucadros. You know him today as the King of the Decies," said Facia, flatly.

Tara jumped up off the bed. "Now that doesn't make any sense."

"Actually, it does, Tara. Queen Mir is not known for her forgiving nature. When she found out that her husband, King Belatucadros was in love with a mortal Earth woman, a human at that, she cursed him. King Belatucadros and his entire race became cursed that day. They became the Decies. The very species that is our enemy. There is some ironic justice in that," stated Facia.

"When King Belatucadros realized who it was who cursed him he used the curse to wreak havoc on her beloved Tir Nan Og. It took us years before we were able to capture the king, which forced his own subjects to follow him into exile."

"But didn't King Belatucadros live on Tir Nan Og?" asked Tara.

Cael stood next to her. "No, Tara, King Belatucadros never lived on Tir Nan Og. He and his subjects are not Tuatha. They are an ancient sky-god race called the Reikas. They lived in a world above our own, called Vil'ash'moy. They were rulers of the sky, and when he was cursed she turned him into a bird-like creature."

"Did you know this before, Cael?" asked Tara.

"No, I only found out when I came here to ask Facia some other questions. Finally, all the pieces make sense."

"Good for you. To me they don't," quipped Tara, now the only one pacing.

"All you need to understand is that King Belatucadros is the only male Queen Mir can have a child with. He has refused her again. King Belatucadros' own bastard child is Dyloulious, and yes, I just informed him today of his true heritage when it became obvious Mir was out to get him killed by his own race."

"That would be the reason for the murderous glare he sent her way," mumbled Tara.

"You need to understand Queen Mir plans to use you, Tara," said Facia.

"I won't let her." Cael flanked Tara's side. Thankfully she didn't flinch.

"I don't follow. How can she use me?" Tara faced Facia.

"You are part Druid and part Tuatha—a first. Your bloodline is pure and because she made your mother, my sister, Rhea submit to her, that call is in your blood. She will use your knowledge to force King Belatucadros to give her the child she needs to stay on as queen and she will do it at any cost. Her time is running out and she is desperate."

Tara stifled a crazed giggle. "It's not like I can make Belatucadros mate with Mir or anything like that."

"Actually, with your combined Druid and Tuatha powers you could," said Cael.

"I haven't the foggiest notion how to use my druid powers and I'm just sort of getting the hang of these Tuatha ones." Tara swept out her hand to indicate how she had wielded her own clothing.

"That doesn't matter. Queen Mir can invade your mind and take what she needs. And she will. Trust me on that score. We need to protect you, Tara. I thought I was doing that when I sent Dyloulious to you," said Facia, moving toward the fireplace.

"Wait a sec...you're saying you sent Dyloulious to compete!" barked Cael, clearly angry. "Why didn't you tell me?"

Facia turned and leveled him with a penetrating look. "I wasn't sure she mattered to you, Cael."

Facia unsheathed a small dagger, belted on her calf muscle. Like with most Tuatha weapons the hilt was beautifully ornate with green emeralds and red rubies.

"You, Cael are also bound to follow Queen Mir's command. The only thing that can protect Tara is if she goes to Earth and never sets foot on Tir Nan Og again. Rhea entrusted the Highlander Druids to keep you safe. Go to them. They will help you master your powers."

Facia spoke directly to Tara, who was clearly stunned by the turn of events. She had plopped back down on the bed.

"But Mir will come after me," said Tara, clearly agitated.

"That is where my plan comes into play. I am sending Dyloulious to protect you."

"Over my dead body, Facia" said Cael, unsheathing his own deadly looking dagger as he moved closer to Tara in a blur of speed that strangely had Facia smiling.

"Good to see your true feelings, Cael. I was beginning to doubt you had it in you."

Women and their words. No matter what world I'm in I will never understand their language. "What are you talking about?"

"No matter. It is your dead body I need."

Tara got up and moved a smidgen closer to Cael. "What?" she squeaked.

"You are getting your wish, Cael...after all these years, isn't that what you wanted?"

Cael didn't say anything for a solid minute. "Yes. I did want that at one time, but not now...not when—"

"Not when what?" asked Facia, toying with the deadly dagger in her hand.

"I will protect Tara," stated Cael, glaring daggers of his own at Facia.

"No, Cael, you will not. Not just yet, anyway. Mir will not let you go. However, she has agreed to let Dyloulious go."

Tara fingered the edge of her shirt. "Why would she let Dyloulious go and not Cael?"

"Because Dyloulious has threatened to expose her, right Facia? You and your sisters can shove all these fucking games right where the sun don't shine...heck, what am I thinking? The sun hasn't shone in Culinibra for two millennia."

In a blink, Facia had the jeweled dagger pushed against Cael's throat.

"You want me dead, Facia, then do it. Show your precious niece how unlike Queen Mir you really are," taunted Cael, standing rigidly straight, all but daring her on.

The tension in the air was almost tangible. Hot gusts of wind once again swept through the bedroom, causing the heavily draped curtains to billow up. The movement drew Tara's eyes.

"Yes, Tara, enjoy the view. This is the cursed dead-zone my sister exiled me to...isn't it sweet...so beautiful, just like the rest of Tir Nan Og."

Cael knew exactly what she saw. After all this was his birth place. A barren wasteland made up mostly of rock, with harsh cold winds complete with a dark, overcast sky for constant cover. There were no trees, only craggy outcrops of mountains and rocks. The sun never shone. Life was cold, dreary, dark and usually deadly. The shadow people that was the nickname of Facia's subjects. And at one time he had been one of them.

During his early years, Cael hadn't known that there was a luxurious, beautiful part of the world called Tir Nan Og. Only once he had pledged servitude to Queen Mir and was willed away by her, did he slowly begin to understand Mir's cruelty. He had asked himself growing up why food was scarce and it was only once he began his warrior training with Facia that he came to discover she used her powers to conjure the basic necessities for her subjects. Facia's power was immense, but even hers wasn't unlimited.

"I think I am beginning to see what is going on, Facia, and why you are willing to force your sister's hand?" said Cael, wishing to Hell she'd move the dagger from his neck.

Two silver eyes searched his face. It took her another few minutes before she removed her weapon and then she did something so unexpected, Cael wondered if he'd imagined it. Facia, the warrior-princess, bowed her head in a subservient manner to him.

"You were ever the smart pupil, Cael."

"Is it always like this?" asked Tara, moving to the window so she could look out for herself.

"Yes," replied Facia and Cael at the same time.

Cael sheathed his own weapon and moved toward the window. He needed to be close to Tara.

"My power is not unlimited like you guessed, Cael. And I will not have my subjects suffer any more for her crimes."

"You plan to free King Belatucadros," said Cael, stopping in mid-stride.

Tara turned toward Cael, her gaze darting to Facia.

"Yes," replied Facia. "The only way to force her hand is to break the curse. I plan to free Belatucadros myself."

"Mir will kill you," said Cael.

"She would like to think she has the power to do so, but we will see," replied Facia. "Come, it is time. Tara I will open the veil to Earth and send you on your way. Dyloulious will come."

On cue another harsh knock on the bedroom door interrupted the conversation. Facia willed the door open and in walked Dyloulious.

"What, running away from me before I claim my kiss?" said Dyloulious, striding toward Tara.

"Kiss her and you die, Dyloulious." Cael moved his body in front of Tara to stop Dyloulious.

"Enough, Cael. Time is not something I have. Tara, when you get to Earth go to your Druids. They will help you. Remember my words well."

Before anyone could say another word, Facia used her jeweled dagger to slice her hand. Two drops of red blood fell while she chanted the ancient Tuatha Dé Danann words. Within seconds a bubble of energy formed, showcasing Earth on the other side. "Now, my niece!"

Cael moved to stop her, but Facia's will was too strong. "Do not overstep your bounds, Cael. These plans took too long to put together. I will not let you get in the way of them. The safety of Tir Nan Og is at stake and if you dare to defy me, I will destroy you."

Cael desperately wanted to move but Facia's power held him in place, as it moved Tara toward the veil. In a blink she was through. He could have sworn she called out his name, but he was too angry to think a coherent thought as Dyloulious grinned wickedly at him the second before he too jumped through the veil. When the veil finally evaporated, he was released. He advanced toward Facia.

"Come now Cael, you are still needed."

Like a bloody fucking leashed dog. He wanted to rip out Facia's heart and tear it to shreds. As it was his body was rigidly taut, already posed for a battle.

"You, my dear Tuatha, have another more important mission to undertake and it will be to your liking. You are going to ask...no, beg, Queen Mir to grant you your final wish. That blessed wish you so desperately wanted on Earth. Get Mir to give you the Stone of Fal and let her think you've wished for death. Then you will get your Tara back."

Cael didn't trust himself to speak. If she thinks Mir is about to hand over that fucking stone to me now, she's insane.

"You underestimate your charms, and those of your friend."

"Friend?"

"Yes, that Druid Priest who exchanged his life for yours. He will aid you in your endeavor. The two of you will work to lure Mir into a state of sexual frenzy she has so desperately wanted all these years—"

"Wait a bloody second. If you think for one minute that I am about to fuck your sister ever again, you're mistaken."

"You will do as I say." Facia's silver eyes were intense. "Whether you fuck her, as you so elegantly put it, depends on you. All I want is her to be horny. I need her concentration on you two. Think you are up to that?" asked Facia, giving his body a thorough once over from head to toe.

Cael desperately wanted to tell her to go fuck herself, but he wisely remained silent. What choice do I have? "Fine. Have it your way."

"Wouldn't that be nice for a change," laughed Facia.

It was the second time in less than an hour Facia had laughed. It unnerved him more than he cared to think.

Chapter Thirty

THE STRONG GUST OF a north wind and the scent of pine trees greeted Tara when her feet landed on Earth. By the bright rays from the sun she judged it to be mid-day. She shielded her eyes with a hand and looked around. She wasn't too far from MacLeod's Tavern, recognizing the secondary road she had landed on, which was used by the locals as a shortcut.

Thank God I'm home. Her second thought was she had two things to do and quickly. She walked down the familiar gravel road, noting the contrast of Earth to Tir Nan Og. The plant life on Earth wasn't nearly as vibrant in its color and while she could see a faint yellow outline from the plants' auras it was nothing like the vibrating life force of the vegetation on Tir Nan Og. The sky was at least a light blue, something she was thankful for. Having a purple-pink sky had been slightly eerie to say the least, she thought.

"There you are!" cried Katie, running down the road with a small black suitcase in hand.

Tara stopped walking. "Where are you going?"

Katie advanced until she was a breath away from Tara. "Shh! I'm going to the mainland. And just where have you been for the past two months?" she huffed, thoroughly annoyed as she reached out to embrace Tara in a warm hug.

Two months! Tara blinked and kicked at the gravel with her sneaker, happy she could materialize her normal clothing. She could have sworn she had only been gone for a day or two. Two whole months, that seems impossible.

"Cat got your tongue, Tara-girl?" asked Katie.

Then her friend shrieked. "Oh my God! A hunk of a man just dropped out of the sky." Katie pointed to a cleared meadow.

Tara's heart sped up. Maybe it's Cael. Maybe he was able to convince Facia to let him go. Then the man approached and all hope vanished.

"Nice of you to wait for me, Tara." Dyloulious eyed her friend like she was candy. "And this beautiful creature is?"

"Katie," answered Katie for herself, striking out her hand for Dyloulious to shake while at the same time Tara answered, "No one."

The man had the gall to turn Katie's hand over and kiss her palm. Tara watched as Katie blushed prettily, a tactic she had mastered like an art.

"I am Dyloulious...your humble servant."

Tara rolled her eyes when Dyloulious actually uttered the word humble.

"Is that Greek or something?" asked Katie, playfully batting her eyes.

Dyloulious placed his hands on his hips, and stared hard at Katie. "Greek? Do I look Greek to you, my dear?"

Tara grabbed her friend by the arm and dragged her away from Dyloulious. A flirting Dyloulious, that's one I wasn't expecting. Over her shoulder she turned her head. "Go home, Dyloulious."

"I am here to protect you, Tara. Need I remind you?"

"I don't need protection. You're not wanted. Go home." Tara hustled her friend toward the tavern.

Katie dragged her feet and then stopped all together. "I'm not going back, Tara. You've been gone for two whole months. Not a word, nothing. Life hasn't been the same. When I found out that Balor was dead...I felt like I didn't have anything to live for. A yearning for adventure awoke within me. I need to experience my own life without all my brothers in tow. Please understand."

Tara turned, her anger flaring to life. "Katie, you didn't even know Balor. What are you talking about?"

Katie cast her eyes downward. "I can't explain it. I felt this connection to him, this strange pull and no, before you begin to lecture me again, I am not simply fantasizing about this. As great looking as that man is who just dropped out of the sky, which I've learned over the years to ignore, he doesn't make me feel the same way as I did when I saw Balor."

Tara wished she had the right to lecture her friend but she realized she didn't. Who am I to give her a lecture about falling in love with a man you hardly know. Tara felt Dyloulious approach. She didn't want him anywhere near her. Knowing he was the bastard son to the King of Decies sent shivers down her spine, even though she knew the king was only that way because of Queen Mir's curse. That thought didn't provide her with any comfort.

"Katie, don't leave. I honestly didn't realize I would be gone so long. It only felt like a day to me."

"What's it like?" asked Katie, already hooked with her imagination.

Tara linked her arm through her friend's and encouraged them to move toward the tavern. "Walk with me back to the tavern and I'll tell you what I can. I need to find your father, though. My mother, Rhea...and yes, I know we all thought she was my grandmother, but she's not. Katie, she's really my mom. I still can't believe it. She's alive and she's young, beautiful and a princess. I have six aunts including the Queen of Tir Nan Og, who isn't at all what I expected. Come," she said, no longer needing to pull her friend along. "I will tell you all I can."

Katie gave Tara's arm a squeeze and leaned in close. "It's really great that you're back. Don't leave me again."

That statement tore at Tara's heart. She longed to say she never would, but she wasn't so certain. Without a doubt she knew Queen Mir would come for her. It was just a matter of when.

"Ignore me, why don't you?" snapped Dyloulious.

"I am," replied Tara, turning to look at him.

Dyloulious seemed genuinely hurt by her actions, which surprised her. "Fine, come along. I will explain a little of Earth to you," she said, urging him to walk beside them.

"Is the sky always blue?" he asked, awe filling his voice. "What is that black, foul creature?" They watched as Dyloulious unsheathed a deadly looking sword which he used to point at the creature he was asking about.

Both Tara and Katie burst out laughing. Dyloulious didn't look one bit pleased by their reactions.

"I'll have you know that I am Queen Mir's warrior," he replied, realizing by their laughter the creature meant no harm. He resheathed his sword without a word to them.

"Sorry Dyloulious, that was precious. That's a raven. They won't hurt you if you don't hurt them." Tara gave a conciliatory wink to her friend.

"I take it you're from Tir Nan Og," said Katie, calmly, as she glanced at Dyloulious.

He nodded.

"Well, welcome to Earth. I will help Tara explain the sights." Katie unlinked her arm from Tara's so she could link it through Dyloulious' arm.

He grinned. "Thank you."

Now it was Tara's turn to be surprised. Hatred and anger had comprised Dyloulious' attitude so much so that Tara was awed to see another side to him. "I'm sorry, Dyloulious, for my earlier rude behavior," said Tara.

"No need. I know you only have eyes for that Damned Fairy," he replied, giving her a playful wink.

Tara didn't say anything else. She couldn't. Thinking about her Damned Fairy, her Cael, caused a rush of emotion to fill her.

"It's going to be okay. You'll see him again," said Katie.

Tara sighed. "Just when did you become psychic?"

"Woman's intuition," giggled Katie.

A few minutes later all three walked through the front door of MacLeod's Tavern. A cluster of people, mostly finishing up their lunches took up the side booths.

"Katie MacLeod, get yourself in here now!" bellowed MacCallah.

"Oops, gotta go and hide this before she gets even madder." Katie swung the black suitcase quickly behind her as she rushed back out the front door.

Tara smiled. Not much had changed.

"Tara, is that you?" shouted MacCallah, marching through the swinging kitchen doors. "Boys, go get your father. Tara's back!"

Tara waited until MacCallah had finished giving her a huge mother bear-hug. "It's good to be home," said Tara, feeling her eyes mist up with longing.

"You were gone long enough. Thought for certain those fairies had eaten you," chuckled MacCallah.

Almost. Then MacCallah's eyes caught sight of the tall male standing next to her. "This is Dyloulious," said Tara, turning her head so Dyloulious would venture forth. He didn't. He stood warrior-ready for battle.

"There are Druids here." Dyloulious sneered, his eyes almost glowing as four of MacCallah's sons strode through the kitchen door toward them.

"And here I was thinking we'd seen the last of those fairies," snapped MacCallah.

"You didn't tell me they were here," accused Dyloulious, pulling Tara closer to him.

Tara brushed off his hand and darted daggers at him with her eyes. "They are my friends."

339

"Druids can never be trusted." Dyloulious let the words equal the challenge he meant them to.

Alec motioned for his mother to get behind him, as he nudged closer to Dyloulious. "Well Tara-girl, looks like you brought us another fucking fairy."

Tara positioned her body between the two glaring men. *He's not really a fairy but I'm not about to tell you that.* "Cut it out, Alec. I need to speak to Devon...be civil." She left the men who seemed to be enjoying their staring contest so she could talk privately with Devon, who sauntered in through the front door.

"Ahh, Tara, it's good to see you girl." He immediately engulfed her in another hug. "See you brought us another treat."

Tara knew he was referring to Dyloulious. She nodded affirmatively. "Did you know Rhea was my real mother, Devon?"

He took a small step back and looked at her, not breaking his hold on her shoulders. "Ahh, now, I was wondering, but it wasn't my place to ask, or intervene. Can I assume she's all right?"

Tara felt tears well up inside her. "She's beautiful. But..."

"But what?"

"Tir Nan Og isn't at all what I thought it would be."

"Isn't it as beautiful and serene as all those fanciful tales make it out to be?" asked Devon.

Tara recognized the twinkle in his eyes. *He knows. He knows exactly what it's like. The old devil.* "Sort of, but that's not why I needed to speak with you. Rhea told me to give you this." Tara held out the small, silver bracelet so she could place it in Devon's large palm.

A blue haze engulfed his hand and Tara watched as he closed his eyes. He was listening to something.

"This is unexpected. I'm going to have to leave you now, Tara. It really is great to have you back home. Hope you plan on staying for a while." He gave her a final parting hug.

"That would be nice." She bowed her head, afraid her true emotions would get the best of her. "I'm going to go home. I need to see it again."

Devon looked at her hard. "You sure you're ready for that?"

Tara nodded.

"MacCallah and me boys made sure everything was neat and tidy for when you returned. Alec chopped up more wood for you and you be knowin' MacCallah, she made sure there was a wee bit of something in the fridge for you when you returned."

Tara looked at him then. "How did you know I would come back?"

"Katie said it would be so and well, it was easier to think that way." A weak smile flew across Devon's face as if he wanted to say more but didn't deem it wise.

Dyloulious brushed past her.

"Something's different about Katie, isn't it?" asked Tara.

"Ahh, now Tara-girl don't you be worryin' your pretty little head about Katie. She's a Druid and a fine one she'll make someday. She's just goin' through a wee bit of a time with all the changes. She'll be fine."

Tara wasn't so sure of that. Change, as she had discovered, wasn't always good.

Devon gave her a wink before he walked away.

"You got another place we can go to, Tara?" asked Dyloulious, holding open the front door, letting the cold air stir restlessly through the tavern.

Boy do I ever. Tara waved a goodbye to MacCallah, Alec and the rest of the Highlanders. She marched out the door and down the dirt road, taking a left into the woods as she rounded the corner. She yearned for the comforts of the forest, and to feel her Earth encompass her.

"What is that stench?" bellowed Dyloulious.

A slow smile spread across Tara's face as the pungent odor of a dead skunk sailed on the wind toward them. She inhaled sharply, welcoming the familiar smell. She didn't bother answering Dyloulious, who had sauntered past her in his haste to escape the ripe odor. The rank smell made her recall her first encounter with Cael. A blush instantly stole across her face when her memory replayed that first Tuatha kiss. *The kiss that changed my life forever. The kiss that took my heart and soul and left it in Tir Nan Og.*

"You walking or do I have to carry you from this stench?" asked Dyloulious, barking at her from ahead. He ducked down to avoid a large evergreen branch only to have the thorny brambles from the thick underbrush dig into his forearms. He cursed in his native tongue. Tara fought not to laugh. She hoped by the time they reached her house from the dense forest he'd have enough scrapes and scratches on him that he'd be forced to tend to them and leave her alone.

What did I do to deserve him for a bodyguard? But the bigger question is why did Facia send him to Earth? Dyloulious needed to learn the arts of tact and silence. His curses, anything but muffled, could wake the dead. Then again, wasn't that exactly what Rhea had ordered Devon to do? Too bad Tara understood the whispered words that had traveled from the bracelet to Devon. She wasn't sure that what her mother envisioned was the right thing to do, but she now understood part of Facia's purpose in sending Dyloulious with her. Without Dyloulious' blood, Cael's brother could not be converted back into the Tuatha he was. The realization Cael hadn't actually killed his brother warmed Tara. No sibling should have to murder one of their own. It wasn't right. Then the stark, cold reality of Mir's plan ricocheted through Tara. That's exactly what Mir was trying to do to Facia—murder her, to secure her position of power.

Tara wondered exactly how Devon was going to convince the mistrusting Dyloulious to help Balor. She had a sinking feeling it wasn't going to be easy. After all, nothing in my life for the past week, wait...make that week plus two months has been easy, so why should this be any different? Tara ducked and swayed to avoid the snapping branches from Dyloulious' cutting path through the forest, knowing he was doing that on purpose, hoping she'd land on her ass.

Not on my own turf! Tara side-stepped around a large tree and strode forward, her house now within sight.

"Is that shack yours?"

So much for his charm. Tara wished she had mastered enough of the Tuatha powers within her to spell Dyloulious far away from her for the time being.

CAEL COULDN'T BELIEVE he'd been talked into this. Every argument he'd had with himself told him it was wrong, but he also hadn't come up with anything better.

"Facia, you had better get that Stone of Fal quickly." He flashed himself to the outside entranceway of Queen Mir's Pleasure Palace, and could have sworn Facia was laughing at him. Again!

"Cael, is that you?"

Queen Mir's sultry voice caused him to see red.

Cael, leash that famous temper of yours, now!

Facia's voice was hard as steel as it radiated loud and clear inside his head. Get the fuck out of my head, Facia, or else I leave.

Now Cael, that wouldn't do at all. Then you'll never see your halfling again.

That stark reminder caused him to grit his teeth in frustration. Fine, let's get this show on the road.

Taking in a shuddering breath, Cael willed his clothing off. There was nothing on his skin except the dark blue and black druid tattoos that lined his arms. He was naked. This would be the first time Queen Mir would see the marks, which he'd received only about one week before his banishment. A part of him wondered what she'd think, while another aspect of him was slightly terrified she'd obliterate him on the spot.

Nice ass! Move it, ordered Facia.

Once again, Cael wondered if he was doing the right thing. Which was the lesser of the two evils—Mir or her warrior-sister, Facia. He hoped he'd picked the correct one, but at the moment Facia was almost as annoying as her sister.

The outer door to Mir's chamber opened of its own accord. He felt a brush of warm air as Facia used her powers to rush past him and hoped Mir would not notice it. His feet padded silently on the cold marble floor. He spied Mir, as usual wearing her translucent gown, idly toying with Xavier's hair. She hadn't bothered to rise—for that he was thankful. She was completely oblivious to the warm air of power that had seeped into the room.

Xavier's eyes narrowed as Cael approached. Cael hoped Facia could explain things fast to him before Mir realized what was going on.

"Well, if this isn't a surprise. I am pleased. You came to offer me your services so soon. But not today." Mir barely glanced his way and dismissed him with a flick of her wrist.

Bitch! Cael didn't slow his stride. Xavier's eyes widened in surprise and Cael could only hope Facia had detailed the plan to him, and that he was on their side.

"I've come to offer my services to both of you," replied Cael, smoothly. He advanced until he was a foot from her. She lay on her favorite gold-embossed settee that was on a raised platform. He saw a moment of interest sparkle her eyes as her pupils dilated in awareness of the marks on his arms.

"So, my Cael, you gained enough druid trust to be marked as one of them, when you are not. Isn't that interesting, Xavier?" Mir turned her amber eyes to look directly at the Druid Priest who was lying next to her, trying to look slightly bored with the scene.

"I was there under your orders," reminded Cael.

"Yes, that is correct. My trusty spy...funny how things turned out, Cael. If you could change something in your past Cael, would it be the moment you challenged me in front of the Druid Constellation?"

Cael closed his eyes. This wasn't what he wanted. He didn't want to discuss the past or his actions, because that would only serve to make Mir angry, which wouldn't let him accomplish the trickery he had to now.

"The past is behind me. I am thankful to be home. I've come to offer my services to both of you," said Cael. Talk about bullshit. Cael's skin bristled. He wondered if Mir would bite.

"The two of us? Really, Cael the things you say do sometimes surprise me. But then again, I always did like surprises." Mir turned her attention to Xavier, who was still playing with one of her nipples through the sheer gown.

Xavier's blue eyes tested Cael's.

"And me," mumbled the Druid Priest.

Cael fought hard with himself to not say anything. The urge to slink out while he could ran like a cold stream through his consciousness. Probably the only sane part left within me. "I have missed you, Mir," he gulped, almost gagging on the lie.

Mir lazily drew a long nail over her other already-pebbled nipple. "You must think I am a fool to fall for that flattery, Cael. But do continue, your actions are amusing me."

Good to know someone is amused, thought Cael.

"And I." Xavier rose from behind Mir's settee to the front. The slight nod was the only indication Xavier knew what was really going on.

Cael watched as his old friend and nemesis moved off the raised platform so he could stand facing him.

"You sure you want to go through with this?" Xavier's voice was a mere whisper.

Cael was one hundred per cent against it! Instead, he nodded affirmatively. He felt Xavier move around to his back and goose bumps formed all over his body. Every warrior instinct within him screamed to turn—never give the enemy your back. Instead he braced himself.

"I don't know Mir, this might be fun," Xavier taunted.

Then Xavier ran a feather-light hand down Cael's naked back. Cael couldn't help but flinch, as his own nipples pebbled to life. *Fuck! I am never going to live this down!* He braced the soles of his feet firmly on the floor and reminded himself, again, why he was doing this. He watched Queen Mir rise to her imposing regal height. She was enjoying the show, of that he had no doubt. Her aroused scent slammed hard into him. After years of screwing her he knew that scent like the back of his hand, which was currently clenched into a tight fist.

"Relax."

Again, Xavier's voice brushed soft against his ears.

"Just get on with it." Cael managed to mumble the words as Mir floated down off her pedestal.

"She wants a show. To do this successfully we are going to have to do just that. You Tuatha enough, Cael?" Xavier brushed his body up against Cael's so he could lean in and quietly whisper his conspiracy to him, making it appear as if he were caressing him.

"Go fuck yourself." Cael couldn't help it. This went again every fiber of his being, but he didn't have a choice. And he knew it. So did Xavier. He closed his eyes, forcing a calm he didn't feel and let Xavier walk around to his front. The entire time, the Druid Priest trailed a finger from his back, over his right hip to his navel. Cael's jaw clenched so hard he thought it might never work again. He eyed where Xavier's hand came to rest. An inch lower and the priest would have his hand on his cock. Xavier took a calculated step back to give Cael's body a thorough once over.

"You're going to have to do better than that," said Xavier, still keeping his back to Queen Mir.

"Boys, enough of the sweet talk. You have my undivided attention, but need I remind you; I am the one you need to please." Mir let her gown fall to the floor as she ambled seductively toward them.

"Think of Tara." That was Xavier's parting advice as he turned his charm back to Mir.

"My Queen, I do believe I have too many layers of clothing on to service both of you..." he turned and gave Cael a heated look, "Properly."

In a blink Xavier was naked as well. Cael caught himself before he rolled his eyes to the ceiling.

"Much better," said Xavier, as he walked up to Mir to boldly pinch both her nipples. A small gasp of pleasure escaped her.

My cue. Cael forced his feet and body to comply. He walked around Xavier, and hoped his face didn't cringe as he lightly reached out to trace the same path the priest's fingers had on him. However once his fingers reached the front he moved them to Queen Mir's body, reaching down to rub her naked mound. As always she kept it smooth, a novelty she found sexually satisfying.

Hurry up, Facia! He let his body brush suggestively up against Mir's back.

"Why Cael, not hard yet?" said Mir. "I do believe I shall enjoy fixing that."

Cael knew it was a challenge. She was testing him. So be it. Cael closed his eyes an envisioned Tara's small hands wrapped snugly around his cock and prayed it would work. A few brisk strokes later he sprang to life. When he opened his eyes, Xavier was looking at him with a calculating stare. Cael wrinkled his nose at him.

Facia if you're taking your time, move your ass or I'm out of here. Cael wanted to shout the words out loud. Instead, he tried with all his might to zone in on her thoughts.

But Cael, you seem to be enjoying yourself.

You have two more minutes before I'm out of here. And he would be. Enough of these games.

"This is fun," said Mir, cupping Cael in her hand, hard.

Again, he fought not to move. The minute she let him go, Cael moved Mir around so that she was now facing Xavier. He nipped her neck hard. She leaned back into him, welcoming his attentions. At the same time, Xavier moved his head down so he could bring one of her peaked nipples into his mouth.

"This I like," purred Mir, giving her ass a squirm against Cael so he would get her meaning.

Got it! Shouted Facia in his ear. He felt the warmth of her power as she brushed past him.

About bloody well time. I'm out of here.

Cael eyed Xavier as Mir leaned back her head more, exposing her vulnerability to the priest.

With a curt nod, Xavier got his meaning, as he moved his lips to Mir's neck. Cael backed up slowly and then a foot away he dashed for the door, knowing his powers were useless inside the Pleasure Palace. Once outside he flashed to Facia's rendezvous site. He hoped Xavier could explain his actions, without getting into too much trouble. Then again, why should I care?

Chapter Thirty-One

"WHAT THE HELL WAS THAT?" asked Dyloulious. "Did you feel that, too?

Tara shivered. She felt it and it wasn't to her liking at all. "Change of plans. We're going somewhere else. Hold my hand. I've only done this once before so let's pray I get it right."

"What are you talking about?" Dyloulious turned weary eyes toward her.

"I'm going to use my Tuatha powers to flash us somewhere."

"You are, are you?" he sneered. "You're only half-Tuatha, this should be interesting." Dyloulious grasped her hand hard. "So, let's do it."

Tara closed her eyes to envision the cave at Kelly's Mountain. When next she opened them, a large smile spread across her face.

"I take it this is it." Dyloulious darted his eyes to the large cave entrance. "And we've got company."

Tara heard the familiar sound of the pickup trucks and knew it would be Devon and his sons. They too had felt what she felt.

"Dyloulious, get the fuck away from my woman."

The voice charmed every nerve ending in Tara's body. "Cael!" she screamed, and raced to the foot of the cave's entrance, needing to feel his solid body up against her own. However, before she managed to reach him she stopped. Emerging from the cave was the King of the Decies and Facia, who looked mighty pleased with herself.

Tara felt Dyloulious flank her other side. What must it be to know that thing, that creature is your father? Tara turned her head to look at Dyloulious.

The King of the Decies stepped forward, his long, spidery wings unfurling with the gust of wind.

"Get back, Tara!" yelled Devon.

Tara didn't move. She watched as Cael placed a hand on the king's spiny shoulder, holding him in place.

Then Facia took the Stone of Fal Tara was beginning to hate with a vengeance and handed it to the King of the Decies. He mouthed the words. The sound coming from his beak felt like someone had raked their nails down a chalkboard. Tara's spine stiffened. Dyloulious moved a fraction of an inch forward. And then before their eyes the king transformed into his true majestic form. He bowed his head low to Facia and then turned his startling violet eyes to his son.

Tara admitted he was a sight to behold. His crystal-clear butterfly wings bespoke power and evoked awe within her. He was as tall as Facia, muscular and moved with regal grace. To see him like this now, Tara found it hard to believe that such a beautiful creature could have been transformed into abject evil by the actions of one sick woman. A part of Tara wept at the injustice Mir had inflicted upon the Reikas, the once proud sky-beings.

"Son." Belatucadros breathed the word into the air and moved with his arms outstretched in a welcoming embrace to greet Dyloulious.

"You don't have long, Belatucadros," reminded Facia.

Dyloulious took a small step back, his posture ram-rod straight and still warrior ready. His father advanced until they were standing face-to-face.

"Is it too late to get to know you?" asked King Belatucadros.

Cael moved her away from the personal scene taking place before her eyes. "They need time alone, Tara. Come with me. We don't have much time."

His voice and words hauled her out of her dream world. "What's going on, Cael?"

"Yes Cael, what's going on?" asked Devon, as he and his sons came to stand next to them on the steep hill outside of the cave.

"Facia can explain it better than me."

"You are right for once, Cael." Facia gave a small nod to Devon as she stepped forward, still wearing her warrior gear. She too was a sight to behold. Her long black hair, streaked with white was tied back in a sharp ponytail and she was armed to the teeth. An array of deadly knives were strapped to her arms, thighs and waist. She was dressed for battle.

"I am Facia, the rightful Queen of Tir Nan Og. I took the Stone of Fal from my sister, Mir, and something else she holds dear. I am finally claiming what was taken from me before Mir can do any more damage to our realm."

Devon stepped forward and gave Facia a low courtly bow. "What service can we be?"

Facia acknowledged his gesture and bowed back at him, a small smile creasing her stony features. "I will need druid help. Do you have the power to create a holding circle?"

Devon nodded.

"Then do so. She will be here soon. And she won't be happy."

Devon motioned for his sons to follow him into the cave.

Cael pulled her to him. "You need to stay in the cave and this time, Tara, no matter what...don't come out."

Tara couldn't believe what she was hearing, again. "Cael, don't do this. I can't stand it when you hide me away and I'm left wondering what's happening to you. Let me help."

"No!"

"Yes," chimed Facia, moving toward her.

"I said no Facia, back off." Cael positioned his body so that he stood in front of her.

"She will help. It's her destiny. Don't say another word, Cael, or I will send you back."

Tara darted her eyes first to Cael and then to Facia. Tension wrung the air.

"Fine. Stay by my side, Tara," demanded Cael. "My brother?"

Facia moved to the fresh mound that rested at the side of the cave. "Belatucadros can't save him, but Dyloulious can. If he's willing."

Cael walked away, mumbling under his breath. "He'll be willing all right." Once he was at the gravesite, he shouted, "Dyloulious, get over here!"

Tara knew Cael didn't care he was interrupting the first father-son chat between the two of them.

Dyloulious turned and marched over. "This had better be good, Cael."

Using Tuatha powers, Cael willed the soil away, revealing the body of his brother, Balor. Once he had removed the fine dusting of soil on his brother's face, he stood up.

"I need your blood," he declared, his eyes cold as he stared at Dyloulious.

Dyloulious backed up a foot. "Why?"

"I put him in a deep druid sleep. It was the only way to stop him from turning into a Decies, because of Mir's lovely curse. Your untainted blood can purge him."

"But my father is no longer—"

"I will be again," declared King Belatucadros, his tone soft, as he came to stand beside the two of them.

Dyloulious turned to stare at his father. "But I thought the Stone of Fal granted you your wish. You can't turn again."

Facia moved to flank Dyloulious' other side. "The Stone of Fal can only work temporarily. Mir's spell is too strong to keep your father like this. I told him all of that before giving him the stone, but he insisted that he wanted to see you with his own eyes. This,

Dyloulious is his one chance, his one time, to talk to you like his true Reikas self. The curse will take hold of him again."

"Is there no way to break Mir's curse?" asked Dyloulious.

Facia shook her head, negatively. "Only Mir can break the curse, and she won't. But you can save Cael's brother. Your blood is the cure for him. Will you do that for him?" Facia placed her hands on Dyloulious' chest, willing him to look at her.

He nodded. "What do I do?"

He didn't need to say anything else. Facia sliced his hand so fast even Cael moved out of her way, as she brought Dyloulious forward so that the blood flowed freely onto Balor's face.

A blinding white light sailed through Balor's body and then his eyes flew open.

"Cael, what the Hell did you do to me?"

Tara watched as Balor shakily attempted to get up.

"He didn't do anything to you. He saved you," said Facia.

"Yeah, right," muttered Balor.

Tara moved toward Cael. "You and your brother need to work on those trust issues."

"She's coming." Facia's voice was soft in its intensity. "Are you ready, Devon?"

"Yes," he replied, standing at the cave's entrance.

A hot gust of wind ripped up the steep incline.

Facia began to chant the Tuatha words, forcing her Tuatha powers and those of the Druids to work their way to the source. Tara heard Devon and his sons chant a druid spell. Tara realized she was beginning to understand more of her druid heritage.

A shrill scream of rage and agony spiraled through the hill. Still Facia kept up her chant. Hail the size of large golf balls materialized in the air, but still Facia didn't flinch or stop chanting. She stood rigidly still, willing the elements to work her way.

Cael moved and Tara wondered where he was going, but it was Facia's words in her mind that made her react.

Stop him, Tara. Mir is using a spell on him to get to Devon so Cael can break the druid holding circle. Use your power to stop him, bind him to you. The words were spoken quickly in her mind and Tara instantly understood what she had to do.

She moved in front of Cael and hugged his body close. Then she closed her eyes, willing her love for him to seep into him. Using the Tuatha powers inherent within her she levitated her body up off the ground so she was eye-level with him. His normally silver-grey eyes had a glazed look to them and she could tell by his tense body language he was attempting to fight Mir's spell.

Tara claimed his lips. She dominated the kiss, working his mouth until she felt him yield to his passion. She twined her hands behind his head, loving the heady feel of power as she made him hers for once. Feeling even more daring she darted a tongue into his mouth and groaned as he answered her duel. They meshed their mouths together in a frenzy, hands flying across each other's bodies, grappling through each other's hair, while they exchanged groans and moans, not caring of what was taking place around them. The wind ripped through their clothing and hail continued to stream down around them but it didn't seem to matter. They were in their own element. They were nature themselves. Their passion, a fiery heat, wiped clear the fury taking place around them.

Cael pressed into her more, allowing her to feel the hard, rigid length of his erection. It thrilled her more than she thought possible. She ached to strip off their clothing and climb onto his cock and ride him hard. Her inner core muscles clenched eagerly for him. Tara wanted his body so much so that a fine sheen of passion-induced sweat coated her skin.

Then heat tingled into her awareness. They had been both flashed somewhere. When Tara next opened her eyes, she gasped.

They were back on Tir Nan Og, only the sky was no longer its eerie pink-purple color.

"She did it." Cael gasped the words into her mouth, as his eyes scanned the horizon.

"What does that mean?" Tara desperately needed to know if she was safe.

"It means, Tara," said Facia, her form solidifying next to both of them, "That Queen Mir is no more. And yes, you are safe."

Not relinquishing his hold on her, Cael asked, "What about Belatucadros?"

"I can't change what happened to Belatucadros, only Mir can. Thanks to your Druid friends I was able to place Mir temporarily in the druid holding circle. I tried to explain to her why I was doing what I was doing but she was too angry to listen to me. It was Belatucadros who insisted I give her back a little of what she gave him." Facia reached out to trail her hands through a lush green bush, which had pink berries.

Tara watched as Facia popped two berries into her mouth.

"I had forgotten how wonderful the food can taste," she declared, clearly in awe.

Tara shook her head. She still didn't understand what had happened to Queen Mir. Before she could ask any more questions, Cael released her and stepped forward to confront Facia.

"What exactly happened to her, Facia?"

"Don't take that tone with me, Cael. You should know I would never do anything to harm my sister, even after all the horribly wicked things she's done to me and to Tir Nan Og. I am not like her. I let Belatucadros change her and claim her. It is his right as her husband, so don't look so astonished."

Tara watched as Facia plucked two more pink berries and popped them into her mouth before she continued.

"You know I do believe he really does have feelings for her. It was Belatucadros who insisted Mir release his race. That's why the sky is turning back to its original light blue color. The Reikas are home again. My heart is rejoicing. As for Belatucadros and Mir, they are finally together. It's just not quite how Mir envisioned it would be."

Facia laughed, causing Cael to run his hands through his hair. Tara noticed he didn't look pleased one bit.

"So, you're telling me you made her into a Decies," said Cael.

"No, I'm telling you Mir wouldn't release Belatucadros from her spell and the only option left to her was for Belatucadros to claim her. I do believe it's just reward. They are both safe here," said Facia, conjuring up the small ivory-jeweled treasure chest.

"I thought we agreed that there wouldn't be any more Decies." Cael's voice was dangerously gruff as he now paced back and forth on the bright yellow grass.

"Cael, I have done nothing wrong. I gave Mir her choices. She picked her own fate. Let it be. Ahh, here comes Rhea." A genuine smile filled Facia's face, softening her normally hard features.

Tara watched as Rhea embraced her sister, then her mother held out her arms for her. Tara didn't hesitate.

"Thank you, Facia," said Rhea.

"A sisterly debt now paid in full, Rhea. And it was my pleasure," answered Facia.

"The preparations are complete for your official coronation," said Rhea, her hand gently stroking Tara's hair.

"Then it's done. You get what you wanted, Facia. And I'm getting what I want." Cael moved Tara from her mother's embrace to his hard, chiseled chest.

"And what is that, Cael?" asked Facia, her eyes calculating.

"Tara," he said, nuzzling the top of her head with a kiss.

Tara watched as her mother stepped forward and before she spoke, she knew she had to say what was in her heart before something else got in the way, or whisked them somewhere else.

She tilted her head up so she could look into those clear silver eyes of his that had claimed her from the first moment Tara gazed at him." I love you, Cael."

"You do understand I am the Damned Fairy," he said, looking at her in earnest.

"No, Cael, you are my Damned Fairy and I like you just the way you are," she replied, moving her hands so she could bring his head down for a claiming kiss.

He read the intent in her eyes and smiled. There was no hesitation on his part. His lips devoured hers, staking her with his passion, his claim, his heart to hers.

Tara knew no matter what was to come, this was what she needed, what she craved—Cael, her Damned Fairy!

About Renee Field

RENEE LOVES TO WRITE a variety of genres. She writes romance for HQN Spice Briefs, and sensual paranormal and contemporary romance as an Indie author. Field also writes nitty gritty young adult and paranormal young adult romance novels under the pen name Renee Pace.

Renee calls Halifax, Nova Scotia, Canada home and loves her view of the Atlantic Ocean. She is a member of Romance Writers' of America, and her local Romance Writers of Atlantic Canada chapter. She juggles work, four children and is a firm believer in soul-mates and the power of the sea.

Renee loves to hear from fans. She can be reached by email at reneefieldauthor@gmail.com.

LINKS:

Renee Field - www.reneefield.com

Facebook - https://www.facebook.com/ReneeFieldRomanceAuthor

Renee Pace (young adult) - www.reneepace.com

Facebook - https://www.facebook.com/ReneePaceYABooks

Twitter @ReneePaceYA

OTHER TITLES BY

Rapture, (Titan series, #1)

Bliss, (Titan series, #2)

Embrace (sweet romance novella)

Spice Me Up
A Siren's Wish
Claiming A Siren's Heart
Claiming Poseidon's Heart
Claiming the Temptress (HQN novella)
Witch Me Good (Sexy Salem Witch Stories)
Love Me Wild (Love Curse, #1)
Love Me Tender (Love Curse, # 2)
Love Me Strong (Love Curse, #3)
Wild and Tender (paperback)
Heart of Mine
Be My Vampire Tonight (Darklander series, #1)
Be My Werecat Tonight (Darklander series, #2)
Be My Warlock Tonight (Darklander series, #3)
Electrify Me
Queen of Dragons
Summer Heat (new adult contemporary novella)

Don't miss out!

Visit the website below and you can sign up to receive emails whenever Renee Field publishes a new book. There's no charge and no obligation.

https://books2read.com/r/B-A-HRN-AWRH

BOOKS 2 READ

Connecting independent readers to independent writers.

Did you love *Fairy Cursed*? Then you should read *Rapture*[1] by Renee Field!

[2]

Mermen aren't real. That's what biologist Jamie Winters thinks until a gorgeous Greek god enters her life and drowns her, forcing her to rapture into a Siren. Used to logic, she can't quite come to terms with Seth Cutter's magical undersea realm or the fact that he's a macho Titan.

Being a Siren causes Jamie's hormones to go into overdrive, which isn't good when she realizes that's exactly what Seth was hoping for. Sure, the sex is out of this world, but she's not about to change her character.

As Prince of the North Seas, Seth is used to having his commands followed. A decade of exile on land was easier than

---

1. https://books2read.com/u/bMRq83

2. https://books2read.com/u/bMRq83

having to deal with the sexy-as-sin Siren who tips the scales of his existence and doesn't listen to one word he says.

They must overcome their prejudices to recover stolen relics that are key to the undersea kingdom, stop a deadly plague and destroy an underwater diva who wants to rule the roost. Are they two souls destined for each other or will the Fates decide otherwise? Seth knows firsthand, Fate can be a bitch.

Read more at www.reneefield.com.

Also by Renee Field

A Warriors of Maida Novella
Love Me Wild
Love Me Tender
Love Me Strong
Love Me Wild

Darklander Lovers
Be My Warlock Tonight
Be My Vampire Tonight
Be My Werecat Tonight

Elemental Love
Heart of Mine

Riverton Cove series
Embrace

Titan series
Rapture
Bliss

Standalone
Claiming A Siren's Heart
Claiming Poseidon's Heart
A Siren's Wish
Fairy Cursed
Summer Heat
Queen of Dragons
Summer Heat
Electrify Me

Watch for more at www.reneefield.com.

About the Author

Renee loves to write a variety of genres. She writes for HQN Spice Briefs and also writes sensual paranormal romance, and contemporary romance as an Indie author. Field also writes nitty gritty young adult and paranormal young adult romance novels under the pen name Renee Pace. Renee calls Halifax, Nova Scotia, Canada home and loves her view of the Atlantic Ocean. She is a member of Romance Writers' of America, and her local Romance Writers of Atlantic Canada. She juggles work, four children and is a firm believer in soul-mates and the power of the sea.

Renee loves to hear from fans. She can be reached by email at reneefieldauthor@gmail.com

Read more at www.reneefield.com.